FEVER DREAM

"This is no dream; it's the authors' best book in years."
—*Library Journal* (**starred review**)

"A thrill a minute."
—*San Jose Mercury News*

"Preston and Child up the emotional ante considerably in this thriller featuring brilliant and eccentric Pendergast...Once again, the bestselling authors show they have few peers at creating taut scenes of suspense."
—*Publishers Weekly* (**starred review**)

"Together [Preston and Child] reach an entirely different level, achieving a stylistic grace and thematic resonance neither has so far matched alone. This may be the best of the Pendergast novels...a definite must-read."
—*Booklist* (**starred review**)

WHITE FIRE
ONE OF THE BEST BOOKS OF THE YEAR
BY *LIBRARY JOURNAL*

"Excellent...Small-town politics, murder, a century-old conspiracy, arson, and a detective who embodies a modern-day Holmes add up to an amazing journey... Preston and Child's best novel to date."
—**Associated Press**

TWO GRAVES

"A good thriller forces the reader to finish the book in one sitting. An exceptional thriller does that plus forces the reader to slow down to savor every word. With TWO GRAVES, Preston and Child have delivered another exceptional book...The gothic atmosphere that oozes from the pages will envelop the reader...Pendergast is a modern-day Sherlock Holmes, quirks and all...The mystery tantalizes, and the shocks throughout the narrative are like bolts of lightning. Fans will love the conclusion to the trilogy, and newcomers will seek out the authors' earlier titles."

—Associated Press

"Pendergast—an always-black-clad pale blond polymath, gaunt yet physically deadly, an FBI agent operating without supervision or reprimand—lurks at the dark, sharp edge of crime fiction protagonists."

—*Kirkus Reviews*

"A lavish story and one that takes the time for some skillful vignettes and characterizations."

—*Charlotte Observer*

"Preston and Child's high-adrenaline thriller wraps up the trilogy...with a bang...[An] intelligent suspense novel."

—*Publishers Weekly*

"TWO GRAVES provides readers exactly what they would expect from a Preston and Child novel—thrills, high adventure, treacherous plot twists, and well-researched scientific intrigue. The story is never predictable, and Pendergast is a multi-layered personality who keeps you guessing throughout."

—BookReporter.com

"The action is constant and starts with a bang."
—*RT Book Reviews*

"Another fast-paced murder mystery that crosses the country, dips into Mexico and then wallops Manhattan hotels. It's the perfect holiday gift for that thriller-genre lover in your life."
—*Asbury Park Press*

COLD VENGEANCE

"Before you even open the cover of a Preston and Child book, you know you're in for a good, if chilling, even thrilling time."
—*Asbury Park Press*

"[Preston and Child are] still going strong...Such is the talent of our authors that we happily follow their characters...all over the globe, from the moors of Scotland to the loony bins of New York City; the recipe is mixed well with a dash of assassins here and a soupcon of Nazis there, a couple of traitors and some really fascinating secondary characters...*Cold Vengeance* is a hot hell of a fun read."
—**Examiner.com**

"4½ stars! Top Pick! Preston and Child continue their dominance of the thriller genre with stellar writing and twists that come at a furious pace. Others may try to write like them, but no one can come close. The best in the business deliver another winner."
—*RT Book Reviews*

FEVER
DREAM

ALSO BY DOUGLAS PRESTON AND LINCOLN CHILD

Agent Pendergast Novels

Crimson Shore
Blue Labyrinth
White Fire
*Two Graves**
*Cold Vengeance**
*Fever Dream**
Cemetery Dance
The Wheel of Darkness
*The Book of the Dead***
*Dance of Death***
*Brimstone***
Still Life with Crows
The Cabinet of Curiosities
Reliquary†
Relic†

Gideon Crew Novels

The Lost Island
Gideon's Corpse
Gideon's Sword

Other Novels

The Ice Limit
Thunderhead
Riptide
Mount Dragon

*The Helen Trilogy
**The Diogenes Trilogy
†*Relic* and *Reliquary* are
  ideally read in sequence

By Douglas Preston

The Kraken Project
Impact
The Monster of Florence
  (with Mario Spezi)
Blasphemy
Tyrannosaur Canyon
The Codex
Ribbons of Time
The Royal Road
Talking to the Ground
Jennie
Cities of Gold
Dinosaurs in the Attic

By Lincoln Child

The Forgotten Room
The Third Gate
Terminal Freeze
Deep Storm
Death Match
Lethal Velocity
  (formerly *Utopia*)
Tales of the Dark 1–3
Dark Banquet
Dark Company

FEVER DREAM

DOUGLAS PRESTON
&
LINCOLN CHILD

GRAND CENTRAL
PUBLISHING

NEW YORK   BOSTON

Authors' note: While most towns and other locations in *Fever Dream* are completely imaginary, we have in a few instances employed our own version of existing places, such as New Orleans and Baton Rouge. In such cases, we have not hesitated to alter geography, topology, history, and other details to suit the needs of the story. All persons, locales, police departments, corporations, institutions, museums, and governmental agencies mentioned in this novel are either fictitious or used fictitiously.

Grand Central Publishing
Hachette Book Group
1290 Avenue of the Americas
New York, NY 10104
www.HachetteBookGroup.com

Grand Central Publishing is a division of Hachette Book Group, Inc.
The Grand Central Publishing name and logo are trademarks of Hachette Book Group, Inc.

The Hachette Speakers Bureau provides a wide range of authors for speaking events. To find out more, go to www.hachettespeakersbureau.com or call (866) 376-6591.

The publisher is not responsible for websites (or their content) that are not owned by the publisher.

Printed in the United States of America

Originally published in hardcover by Hachette Book Group

First oversize mass market edition: April 2011
Reissued: November 2014

10 9 8 7
OPM

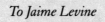

To Jaime Levine

FEVER
DREAM

1

Musalangu, Zambia

The setting sun blazed through the African bush like a forest fire, hot yellow in the sweltering evening that gathered over the bush camp. The hills along the upper Makwele Stream rose in the east like blunt green teeth, framed against the sky.

Several dusty canvas tents circled a beaten area shaded by a grove of old musasa trees, their branches spreading like emerald umbrellas over the safari camp. A thread of smoke from a cooking fire twisted up through the cover, carrying with it the tantalizing scent of burning mopane wood and roasting kudu.

In the shade of the central tree, two figures, a man and a woman, were seated in camp chairs on either side of a table, drinking iced bourbon. They were dressed in dusty khakis, long pants and sleeves, protection against the tsetse flies that came out in the evening. They were in their late twenties. The man, slender and tall, was remarkable for a cool, almost icy paleness that seemed impervious to the heat. The coolness did not extend to the woman, who was lazily fanning herself with a large banana leaf, stirring the thick mane of auburn hair she had loosely tied back with a bit of salvaged twine. She was tanned and relaxed. The low murmur of their conversation, punctuated by an occasional laugh from the woman, was almost indistinguishable amid the sounds of the African bush: the calls of vervet monkeys, the screech of francolins and chattering of fire-finches, which mingled with the clattering of pots and pans in the kitchen tent. The evening chatter was underlain by the distant roar of a lion deep in the bush.

The seated figures were Aloysius X. L. Pendergast and his wife of two years, Helen. They were at the tail end of a hunting safari in the Musalangu Game Management Area, where they had been shooting bushbuck and duiker under a herd reduction program granted by the Zambian government.

"Care for another sundowner?" Pendergast asked his wife, raising the cocktail pitcher.

"Another?" she replied with a laugh. "Aloysius, you wouldn't be planning an assault on my virtue, would you?"

"The thought never entered my mind. I was hoping perhaps we could spend the night discussing Kant's concept of the categorical imperative."

"Now you see, this is exactly what my mother warned me about. You marry a man because he's good with a rifle, only to find he has the brains of an ocelot."

Pendergast chuckled, sipped his drink, glanced down at it. "African mint is rather harsh on the palate."

"Poor Aloysius, you miss your juleps. Well, if you take that FBI job Mike Decker's offering, you can drink juleps day and night."

He took another thoughtful sip and gazed at his wife. It was remarkable how quickly she tanned in the African sun. "I've decided not to take it."

"Why not?"

"I'm not sure I'm ready to stay in New Orleans with all that it entails—the family complications, the unpleasant memories. And I've seen enough violence already, don't you think?"

"I don't know—have you? You tell me so little about your past, even now."

"I'm not cut out for the FBI. I don't like rules. In any case, you're all over the world with that Doctors With Wings outfit; we can live anywhere, as long as it's close to an international airport. *'Our two souls therefore endure not a breach, but an expansion, like gold to airy thinness beat.'*"

"Don't bring me to Africa and quote John Donne. Kipling, maybe."

"*'Every woman knows all about everything,'*" he intoned.

"On second thought, spare me the Kipling as well. What did you do as a teenager, memorize *Bartlett's*?"

"Among other things." Pendergast glanced up. A figure was approaching along the trail from the west. He was a tall Nyimba tribesman, dressed in shorts and a dirty T-shirt, an ancient rifle slung over his shoulders, carrying a forked walking stick. As he approached the camp, he paused and cried out a greeting in Bemba, the local lingua franca, which was answered by welcoming shouts from the kitchen tent. He then proceeded into camp and approached the table at which the Pendergasts were seated.

Both rose. *"Umú-ntú ú-mó umú-sumá á-áfíká,"* Pendergast said by way of greeting, and grasped the man's dusty, warm hand, Zambian-fashion. The man proffered his walking stick to Pendergast; there was a note wedged into its fork.

"For me?" Pendergast asked, switching to English.

"From the district commissioner."

Pendergast shot a glance at his wife, then removed the note and unfolded it.

My dear Pendergast,
I wish to have a conversation with you immediately via SSB. There has been a nasty business at Kingazu Camp—very nasty.

                                    Alistair Woking, DC
                                    South Luangwa

PS. Dear chap, you know perfectly well that regulations require you to have SSB communications set up at every bush camp. It is most annoying to have to send a runner like this.

"I don't like the sound of that," said Helen Pendergast, looking over her husband's shoulder. "What do you think this 'nasty business' is?"

"Perhaps a photo tourist has suffered the amorous advances of a rhinoceros."

"That's not funny," Helen said, laughing all the same.

"It is rutting season, you know." Pendergast folded the note and shoved it in his breast pocket. "I'm very much afraid this means our shooting safari is over."

He walked over to the tent, opened a box, and began screwing together the battered pieces of an aerial antenna, which he then carried up into a musasa tree and wired to an upper branch. Climbing back down, he plugged the wire into the single side-band radio he had placed on the table, turned on the unit, adjusted the dials to the correct frequency, and sent out a call. In a moment the irritated voice of the district commissioner came back, squawking and scratchy.

"Pendergast? For God's sake, where are you?"

"Upper Makwele Stream camp."

"Blast. I was hoping you were nearer the Banta Road. Why the devil don't you keep your SSB connected? I've been trying to reach you for hours!"

"May I ask what's happened?"

"Over at Kingazu Camp. A German tourist was killed by a lion."

"What idiot allowed that to happen?"

"It wasn't like that. The lion came right into camp in broad daylight, jumped the man as he was walking back to his hut from the dining tent, and dragged him screaming into the bush."

"And then?"

"Surely you can imagine 'and then'! The wife was hysterical, the whole camp went into an uproar, they had to bring in a helicopter to airlift out the tourists. The camp staff left behind are scared shiteless. This fellow was a well-known photographer in Germany— bloody bad for business!"

"Did you track the lion?"

"We have trackers and guns, but nobody who'll go into the bush after *this* lion. Nobody with the experience—or the ballocks. That's why we need you, Pendergast. We need you down here to track that bugger and...well...recover the remains of the poor German before there's nothing left to bury."

"You haven't even recovered the body?"

"Nobody will go out there after the bloody thing! You know what Kingazu Camp is like, all the dense brush that's come up because of the elephant poaching. We need a damned experienced hunter. And I needn't remind you that terms of your professional hunting license require you to deal with rogue man-eaters as, and if, it becomes necessary."

"I see."

"Where'd you leave your Rover?"

"At the Fala Pans."

"Get cracking as fast as you can. Don't bother breaking camp, just grab your guns and get down here."

"It'll take a day, at least. Are you sure there isn't anyone closer who can help you?"

"Nobody. At least, nobody I'd trust."

Pendergast glanced at his wife. She smiled, winked, mimed the shooting of a pistol with one bronzed hand. "All right. We'll get moving right away."

"One other thing." The DC's voice hesitated and there was a silence over the radio, filled with hissing and crackling.

"What?"

"Probably not very important. The wife who witnessed the attack. She said..." Another pause.

"Yes?"

"She said the lion was peculiar."

"How so?"

"It had a red mane."

"You mean, a little darker than usual? That's not so uncommon."

"Not darker than usual. This lion's mane was deep red. Almost blood red."

There was a very long silence. And then the DC spoke again. "But of course it can't be the same lion. That was forty years ago in northern Botswana. I've never heard of a lion living more than twenty-five years. Have you?"

Pendergast said nothing as he switched off the radio, his silvery eyes glittering in the dying twilight of the African bush.

2

Kingazu Camp, Luangwa River

The Land Rover banged and lurched along the Banta Road, a bad track in a country legendary for them. Pendergast turned the wheel violently left and right to avoid the yawning potholes, some almost half as deep as the bashed-up Rover. The windows were wide open—the air-conditioning was broken—and the interior of the car was awash in dust blown in by the occasional vehicle passing in the other direction.

They had left Makwele Stream just before dawn, making the twelve-mile trek through the bush without guides, carrying nothing but their weapons, water, a hard salami, and chapati bread. They reached their car around noon. For several hours now they had been passing through sporadic, hardscrabble villages: circular buildings of lashed sticks with conical roofs of thatch, dirt streets clogged with loose cattle and sheep. The sky was a cloudless, pale, almost watery blue.

Helen Pendergast fiddled with her scarf, pulling it more tightly around her hair in a losing battle with the omnipresent dust. It stuck to every exposed inch of their sweaty skin, giving them a scrofulous appearance.

"It's strange," she said as they crawled through yet another village, avoiding chickens and small children. "I mean, that there isn't a hunter closer by to take care of this lion problem. After all, you're not exactly a crack shot." She smiled wryly; this was a frequent tease.

"That's why I'm counting on you."

"You know I don't like killing animals I can't eat."

"How about killing animals that can eat us?"

"Perhaps I can make an exception there." She angled the sun visor into a new position, then turned toward Pendergast, her eyes—blue with flecks of violet—narrowed by the bright light. "So. What was that business about the red mane?"

"A lot of nonsense. There's an old legend knocking about this part of Africa concerning a red-maned, man-eating lion."

"Tell me about it." Her eyes sparkled with interest; the local stories fascinated her.

"Very well. About forty years ago—the story goes—a drought struck the southern Luangwa Valley. Game grew very scarce. A pride of lions that hunted in the valley starved to death, one by one, until only a single survivor remained—a pregnant lioness. She survived by digging up and eating the corpses at a local Nyimba cemetery."

"How horrible," Helen said with relish.

"They say she gave birth to a cub with a flaming red mane."

"Go on."

"The villagers were angry with this continuing desecration of their burial grounds. Eventually they tracked down the lioness, killed her, skinned her, and nailed her hide to a frame in the village square. Then they held a dance to celebrate her demise. At dawn, while the villagers were sleeping off the effects of all the maize beer they'd downed, a red-maned lion snuck into the village, killed three of the sleeping men, then carried off a boy. They found his gnawed bones a couple of days later in a stand of long grass a few miles off."

"Good Lord."

"Over the years, the Red Lion, or the *Dabu Gor* as it was called in the Bemba language, killed and ate a large number of locals. It was very clever, they said: as clever as a man. It shifted ranges frequently and sometimes crossed borders to evade capture. The local Nyimba claimed the Red Lion could not survive without the nourishment of human flesh—but with it, he would live forever."

Pendergast paused to circumnavigate a pothole almost lunar in its depth and extent.

"And?"

"That's the story."

"But what happened to the lion? Was he ever killed?"

"A number of professional hunters tried to track him, without success. He just kept killing until he died of old age—if he *did* die, that is." Pendergast rolled his eyes toward her dramatically.

"Really, Aloysius! You know it can't be the same lion."

"It might be a descendant, carrying the same genetic mutation."

"And perhaps the same tastes," said Helen, with a ghoulish smile.

As the afternoon turned to evening, they passed through two more deserted villages, the usual cries of children and lowing of cattle replaced by the drone of insects. They arrived at Kingazu Camp after sunset, as a blue twilight was settling over the bush. The camp stood on the Luangwa River, a cluster of *rondevaals* arranged along the banks, with an open-air bar and a dining shelter.

"What a delightful setting," Helen said as she looked around.

"Kingazu is one of the oldest safari camps in the country," Pendergast replied. "It was founded in the 1950s, when Zambia was still part of Northern Rhodesia, by a hunter who realized that taking people out to photograph animals could be just as exciting as killing them—and a lot more remunerative."

"Thank you, Professor. Will there be a quiz after the lecture?"

When they pulled into the dusty parking area, the bar and dining shelter were empty, the camp staff having taken refuge in the surrounding huts. All the lights were on, the generator chugging full blast.

"Nervous bunch," said Helen, flinging open the door and climbing out into the hot evening, the air shrill with cicadas.

The door of the closest *rondevaal* opened, striping yellow light across the beaten earth, and a man in pressed khakis with knife-edge creases, leather bush-boots, and high socks stepped out.

"The district commissioner, Alistair Woking," Pendergast whispered to his wife.

"I'd never have guessed."

"And the fellow with him in the Australian cowboy hat is Gordon Wisley, the camp concessionaire."

"Come inside," said the district commissioner, shaking their hands. "We can talk more comfortably in the hut."

"Heavens, no!" said Helen. "We've been cooped up in a car all day—let's have a drink at the bar."

"Well...," the commissioner said dubiously.

"If the lion comes into camp, so much the better. Then we won't have the bother of stalking him in the bush. Right, Aloysius?"

"Flawlessly argued."

She lifted the soft-canvas bag that held her gun out of the back of the Land Rover. Pendergast did the same, hefting a heavy metal canister of ammunition over his shoulder.

"Gentlemen?" he said. "To the bar?"

"Very well." The DC eyed their heavy-bore safari guns with a certain look of reassurance. "Misumu!"

An African in a felt fez and red sash ducked his head out a door of the staff camp.

"We'd like a drink at the bar," said Woking. "If you don't mind."

They retired to the thatched bar, the barman taking his place behind the polished wood counter. He was sweating, and not because of the heat.

"Maker's Mark," said Helen. "On the rocks."

"Two," said her husband. "And muddle in some mint, if you have it."

"Make it the same all 'round," said the DC. "Is that all right with you, Wisley?"

"Just so long as it's strong," said Wisley with a nervous laugh. "What a day."

The barman poured the drinks, and Pendergast washed the dust from his throat with a good slug. "Tell us what happened, Mr. Wisley."

Wisley was a tall redhead with a New Zealand accent. "It was after lunch," he began. "We had twelve guests in camp—a full house."

As he spoke, Pendergast unzipped the canvas carrying case and removed his gun, a Holland & Holland .465 "Royal" double rifle. He broke the action and began cleaning the weapon, wiping off dust from the long drive. "What was lunch?"

"Sandwiches. Roast kudu, ham, turkey, cucumber. Iced tea. We always serve a light lunch during the heat of the day."

Pendergast nodded, polishing the walnut stock.

"A lion had been roaring most of the night off in the bush, but during the day it settled down. We often hear roaring lions—it's one of the attractions of the camp, actually."

"Charming."

"But they've never bothered us before. I just can't understand it."

Pendergast glanced at him, then returned his attention to the gun. "This lion, I take it, was not local?"

"No. We have several prides here—I know every individual by sight. This was a rogue male."

"Large?"

"Large as hell."

"Big enough to make the book?"

Wisley grimaced. "Bigger than anything *in* the book."

"I see."

"The German, a fellow named Hassler, and his wife were the first to leave the table. I think it was around two. They were heading back to their *rondevaal* when—according to the wife—the lion leapt from the cover along the riverbank, knocked her husband down, and sank his teeth into the poor man's neck. The wife started screaming bloody murder, and of course the poor bloke was screaming, too. We all came running, but the lion had dragged him off into the bush and vanished. I can't tell you how terrible it was—we could hear him scream, again and again. Then all went quiet except for the sounds of…" He stopped abruptly.

"Good God," said Helen. "Didn't anyone fetch a rifle?"

"I did," said Wisley. "I'm not much of a shot, but as you know we're required to carry rifles during outings with tourists. I didn't dare follow him into the long grass—I don't hunt, Mr. Pendergast—but I fired several times at the sounds and it seemed to drive the lion deeper into the bush. Perhaps I wounded him."

"That would be unfortunate," said Pendergast dryly. "No doubt he dragged the body with him. Did you preserve the spoor at the scene of the attack?"

"Yes, we did. Of course, there was some initial disturbance during the panic, but then I blocked off the area."

"Excellent. And no one went into the bush after him?"

"No. Everyone was simply hysterical—we haven't had

a lion killing in decades. We evacuated all but essential staff."

Pendergast nodded, then glanced at his wife. She, too, had cleaned her rifle—a Krieghoff .500/.416 "Big Five"—and was listening intently.

"Have you heard the lion since then?"

"No. It was bloody silent all last night and today. Perhaps he's gone off."

"Not likely, until he's finished his kill," said Pendergast. "A lion won't drag a kill more than a mile. You can be sure he's still around. Did anyone else see him?"

"Just the wife."

"And she said he was red-maned?"

"Yes. At first, in her hysteria, she said he was soaked in blood. But when she calmed down a bit we were able to question her more exactly, and it appears the lion's mane was deep red."

"How do you know it *wasn't* blood?"

Helen spoke up. "Lions are very fussy about their manes. They clean them regularly. I've never seen a lion with blood on its mane—only its face."

"So what do we do, Mr. Pendergast?" Wisley asked.

Pendergast took a long sip of his bourbon. "We'll have to wait until dawn. I'll want your best tracker and a single gun bearer. And of course, my wife will be the second shooter."

A silence. Wisley and the DC were both looking at Helen. She returned their looks with a smile.

"I'm afraid that might be somewhat, ah, irregular," said Woking, clearing his throat.

"Because I'm a woman?" Helen asked, amused. "Don't worry, it isn't catching."

"No, no," came the hasty reply. "It's just that we're in a national park, and only someone with a government-issued professional license is authorized to shoot."

"Of the two of us," said Pendergast, "my wife is the better shot. On top of that, it's essential to have two expert shooters when stalking lion in the bush." He paused. "Unless, of course, you'd care to be the second shooter?"

The DC fell silent.

"I won't allow my husband to go in there alone," said Helen. "It would be too dangerous. The poor dear might get mauled—or worse."

"Thank you, Helen, for your confidence," said Pendergast.

"Well, you know, Aloysius, you *did* miss that duiker at two hundred yards. That was as easy as hitting a barn door from the inside."

"Come now, there was a strong cross-wind. And the animal moved at the last moment."

"You spent too long setting up your shot. You think too much, that's your problem."

Pendergast turned to Woking. "As you can see, this is a package deal. It's both of us or neither."

"Very well," said the DC with a frown. "Mr. Wisley?"

Wisley nodded reluctantly.

"We'll meet tomorrow morning at five," Pendergast went on. "I'm quite serious when I say we'll need a very, very good tracker."

"We have one of the best in Zambia—Jason Mfuni. Of course, he's rarely tracked for hunting, only for photographers and tourists."

"As long as he has nerves of steel."

"He does."

"You'll need to spread the word to the locals, make sure they stay well away. The last thing we'll need is a distraction."

"That won't be necessary," said Wisley. "Perhaps you noticed the empty villages on your way in to the camp? Except for us, you won't find a single human being within twenty miles."

"The villages emptied that quickly?" Helen said. "The attack only took place yesterday."

"It's the Red Lion," the DC said, as if this were explanation enough.

Pendergast and Helen exchanged glances. For a moment, the bar went silent.

Then Pendergast rose, took Helen's hand, and helped her to her feet. "Thanks for the drink. And now, if you will show us to our hut?"

3

The Fever Trees

The night had been silent. Even the local prides that often tattooed the darkness with their roars were lying low, and the usual chatter of night animals seemed subdued. The sound of the river was a faint gurgle and shush that belied its massive flow, perfuming the air with the smell of water. Only with the false dawn came the first noises of what passed for civilization: hot water being poured into shower-drums in preparation for morning ablutions.

Pendergast and his wife had left their hut and were in the dining shelter, guns beside them, sitting by the soft glow of a single bulb. There were no stars—the night had been overcast, the darkness absolute. They had been sitting there, unmoving and silent, for the last forty-five minutes, enjoying each other's company and—with the kind of unspoken symbiosis that characterized their marriage—preparing mentally and emotionally for the hunt ahead. Helen Pendergast's head was resting on her husband's shoulder. Pendergast stroked her hand, toying now and then with the star sapphire on her wedding band.

"You can't have it back, you know," she said at last, her voice husky from the long silence.

He simply smiled and continued his caresses.

A small figure appeared in the shadows, carrying a long spear and wearing long pants and a long shirt, both of dark color.

The two straightened up. "Jason Mfuni?" Pendergast asked, his voice low.

"Yes, sir."

Pendergast extended his hand. "I'd rather you didn't 'sir' me, Jason. The name's Pendergast. And this is my wife, Helen. She prefers to be called by her first name, I by my last."

The man nodded, shook Helen's hand with slow, almost phlegmatic movements. "The DC want to talk to you, Miss Helen, in the mess."

Helen rose. So did Pendergast.

"Excuse me, Mr. Pendergast, he want it private."

"What's this all about?"

"He worry about her hunting experience."

"This is ridiculous," Pendergast said. "We've settled that question."

Helen waved her hand with a laugh. "Don't worry about it—apparently it's still the British Empire out here, where women sit on the veranda, fan themselves, and faint at the sight of blood. I'll set him straight."

Pendergast eased back down. The tracker waited by him, shifting uncomfortably from foot to foot.

"Would you care to sit down, Jason?"

"No thank you."

"How long have you been tracking?" Pendergast asked.

"A few years," came the laconic reply.

"Are you good?"

A shrug.

"Are you afraid of lions?"

"Sometimes."

"Ever killed one with that spear?"

"No."

"I see."

"This is a new spear, Mr. Pendergast. When I kill lion with spear, it usually break or bend, have to get new one."

A silence settled over the camp as the light crept up behind the bush. Five minutes passed, and then ten.

"What's taking them?" asked Pendergast, annoyed. "We don't want to get a late start." Mfuni shrugged and leaned on his spear, waiting.

Suddenly Helen appeared. She quickly seated herself.

"Did you set the blighter straight?" asked Pendergast with a laugh.

For a moment, Helen didn't answer. He turned to her quizzically and was startled at the whiteness of her face. "What is it?" he asked.

"Nothing. Just...butterflies before a hunt."

"You can always remain back in camp, you know."

"Oh, no," she said with vehemence. "No, I can't miss this."

"In that case, we'd better get moving."

"Not yet," she said, her voice low. He felt her cool

hand on his arm. "Aloysius...do you realize we forgot to watch the moonrise last evening? It was full."

"With all the lion excitement, I'm not surprised."

"Let's take just a moment to watch it set." She took his hand and enclosed it in hers, an unusual gesture for her. Her hand was no longer cool.

"Helen..."

She squeezed his hand. "No talking."

The full moon was sinking into the bush on the far side of the river, a buttery disk descending through a sky of mauve, its reflection rippling like spilled cream over the swirling waters of the Luangwa River. They had first met the night of a full moon and, together, had watched it rise; ever since it had been a tradition of their courtship and marriage that no matter what else was happening in their lives, no matter what travel or commitments they faced, they would always contrive to be together to watch the rise of the full moon.

The moon touched the distant treetops across the river, then slid down behind them. The sky brightened and, finally, the gleam of the moon vanished in the tangle of bush. The mystery of the night had passed; day had arrived.

"Good-bye, old moon," said Pendergast lightly.

Helen squeezed his hand, then stood up as the DC and Wisley materialized on the path from the kitchen hut. With them was a third man, hollow-faced, very tall and lanky. His eyes were yellow.

"This is Wilson Nyala," said Wisley. "Your gun bearer."

Handshakes. The bartender from the previous night came from the kitchen with a large pot of lapsang souchong tea, and steaming cups of the strong brew were poured all around.

They drank quickly in silence. Pendergast set his cup down. "It's light enough to take a look at the scene of the attack."

Nyala slung one gun over each shoulder, and they walked down a dirt path that ran along the river. Where it passed a dense stand of miombo brush, an area had been marked out with rope and wooden stakes. Pendergast knelt, examining the spoor. He could see a pair of enormous pug marks in the dust, next to a puddled mass of black blood, now dry and cracking. As he looked about, he reconstructed the attack in his mind. What had happened was clear enough: the man had been jumped from the brush, knocked down, bitten. The initial reports were accurate. The dust showed where the lion had dragged his thrashing victim back into the brush, leaving a trail of blood.

Pendergast rose. "Here's how it'll work. I'll stay eight feet behind Jason, slightly to his left. Helen will be behind me another eight feet, to the right. Wilson, you float just behind us." He glanced over at his wife, who gave a subtle nod of approval.

"When the time comes," he continued, "we'll gesture for the guns—bring them up with safeties on. For my rifle, detach the strap—I would rather not hitch it up on brush."

"I prefer my strap on," said Helen curtly.

Wilson Nyala nodded his bony head.

Pendergast extended an arm. "My rifle, please?"

Wilson handed him his rifle. Pendergast broke the action, examined the barrel, dunked in two soft-point

.465 nitro express cartridges—big as Macanudos—closed it, locked it, made sure the safety was on, and handed it back. Helen did the same with her rifle, loading it with .500/.416 flanged soft points.

"That's a rather big gun for such a slender woman," said Woking.

"I think a big-bore weapon is rather fetching," replied Helen.

"All I can say," Woking continued, "is I'm glad I'm not going into the bush after that brute, big rifle or no."

"Keep the long-triangle formation as closely as possible as we advance," said Pendergast, glancing from Mfuni to Nyala and back again. "The wind's in our favor. No talking unless absolutely necessary. Use hand signals. Leave the flashlights here."

Everyone nodded. The atmosphere of false jollity quickly evaporated as they waited in silence for the sun to come up enough to fill the underbrush with dim blue twilight. Then Pendergast motioned for Mfuni to proceed.

The tracker moved into the bush, carrying his spear in one hand, following the blood spoor. The trail moved away from the river, through the dense thorn scrub and second-growth mopane brush along a small tributary of the Luangwa called Chitele Stream. They moved slowly, following the spoor that coated the grass and leaves. The tracker paused to point with his spear at a brake of flattened grass. There was a large stained area, still damp, the leaves around splattered with arterial blood. This was where the lion had first put down his victim and begun eating, even while the victim still lived, before being shot at.

Jason Mfuni bent down and silently held up an object: half of a lower jawbone with teeth, gnawed around the edges and licked clean. Pendergast looked at it without speaking. Mfuni laid it down again and pointed to a hole in the wall of vegetation.

They proceeded through the hole into heavy green bush. Mfuni paused every twenty yards to listen and smell the air, or to examine a smear of blood on a leaf. The corpse had bled out by this point, and the spoor grew fainter: all that marked the trail were tiny smears and spots.

The tracker stopped twice to point out areas of broken grass where the lion had put the body down to shift its fang-hold and then pick it up again. The day was coming up rapidly, the sun breaking over the treetops. Except that, save for the constant drone of insects, this particular morning was unusually silent and watchful.

They followed the spoor for more than a mile. The sun boiled over the horizon, beaming furnace-like heat into the brush, and the tsetse flies rose in whining clouds. The air carried the heavy smell of dust and grass. The trail finally broke free of the bushveldt into a dry pan under the spreading branches of an acacia tree, a single termite mound rising like a pinnacle against the incandescent sky. In the center of the pan was a jumble of red and white, surrounded by a roaring cloud of flies.

Mfuni moved out cautiously, Pendergast, Helen, and the gun bearer following. They silently gathered around the half-eaten body of the German photographer. The lion had opened the cranium, eaten his face, brain, and much of the upper torso, leaving two perfectly white, unscathed legs, licked clean of blood, and one detached arm, its fist still clenching a tuft of fur. Nobody spoke. Mfuni bent down, tugged the hair from the fist, shaking the arm free in the process, and inspected it carefully. He then placed it in Pendergast's hand. It was deep red in color. Pendergast passed it to Helen, who examined it in turn, then handed it back to Mfuni.

While the others remained near the body, the tracker slowly circled the pan, looking for tracks in the alkaline crust. He placed a finger on his mouth and pointed across the dry pan into a *vlei*, a swampy depression during the wet season that—now the dry season was advanced—had grown up into an extremely dense stand of grass, ten to twelve feet high. Several hundred yards into the *vlei* rose a large, sinuous grove of fever trees, their umbrella-like crowns spreading against the horizon. The tracker was pointing at a slot bent into the tall grass, made by the lion in its retreat. He came back over, his face serious, and whispered into Pendergast's ear. "In there," he said, pointing with his spear. "Resting."

Pendergast nodded and glanced at Helen. She was still pale but absolutely steady, the eyes cool and determined.

Nyala, the gun bearer, was nervous. "What is it?" Pendergast asked in a low tone, turning to him.

He nodded toward the tall grass. "That lion smart. Too smart. Very bad place."

Pendergast hesitated, looking from the bearer, to the tracker, to the stand of grass and back again. Then he gestured for the tracker to proceed.

Slowly, stealthily, they entered the tall grass. The visibility dropped to less than five yards. The hollow stalks rustled and whispered with their movements, the cloying smell of heated grass stifling in the dead air. Green twilight enveloped them as they moved deeper into the stand. The drone of insects merged into a steady whine.

As they approached the grove of fever trees, the tracker slowed; held up his hand; pointed to his nose. Pendergast inhaled and caught the faint, musky scent of lion, overlaid with the sweetish whiff of carrion.

The tracker crouched and signaled for the others to do likewise—the visibility in the bunch grass was better closer to the ground, where they had a greater chance of seeing the tawny flash of the lion before he was actually on top of them. They slowly entered the fever grove, inching along at a crouch. The dried, silty mud was baked hard as rock and it retained no spoor, but broken and bent stems told a clear tale of the lion's passage.

Again the tracker paused, motioning for a talk. Pendergast and Helen came up and the three huddled in the close grass, whispering just loud enough to be heard over the insects.

"Lion somewhere in front. Twenty, thirty yards. Moving slowly." Mfuni's face was creased with concern. "Maybe we should wait."

"No," whispered Pendergast. "This is our best chance at bagging him. He's just eaten."

They moved forward, into a small open area with no grass, no more than ten feet square. The tracker paused, sniffed the air, then pointed left. *"Lion,"* he whispered.

Pendergast stared ahead, looked left, then shook his head and pointed straight ahead.

The tracker scowled, leaned to Pendergast's ear. "Lion circle around to left. He very smart."

Still Pendergast shook his head. He leaned over Helen. "You stay here," he whispered, his lips brushing her ears.

"But the tracker—"

"The tracker's wrong. You stay, I'll go ahead just a few yards. We're nearing the far end of the *vlei*. He'll want to remain in cover; with me moving toward him he'll feel pressed. He might rush. Be ready and keep a line of fire open to my right."

Pendergast signaled for his gun. He grasped the metal barrel, warm in the heat, and pulled it forward under his arm. He thumbed off the safety and flipped up the night sight—a bead of ivory—for better sighting in the grassy half-light. Nyala handed Helen her rifle.

Pendergast moved into the dense grass straight ahead, the tracker following in frozen silence, his face a mask of terror.

Pushing through the grass, placing each foot with exceeding caution on the hardpan ground, Pendergast listened intently for the peculiar cough that would signal the beginning of a rush. There would be time for only one shot: a charging lion could cover a hundred yards in as little as four seconds. He felt more secure with Helen behind him; two chances at the kill.

After ten yards, he paused and waited. The tracker came alongside, deep unhappiness written on his face. For a full two minutes, neither man moved. Pendergast listened intently but could hear only insects. The gun was slippery in his sweaty hands, and he could taste the alkali dust on his tongue. A faint breeze, seen but not felt, swayed the grass around them, making a soft clacking sound. The insect drone fell to a murmur, then died. Everything grew utterly still.

Slowly, without moving any other part of his body, Mfuni extended a single finger—again ninety degrees to his left.

Remaining absolutely still, Pendergast followed the gesture with his eyes. He peered into the dim haze of grass, trying to catch a glimpse of tawny fur or the gleam of an amber eye. Nothing.

A low cough—and then a terrible, earthshaking explosion of sound, a massive roar, came blasting at them like a freight train. Not from the left, but from straight ahead.

Pendergast spun around as a blur of ocher muscle and reddish fur exploded out of the grass, pink mouth agape, daggered with teeth; he fired one barrel with a massive *ka-whang!* but he hadn't time to compose the shot and the lion was on him, six hundred pounds of enormous stinking cat, knocking him flat, and then he felt the red-hot fangs slice into his shoulder and he cried out, twisting under the suffocating mass, flailing with his free arm, trying to recover the rifle that had been knocked away by the massive blow.

The lion had been so well hidden, and the rush so fast and close, that Helen Pendergast was unable to shoot before it was on top of her husband—and then it was too late; they were too close together to risk a shot. She leapt from her spot ten yards behind and bulled through the tall grass, yelling, trying to draw the monstrous lion's attention as she raced toward the hideous sound of muffled, wet growling. She burst onto the scene just as Mfuni sank his spear into the lion's gut; the beast—bigger than any lion should rationally be—leapt off Pendergast and swiped at the tracker, tearing away part of his leg, then bounded into the grass, the spear dragging from its belly.

Helen took careful aim at the lion's retreating back and fired, the recoil from the massive .500/.416 nitro express cartridge jolting her hard.

The shot missed. The lion was gone.

She rushed to her husband. He was still conscious. "No," Pendergast gasped. *"Him."*

She glanced at Mfuni. He was lying on his back, arterial blood squirting into the dirt from where the calf muscle of his right leg was hanging by a thread of skin.

"Oh, Jesus." She tore off the lower half of her shirt, twisted it tight, and wrapped it above the severed artery. Groping around for a stick, she slid it under the cloth and twisted it tight to form a tourniquet.

"Jason?" she said urgently. "Stay with me! *Jason!*"

His face was slick with sweat, his eyes wide and trembling.

"Hold that stick. Loosen it if you start going numb."

The tracker's eyes widened. "Memsahib, the lion is coming back."

"Just hold that—"

"It's coming back!" Mfuni's voice broke in terror.

Ignoring him, she turned her attention to her husband. He lay on his back, his face gray. His shoulder was misshapen and covered with a clotted mass of blood. "Helen," he said hoarsely, struggling to rise. "Get your gun. *Now.*"

"Aloysius—"

"For the love of God, get your gun!"

It was too late. With another earsplitting roar, the lion burst from the cover, sending up a whirlwind of dust and flying grass—and then he was on top of her. Helen screamed once and tried to fight him off as the lion seized her by the arm; there was a sharp crackling of bone as the lion sank his teeth in—and then the last thing Pendergast saw before he passed out was the sight of her struggling, screaming figure being dragged off into the deep grass.

4

The world came back into focus. Pendergast was in one of the *rondevaals*. The distant throb of a chopper sounded through the thatch roof, rapidly increasing in volume.

He sat up with a cry to see the DC, Woking, leap out of a chair he'd been sitting in at the far side of the hut.

"Don't exert yourself," Woking said. "The medevac's here, everything'll be taken care of—"

Pendergast struggled up. "My wife! Where is she?"

"Be a good lad and—"

Pendergast swung out of bed and staggered to his feet, driven by pure adrenaline. "My *wife*, you son of a bitch!"

"It couldn't be helped, she was dragged off, we had a man unconscious and another bleeding to death—"

Pendergast staggered to the door of the hut. His rifle was there, set in the rack. He seized it, broke it, saw that it still contained a single round.

"What in God's name are you doing—?"

Pendergast closed the action and swung the rifle toward the DC. "Get out of my way."

Woking scrambled aside and Pendergast lurched out of the hut. The sun was setting. Twelve hours had passed. The DC came rushing out after him, waving his arms. "Help! I need help! The man's gone mad!"

Crashing into the wall of brush, Pendergast pushed through the long grass until he had picked up the trail. He did not even hear the ragged shouts from the camp behind. He charged along the old spoor trail, thrusting the brush aside, heedless of the pain. Five minutes passed, then ten, then fifteen—and then he burst into the dry pan. Beyond lay the *vlei*, the dense grass, the grove of fever trees. With a gasp he lurched forward across the pan and into the grass, swiping his weapon back and forth with his good arm to clear a path, the birds overhead screaming at the disturbance. His lungs burned, his arm was drenched in blood. Still he advanced, bleeding freely from his torn shoulder, vocalizing inarticulately. And then he stopped, the ragged incoherent sounds dying in his throat. There was something in the grass ahead, small, pale, lying on the hardpacked mud. He stared down at it. It was a severed hand—a hand whose ring finger was banded with a star sapphire.

With an animalistic cry of rage and grief, he staggered forward, bursting from the long grass into an open area where the lion, its mane ablaze with color, was crouching and quietly feeding. He took in the horror all at once: the bones decorated with ribbons of flesh, his wife's hat, the tattered pieces of her khaki outfit, and then suddenly the smell—the faint smell of her perfume mingling with the stench of the cat.

Last of all he saw the head. It had been severed from her body but—with a cruel irony—was otherwise intact compared with the rest. Her blue-and-violet eyes stared up sightlessly at him.

Pendergast walked unsteadily up to within ten yards of the lion. It raised its monstrous head, slopped a tongue around its bloody chops, and looked at him calmly. His breath coming in short, sharp gasps, Pendergast raised the Holland & Holland with his good arm, propped it on his bad, sighted along the top of the ivory bead. And pulled the trigger. The massive round, packing five thousand foot-pounds of muzzle energy, struck the lion just between and above the eyes, opening the top of its head like a sardine can, the cranium exploding in a blur of red mist. The great red-maned lion hardly moved; it merely sank down on top of its meal, and then lay still.

All around, in the sunbaked fever trees, a thousand birds screamed.

5

St. Charles Parish, Louisiana

The Rolls-Royce Grey Ghost crept around the circular drive, the crisp crunch of gravel under the tires muffled in places by patches of crabgrass. The motorcar was followed by a late-model Mercedes, in silver. Both vehicles came to a stop before a large Greek Revival plantation house, framed by ancient black oaks draped in fingers of Spanish moss. A small bronze plaque screwed into the façade announced that the mansion was known as Penumbra; that it had been built in 1821 by the Pendergast family; and that it was on the National Register of Historic Places.

A. X. L. Pendergast stepped out of the rear compartment of the Rolls and looked around, taking in the scene. It was the end of an afternoon in late February. Mellow light played through the Greek columns, casting bars of gold into the covered porch. A thin mist drifted across the overgrown lawn and weed-heavy gardens. Beyond, cicadas droned sleepily in the cypress groves and mangrove swamps. The copper trim on the second-floor balconies was covered in a dense patina of verdigris. Small curls of white paint hung from the pillars, and an atmosphere of dampness, desuetude, and neglect hung over the house and grounds.

A curious gentleman emerged from the Mercedes, short and stocky, wearing a black cutaway with a white carnation in his boutonniere. He looked more like a maître d' from an Edwardian men's club than a New Orleans lawyer. Despite the limpid sunlight, a tightly rolled umbrella was tucked primly beneath one arm. An alligator-skin briefcase was clutched in one fawn-gloved hand. He placed a bowler hat on his head, gave it a smart tap.

"Mr. Pendergast. Shall we?" The man extended a hand toward an overgrown arboretum, enclosed by a hedge, that stood to the right of the house.

"Of course, Mr. Ogilby."

"Thank you." The man led the way, walking briskly, his wingtips sweeping through the moisture-laden grass. Pendergast followed more slowly, with less sense of purpose. Reaching a gate in the hedge, Mr. Ogilby pushed it open, and together they entered the arboretum. At one point he glanced back with a mischievous smile and said, "Let us keep an eye out for the ghost!"

"That would be a thrill," said Pendergast, in the same jocular vein.

Continuing his brisk pace, the lawyer followed a once-graveled path now overgrown with weeds toward a specimen-size weeping hemlock, beyond which could be seen a rusting iron fence enclosing a small plot of ground. Peeking up from the grass within was a scattering of slate and marble headstones, some vertical, some listing.

The gentleman, his creased black trouser cuffs now soaked, came to a halt before one of the larger tombstones, turned, and then grasped the briefcase in both hands, waiting for his client to catch up. Pendergast took a thoughtful turn around the private graveyard, stroking his pale chin, before ending up next to the dapper little man.

"Well!" the lawyer said, "here we are again!"

Pendergast nodded absently. He knelt, pushed aside the grass from the face of the tombstone, and read aloud:

Hic Iacet Sepultus
Louis de Frontenac Diogenes Pendergast
Apr 2, 1899–Mar 15, 1975
Tempus Edax Rerum

Mr. Ogilby, standing behind Pendergast, propped his briefcase on the top of the tombstone, undid the latches, raised the cover, and slipped out a document. On the cover of the briefcase, balancing it on the headstone, he laid down the document.

"Mr. Pendergast?" He proffered a heavy silver fountain pen.

Pendergast signed the document.

The lawyer took the pen back, signed it himself with a flourish, impressed it with a notary public seal, dated it, and slipped it back in his briefcase. He shut it with a snap, latched it, and locked it.

"Done!" he said. "You are now certified to have visited

your grandfather's grave. I shall not have to disinherit you from the Pendergast family trust—at least, not for the present!" He gave a short chuckle.

Pendergast rose, and the little man stuck out a pudgy hand. "Always a pleasure, Mr. Pendergast, and I trust I shall have the favor of your company in another five years?"

"The pleasure is, and shall be, mine," said Pendergast with a dry smile.

"Excellent! I'll be heading back to town, then. Will you follow?"

"I think I'll drop in on Maurice. He'd be crushed if I left without paying him my respects."

"Quite, quite! To think he's been looking after Penumbra unassisted for—what?—twelve years now. You know, Mr. Pendergast—" Here the little man leaned in and lowered his voice, as if to impart a secret. "—you really should fix this place up. You could get a handsome sum for it—a handsome sum! Antebellum plantation houses are all the rage these days. It would make a charming B and B!"

"Thank you, Mr. Ogilby, but I think I shall hold on to it a while longer."

"As you wish, as you wish! Just don't stay out after dark—what with the old family ghost, and all." The little man strode off chuckling to himself, briefcase swinging, and soon vanished, leaving Pendergast alone in the family plot. He heard the Mercedes start up; heard the crunch of gravel fade quickly back into silence.

He strolled about for another few minutes, reading the inscriptions on the stones. Each name resurrected memories stranger and more eccentric than the last.

Many of the remains were of family members disinterred from the ruins of the basement crypt of the Pendergast mansion on Dauphine Street after the house burned; other ancestors had expressed wishes to be buried in the old country.

The golden light faded as the sun sank below the trees. Pallid mists began to drift across the lawn from the direction of the mangrove swamp. The air smelled of verdure, moss, and bracken. Pendergast stood in the graveyard for a long time, silent and unmoving, as evening settled over the land. Yellow lights—coming up in the windows of the plantation house—filtered through the trees of the arboretum. The scent of burning oak wood drifted on the air; a smell that brought back irresistible memories of childhood summers. Glancing up, Pendergast could see one of the great brick chimneys of the plantation house issuing a lazy stream of blue smoke. Rousing himself, he left the graveyard, walked through the arboretum, and gained the covered porch, the warped boards protesting under his feet.

He knocked on the door, then stood back to wait. A creaking from inside; the sound of slow footsteps; an elaborate unlatching and unchaining; and the great door swung open to reveal a stooped old man of indeterminate race, dressed in an ancient butler's uniform, his face grave. "Master Aloysius," he said, with fine reserve, not offering his hand immediately.

Pendergast extended his and the old man responded, the ribbed old hand getting a friendly shake. "Maurice. How are you?"

"Middling," the old man replied. "I saw the cars drive up. Glass of sherry in the library, sir?"

"That will be fine, thank you."

Maurice turned and moved slowly through the entry hall toward the library. Pendergast followed. A fire was burning on the hearth, not so much for warmth as to drive out the damp.

With a clinking of bottles, Maurice muddled about the sideboard and poured a measure into a tiny sherry glass, placed it on a silver tray, and carried it over with great ceremony. Pendergast took it, sipped, then glanced around. Nothing had changed for the better. The wallpaper was stained, and balls of dust lay in the corners. He could hear the faint rustle of rats in the walls. The place had gone downhill significantly in the five years since he had last been here.

"I wish you'd let me hire a live-in housekeeper, Maurice. And a cook. It would greatly relieve your burden."

"Nonsense! I can take care of the house myself."

"I don't think it's safe for you to be here alone."

"Not safe? Of course it's safe. I keep the house well locked at night."

"Naturally." Pendergast sipped the sherry, which was an excellent dry oloroso. He wondered, a little idly, how many bottles were left in the extensive cellars. Many more, probably, than he could drink in a lifetime, not to mention the wine, port, and fine old cognac. As the collateral branches of his family had died out, all the various wine cellars—like the wealth—had concentrated around him, the last surviving member of sound mind.

He took another sip and put down the glass. "Maurice, I think I'll take a turn through the house. For old times' sake."

"Yes, sir. I'll be here if you need me."

Pendergast rose and, opening the pocket doors, stepped into the entry hall. For fifteen minutes, he wandered through the rooms of the first floor: the empty kitchen and sitting rooms, the drawing room, the pantry and saloon. The house smelled faintly of his childhood—of furniture polish, aged oak, and, infinitely distant, his mother's perfume—all overlaid with a much more recent odor of damp and mildew. Every object, every knickknack and painting and paperweight and silver ashtray, was in its place, and every little thing carried a thousand memories of people long since under earth, of weddings and christenings and wakes, of cocktail parties and masked balls and children stampeding the halls to the warning exclamations of aunts.

Gone, all gone.

He mounted the stairs to the upper landing. Here, two hallways led to bedrooms in the opposite wings of the house, with the upstairs parlor straight ahead, through an arched doorway protected by a brace of elephant tusks.

He entered the parlor. A zebra rug lay on the floor, and the head of a Cape buffalo graced the mantel above the massive fireplace, looking down at him with furious glass eyes. On the walls were numerous other heads: kudu, bushbuck, stag, deer, hind, wild boar, elk.

He clasped his hands behind his back and slowly paced the room. Seeing this array of heads, these silent sentinels to memory and events long past, his thoughts drifted irresistibly to Helen. He'd had the old nightmare the previous night—as vivid and terrible as ever—and the malevolent effects still lingered like a canker in the pit of his stomach. Perhaps this room might exorcise that particular demon, at least for a while. It would never disappear, of course.

On the far side, against the wall, stood the locked gun case that displayed his collection of hunting rifles. It was a savage, bloody sport—driving a five-hundred-grain slug of metal at two thousand feet per second into a wild animal—and he wondered why it attracted him. But it was Helen who had truly loved hunting, a peculiar interest for a woman—but then Helen had been an unusual woman. A most unusual woman.

He gazed through the rippled, dusty glass at Helen's Krieghoff double-barreled rifle, the side plates exquisitely engraved and inlaid with silver and gold, the walnut stock polished with use. It had been his wedding present to her, just before they went on their honeymoon safari, after Cape buffalo in Tanzania. A beautiful thing, this rifle: six figures' worth of the finest woods and precious metals—designed for a most cruel purpose.

As he looked, he noted a small edge of rust creeping around the muzzle rim.

He strode to the door of the parlor and called down the stairs. "Maurice? Would you kindly bring me the key to the gun cabinet?"

After a long moment, Maurice appeared in the hall. "Yes, sir." He turned, disappearing once again. Moments later, he slowly mounted the groaning stairs, an iron key gripped in his veined hand. He creaked past Pendergast and stopped before the gun case, inserted the key, and turned it.

"There you are, sir." His face remained impassive,

but Pendergast was glad to sense in Maurice a feeling of pride: for having the key at his fingertips, for simply being of service.

"Thank you, Maurice."

A nod and the manservant was gone.

Pendergast reached inside the case and—slowly, slowly—grasped the cold metal of the double barrel. His fingers tingled at the mere touch of her weapon. For some reason his heart was accelerating—the lingering effects of the nightmare, no doubt. He brought it out and placed it on the refectory table in the middle of the room. From a drawer below the cabinet he removed the gun-cleaning paraphernalia, arranging it beside the rifle. He wiped his hands, picked up the gun, and broke open the action, peering down both barrels.

He was faintly surprised: the right barrel was badly fouled; the left one clean. He laid the gun down, thinking. Again he walked to the top of the stairs.

"Maurice?"

The servant appeared once more. "Yes, sir?"

"Do you know if anyone has fired the Krieghoff since…my wife's death?"

"It was your explicit request, sir, that no one be allowed to handle it. I've kept the key myself. No one has even been near the case."

"Thank you, Maurice."

"You're quite welcome, sir."

Pendergast went back into the parlor, this time shutting the doors. From a writing desk he extracted an old sheet of stationery, which he flipped over and laid on the table. Then he inserted a brush into the right barrel, pushed out some of the fouling onto the paper, and examined it: bits and flakes of some burned, papery substance. Reaching into his suit pocket, he pulled out the loupe he always carried, fixed it to his eye, and examined the bits more intently. There was no doubt: they were the scorched, carbonized fragments of wadding.

But the .500/.416 NE cartridge had no wadding: just the bullet, the casing, and the propellant. Such a cartridge, even a defective one, would never leave this kind of fouling behind.

He examined the left barrel, finding it clean and well oiled. With the cleaning brush he pushed a rag through. There was no fouling at all.

Pendergast straightened up, his mind suddenly in furious thought. The last time the gun had been fired had been on that terrible day. He forced himself to think back. This was something he had avoided—while awake—at all costs. But once he began to remember, it wasn't hard to recall the details: every moment of that hunt was seared forever into his memory.

She had fired the gun only once. The Krieghoff had two triggers, one behind the other. The front trigger fired the right barrel, and that was the trigger normally pulled first. It was the one she pulled. And that shot had fouled the right barrel.

With that single shot, she missed the Red Lion. He'd always chalked it up to bush deflection, or perhaps extreme agitation.

But Helen wasn't one to display agitation, even under the most extreme of circumstances. She rarely missed. And she hadn't missed that last time, either… or wouldn't have missed, if the right barrel had been loaded with a bullet.

Except that it *wasn't* loaded with a bullet: it was loaded with a blank.

For a blank to generate a similar sound and recoil, it would have to have a large, tightly wadded plug, which would foul the barrel exactly as he'd observed.

Had Pendergast been a man of lesser control, the hinges of his sanity might have weakened under the emotional intensity of his thoughts. She had loaded the gun with .500/.416 NE soft-points at the camp that morning, just before heading into the bush after the lion. He knew that for a fact: he had watched her. And he knew they were live rounds, not blanks—nobody, especially not Helen, would mistake a wadded blank for a two-ounce round. He himself clearly recalled the blunt heads of the soft-points as she dunked them into the barrels.

Between the time she loaded the Krieghoff with soft-points and the time she fired, someone had removed her unfired cartridges and replaced them with blanks. And then, after the hunt, someone had removed the two blanks—one fired, one not—to cover up what they had done. Only they made a small mistake: they did not clean the fired barrel, leaving the incriminating fouling.

Pendergast sat back in the chair. One hand—trembling ever so slightly—rose to his mouth.

Helen Pendergast's death had not been a tragic accident. It had been murder.

6

Four AM, Saturday. Lieutenant Vincent D'Agosta pushed through the crowd, ducked under the crime-scene tape, and walked over to where the body lay sprawled across the sidewalk outside one of the countless identical Indian restaurants on East 6th Street. A large pool of blood had collected beneath it, reflecting the red and purple neon light in the restaurant's grimy window with surreal splendor.

The perp had been shot at least half a dozen times and he was dead. Very dead. He lay crumpled on his side, one arm thrown wide, his gun twenty feet away. A crime-scene investigator was laying a tape measure, measuring the distance from the open hand to the gun.

The corpse was a scrawny Caucasian, thirtysomething, with thinning hair. He looked like a broken stick, his legs crooked, one knee hitched up to his chest, the other extended out and back, the arms flung wide.

The two cops who had done the shooting, a beefy black guy and a wiry Hispanic, were off to one side, talking with Internal Affairs.

D'Agosta went over, nodded to the Internal Affairs officer, and clasped the hands of the cops. They felt sweaty, nervous.

It's damn hard, D'Agosta thought, *to have killed someone. You never really get over it.*

"Lieutenant," said one of the cops in a rush, anxious to explain yet again to a fresh ear, "the guy had just robbed the restaurant at gunpoint and was running down the street. We identified ourselves, showed our badges, and that's when he opened on us, motherfucker just emptied his gun, firing while he ran, there were civilians on the street and we had no choice, we *had* to take him down. No choice, man, *no choice—*"

D'Agosta grasped the man's shoulder, gave it a friendly squeeze as he glanced at his nameplate. "Ocampo, don't sweat it. You did what you had to do. The investigation will show that."

"I mean, he just opened up like there was no tomorrow—"

"For him there won't be." D'Agosta walked aside with the Internal Affairs investigator. "Any problems?"

"I doubt it, sir. These days, of course, there's always a hearing. But this is about as clear-cut as they come." He slapped his notebook shut.

D'Agosta lowered his voice. "See those guys get some psychological counseling. And make sure they meet with the union lawyers before they do any more talking."

"Will do."

D'Agosta looked thoughtfully at the corpse. "How much did he get?"

"Two hundred and twenty, give or take. Fucking addict, look at him, all eaten up by horse."

"Sad. Any ID?"

"Warren Zabriskie, address in Far Rockaway."

D'Agosta shook his head as he glanced over the scene. It was about as straightforward as you could ask for: two cops, both minorities; the dead perp white; witnesses up the wazoo; everything caught on security cams. Open and shut. There would be no protest marches or accusations of police brutality. The shooter got what he deserved—everyone would reluctantly agree on that.

D'Agosta glanced around. Despite the cold, a pretty big crowd had developed beyond the tape, East Village rockers and yupsters and metrosexuals and whatever the hell else you called them these days. The forensic unit was still working the body, the EMTs waiting to one side, the owner of the victimized restaurant being interviewed by detectives. Everyone doing their job. Everything under control. A senseless, stupid, piece-of-shit case that would generate a blizzard of paperwork, interviews, reports, analyses, boxes of evidence, hearings, press conferences. All because of two hundred lousy bucks for a fix.

He was wondering how long it would be before he could gracefully escape when he heard a shout and saw a disturbance at the far edge of the cordoned area. Someone had ducked under the tape and trespassed onto the scene. He turned angrily—only to come face-to-face with Special Agent A. X. L. Pendergast, pursued by two uniformed officers.

"Hey, you—!" one of the cops shouted, grabbing Pendergast roughly by the shoulder. With a deft movement the agent freed himself, extracted his badge, and flashed it into the officer's face.

"What the—?" the cop said, backing off. "FBI. He's FBI."

"What's he doing here?" asked the other.

"Pendergast!" D'Agosta cried, stepping toward him quickly. "What the hell brings you here? This killing isn't exactly your kind of—"

Pendergast silenced him with a violent gesture, slashing his hand through the air between them. In the neon gloom, his face was so white he almost looked spectral, dressed as usual like a wealthy undertaker in his trademark tailored black suit. Except this time he somehow looked different—very different. "I must speak with you. Now."

"Sure, of course. As soon as I wrap things up—"

"I mean *now*, Vincent."

D'Agosta stared. This was not the cool, collected Pendergast he knew so well. This was a side of the man he had never seen before, angry, brusque, his movements rushed. Not only that, but—D'Agosta noticed on closer inspection—his normally immaculate suit was creased and rumpled.

Pendergast grasped him by the lapel. "I have a favor to ask you. More than a favor. Come with me."

D'Agosta was too surprised by his vehemence to do anything but obey. Leaving the scene under the stares of his fellow cops, he followed Pendergast past the crowd and down the street to where the agent's Rolls was idling. Proctor, the chauffeur, was behind the wheel, his expression studiously blank.

D'Agosta had to practically run to keep up. "You know I'll help you out any way I can—"

"Don't say anything, do not *speak*, until you've heard me out."

"Right, sure," D'Agosta added hastily.

"Get in."

Pendergast slipped into the rear passenger compartment, D'Agosta climbing in behind. The agent pulled open a panel in the door and swung out a tiny bar. Grasping a cut-glass decanter, he sloshed three fingers of brandy into a glass and drank half of it off with a single gulp. He replaced the decanter and turned to D'Agosta, his silvery eyes glittering with intensity. "This is no ordinary request. If you can't do it, or won't do it, I'll understand. But you must not burden me with questions, Vincent—I don't have time. I simply *don't—have—time*. Listen, and then give me your answer."

D'Agosta nodded.

"I need you to take a leave of absence from the force. Perhaps as long as a year."

"A *year*?"

Pendergast knocked back the rest of the drink. "It could be months, or weeks. There's no way to know how long this is going to take."

"What is *'this'*?"

For a moment, the agent did not reply. "I've never spoken to you about my late wife, Helen?"

"No."

"She died twelve years ago, when we were on safari in Africa. She was attacked by a lion."

"Jesus. I'm sorry."

"At the time, I believed it to be a terrible accident. Now I know different."

D'Agosta waited.

"Now I know she was murdered."

"Oh, God."

"The trail is cold. I need you, Vincent. I need your skills, your street smarts, your knowledge of the working classes, your way of thinking. I need you to help me track down the person—or persons—who did this. I will of course pay all your expenses and see to it that your salary and health benefits are maintained."

A silence fell in the car. D'Agosta was stunned. What would this mean for his career, his relationship with Laura Hayward . . . his future? It was irresponsible. No—it was more than that. It was utterly crazy.

"Is this an official investigation?"

"No. It would be just you and me. The killer might be anywhere in the world. We will operate completely outside the system—*any* system."

"And when we find the killer? What then?"

"We will see to it that justice is served."

"Meaning?"

Pendergast sloshed more brandy into the glass with a fierce gesture, gulped it down, and fixed D'Agosta once again with those cold, platinum eyes.

"We kill him."

7

The Rolls-Royce tore up Park Avenue, late-cruising cabs flashing by in blurs of yellow. D'Agosta sat in the back with Pendergast, feeling awkward, trying not to turn a curious eye toward the FBI agent. This Pendergast was impatient, unkempt, and—most remarkable—openly emotional.

"When did you find out?" he ventured to ask.

"This afternoon."

"How'd you figure it out?"

Pendergast did not answer immediately, glancing out the window as the Rolls turned sharply onto 72nd Street, heading toward the park. He placed the empty brandy glass—which he had been holding, unheeded, the entire uptown journey—back into its position in the tiny bar. Then he took a deep breath. "Twelve years ago, Helen and I were asked to kill a man-eating lion in Zambia—a lion with an unusual red mane. Just such a lion had wreaked havoc in the area forty years before."

"Why did *you* get asked?"

"Part of having a professional hunting license. You're obligated to kill any beasts menacing the villages or camps, if the authorities request it." Pendergast was still looking out the window. "The lion had killed a German tourist at a safari camp. Helen and I drove over from our own camp to put it down."

He picked up the brandy bottle, looked at it, put it back into its holder. The big car was now moving through Central Park, the skeletal branches overhead framing a threatening night sky. "The lion charged us from deep cover, attacked me and the tracker. As he ran back into the bush, Helen shot at him and apparently missed. She went to attend to the tracker..." His voice wavered and he stopped, composing himself. "She went to attend to the tracker and the lion burst out of the brush a second time. It dragged her off. That was the last time I saw her. Alive, anyway."

"Oh, my God." D'Agosta felt a thrill of horror course through him.

"Just this afternoon, at our old family plantation, I happened to examine her gun. And I discovered that—on that morning, twelve years ago—somebody had taken the bullets from her gun and replaced them with blanks. She hadn't missed the shot—because there *was* no shot."

"Holy shit. You sure?"

Now Pendergast looked away from the window to fix him with a stare. "Vincent, would I be telling you this—would I be here now—if I wasn't *absolutely* sure?"

"Sorry."

There was a moment of silence.

"You just discovered it this afternoon in New Orleans?"

Pendergast nodded tersely. "I chartered a private jet back."

The Rolls pulled up before the 72nd Street entrance of the Dakota. Almost before the vehicle had come to a stop Pendergast was out. He strode past the guardhouse and through the vaulted stone archway of the carriage entrance, ignoring the fat drops of rain that were now splattering the sidewalk. D'Agosta followed at a jog as the agent strode across a wide interior courtyard, past manicured plants and muttering bronze fountains, to a narrow lobby in the southwest corner of the apartment building. He pressed the elevator button, the doors whispered open, and they ascended in silence. A minute later the doors opened again on a small space, a single door set into the far wall. It had no obvious locking mechanism, but when Pendergast moved his fingertips across the surface in an odd gesture D'Agosta heard the unmistakable click of a deadlock springing free. Pendergast pushed the door open, and the reception room came into view: dimly lit, with three rose-painted walls and a fourth wall of black marble, covered by a thin sheet of falling water.

Pendergast gestured at the black leather sofas arrayed around the room. "Take a seat. I'll be back shortly."

D'Agosta sat down as the FBI agent slipped through a door in one of the walls. He sat back, taking in the soft gurgle of water, the bonsai plants, the smell of lotus blossoms. The walls of the building were so thick, he could barely hear the opening peals of thunder outside. Everything about the room seemed designed to induce tranquility. Yet tranquil was the last thing he felt. He wondered again just how he'd swing a sudden leave of absence—with his boss, and especially with Laura Hayward.

It was ten minutes before Pendergast reappeared. He had shaved and changed into a fresh black suit. He also seemed more composed, more like the old Pendergast—although D'Agosta could still sense a great tension under the surface.

"Thank you for waiting, Vincent," he said, beckoning. "Let us proceed."

D'Agosta followed the agent down a long hallway, as dimly lit as the reception room. He glanced curiously left and right: at a library; a room hung with oil paintings floor-to-ceiling; a wine cellar. Pendergast stopped at the only closed door in the hallway, opening it with the same strange movement of his fingers against the wood. The room beyond was barely large enough for the table and two chairs that it contained. A large steel bank-style vault, at least four feet in width, dominated one of the side walls.

Again Pendergast motioned D'Agosta to take a seat, then vanished into the hall. Within moments he returned, a leather Gladstone bag in one hand. He set this on the table, opened it, and drew out a rack of test tubes and several glass-stoppered bottles, which he arrayed carefully on the polished wood. His hand trembled once—only once—and the test tubes clinked quietly in response. After the apparatus was unpacked, Pendergast turned to the vault and with five or six turns of the dial unlocked it. As he swung the heavy door open, D'Agosta could see a grid of metal-fronted containers within, not unlike safe-deposit boxes. Pendergast selected one, withdrew it, and placed it on the table. Then, closing the vault, he took the seat opposite D'Agosta.

For a long moment, he remained motionless. Then came another rumble of thunder, muffled and distant, and it seemed to rouse him. He removed a white silk handkerchief from the Gladstone bag and spread it on the table. Then he slid the steel box closer, lifted its lid, and took from it two items: a tuft of coarse red hair and a gold ring, set with a beautiful star sapphire. He took away the tuft of hair with a set of forceps; the ring he gently removed with his bare hand, in a gesture so unconsciously tender D'Agosta felt himself pierced to the heart.

"These are the items I took from Helen's corpse," Pendergast said. The indirect lighting exaggerated the hollows of his drawn face. "I haven't looked at these in almost twelve years. Her wedding ring...and the tuft of mane she tore from the lion as it devoured her. I found it clutched in her severed left hand."

D'Agosta winced. "What are you going to do?" he asked.

"I'm going to play a hunch." Opening the glass-stoppered bottles, Pendergast poured a selection of different powders into the test tubes. Then, using the forceps, he pulled bits of mane from the reddish tuft and dropped a few strands carefully into each tube in turn. Finally, he pulled a small brown bottle from the bag, its top sealed with a rubber eyedropper. He unscrewed the eyedropper from the bottle and let several drops of clear liquid fall into each tube. There was no obvious reaction in the first four test tubes. But in the fifth, the liquid immediately turned a pale green, the color of green tea. Pendergast stared intently at this tube for a moment. Then, using a pipette, he removed a small sample of the liquid and applied it to a small strip of paper he took from the bag.

"A pH of three point seven," he said, examining the strip of paper. "Precisely the kind of mild acid required to release the lawsone molecules from the leaf."

"The leaf of what?" D'Agosta asked. "What is it?"

Pendergast glanced from the strip of paper to him and back again. "I could do further tests, but there seems little point. The mane of the lion that killed my wife had been treated with molecules originally from the plant *Lawsonia inermis*. More commonly known as henna."

"Henna?" D'Agosta repeated. "You mean the mane was *dyed* red?"

"Precisely." And Pendergast looked up again. "Proctor will drive you home. I can spare you three hours to make the necessary arrangements—not a minute more."

"I'm sorry?"

"Vincent, *we're headed for Africa*."

8

D'Agosta stood, a little uncertainly, in the hallway of the tidy two-bedroom he shared with Laura Hayward. It was technically her apartment, but recently he'd finally begun splitting the rent with her. Just getting her to concede to that had taken months. Now he fervently hoped this sudden turn of events wouldn't undo all the hard work he'd put into repairing their relationship.

He stared through the doorway into the master bedroom. Hayward was sitting up in bed, delicious looking despite having been roused from a sound sleep a quarter of an hour earlier. The clock on the dresser read ten minutes to six. Remarkable, how his whole life had been turned upside down in just ninety minutes.

She returned his look, her expression unreadable. "So that's it?" she said. "Pendergast arrives out of nowhere with some crazy story, and, wham, you're going to let him spirit you off?"

"Laura, he's just found out his wife was murdered. He feels I'm the only one who can help him do this."

"Help? What about helping yourself? You know, you're still pulling yourself out of the hole you got in over the Diogenes case—a hole that, by the way, Pendergast dug for you."

"He's my friend," D'Agosta replied. It sounded lame even to his own ears.

"This is unbelievable." She shook out her long black hair. "When I go to sleep, you're called out on a routine homicide. Now I wake up to find you packing for a trip—and you can't even tell me when you'll be back?"

"Honey, it won't be that long. My job here is important to me, too."

"And me? What about me? The job isn't the only thing you're walking out on here."

D'Agosta stepped into the room, sat down on the edge of the bed. "I swore I'd never lie to you, ever again. That's why I'm telling you everything. Look— you're the most important thing in my life." He took a breath. "If you tell me to stay, I'll stay."

For a minute, she just stared back at him. Then her expression softened and she shook her head. "You know I can't do that. I couldn't put myself between you and this—this *task*."

He took her hand. "I'll be back as soon as possible. And I'll call you every day."

With a fingertip she tucked a stray strand of hair behind her ear. "Have you told Glen yet?"

"No. I came here directly from Pendergast's apartment."

"Well, you'd better call him and break the news that you're taking a leave of absence, date of return unknown. You realize he might say no—and then what?"

"It's something I've just got to do."

Hayward pulled back the covers, swung her legs out of the bed. As his eyes drifted to them, D'Agosta felt a sudden sting of desire. How could he leave this beautiful woman, even for a day—let alone a week, a month . . . a year?

"I'll help you pack," she said.

He cleared his throat. "Laura—"

She put a finger to his lips. "It's better if you don't say any more."

He nodded.

She leaned toward him, kissed him lightly. "Just promise me one thing."

"Anything."

"Promise me that you'll take care of yourself. I don't much mind if Pendergast gets himself killed on this wild goose chase. But if anything happens to you, I'll be very angry. And you know how ugly that can get."

9

The Rolls, Proctor again at the wheel, hummed along the Brooklyn-Queens Expressway south of the Brooklyn Bridge. D'Agosta watched a pair of tugboats pushing a giant barge heaped with cubed cars up the East River, leaving a frothy wake behind. It had all happened so fast, he still wasn't quite able to wrap his head around it. They were heading for JFK, but first—Pendergast explained—they would have to make a brief, but necessary, detour.

"Vincent," said Pendergast, sitting across from him, "we must prepare ourselves for a deterioration. They tell me Great-Aunt Cornelia has been poorly of late."

D'Agosta shifted in his seat. "I'm not sure I get why it's so important to see her."

"It's just possible she can shed some light on the situation. Helen was a great favorite of hers. Also, I wish to consult her on a few points regarding some family history that may—I fear—have bearing on the murder."

D'Agosta grunted. He didn't care much about Great-

Aunt Cornelia—in fact he couldn't stand the murderous old witch—and his few visits to the Mount Mercy Hospital for the Criminally Insane had not exactly been pleasant. But it was always better, when working with Pendergast, to go with the flow.

Exiting the expressway, they worked their way through various side streets and eventually crossed a narrow bridge over to Little Governor's Island, the road meandering through marshland and meadows, hung with morning mists that drifted among the cattails. A colonnade of old oaks appeared on either side of the road, once part of the magnificent approach to a grand estate, the trees now reduced to a series of dead claws held against the sky.

Proctor stopped at a guardhouse, and the uniformed man stepped out. "Why, Mr. Pendergast, that was quick." He waved them through without the usual formalities of signing them in.

"What'd he mean by that?" D'Agosta asked, looking over his shoulder at the guard.

"I have no idea."

Proctor parked in the small lot and they got out. Passing through the front door, D'Agosta was mildly surprised to see the attendant missing from the ornate reception desk, with some evidence of hurry and confusion. As they cast about for someone to speak with, a rattling gurney approached down the marble transverse hall, carrying a body draped in a black sheet, being wheeled by two burly attendants. D'Agosta could see an ambulance pulling into the porte cochere, with no siren or flashing lights to indicate any hurry.

"Good morning, Mr. Pendergast!" Dr. Ostrom,

Great-Aunt Cornelia's attending physician, appeared in the foyer and hastened over, his hand extended, a look of surprise and consternation blooming on his face. "This is . . . well, I was just about to telephone you. Please come with me."

They followed the doctor down the once-elegant hallway, somewhat reduced now to institutional austerity. "I have some unfortunate news," he said as they walked along. "Your great-aunt passed away not thirty minutes ago."

Pendergast stopped. He let out a slow breath, and his shoulders slumped visibly. D'Agosta realized with a shudder that the body they had seen was probably hers.

"Natural causes?" Pendergast asked in a low monotone.

"More or less. The fact is, she'd been increasingly anxious and delusional these past few days."

Pendergast seemed to consider this a moment. "Any delusions in particular?"

"Nothing worth repeating, the usual family themes."

"Nevertheless, I should like to hear about them."

Ostrom seemed reluctant to proceed. "She believed . . . believed that a fellow named, ah, Ambergris was coming to Mount Mercy to exact revenge on her for an atrocity she claims to have committed years ago."

Once again, they resumed walking down the corridor. "Did she go into any detail on this atrocity?" Pendergast asked.

"It was all quite fantastical. Something about punishing some child for swearing by . . ." A second hesitation. "Well, by splitting his tongue with a razor."

An ambiguous head movement from Pendergast. D'Agosta felt his own tongue curling at the thought.

"At any rate," Ostrom continued, "she became violent—more violent, that is, than usual—and had to be completely restrained. And medicated. At the time of this alleged appointment with Ambergris, she had a series of seizures and passed away abruptly. Ah, here we are."

He entered a small room, windowless and sparely furnished with antique, unframed paintings and various soft knickknacks—nothing, D'Agosta noted, that could be fashioned into a weapon or cause harm. Even the stretchers had been removed from the canvases, the paintings hung on the wall with kite string. As D'Agosta looked around at the bed, the table, silk flowers in a basket, a peculiar butterfly-shaped stain on the wall, it all seemed so forlorn. He suddenly felt sorry for the homicidal old lady.

"There is the question of the disposition of the personal effects," the doctor went on. "I understand these paintings are quite valuable."

"They are," said Pendergast. "Send them over to the nineteenth-century painting department at Christie's for public auction, and consider the proceeds a donation to your good work."

"That's very generous of you, Mr. Pendergast. Would you care to order an autopsy? When a patient dies in custody, you have the legal right—"

Pendergast interrupted him with a brusque wave of his hand. "That won't be necessary."

"And the funeral arrangements—?"

"There will be no funeral. The family attorney,

Mr. Ogilby, will be in touch with you about disposition of the remains."

"Very well."

Pendergast looked around the room for a moment, as if committing its details to memory. Then he turned to D'Agosta. His expression was neutral, but his eyes spoke of sorrow, even desolation.

"Vincent," he said. "We have a plane to catch."

10

Zambia

The smiling, gap-toothed man at the dirt airstrip had called the vehicle a Land Rover. That description, D'Agosta thought as he hung on for dear life, was more than charitable. Whatever it might have been, now it barely deserved to be called an automobile. It had no windows, no roof, no radio, and no seat belts. The hood was fixed to the grille by a tangle of baling wire. He could see the dirt road below through giant rust holes in the chassis.

At the wheel, Pendergast—attired in khaki shirt and pants, and wearing a Tilley safari hat—swerved around a massive pothole in the road, only to hit a smaller one. D'Agosta rose several inches out of his seat at the impact. He gritted his teeth and took a fresh hold on the roll bar. *This is frigging awful,* he thought. He was hot as hell, and there was dust in his ears, eyes, nose, hair, and crevices he hadn't even known he had. He contemplated asking Pendergast to slow down, then thought better of it. The closer they came to the site of Helen Pendergast's death, the grimmer Pendergast became.

Pendergast slowed just slightly as they came to a village—yet another sorry-looking collection of huts built of sticks and dried mud, baking in the noonday sun. There was no electricity, and a single communal well stood in the middle of the lone crossroads. Pigs, chickens, and children roamed aimlessly.

"And I thought the South Bronx was bad," D'Agosta muttered more to himself than to Pendergast.

"Kingazu Camp is ten miles ahead," was Pendergast's reply as he stepped on the accelerator.

They hit another pothole and D'Agosta was again thrown in the air, coming down hard on his tailbone. Both arms were smarting from the inoculations, and his head hurt from the sun and vibration. About the only painless thing he'd endured in the past thirty-six hours was the phone call to his boss, Glen Singleton. The captain had approved his leave of absence with barely a question. It was almost as if he was relieved to see D'Agosta go.

Half an hour brought them to Kingazu Camp. As Pendergast maneuvered the vehicle into a makeshift lot beneath a grove of sausage trees, D'Agosta took in the trim lines of the photographic safari camp: the immaculate reed-and-thatch huts, the large canvas structures labeled DINING TENT and BAR, the wooden walkways linking each building to the next, the linen pavilions that sheltered comfortable deck chairs on which a dozen fat and happy tourists dozed, cameras dangling from their necks. Strings of tiny lights were strung along the rooflines. A generator purred off in the bush. Everything was done up in bright—almost gaudy—colors.

"This is straight out of Disney," D'Agosta said, getting out of the vehicle.

"A great deal has changed in twelve years," Pendergast replied, his voice flat.

They stood there a moment, motionless, without speaking, in the shade of the sausage trees. D'Agosta took in the fragrant smell of burning wood, the tang of crushed grass, and—more faintly—an earthy, animal muskiness he couldn't identify. The bagpipe drone of insects mingled with other sounds: the whine of the generators, the cooing of doves, the restless mutterings of the nearby Luangwa River. D'Agosta shot a covert glance at Pendergast: the agent was stooped forward, as if he bore a terrific weight; his eyes glittered with a haunted fire, and—as he took in the scene with what seemed like a strange mixture of hunger and dread—a single muscle in his cheek twitched erratically. He must have realized he was being scrutinized, because the FBI agent composed himself, straightening up and smoothing his safari vest. But the strange glitter did not leave his eyes.

"Follow me," he said.

Pendergast led the way past the pavilions and dining tent to a smaller structure, set apart from the rest of the camp in a copse of trees near the banks of the Luangwa. A single elephant was standing, knee-deep, in the mud of the river. As D'Agosta watched, the animal scooped up a trunkful of water, sprayed it over its back, then lifted its wrinkled head and emitted a harsh trumpeting sound that momentarily drowned out the hum of insects.

The small structure was clearly the administrative building for the camp. It consisted of an outer office, currently empty, and an inner office occupied by a lone man, sitting behind a desk and writing industriously in a notebook. He was about fifty, thin and wiry, his fair hair bleached by the sun and his arms deeply tanned.

The man looked up as he heard them approach. "Yes, what can I . . ." The words died in his throat as he caught sight of Pendergast. Clearly he'd been expecting to see one of the guests.

"Who are you?" he asked, rising.

"My name is Underhill," Pendergast said. "And this is my friend, Vincent D'Agosta."

The man looked at them in turn. "What can I do for you?" It seemed to D'Agosta that this was a man who didn't get many unexpected visitors.

"May I ask your name?" Pendergast asked.

"Rathe."

"My friend and I were on safari here, about twelve years ago. We happened to be back in Zambia again— on our way to Mgandi hunting camp—and thought we'd drop in." He smiled coldly.

Rathe glanced out the window, in the general direction of the makeshift parking area. "Mgandi, you say?"

Pendergast nodded.

The man grunted and extended a hand. "Sorry. All the goings-on these days, the rebel incursions and whatnot, a fellow gets a little jumpy."

"Understandable."

Rathe gestured at two well-worn wooden chairs before the desk. "Please, sit down. Can I get you anything?"

"A beer would be nice," D'Agosta said instantly.

"Of course. Just a minute." The man disappeared, returning a minute later with two bottles of Mosi beer. D'Agosta accepted his bottle, mumbling his thanks and taking a grateful swig.

"Are you the camp concessionaire?" Pendergast asked as the man took a seat behind his desk.

Rathe shook his head. "I'm the administrator. The chap you want is Fortnum. He's still out with this morning's group."

"Fortnum. I see." Pendergast glanced around the office. "I suppose there have been a number of personnel changes since we were here. The entire camp looks rather different."

Rathe gave a mirthless smile. "We have to keep up with the competition. Today our clients demand comfort in addition to scenery."

"Of course. Still, it's a shame, isn't it, Vincent? We'd been hoping to see a few familiar faces."

D'Agosta nodded. It had taken five swallows just to get the dust out of his throat.

Pendergast gave the impression of thinking a moment. "What about Alistair Woking? Is he still the district commissioner?"

Rathe shook his head again. "He died quite some time ago. Let's see, it must have been almost ten years back."

"Really? What happened?"

"Hunting accident," the administrator replied. "They

were culling elephants, and Woking went along to observe. Shot in the back by mistake. Bloody balls-up."

"How regrettable," Pendergast said. "And the current camp concessionaire is named Fortnum, you say? When we were on safari here, it was Wisley. Gordon Wisley."

"He's still around," Rathe said. "Retired the year before last. They say he lives like a king on that hunting concession of his near Victoria Falls. Boys waiting on him hand and foot."

Pendergast turned to D'Agosta. "Vincent, do you recall the name of our gun bearer?"

D'Agosta, quite truthfully, said that he did not.

"Wait, I recall it now. Wilson Nyala. Any chance of our saying hello to him, Mr. Rathe?"

"Wilson died in the spring. Dengue fever." Rathe frowned. "Just a moment. Did you say gun bearer?"

"Pity." Pendergast shifted in his seat. "What about our tracker? Jason Mfuni."

"Never heard of him. But then, that kind of help comes and goes so quickly. Now, listen, what's all this about a gun bearer? We only handle photographic expeditions here at Kingazu."

"As I said—it was a *memorable* safari." And hearing Pendergast say "memorable," D'Agosta felt a chill despite the heat.

Rathe did not reply. He was still frowning.

"Thank you for your hospitality." Pendergast rose, and D'Agosta did the same. "Wisley's hunting concession is near Victoria Falls, you say? Does it have a name?"

"Ulani Stream." Rathe stood as well. His initial suspicion seemed to have returned.

"Would you mind if we take a brief look around?"

"If you wish," Rathe replied. "Don't disturb the guests."

Outside the administration building, Pendergast stopped, glancing left and right, as if orienting himself. He hesitated briefly. And then, without a word, he struck out along a well-beaten path that led away from the camp. D'Agosta hurried to catch up.

The sun beat down mercilessly, and the drone of insects swelled. On one side of the footpath was a dense stand of brush and trees; on the other, the Luangwa River. D'Agosta felt the unfamiliar khaki shirt clinging damply to his back and shoulders. "Where are we going?" he panted.

"Into the long grass. Where..." He didn't finish the sentence.

D'Agosta swallowed. "Okay, sure. Lead the way."

Pendergast stopped suddenly and turned. An expression had come over his features D'Agosta had never seen before—a look of sorrow, regret, and almost unfathomable weariness. He cleared his throat, then spoke in a low tone. "I'm very sorry, Vincent, but this is something I must do alone."

D'Agosta took a deep breath, relieved. "I understand."

Pendergast turned, fixed him briefly with his pale eyes. He nodded once. Then he turned back and walked away, stiff-legged, determined, off the path and into the bush, vanishing almost immediately into the woven shade beneath the trees.

11

Everyone, it seemed, knew where the Wisley "farm-stead" was. It lay at the end of a well-maintained dirt track on a gently sloping hill in the forests north-west of Victoria Falls. In fact—as Pendergast paused the decrepit vehicle just before the final bend in the road—D'Agosta thought he could hear the falls: a low, distant roar that was more sensation than sound.

He glanced at Pendergast. The drive from Kingazu Camp had taken hours, and in all that time the agent had spoken maybe half a dozen words. D'Agosta had wanted to ask what, if anything, he'd learned in his investigation in the long grass, but this was clearly not the time. When he was ready to talk about it, he would.

Pendergast eased the vehicle around the bend, and the house came into view: a lovely old colonial, painted white, with four squat columns and a wraparound porch. The formal lines were softened by beautifully tended shrubs: azalea, boxwood, bougainvillea. The entire plot—maybe five or six acres—appeared to have been cut wholesale out of the surrounding jungle. A lawn of emerald green swept down toward them, punctuated by at least half a dozen flower beds filled with roses of every imaginable shade. Except for the almost fluorescent brilliance of the flowers, the tidy estate wouldn't have looked out of place in Greenwich or Scarsdale. D'Agosta thought he saw figures on the porch, but from this distance he could not make them out.

"Looks like old Wisley has done all right for himself," he muttered.

Pendergast nodded, his pale eyes focused on the house.

"That guy, Rathe, mentioned Wisley's boys," D'Agosta went on. "What about the wife? You suppose he's divorced?"

Pendergast gave a wintry smile. "I believe we'll find Rathe meant something else entirely."

He drove slowly up the path to a turnaround in front of the house, where he stopped the vehicle and killed the engine. D'Agosta glanced up at the porch. A heavy-set man about sixty years old was seated in an immense wicker chair, his feet propped up on a wooden stool. He wore a white linen suit that made his fleshy face look even more florid than it was. A thin circle of red hair, like a monk's tonsure, crowned his head. The man took a sip of a tall icy drink, then set the glass down hard on a table, next to a half-full pitcher of the same beverage. His movements had the flaccid generosity of a drunk's. Standing on either side of him were middle-aged Africans, gaunt looking, in faded madras shirts. One had a bar towel draped over his forearm; the other held a fan attached to a long handle, which he was waving slowly over the wicker chair.

"That's Wisley?" D'Agosta asked.

Pendergast nodded slowly. "He has not aged well."

"And the other two—those are his 'boys'?"

Pendergast nodded again. "It would seem this place has yet to enter the twentieth century—let alone the twenty-first."

And then—slowly, with great deliberation—he eased out of the vehicle, turned to face the house, and raised himself to his full height.

On the porch, Wisley blinked once, twice. He glanced from D'Agosta to Pendergast, opening his mouth to speak. But his expression froze as he stared at the FBI agent. Blankness gave way to horrified recognition. With a curse, the man abruptly struggled out of the chair and rose to his feet, knocking over the glassware in the process. Grabbing an elephant gun that had been propped against the wooden siding, he pulled open a screen door and lurched into the house.

"Can't get much guiltier than that," D'Agosta said. "I don't—oh, shit."

The two attendants had dropped out of sight below the porch railing. A gunshot boomed from the porch and a spout of dirt erupted behind them.

They threw themselves behind the car. "What the *fuck*?" D'Agosta said, scrambling to pull his Glock.

"Stay put and down." Pendergast leapt up and ran.

"Hey!"

Another report, and a bullet smacked the side of the jeep with a *whang!* sending up a cloud of shredded upholstery stuffing. D'Agosta peered around the tire up at the house, gun in hand. Where the hell had Pendergast gone?

He ducked back and winced as he heard a third shot ricochet off the steel frame of the jeep. Christ, he couldn't just sit here like a target at a shooting gallery. He waited until a fourth shot sailed over his head, then raised his head above the vehicle's fender, aiming his weapon as the shooter ducked behind the railing. He was about to pull the trigger when he saw Pendergast emerge from the shrubbery below the porch. With remarkable speed he vaulted the railing, felled the African shooter with a savage chop to the neck, and pointed his .45 at the other attendant. The man slowly raised his hands.

"You can come up now, Vincent," Pendergast said as he retrieved the gun that lay beside the groaning form.

They found Wisley in the fruit cellar. As they closed in on him, he fired the elephant gun, but his aim was off—through drink or fear—and the kick sent him sprawling. Before he could fire again Pendergast had darted forward, pinned the rifle with his foot, and subdued Wisley with two swift, savage blows to the face. The second blow broke Wisley's nose; and bright blood fountained over the man's starched white shirt. Reaching into his own breast pocket and plucking out a handkerchief, Pendergast handed it to him. Then, seizing Wisley by the upper arm, the FBI agent propelled him out of the fruit cellar, up the basement stairs, and out the front door to the porch, where he dropped him back into the wicker chair.

The two attendants were still standing there, as if dumbstruck. D'Agosta waved his weapon at them.

"Walk down the road a hundred yards," he said. "Stay where we can see you, hands up in the air."

Pendergast tucked his Les Baer into his waistband and stood before Wisley. "Thank you for the warm welcome," he said.

Wisley pressed the handkerchief to his nose. "I must've mistaken you for someone else." He spoke in what sounded to D'Agosta like an Australian accent.

"On the contrary, I commend you on your prodigious recall. I think you have something to tell me."

"I've nothing to tell you, mate," Wisley replied.

Pendergast crossed his arms. "I will ask you only once: who arranged my wife's death?"

"I don't know what you're talking about," came the muffled response.

Pendergast looked down on the man, his lip twitching. "Let me explain something, Mr. Wisley," he said after a moment. "I can assure you, without the slightest possibility of error, that you *will* tell me what I want to know. The degree of mortification and inconvenience you will endure *before* telling me is a choice you are free to make."

"Sod off."

Pendergast contemplated the sweating, bleeding figure sprawled in the chair. Then, leaning forward, he pulled Wisley to his feet.

"Vincent," he said over his shoulder, "escort Mr. Wisley to our vehicle."

Gun pressed into the bulging back, D'Agosta prodded Wisley toward the jeep and into the passenger seat, then climbed into the rear, brushing debris off the seat. Pendergast started the engine and drove back down the path, past the emerald grass and the Technicolor flowers, past the two attendants—who stood motionless as statues—and into the jungle.

"Where are you taking me?" Wisley demanded as they rounded the bend and the house disappeared from view.

"I don't know," Pendergast replied.

"What do you mean, you don't *know*?" Wisley's voice sounded a little less assured now.

"We're going on safari."

They drove on, without hurry, for fifteen minutes. The tall grass gave way to savanna, and a wide, chocolate-brown river that looked too lazy even to flow. D'Agosta saw two hippos playing by the riverbank, and a vast flock of stork-like birds with thin yellow legs and immense wingspans, rising like a white cloud from the water. The sun had begun to descend toward the horizon, and the fierce heat of midday had abated.

Pendergast took his foot off the accelerator and let the vehicle coast to a stop on the grassy shoulder. "This looks like a good spot," he said.

D'Agosta glanced around in confusion. The vista here seemed little different from the landscape they'd been traveling through for the last five miles.

Then he froze. About a quarter mile off, away from the river, he made out a pride of lions, gnawing at a skeleton. Their sandy-colored fur had made them difficult to see at first against the low grassland.

Wisley was sitting rigid in the front seat, staring intently. He'd noticed them right away.

"Get out of the car, please, Mr. Wisley," Pendergast said mildly.

Wisley did not move.

D'Agosta placed his gun at the base of Wisley's skull. "Move."

Stiffly, slowly, Wisley exited the vehicle.

D'Agosta climbed out of the backseat. He felt hugely reluctant to even stop the car this close to half a dozen lions, let alone get out. Lions were to be looked at from the safety of the Bronx Zoo, with at least two layers of tall strong steel fencing in between.

"Looks like an old kill, doesn't it?" Pendergast said, motioning with his gun at the pride. "I imagine they're hungry."

"Lions aren't man-eaters," Wisley said, handkerchief pressed to his nose. "It's very rare." But the bluster had gone from his voice.

"They don't need to eat you, Mr. Wisley," Pendergast said. "That would merely be icing on the cake, so to speak. If they think you're after their kill, they will attack. But then, you know all about lions, don't you?"

Wisley said nothing. He was staring at the lions.

Pendergast reached over and plucked the handkerchief away. Immediately fresh blood began streaming down Wisley's face. "That should attract some interest, at any rate."

Wisley shot him a hunted glance.

"Walk toward them, if you please," Pendergast said.

"You're crazy," Wisley replied, voice rising.

"No. I'm the one with the gun." Pendergast aimed it at Wisley. "Walk."

For a moment, Wisley remained motionless. Then—very slowly—he put one foot before the other and began moving toward the lions. Pendergast followed close behind, gun at the ready. D'Agosta followed, staying several paces back. He was inclined to agree with Wisley—this *was* insane. The pride was watching their approach intently.

After forty yards of snail-like progress, Wisley stopped again.

"Keep going, Mr. Wisley," Pendergast called.

"I can't."

"I'll shoot you if you don't."

Wisley's mouth worked frantically. "That handgun of yours will barely stop a single lion, let alone an entire pride."

"I'm aware of that."

"If they kill me, they'll kill you, too."

"I'm aware of that, as well." Pendergast turned. "Vincent, stay back, will you?" He fished in his pocket, withdrew the keys to the jeep, tossed them to D'Agosta. "Get to a safe distance if things go badly."

"Are you bloody daft?" Wisley said, his voice shrill. "Didn't you hear me? You'll die, too!"

"Mr. Wisley, be a good fellow and walk forward. I do hate having to repeat myself."

Still Wisley did not move.

"Indeed, I *won't* ask again. In five seconds I will put a bullet through your left elbow. You'll still be able to walk—and the shot will no doubt arouse the lions."

Wisley took a step, stopped again. Then he took another step. One of the lions—a big male, with a wild tawny mane—rose lazily to his feet. He looked toward them, licking bloody chops. D'Agosta, hanging back, felt his stomach churn.

"All right!" Wisley said. "All right, I'll tell you!"

"I'm all ears," Pendergast said.

Wisley was shaking violently. "Let's get back to the car!"

"Right here is fine with me. Better speak fast."

"It was a, it was a setup."

"Details, if you please."

"I don't know the details. Woking was the contact."

Now two of the lionesses had risen, as well.

"Please, *please*," Wisley begged, voice breaking. "For God's sake, can't we talk in the jeep?"

Pendergast seemed to consider this a moment. Then he nodded.

They returned to the vehicle at a rather brisker pace than they'd left it. As they climbed in and D'Agosta passed Pendergast the keys, he noticed the male lion moving toward them at a walk. Pendergast cranked the engine. The walk became a lope. The engine finally caught; Pendergast threw it into gear and slewed around just as the lion caught up, roaring and raking the side of the vehicle as it lurched past. D'Agosta glanced over his shoulder, heart hammering in his throat. The lion slowly dwindled behind them, finally disappearing.

They drove ten minutes in silence. Then Pendergast pulled over again, got out, and motioned for Wisley to do the same. D'Agosta followed suit, and they walked a short distance from the car.

Pendergast waved his Les Baer at Wisley. "On your knees."

Wisley complied.

Pendergast handed him the bloody handkerchief. "All right. Tell me the rest."

Wisley was still shaking violently. "I, I don't know

much else. There were two men. One was American, the other European. German, I think. They...they supplied the man-eating lion. Supposedly trained. They were well funded."

"How did you know their nationalities?"

"I heard them. Behind the dining tent, talking to Woking. The night before the tourist was killed."

"What did they look like?"

"It was night. I couldn't see."

Pendergast paused. "What did Woking do, exactly?"

"He set up the death of the tourist. He knew where the lion was waiting, he steered the tourist in that direction. Told him a warthog, a photo-op, was there." Wisley swallowed. "He...he arranged for Nyala to load your wife's gun with blanks."

"So Nyala was in on it, too?"

Wisley nodded.

"What about Mfuni? The tracker?"

"Everyone was in on it."

"These men you mention—you said they were well funded. How do you know?"

"They paid very well. Woking got fifty thousand to carry out the plan. I...I got twenty thousand for the use of the camp and to look the other way."

"The lion was trained?"

"That's what someone said."

"How?"

"I don't know how. I only know it was trained to kill on command—though anybody who thinks that can be done reliably is crazy."

"Are you sure there were only two men?"

"I only heard two voices."

Pendergast's face set in a hard line. Once again, D'Agosta watched the FBI agent bring himself under control by the sheer force of his will. "Is there anything else?"

"No. Nothing. That's all, I swear. We never spoke of it again."

"Very well." And then—with sudden, frightening speed—Pendergast grabbed Wisley by the hair, placed his gun against the man's temple.

"No!" D'Agosta cried, placing a restraining hand on Pendergast's arm.

Pendergast turned to look at him and D'Agosta was almost physically knocked back by the intensity of the agent's gaze.

"Not a good idea to kill informants," D'Agosta said, modulating his voice carefully, making it as casual as possible. "Maybe he isn't done talking. Maybe the gin and tonics will kill him for us, save you the trouble. Don't worry—the fat fuck isn't going anywhere."

Pendergast hesitated, gun still pressed to Wisley's temple. Then, slowly, he released his grip on Wisley's thin tonsure of reddish hair. The ex-concessionaire sank to the ground and D'Agosta noted, with disgust, that he had wet himself.

Without speaking, Pendergast slipped back into the vehicle. D'Agosta climbed in beside him. They pulled back onto the road and headed for Lusaka without a backward glance.

It was half an hour before D'Agosta spoke. "So," he said. "What's next?"

"The past," Pendergast replied, not taking his eyes from the road. "The past is what's next."

12

Savannah, Georgia

Whitfield Square dozed placidly in the failing light of a Monday evening. Streetlights came up, throwing the palmettos and the Spanish moss hanging from gnarled oak limbs into gauzy relief. After the cauldron-like heat of Central Africa, D'Agosta found the humid Georgia air almost a relief.

He followed Pendergast across the manicured carpet of grass. In the center of the square stood a large cupola, surrounded by flowers. A wedding party stood beneath its scalloped roof, obediently following the instructions of a photographer. Elsewhere, people strolled slowly by or sat on black-painted benches, chatting or reading. Everything seemed just a little soft and out of focus, and D'Agosta shook his head. Following the mad dash from New York to Zambia to this center of southern gentility, he felt numb.

Pendergast stopped, pointing across Habersham

Street at a large gingerbread Victorian house, white and immaculate and very much like its neighbors. As they headed over, Pendergast said, "Keep in mind, Vincent—he doesn't yet know."

"Got it."

They crossed the street and mounted the wooden steps. Pendergast pressed the doorbell. After about ten seconds, the overhead light came on and the door was opened by a man in his mid-forties. D'Agosta looked at him curiously. He was tall and strikingly handsome, with high cheekbones, dark eyes, and a thick head of brown hair. He was as tanned as Pendergast was pale. A folded magazine was in one hand. D'Agosta glanced at the open page: the footer read *Journal of American Neurosurgery*.

The sun, dipping behind the houses on the far side of the square, was in the man's keen eyes, and he couldn't see them well. "Yes?" he asked. "May I help you?"

"Judson Esterhazy," Pendergast said, extending his hand.

Esterhazy started, and a look of surprise and delight blossomed over his features. "Aloysius?" he said. "My God! Come in."

Esterhazy led the way through a front hall, down a narrow, book-lined corridor, and into a cozy den. *Cozy* wasn't a word D'Agosta used very often, but he could think of no other way to describe the space. Warm yellow light imparted a mellow sheen to the antique mahogany furniture: chiffonier, rolltop desk, gun case, still more bookshelves. Rich Persian rugs covered the floor. Two large diplomas—a medical degree, and a PhD—hung on one wall. The furniture was overstuffed and looked exceptionally comfortable. Antiques from all over the world—African sculpture, Asian jades—adorned every horizontal surface. Two windows, framed by delicate curtains, looked out over the square. It was a room stuffed full of objects that somehow managed not to appear cluttered—the den of a well-educated, well-traveled man of taste.

Pendergast turned and introduced D'Agosta to Esterhazy. The man couldn't hide his surprise upon learning D'Agosta was a cop; nevertheless he smiled and shook his hand warmly.

"This is an unexpected pleasure," he said. "Would you care for anything? Tea, beer, bourbon?"

"Bourbon, please, Judson," said Pendergast.

"How'd you like it?"

"Neat."

Esterhazy turned to D'Agosta. "And you, Lieutenant?"

"A beer would be great, thanks."

"Of course." Still smiling, Esterhazy stepped over to a dry sink in the corner and deftly poured out a measure of bourbon. Then, excusing himself, he went to the kitchen to retrieve the beer.

"Good Lord, Aloysius," he said as he returned, "how long has it been—nine years?"

"Ten."

"Ten years. When we took that hunting trip to Kilchurn Lodge."

D'Agosta sipped the beer and glanced around as the two chatted. Earlier, Pendergast had filled him in on Esterhazy: a neurosurgeon and medical researcher, who—having risen to the top of his profession— now devoted part of his time to pro bono work, both at local hospitals and for Doctors With Wings, the charity that flew doctors into Third World disaster areas and where his sister had worked. He was a committed sportsman and, according to Pendergast, an even better shot than his sister had been. D'Agosta, glancing around at the various hunting trophies displayed on the walls, decided Pendergast hadn't been exaggerating. A doctor who was also an avid hunter: interesting combination.

"So tell me," Esterhazy said in his deep, sonorous voice. "What brings you to the Low Country? Are you on a case? Please, give me all the sordid details." He chuckled.

Pendergast took a sip of his bourbon. He hesitated just a moment. "Judson, I'm afraid there's no easy way to say this. I'm here about Helen."

The chuckle died in Esterhazy's throat. A look of confusion gathered on the patrician features. "Helen? What about Helen?"

Pendergast took another, deeper sip. "I've learned her death was no accident."

For a minute, Esterhazy stood, frozen, staring at Pendergast. "What on earth do you mean?"

"I mean, your sister was murdered."

Esterhazy rose, a stricken look on his face. He turned his back on them and walked—slowly, as in a dream—to a bookcase in the far wall. He picked up an object apparently at random, turned it over in his hand, put it down again. And then—after a long moment—he turned back. Walking to the dry sink, he reached for a tumbler and, with fumbling fingers, poured himself a stiff drink. Then he took a seat across from them.

"Knowing you, Aloysius, I don't suppose I need ask if you're sure about this," he said, very quietly.

"No, you don't."

Esterhazy's whole demeanor changed, his face becoming pale, his hands clenching and unclenching. "What are you—are *we*—going to do about it?"

"I—with Vincent's help—will find the person or persons ultimately responsible. And we will see that justice is served."

Esterhazy looked Pendergast in the face. "I want to be there. I want to be there when the man who murdered my little sister pays for what he did."

Pendergast did not answer.

The anger, the power of the man's emotions, were so intense they almost frightened D'Agosta. Esterhazy sank back in his chair, his dark eyes restless and glittering. "How did you find this out?"

Briefly, Pendergast sketched out the events of the last few days. Although shaken, Esterhazy nevertheless listened intently. When Pendergast finished, he rose and poured himself a fresh drink.

"I believed…" Pendergast paused. "I believe I knew Helen extremely well. And yet—for someone to have killed her, and taken such extraordinary pains and expense to disguise her death as an accident—it's clear there must be a part of her life I knew nothing about. Since we spent most of her last two years on earth together, I have to believe that, whatever it was, it lay farther back in her past. This is where I need your help."

Esterhazy passed a hand across his broad forehead, nodded.

"Do you have any idea, any, of a person who might have had a motive to kill her? Enemies? Professional rivals? Old lovers?"

Esterhazy was silent, his jaw working. "Helen was... wonderful. Kind. Charming. She *had* no enemies. Everyone loved her at MIT, and in her graduate work she was always scrupulous in sharing credit."

Pendergast nodded. "What about after her graduation? Any rivals at Doctors With Wings? Anyone passed over for a promotion in favor of her?"

"DWW didn't operate like that. Everyone worked together. No egos. She was much appreciated there." He swallowed painfully. "Even loved."

Pendergast sat back in his chair. "In the months before her death, she took several short trips. Research, she told me, but she was vague about the details. In retrospect it seems a little odd—Doctors With Wings was more about education and treatment than it was about research. I now wish I had pressed her for more information. You're a doctor—do you know what she might have been up to, if anything?"

Esterhazy paused to think. Then he shook his head. "Sorry, Aloysius. She told me nothing. She loved traveling to faraway places—as you know. And she was fascinated by medical research. Those twin loves were what led her to DWW in the first place."

"What about your family history?" D'Agosta asked. "Any instances of familial conflict, childhood grievances, that sort of thing?"

"Everybody loved Helen," Esterhazy said. "I used to be a little jealous of her popularity. And, no, there have been no family problems to speak of. Both our parents died more than fifteen years ago. I'm the only Esterhazy left." He hesitated.

"Yes?" Pendergast leaned forward.

"Well, I'm sure there's nothing to it, but long before she met you she had...an unhappy love affair. With a real bounder."

"Go on."

"It was her first year in graduate school, seems to me. She brought the fellow down from MIT for the weekend. Blond, clean-cut, blue eyes, tall and athletic, always seemed to go about in tennis whites and crew sweaters, came from a rich old WASP family, grew up in Manhattan with a summer cottage on Fishers Island, talked about going into investment banking—you know the type."

"Why was it unhappy?"

"Turned out he had some kind of sexual problem. Helen was vague about it, some kind of perverse behavior or cruelty in that area."

"And?"

"She dumped him. He annoyed her for a while, phone calls, letters. I don't think it reached the level of stalking. And then it seemed to fade away." He waved his hand. "That was six years before you met and nine years before her death. I can't see there being anything in it."

"And the name?"

Esterhazy clutched his forehead in his hands. "Adam...First name was Adam. For the life of me I can't remember his last name—if I ever knew it."

A long silence. "Anything else?"

Esterhazy shook his head. "It seems inconceivable to me anyone would want to hurt Helen."

There was a brief silence. Then Pendergast nodded

to a framed print on one of the walls: a faded picture of a snowy owl sitting in a tree at night. "That's an Audubon, isn't it?"

"Yes. A reproduction, I'm afraid." Esterhazy glanced at it. "Odd you should mention it."

"Why?"

"It used to hang in Helen's bedroom when we were children. She told me how, when she was sick, she would stare at it for hours on end. She was fascinated by Audubon. But of course you know all that," he concluded briskly. "I kept it because it reminded me of her."

D'Agosta noticed something very close to a look of surprise on the FBI agent's face, quickly concealed.

There was a brief silence before Pendergast spoke again. "Is there anything you can add about Helen's life in the years immediately before we met?"

"She was very busy with her work. There was also a period where she was heavily into rock climbing. Spent almost every weekend in the Gunks."

"The Gunks?"

"The Shawangunk Mountains. She was living in New York then, for a time. She did a lot of traveling. Part of it was for Doctors With Wings, of course—Burundi, India, Ethiopia. But part of it was just for adventure. I still remember bumping into her one afternoon, it must have been—oh, fifteen, sixteen years ago. She was packing frantically, on her way to New Madrid, of all places."

"New Madrid?" Pendergast said.

"New Madrid, Missouri. She wouldn't tell me why she was going—said I'd just laugh. She could be a very private person in her own way. You must know that better than anyone, Aloysius."

D'Agosta stole another private glance at Pendergast. *That would make two*, he thought. He could not imagine anyone more private, more reluctant to share his thoughts, than Pendergast.

"I wish I could help you more. If I recall the last name of that old boyfriend, I'll let you know."

Pendergast stood up. "Thank you, Judson. It's most kind of you to see us like this. And I'm sorry you had to learn the truth this way. I'm afraid there—well, there simply wasn't time for me to break it in a gentler fashion."

"I understand."

The doctor saw them through the hallway and into the front passage. "Wait," he began, then hesitated, front door half open. For a moment the mask of stoic anger dropped, and D'Agosta saw the handsome face disfigured by a mixture of emotions—what? Raw fury? Anguish? Devastation? "You heard what I said earlier. I want to—I *have* to..."

"Judson," Pendergast said quickly, taking his hand. "You need to let me handle this. I understand the grief and rage you feel, but you *need to let me handle this*."

Judson frowned, gave his head a brief, savage shake.

"I know you," Pendergast went on, his voice gentle but firm. "I must warn you—don't take the law into your own hands. Please."

Esterhazy took a deep breath, then another, not replying. At last Pendergast gave a slight nod and stepped out into the evening.

After closing the door, Esterhazy stood in the darkened front hall, still breathing hard, for perhaps five minutes. When at last he had mastered his fearful anger and shock, he turned and walked quickly back into the den. Moving straight to the gun case, he unlocked it, dropping the key twice in his agitation. He moved his hands over the beautifully polished rifles, then selected one: a Holland & Holland Royal Deluxe .470 NE with a Leupold VX-III custom scope. He pulled it from the case, turned it with hands that trembled slightly, then put it back and carefully relocked the case.

Pendergast could preach all he wanted to about the rule of law, but the fact was it was time to take matters into his own hands. Because Judson Esterhazy had learned that the only way to do something right was to do it yourself.

13

New Orleans

Pendergast turned the Rolls-Royce into the private parking lot on Dauphine Street, harshly lit with sodium lamps. The attendant, a man with thick ears and heavy pouches below his eyes, lowered the gate behind them and handed Pendergast a ticket, which the agent tucked in the visor.

"In the back on the left, slot thirty-nine!" the man bawled in a heavy Delta accent. He examined the Rolls with bug eyes. "On second thought, take slot thirty-two—it's bigger. And we ain't responsible for damage. You might want to think of parking in LaSalle's on Toulouse, where they got a covered garage."

"Thank you, I prefer this one."

"Suit yourself."

Pendergast maneuvered the massive car through the tight lot and eased it into the designated space. They both got out. The lot was large, yet it felt claustrophobic, surrounded on all sides by a motley collection of old buildings. It was a mild winter night, and despite the extreme lateness of the hour, groups of young men and women, some carrying foaming beers in plastic glasses, could be seen stumbling along the sidewalks, calling out to one another, laughing and making noise. A muffled din wafted into the parking lot from the streets beyond, a mixture of shouts and cries, honking cars, and Dixieland jazz.

"A typical night in the French Quarter," said Pendergast, leaning against the car. "Bourbon is the next street over—nexus of the nation's public display of moral turpitude." He inhaled the night air, and a strange half smile seemed to spread over his pale features.

D'Agosta waited, but Pendergast didn't move. "Are we going?" he finally asked.

"In a moment, Vincent." Pendergast closed his eyes and slowly inhaled again, as if absorbing the spirit of the place. D'Agosta waited, reminding himself that Pendergast's odd mood shifts and strange ways were going to require patience—a lot of it. But the drive from Savannah had been long and exhausting—it seemed Pendergast kept another Rolls down here identical to the one in New York—and D'Agosta was famished. On top of that, he had been looking forward to a beer for some time, and seeing revelers going past with frosty brews was not improving his mood.

A minute passed, and D'Agosta cleared his throat. The eyes opened.

"Aren't we going to see your old digs?" D'Agosta asked. "Or at least what's left of them?"

"Indeed we are." Pendergast turned. "This is one

of the oldest parts of Dauphine Street, right here, the very heart of the French Quarter—the *real* French Quarter."

D'Agosta grunted. He noticed the attendant, across the lot, watching them with a certain amount of suspicion.

Pendergast pointed. "That lovely Greek Revival town house, for example, was built by one of the most famous of the early New Orleans architects, James Gallier Senior."

"Seems they turned it into a Holiday Inn," said D'Agosta, eyeing the sign in front.

"And that magnificent house, there, is the Gardette–Le Prêtre House. Built for a dentist who came here from Philadelphia when this was a Spanish city. A planter named Le Prêtre bought it in 1839 for over twenty thousand dollars—an immense fortune at the time. The Le Prêtres owned it until the '70s, but the family sadly declined... It is now, I believe, luxury apartments."

"Right," said D'Agosta. The attendant was now walking over, a frown on his face.

"And right across the street," said Pendergast, "is the old Creole cottage where John James Audubon stayed with his wife, Lucy Bakewell, for a time. It's now a curious little museum."

"Excuse me," the attendant said, his eyes narrowed to frog-like slits. "No loitering allowed."

"My apologies!" Pendergast reached into his suit and flipped out a fifty-dollar bill. "How careless of me not to offer you a gratuity. I commend you on your vigilance."

The man broke into a smile. "Well, I wasn't... but

that's much appreciated, sir." He took the bill. "You take your time, no rush." Nodding and smiling, he headed back to his booth.

Pendergast still seemed in no hurry to move on. He loitered about, hands clasped behind his dark suit, gazing this way and that as if he were in a museum gallery, his expression a curious mixture of wistfulness, loss, and something harder to identify. D'Agosta tried to suppress his growing irritation. "Are we going to find your old house now?" he finally asked.

Pendergast turned to him and murmured, "But we have, my dear Vincent."

"Where?"

"Right here. *This* was Rochenoire."

D'Agosta swallowed and looked about the asphalt parking lot with a fresh eye. A stray breeze kicked up a piece of greasy trash, whirling it around and around. Somewhere, a cat howled.

"After the house was burned," said Pendergast, "the underground crypts were moved, the basement filled in, and the remains bulldozed. It was a vacant lot for years, until I leased it to the company that runs this parking lot."

"You still own this land?"

"The Pendergasts never sell real estate."

"Oh."

Pendergast turned. "Rochenoire was set well back from the street, formal gardens in front, originally a monastic retreat, a big stone structure with oriel windows, battlements, and a widow's walk. Gothic Revival, rather unusual for the street. My room was in the corner, on the second floor, up there." He pointed into space. "It looked over the Audubon cottage to the river, and the other window looked toward the Le Prêtre house. Ah, the Le Prêtres...I used to watch them for hours, the people going back and forth in the lit windows, listening to the histrionics."

"And you met Helen at the Audubon museum across the street?" D'Agosta hoped to steer the conversation back to the task at hand.

Pendergast nodded. "Some years ago I loaned them our double elephant folio for an exhibition, and I was invited to the opening. They were always keen to get their hands on our family copy, which my great-great-grandfather subscribed to directly from Audubon." Pendergast paused, his face spectral in the stark light of the parking lot. "When I entered the little museum, I immediately saw a young woman across the room, staring at me."

"Love at first sight?" D'Agosta asked.

The ghostly half smile returned. "It was as if the world suddenly vanished, no one else existed. She was utterly striking. Dressed in white. Her eyes were so blue they verged on indigo, flecked throughout with violet. Most unusual—in fact, in my experience, unique. She came straight over and introduced herself, taking my hand even before I could collect myself..." He hesitated. "There was never any coyness about Helen; she was the only person I could trust implicitly."

Pendergast's voice seemed to thicken and he fell silent. Then he roused himself. "Except perhaps for you, my dear Vincent."

D'Agosta was startled by this sudden praise thrown his way. "Thanks."

"What indulgent rubbish I've been spouting," said Pendergast briskly. "The answers lie in the past, but we mustn't wallow there ourselves. Even so, I think it was important for us—for *both* of us—to start from this place."

"Start," D'Agosta repeated. Then he turned. "Say, Pendergast..."

"Yes?"

"Speaking of the past, there's something I've been wondering. Why did they—whoever *they* were—go to all the trouble?"

"I'm not sure I follow you."

"Acquiring the trained lion. Setting up the death of the German photographer in order to lure you and Helen to the camp. Buying off all those people. That took a lot of time and money. It's an awfully elaborate plot. Why not just stage a kidnapping, or a car accident back here in New Orleans? I mean, that would have been a much easier way to..." His voice trailed off.

For a moment Pendergast didn't reply. Then he nodded slowly. "Quite. It's a very curious thought. But don't forget our friend Wisley said one of the conspirators he heard speak was German. And that tourist who the lion killed first was also German. Perhaps that first murder was more than just a diversion."

"I'd forgotten that," D'Agosta said.

"If so, the trouble and expense become more justifiable. But let's hold that thought for the time being, Vincent. I'm convinced our own first step must be to learn more—if we can—about Helen herself." He reached into his pocket and took out a folded paper, handing it to D'Agosta.

D'Agosta unfolded it. Written in Pendergast's elegant hand was an address:

214 Mechanic Street
Rockland, Maine

"What's this?" D'Agosta asked.

"The past, Vincent—the address where *she* grew up. That is your next task. My own...lies here."

14

Penumbra Plantation

"Would you care for another cup of tea, sir?"

"No thank you, Maurice." Pendergast regarded the remains of an early dinner—succotash, field peas, and ham with redeye gravy—with as much complacency as he could muster. Outside the tall windows of the dining room, dusk was gathering among the hemlocks and cypresses, and somewhere in the shadows a mockingbird was singing a long and complex dirge.

Pendergast dabbed at the corners of his mouth with a white linen napkin, then rose from the table. "Now that I've eaten, I wonder if I couldn't see the letter that arrived for me this afternoon."

"Certainly, sir." Maurice stepped out of the dining room into the hall, returning shortly with a letter. It was much battered, and had been re-addressed more than once. Judging by the postmark, it had taken almost three weeks to ultimately reach him. Even if he hadn't recognized the elegant, old-fashioned hand-writing, the Chinese stamps would have indicated the sender: Constance Greene, his ward, who was currently residing at a remote monastery in Tibet with her infant son. He slit the envelope with his knife, pulled out the single sheet of paper within, and read the note.

Dear Aloysius,

I do not know precisely what trouble you are in, but in dreams I see that you are—or soon will be—in great distress. I am very sorry. As flies to wanton boys are we to the gods; they kill us for their sport.

I am coming home soon. Try to rest easy, everything is under control. And what isn't, soon will be.

Know that you are in my thoughts. You are in my prayers, as well—or would be, if I prayed.

                                        Constance

Pendergast re-read the letter, frowning.

"Is there something wrong, sir?" Maurice asked.

"I'm not sure." Pendergast seemed to consider the letter a moment longer. Then he put it aside and turned toward his factotum. "But in any case, Maurice, I was hoping you could join me in the library."

The elderly man paused in the act of clearing the table. "Sir?"

"I thought perhaps we could have a postprandial glass of sherry, reminisce about the old days. I find myself in a nostalgic frame of mind."

This was a most unusual invitation, and the look on Maurice's face implied as much. "Thank you, sir. Let me just finish clearing away here."

"Very good. I'll head down to the cellar and find us a nice moldy bottle."

The bottle was, in fact, more than nice: a Hidalgo Oloroso Viejo VORS. Pendergast took a sip from his glass, admiring the sherry's complexity: woody and fruity, with a finish that seemed to linger forever on the palate. Maurice sat on an ottoman across the old Kashan silk carpet, very erect and stiff in his butler's uniform, almost comically uncomfortable.

"Sherry to your liking?" Pendergast asked.

"It's very fine, sir," the butler replied.

"Then drink up, Maurice—it will help drive out the damp."

Maurice did as requested. "Would you like me to place another log on the fire?"

Pendergast shook his head, then looked around again. "Amazing, how being back here brings on such a flood of memories."

"I'm sure it must, sir."

Pendergast pointed at a large freestanding globe, set into a wooden framework. "For example, I recall having a violent argument with Nurse over whether Australia was a continent or not. She insisted it was only an island."

Maurice nodded.

"And the exquisite set of Wedgwood plates that used to sit on the top shelf of that bookcase." Pendergast indicated the spot with a nod. "I remember the day that my brother and I were reenacting the Roman assault on Silvium. The siege engine Diogenes built proved rather too effective. The very first volley landed directly on that shelf." Pendergast shook his head. "No cocoa for a month."

"I recall it only too clearly, sir," Maurice said, finishing his glass. The sherry seemed to be growing on him.

Quickly Pendergast made to refill their glasses. "No, no, I insist," he said when Maurice tried to demur.

Maurice nodded and murmured his thanks.

"This room was always the focal point of the house," Pendergast said. "This was where we held the party after I won top honors at Lusher. And Grandfather used to practice his speeches here—do you remember how we'd all sit around, acting as audience, cheering and whistling?"

"Like it was yesterday."

Pendergast took another sip. "And this was where we held the reception, after our wedding ceremony in the formal garden."

"Yes, sir." The sharp edge of reserve had dulled somewhat, and Maurice appeared to sit more naturally on the ottoman.

"Helen loved this room, too," Pendergast went on.

"Indeed she did."

"I remember how she'd often sit here in the evenings, working on her research or catching up on the technical journals."

A wistful, reflective smile crossed Maurice's face.

Pendergast examined his glass and the autumn-colored liquid within it. "We could spend hours here without speaking, simply enjoying each other's company." He paused and said, casually, "Did she ever speak to you, Maurice, of her life before she met me?"

Maurice drained his glass, set it aside with a delicate gesture. "No, she was a quiet one."

"What's your strongest memory of her?"

Maurice thought a moment. "Bringing her pots of rose hip tea."

Now it was Pendergast's turn to smile. "Yes, that was her favorite. It seemed she could never get enough. The library always smelled of rose hips." He sniffed the air. Now the room smelled only of dust, damp, and sherry. "I fear I was away from home rather more frequently than was good. I often wonder what Helen did for amusement in this drafty old house while I was out of town."

"She sometimes went on trips for her own work, sir. But she spent a lot of time right in here," Maurice said. "She used to miss you so."

"Indeed? She always put on such a brave face."

"I used to come across her in here all the time in your absences," Maurice said. "Looking at the birds."

Pendergast paused. "The birds?"

"You know, sir. Your brother's old favorite, back before...before the bad times started. The great book with all the bird prints in that drawer there." He nodded toward a drawer in the base of an old chestnut armoire.

Pendergast frowned. "The Audubon double elephant folio?"

"That's the one. I'd bring her tea and she wouldn't even notice I was here. She'd sit turning the pages for hours."

Pendergast put down his glass rather abruptly. "Did she ever talk to you about this interest in Audubon? Ask you questions, perhaps?"

"Now and then, sir. She was fascinated with great-

great-grandfather's friendship with Audubon. It was nice to see her taking such an interest in the family."

"Grandfather Boethius?"

"That's the one."

"When was this, Maurice?" Pendergast asked after a moment.

"Oh, shortly after you were married, sir. She wanted to see his papers."

Pendergast allowed himself a contemplative sip. "Papers? Which ones?"

"The ones in there, in the drawer below the prints. She was always going through those old documents and diaries. Those, and the book."

"Did she ever say why?"

"I expect she admired those pictures. Those are some lovely birds, Mr. Pendergast." Maurice took another sip of his sherry. "Say—wasn't that where you first met her? At the Audubon Cottage on Dauphine Street?"

"Yes. At a show of Audubon prints. But she exhibited little interest in them at the time. She told me she'd only come for the free wine and cheese."

"You know women, sir. They like their little secrets."

"So it would seem," Pendergast replied, very quietly.

15

Rockland, Maine

Under ordinary conditions, The Salty Dog Tavern would have been just the kind of bar Vincent D'Agosta liked: honest, unassuming, working class, and cheap. But these were not ordinary conditions. He had flown or driven among four cities in as many days; he missed Laura Hayward; and he was tired, bone-tired. Maine in February was not exactly charming. The last thing he felt like doing at the moment was hoisting beers with a bunch of fishermen.

But he was becoming a little desperate. Rockland had turned out to be a dead end. The old Esterhazy house had changed hands numerous times since the family moved out twenty years ago. Of all the neighbors, only one old spinster seemed to remember the family—and she had shut the door in his face. Newspapers in the public library had no mention of the Esterhazys, and the public records office held nothing pertinent but tax rolls. So much for small-town gossip and nosiness.

And so D'Agosta found himself resorting to the Salty Dog Tavern, a waterfront dive where—he was informed—the oldest of the old salts hung out. It proved to be a shabby shingled building tucked between two warehouses on the landward end of the commercial fishing wharf. A squall was fast approaching, a few preliminary flakes of snow whirling in from the sea, the wind lashing up spume from the ocean and sending abandoned newspapers tumbling across the rocky strand. *Why the hell am I here, anyway?* he wondered. But he knew the reason—Pendergast had explained it himself. *I'm afraid you'll have to go,* he'd said. *I'm too close to the subject. I lack the requisite investigative distance and objectivity.*

Inside the bar it was dark, and the close air smelled of deep-fried fish and stale beer. As D'Agosta's eyes adjusted to the gloom, he saw that the bar's denizens—a bartender and four patrons in peacoats and sou'westers—had stopped talking and were staring at him. Clearly, this was an establishment that catered to regulars. At least it was warm, heat radiating from a woodstove in the middle of the room.

Taking a seat at the far end of the bar, he nodded to the bartender and asked for a Bud. He made himself inconspicuous, and the conversation gradually resumed. From it, he quickly learned that the four patrons were all fishermen; that the fishing was currently bad; that the fishing was, in fact, always bad.

He took in the bar as he sipped his beer. The decor was, unsurprisingly, early nautical: shark jaws, huge lobster claws, and photos of fishing boats covered the walls, and nets with colored glass balls hung from the ceiling. A heavy patina of age, smoke, and grime coated every surface.

He downed one beer, then a second, before deciding it was time to make his move. "Mike," he said—using the bartender's Christian name, which he had earlier gleaned from listening to the conversation—"let me buy a round for the house. Have one yourself, while you're at it."

Mike stared at him a moment, then with a gruff word of thanks he complied. There were nods and grunts from the patrons as the drinks were handed out.

D'Agosta took a big swig of his beer. It was important, he knew, to seem like a regular guy—and in the Salty Dog, that meant not being a piker when it came to drinking. He cleared his throat. "I was wondering," he said out loud, "if maybe some of you men could help me."

The stares returned, some curious, some suspicious. "Help you with what?" said a grizzled man the others had referred to as Hector.

"There's a family used to live around here. Name of Esterhazy. I'm trying to track them down."

"What's your name, mister?" asked a fisherman called Ned. He was about five feet tall, with a wind- and sun-wizened face and forearms thick as telephone poles.

"Martinelli."

"You a cop?" Ned asked, frowning.

D'Agosta shook his head. "Private investigator. It's about a bequest."

"Bequest?"

"Quite a lot of money. I've been hired by the trustees to locate any surviving Esterhazys. If I can't find them, I can't give them their inheritance, can I?"

The bar was silent a minute while the regulars digested this. More than one pair of eyes brightened at the talk of money.

"Mike, another round, please." D'Agosta took a generous swig from the foamy mug. "The trustees have also authorized a small honorarium for those who help locate any surviving family members."

D'Agosta watched as the fishermen glanced at one another, then back at him. "So," he said, "can anybody here tell me anything?"

"Aren't no Esterhazys in this town anymore," said Ned.

"Aren't no Esterhazys in this entire part of the *world* anymore," said Hector. "There wouldn't be any—not after what happened."

"What was that?" D'Agosta asked, trying not to show too much interest.

More glances among the fishermen. "I don't know a whole lot," said Hector. "But they sure left town in a big hurry."

"They kept a crazy aunt locked up in the attic," said the third fisherman. "Had to, after she began killing and eating the dogs in town. Neighbors said they could hear her up there at night, crying and banging on the door, demanding dog meat."

"Come on, now, Gary," said the bartender, with a laugh. "That was just the wife screaming. She was a real harpy. You've been watching too many late-night movies."

"What really happened," said Ned, "was the wife tried to poison the husband. Strychnine in his cream of wheat."

The bartender shook his head. "Have another beer, Ned. I heard the father lost his money in the stock market—that's why they blew town in a hurry, owed money all over."

"A nasty business," Hector said, draining his beer. "Very nasty."

"What kind of a family were they?" D'Agosta asked.

One or two of the fishermen looked longingly at the empty glasses they'd downed with frightening rapidity.

"Mike, set us up again, if you please," D'Agosta asked the bartender.

"I heard," said Ned as he accepted his glass, "that the father was a real bastard. That he beat his wife with an electrical cord. That's why she poisoned him."

The stories just seemed to get wilder and less likely; the one fact Pendergast had been able to pass on was that Helen's father had been a doctor.

"That's not what *I* heard," said the bartender. "It was the wife who was crazy. The whole family was afraid of her, tiptoed around for fear of setting her off. And the husband was away a lot. Always traveling. South America, I think."

"Any arrests? Police investigations?" D'Agosta already knew the answer: the Esterhazy police record was clean as a whistle. There were no records anywhere of brushes with the law or police responses to domestic trouble. "You mentioned family. There was a son and daughter, wasn't there?"

A brief silence. "The son was kind of strange," said Ned.

"Ned, the son was junior-class valedictorian," said Hector.

Class valedictorian, thought D'Agosta, *at least that can be checked out.* "And the daughter? What was she like?"

He was met with shrugs all around. He wondered if the high school would still have the records. "Anybody know where they might be now?"

Glances were exchanged. "I heard the son was down south somewhere," said Mike the bartender. "No idea what happened to the daughter."

"Esterhazy isn't a common name," offered Hector. "Ever think of trying the Internet?"

D'Agosta looked around at a sea of blank faces. He couldn't think of any other questions that wouldn't lead to another chorus of conflicting rumors and unhelpful advice. He also realized—with dismay—that he was slightly drunk.

He stood, holding the bar to steady himself. "What do I owe you?" he asked Mike.

"Thirty-two fifty," came the reply.

D'Agosta fished two twenties from his wallet and placed them on the bar. "Thank you all for your help," he said. "Have a good evening."

"Say, what about that honorarium?" asked Ned.

D'Agosta paused, then turned. "Right, the honorarium. Let me give you my cell number. Any of you think of something else—something *specific*, not just rumors—you give me a call. If it leads to something, you might just get lucky." He pulled a napkin toward him and wrote down his number.

The fishermen nodded at him; Hector raised a hand in farewell.

D'Agosta clutched his coat up around his collar and staggered out of the bar into the stinging blizzard.

16

New Orleans

Desmond Tipton liked this time of day more than any other, when the doors were shut and barred, the visitors gone, and every little thing in its place. It was the quiet period, from five to eight, before the drink tourists descended on the French Quarter like the Mongolian hordes of Genghis Khan, infesting the bars and jazz joints, swilling Sazeracs to oblivion. He could hear them outside every night, their boozy voices, whoops, and infantile caterwaulings only partly muffled by the ancient walls of the Audubon Cottage.

On this particular evening, Tipton had decided to clean the waxwork figure of John James Audubon, who was the centerpiece of and motive purpose behind the museum. In the life-size diorama, the great naturalist sat in his study by the fireplace, sketchboard and pen in hand, making a drawing of a dead bird—a scarlet tanager—on a table. Tipton grabbed the DustBuster and feather duster and climbed over the Plexiglas barrier. He began cleaning Audubon's clothing, running the little vacuum up and down, and then he turned it on the figure's beard and hair while whisking bits of dirt from the handsome waxwork face with the feather duster.

There came a sound. He paused, switching off the DustBuster. It came again: a knock at the front door.

Irritated, Tipton jammed the switch back on and continued—only to hear a more insistent knocking. This went on almost every night: inebriated morons who, having read the historic plaque affixed beside the door, for some reason decided to knock. For years it had been like that, fewer and fewer visitors during the day, more knocking and revelry at night. The only respite had been the few months after the hurricane.

Another insistent set of knocks, measured and loud.

He put down the hand vacuum, climbed back out, and marched over to the door on creaky bow legs. "We're closed!" he shouted through the oaken door. "Go away or I'll call the police!"

"Why, that isn't you, is it, Mr. Tipton?" came the muffled voice.

Tipton's white eyebrows shot up in consternation. Who could it be? The visitors during the day never paid any attention to him, while he assiduously avoided engaging with them, sitting dourly at his desk with his face buried in research.

"Who is it?" asked Tipton, after he had recovered from his surprise.

"May we carry on this conversation inside, Mr. Tipton? It's rather chilly out here."

Tipton hesitated, then unbolted the door to see a slender gentleman in a dark suit, pale as a ghost, his silvery eyes gleaming in the twilight of the darkening street. There was something instantly recognizable about the man, unmistakable, and it gave Tipton a start.

"Mr.... *Pendergast*?" he ventured, almost in a whisper.

"The very same." The man stepped in and took Tipton's hand, giving it a cool, brief shake. Tipton just stared.

Pendergast gestured toward the visitor's chair opposite Tipton's desk. "May I?"

Tipton nodded and Pendergast seated himself, throwing one leg over the other. Tipton silently took his own chair.

"You look like you've just seen a ghost," said Pendergast.

"Well, Mr. Pendergast..." Tipton began, his mind awhirl, "I thought—I thought the family was gone...I had no idea..." His voice stammered into silence.

"The rumors of my demise are greatly exaggerated."

Tipton fumbled in the vest pocket of his dingy three-piece woolen suit, extracted a handkerchief, and patted his brow. "Delighted to see you, just delighted..." Another pat.

"The feeling is mutual."

"What brings you back here, if I may ask?" Tipton made an effort to recover himself. He had been curator of the Audubon Cottage for almost fifty years, and he knew a great deal about the Pendergast family. The last thing he'd expected was to see one of them again, in the flesh. He remembered the terrible night of the fire as if it were yesterday: the mob, the screams from the upper stories, the flames leaping into the night sky... Although he'd been a trifle relieved when the surviving family members left the area: the Pendergasts had always given him the willies, especially that strange brother, Diogenes. He had heard rumors that Diogenes had died in Italy. He'd also heard that Aloysius had disappeared. He believed it only too well: it was a family that seemed destined for extinction.

"Just paying a visit to our little property across the street. Since I was in the neighborhood, I thought I'd drop in and pay my respects to an old friend. How is the museum business these days?"

"Property? You mean..."

"That's right. The parking lot where Rochenoire once stood. I've never been able to let it go, for—for *sentimental* reasons." This was followed by a thin smile.

Tipton nodded. "Of course, of course. As for the museum, you can see, Mr. Pendergast, the neighborhood has changed much for the worse. We don't get many visitors these days."

"It has indeed changed. How pleasant to see the Audubon Cottage museum is still exactly the same."

"We try to keep it that way."

Pendergast rose, clasped his hands behind his back. "Do you mind? I realize that you're closed at present, but nevertheless I'd love to take a turn through. For old times' sake."

Tipton hastily rose. "Of course. Please excuse the Audubon diorama, I was just cleaning it." He was mortified to see that he had laid the DustBuster in

Audubon's lap, with the feather duster propped up against his arm, as if some jokester had tried to turn the great man into a charwoman.

"Do you recall," Pendergast said, "the special exhibition you mounted, fifteen years ago, for which we loaned you our double elephant folio?"

"Of course."

"That was quite a festive opening."

"It was." Tipton remembered it all too well: the stress and horror of watching crowds of people wandering about his exhibits with brimming glasses of wine. It had been a beautiful summer evening, with a full moon, but he'd been too harassed to notice it much. That was the first and last special exhibit he had ever mounted.

Pendergast began strolling through the back rooms, peering into the glass cases with their prints and drawings and birds, the Audubon memorabilia, the letters and sketches. Tipton followed in his wake.

"Did you know this is where my wife and I first met? At that very opening."

"No, Mr. Pendergast, I didn't." Tipton felt uneasy. Pendergast seemed strangely excited.

"My wife—Helen—I believe she had an interest in Audubon?"

"Yes, she certainly did."

"Did she . . . ever visit the museum afterward?"

"Oh, yes. Before and afterward."

"Before?"

The sharpness of the question brought Tipton up short. "Why, yes. She was here off and on, doing her research."

"Her research," Pendergast repeated. "And this was how long before we met?"

"For at least six months before that opening. Maybe longer. She was a lovely woman. I was so shocked to hear—"

"Quite," came the reply, cutting him off. Then the man seemed to soften, or at least get control of himself. *This Pendergast is a strange one*, thought Tipton, *just like the others.* Eccentricity was all well and good in New Orleans, the city was known for it—but this was something else altogether.

"I never knew much about Audubon," Pendergast continued. "And I never really quite understood this research of hers. Do you remember much about it?"

"A little," said Tipton. "She was interested in the time Audubon spent here in 1821, with Lucy."

Pendergast paused at a darkened glass case. "Was there anything about Audubon in particular she was curious about? Was she perhaps planning to write an article, or a book?"

"You would know that better than I, but I do recall she asked more than once about the Black Frame."

"The Black Frame?"

"The famous lost painting. The one Audubon did at the sanatorium."

"Forgive me, my knowledge of Audubon is so limited. Which lost painting is that?"

"When Audubon was a young man, he became seriously ill. While convalescing, he made a painting. An extraordinary painting, apparently—his first really great work. It later disappeared. The curious thing is that nobody who saw it mentioned what it depicted—just that it was brilliantly lifelike and set in an unusual black-painted frame. What he actually painted seems to have been lost to history." On familiar ground now, Tipton found his nervousness receding slightly.

"And Helen was interested in it?"

"Every Audubon scholar is interested in it. It was the beginning of that period of his life that culminated in *The Birds of America*, by far the greatest work of natural history ever published. The Black Frame was—so people who saw it said—his first work of true genius."

"I see." Pendergast fell silent, his face sinking into thoughtfulness. Then he suddenly started and examined his watch. "Well! How good it was to see you, Mr. Tipton." He grasped the man's hand in his own, and Tipton was disconcerted to find it even colder than when he had entered, as if the man were a cooling corpse.

Tipton followed Pendergast to the door. As Pendergast opened it, he finally screwed up the courage to ask a question of his own. "By any chance, Mr. Pendergast, do you still have the family's double elephant folio?"

Pendergast turned. "I do."

"Ah! If I may be so bold to suggest, and I hope you will forgive my directness, that if for any reason you wish to find a good home for it, one where it would be well taken care of and enjoyed by the public, naturally we would be most honored . . ." He let his voice trail off hopefully.

"I shall keep it in mind. A good evening to you, Mr. Tipton."

Tipton was relieved he did not extend his hand a second time.

The door closed and Tipton turned the lock and barred it, then stood for a long time at the door, thinking. Wife eaten by a lion, parents burned to death by a mob...What a strange family. And clearly the passage of years had not made this one any more normal.

17

The Downtown campus of Tulane University Health Sciences Center, on Tulane Street, was housed in a nondescript gray skyscraper that would not have looked out of place in New York's financial district. Pendergast exited the elevator at the thirty-first floor, made his way to the Women's Health Division, and—after a few inquiries—found himself before the door of Miriam Kendall.

He gave a discreet knock. "Come in," came a strong, clear voice.

Pendergast opened the door. The small office beyond clearly belonged to a professor. Two metal bookcases were stuffed full of textbooks and journals. Stacks of examination bluebooks were arranged on the desktop. Sitting on the far side of the desk was a woman of perhaps sixty years of age. She rose as Pendergast entered.

"Dr. Pendergast," she said, accepting the proffered hand with a certain reserve.

"Call me Aloysius," he replied. "Thanks for seeing me."

"Not at all. Please take a seat."

She sat back behind her desk and looked him over with a detached—almost clinical—manner. "You haven't aged a day."

The same could not be said of Miriam Kendall. Haloed in yellow morning light from the tall, narrow windows, she nevertheless looked a great deal older than she had during the time she shared an office with Helen Esterhazy Pendergast. Yet her manner was just as Pendergast remembered it: crisp, cool, professional.

"Looks can be deceiving," Pendergast replied. "However. I thank you. How long have you been at Tulane?"

"Nine years now." She laid her hands on the desk, tented her fingers. "I have to say, Aloysius, I'm surprised you didn't take your inquiries directly to Helen's old boss, Morris Blackletter."

Pendergast nodded. "I did, actually. He's retired now—as you probably know, after Doctors With Wings he went on to consulting positions with various pharmaceutical companies—but at present he's on vacation in England, not due back for several days."

She nodded. "And what about Doctors With Wings?"

"I was there this morning. The place was a madhouse, everybody mobilizing for Azerbaijan."

Kendall nodded. "Ah, yes. The earthquake. Many feared dead, I understand."

"There wasn't a face there over thirty—and nobody who took a minute to speak with me had the least recollection of my wife."

Kendall nodded again. "It's a job for the young. That's one of the reasons I left DWW to teach women's health issues." The desk phone rang. Kendall ignored it. "In any case," she said briskly, "I'm more than happy to share my memories of Helen with you, Aloysius—though I find myself curious as to why you should approach me now, after all these years."

"Most understandable. The fact is, I'm planning to write a memoir of my wife. A sort of celebration of her life, brief as it was. Doctors With Wings was Helen's first and only job after she obtained her MS in pharmaceutical biology."

"I thought she was an epidemiologist."

"That was her subspecialty." Pendergast paused. "I've realized just how little I knew of her work with DWW—a fault that's entirely my own, and something I am trying to remedy now."

Hearing this, the hard lines of Kendall's face softened a little. "I'm glad to hear you say that. Helen was a remarkable woman."

"So if you'd be kind enough to reminisce a little about her time at Doctors With Wings? And please—don't sugarcoat anything. My wife was not without imperfection—I'd prefer the unvarnished truth."

Kendall looked at him a minute. Then her eyes traveled to some indeterminate spot behind him and grew distant, as if looking into the past. "You know about DWW—we worked on sanitation, clean water, and nutrition programs in the Third World. Empowering people to better their own health and living conditions. But when there was a disaster—like the earthquake in Azerbaijan—we mobilized teams of doctors and health workers and flew them into the target areas."

"That much I know."

"Helen..." She hesitated.

"Go on," Pendergast murmured.

"Helen was very effective, right from the beginning. But I often had the feeling she loved the adventure of it even more than the healing. As if she put in the months of office work just for the chance to be dropped into the epicenter of some disaster."

Pendergast nodded.

"I recall..." She stopped again. "Aren't you going to take notes?"

"I have an excellent memory, Ms. Kendall. Pray continue."

"I remember when a group of us were surrounded by a machete-wielding mob in Rwanda. There must have been at least fifty of them, half drunk. Helen suddenly produced a two-shot derringer and disarmed the whole lot. Told them to chuck their weapons in a pile and get lost. And they did!" She shook her head. "Did she ever tell you about that?"

"No, she didn't."

"She knew how to use that derringer, too. She learned to shoot in Africa, didn't she?"

"Yes."

"I always thought it a little strange."

"What?"

"Shooting, I mean. A strange hobby for a biologist. But then, everyone has their own way of relieving the stress. And when you're in the field, the pressure can be unbearable: the death, cruelty, savagery." She shook her head at some private memory.

"I'd hoped to see her personnel file at DWW—to no avail."

"You saw the place. As you might imagine, they aren't big on paperwork—especially paperwork more than a decade old. Besides, Helen's file would be slimmer than most."

"Why is that?"

"She was only part-time, of course."

"Not...her full-time job?"

"Well, 'part-time' isn't exactly correct. I mean, most of the time she *did* put in a full forty hours—or, when in the field, a great deal more—but she was often gone from the office, sometimes days at a time. I had always assumed she had a second job, or maybe some kind of private project she was working on, but you just said this was her only job." Kendall shrugged.

"She had no other job." Pendergast fell silent a moment. "Any other recollections of a personal nature?"

Kendall hesitated. "She always struck me as a very private person. I didn't even know she had a brother until he showed up at the office one day. Very handsome fellow he was, too. He's also in the medical field, I recollect."

Pendergast nodded. "Judson."

"Yes, that was his name. I imagine medicine ran in the family."

"It did. Helen's father was a doctor," Pendergast said.

"I'm not surprised."

"Did she ever talk to you about Audubon?"

"The painter? No, she never did. But it's funny you should mention him."

"Why, exactly?"

"Because in a way it reminds me of the one and only time I ever caught her at a loss for words."

Pendergast leaned forward slightly in the chair. "Please tell me about it."

"We were in Sumatra. There had been a tsunami, and the devastation was extensive."

Pendergast nodded. "I recall that trip. We'd been married just a few months at the time."

"It was utter chaos; we were all being worked to the bone. One night I came back to the tent I shared with Helen and another aid worker. Helen was there, alone, in a camp chair. She was dozing, with a book open in her lap, showing a picture of a bird. I didn't want to wake her, so I gently removed the book. She woke up with a start and snatched it from me and shut it. She was very flustered. Then she seemed to recover, tried to laugh it off, saying I'd startled her."

"What sort of bird?"

"A small bird, quite colorful. It had an unusual name..." She stopped, trying to recall. "Part of it was the name of a state."

Pendergast thought a moment. "Virginia Rail?"

"No, I'd have remembered that."

"California Towhee?"

"No. It was green and yellow."

There was a lengthy silence. "Carolina Parakeet?" Pendergast finally asked.

"That's it! I knew it was strange. I recall saying at the time I didn't know there were any parrot species in America. But she brushed off the question and that was it."

"I see. Thank you, Ms. Kendall." Pendergast sat

quite still, and then he rose and extended his hand. "Thank you for your help."

"I should like to see a copy of the memoir. I was very fond of Helen."

Pendergast gave a little bow. "And so you shall, as soon as it is published." He turned and left, riding the elevator down to the street in silence, his thoughts far, far away.

18

Pendergast said good night to Maurice and, taking the remains of a bottle of Romanée-Conti 1964 he had opened at dinner, walked down the echoing central hall of Penumbra Plantation to the library. A storm had swept north from the Gulf of Mexico and the wind moaned about the house, worrying the shutters and thrashing the bare limbs of the surrounding trees. Rain beat on the windows, and heavy, swollen clouds obscured the full moon.

He approached the glass-fronted bookcase housing the family's most valuable books: a second printing of the Shakespeare *First Folio;* the two-volume 1755 edition of Johnson's *Dictionary;* a sixteenth-century copy of *Les Très Riches Heures du Duc de Berry,* in the original Limbourg illumination. The four volumes of Audubon's double elephant folio edition of *The Birds of America* were accorded their own private drawer at the bottom of the case.

Donning a pair of white cotton gloves, he removed

the four giant books and laid them side by side on the refectory table in the center of the library. Each one was more than three feet by four feet. Turning to the first, he opened it with exquisite care to the first print: *Wild Turkey, Male.* The dazzling image, as fresh as the day it was struck, was so lifelike it seemed as if it could step off the page. This set, one of only two hundred, had been subscribed directly from Audubon by Pendergast's own ancestor, whose ornate bookplate and signature inscription still graced the endpapers. The most valuable book ever produced in the New World, it was worth close to ten million dollars.

Slowly, he turned the pages: the *Yellow-billed Cuckoo*, the *Prothonotary Warbler*, the *Purple Finch*... one after another, he looked at them with a keen eye, plate after plate, until he arrived at Plate 26: the *Carolina Parakeet*.

Reaching into his coat pocket, he removed a sheet of notes he had scribbled.

Carolina Parakeet (*Conuropsis carolinensis*)
Only parrot species native to the Eastern US.
  Declared extinct 1939.
Last wild specimen killed in Florida in 1904; last
  captive bird, "Incas," died at the Cincinnati Zoo
  in 1918.
Forests cut; killed for feathers to make ladies' hats,
  killed by farmers who thought them pests, taken
  in large numbers as pets.
Prime reason for extinction: Flocking behavior.
  When individual birds were shot and fell to the
  ground, the flock, instead of fleeing, alighted

on the ground and gathered about the
dead and wounded as if to help, resulting
in the extermination of the entire flock.

Folding up the sheet and putting it away again, Pendergast poured himself a glass of Burgundy. As he drank it off, he seemed barely to taste the remarkable vintage.

He now knew—to his great mortification—that his initial meeting with Helen had been no accident. And yet he could hardly believe it. Surely, his family's connection to John James Audubon wasn't the reason she had married him? He knew she had loved him—and yet it was becoming increasingly clear that his wife led a double life. It was a bitter irony: Helen had been the one person in the world he had been able to trust, to open up to—and all the while she had been keeping a secret from him. As he poured another glass of wine he reflected that, because of that very trust, he'd never suspected her secret, which would have been obvious to him in any other friend.

He knew all this. And yet it was nothing compared with the remaining questions that almost shouted out at him:

What was behind Helen's apparent fascination with Audubon—and why had she been so careful to conceal her interest in the artist from him?

What was the relation between Helen's interest in Audubon's famous engravings and an obscure breed of parrot, extinct now for almost a century?

Where was Audubon's first mature work, the mysterious Black Frame, and why was Helen searching for it?

And most perplexing, and most important: why had this interest of Helen's ultimately caused her death? Because, while he was sure of little else, Pendergast was certain—beyond doubt—that somewhere, hiding behind this curtain of questions and suppositions, lurked not only the motive for her death, but the murderers themselves.

Putting aside the glass, he rose from the armchair and strode over to a telephone on a nearby table. He picked it up, dialed a number.

It was answered on the second ring. "D'Agosta."

"Hello, Vincent."

"Pendergast. How you doing?"

"Where are you at present?"

"At the Copley Plaza hotel, resting my dogs. Do you have any idea how many men named Adam attended MIT while your wife was there?"

"No."

"Thirty-one. I've managed to track down sixteen. None of them says he knew her. Five others are out of the country. Two more are dead. The other eight are unaccounted for: lost alumni, the university says."

"Let us put friend Adam on the back burner for the time being."

"Fine by me. So, where to next? New Orleans? New York, maybe? I'd really like to spend a little time with—"

"North of Baton Rouge. Oakley Plantation."

"Where?"

"You will be going to Oakley Plantation House, just outside St. Francisville."

A long pause. "So what am I going to be doing there?" D'Agosta asked in a dubious voice.

"Examining a brace of stuffed parrots."

Another, even longer pause. "And you?"

"I'll be at the Bayou Grand Hotel. Tracking down a missing painting."

19

Bayou Goula, Louisiana

Pendergast sat in the palm-lined courtyard in front of the elegant hotel, one black-clad leg draped over the other, arms crossed, motionless as the alabaster statues that framed the gracious space. The previous night's storm had passed, ushering in a warm and sunny day full of the false promise of spring. Before him lay a wide driveway of white gravel. A small army of valets and caddies were busy ferrying expensive cars and gleaming golf carts here and there. Beyond the driveway was a swimming pool, sparkling azure in the late-morning light, empty of swimmers but surrounded by sunbathers drinking Bloody Marys. Beyond the pool lay an expansive golf course, immaculate fairways and raked bunkers, over which strolled men in pastel-colored blazers and women in golf whites. Beyond passed the broad brown swath of the Mississippi River.

There was a movement at his side. "Mr. Pendergast?"

Pendergast looked up to see a short, rotund man in his late fifties, wearing a dark suit, the jacket buttoned, and a deep red tie bearing only the subtlest of designs. His bald pate gleamed so strikingly in the sun it might have been gilded, and identical commas of white hair were combed back above both ears. Two small blue eyes were set deep in a florid face. Below them, the prim mouth was fixed in a businesslike smile.

Pendergast rose. "Good morning."

"I'm Portby Chausson, general manager of the Bayou Grand Hotel."

Pendergast shook the proffered hand. "Pleased to make your acquaintance."

Chausson gestured toward the hotel with a pink hand. "Delighted. My office is this way."

He led the way through the courtyard into an echoing lobby, draped in cream-colored marble. Pendergast followed the manager past well-fed businessmen with sleek women on their arms to a plain door just beyond the front desk. Chausson opened it to reveal an opulent office in the French Baroque style. He ushered Pendergast into a chair before the ornate desk.

"I see from your accent you're from this part of the country," Chausson said as he took a seat behind the desk.

"New Orleans," Pendergast replied.

"Ah." Chausson rubbed his hands together. "But I believe you are a new guest?" He consulted a computer. "Indeed. Well, Mr. Pendergast, thank you for considering us for your holiday needs. And allow me to commend you on your exquisite taste: the Bayou Grand is the most luxurious resort in the entire Delta."

Pendergast inclined his head.

"Now, over the phone you indicated you were interested in our Golf and Leisure Packages. We have two: the one-week Platinum Package, and the two-week Diamond Package. While the one-week packages begin at twelve thousand five hundred, I might suggest upgrading to the two-week because of the—"

"Excuse me, Mr. Chausson?" Pendergast interrupted gently. "But if you'd allow me to interject for just a moment, I think I could save both of us valuable time."

The general manager paused, looking at Pendergast with an expectant smile.

"It's true I did express some interest in your golf packages. Please forgive my little deception."

Chausson looked blank. "Deception?"

"Correct. I merely wished to gain your attention."

"I don't understand."

"I'm not sure how much plainer I can express myself, Mr. Chausson."

"Do you mean to say"—the blank look darkened—"that you have no intention of staying at the Bayou Grand?"

"Alas, no. Golf is not my sport."

"That you deceived me so that you could...gain *access* to me?"

"I see the light has finally dawned."

"In that case, Mr. Pendergast, we have no further business to discuss. Good day."

Pendergast examined his perfectly manicured fingernails a moment. "Actually, we do have business to discuss."

"Then you should have approached me directly, without subterfuge."

"Had I done that, I would almost certainly never have made it into your office."

Chausson reddened. "I have heard just about enough. I'm a very busy man. Now, if you'll excuse me, I have *valid* guests to attend to."

But Pendergast showed no signs of rising. Instead, with a sigh of something like regret, he reached into his suit jacket, withdrew a small leather wallet, and flipped it open to reveal a gold shield.

Chausson stared at it for a long moment. "FBI?"

Pendergast nodded.

"Has there been a crime?"

"Yes."

Beads of sweat appeared on Chausson's brow. "You aren't going to...make an arrest at my hotel, are you?"

"I had something else in mind."

Chausson looked hugely relieved. "Is this some kind of criminal matter?"

"Not one related to the hotel."

"Do you have a warrant or subpoena?"

"No."

Chausson seemed to regain much of his poise. "I'm afraid, Mr. Pendergast, that we shall have to consult our attorneys before we can respond to any request. Company policy. So sorry."

Pendergast put away the shield. "Such a pity."

Complacency settled over the general manager's features. "My assistant will show you out." He pressed a button. "Jonathan?"

"Is it true, Mr. Chausson, that this hotel building was originally the mansion of a cotton baron?"

"Yes, yes." A slender young man entered. "Will you kindly show Mr. Pendergast out?"

"Yes, sir," the young man said.

Pendergast made no effort to rise. "I wonder, Mr. Chausson—what do you think your guests would say if they were to learn that, in fact, this hotel used to be a sanatorium?"

Chausson's face abruptly shut down. "I have no idea what you're talking about."

"A sanatorium for all kinds of nasty, highly communicable diseases. Cholera, tuberculosis, malaria, yellow fever—"

"Jonathan?" Chausson said. "Mr. Pendergast won't be leaving quite yet. Please close the door on your way out."

The young man retreated. Chausson turned on Pendergast, sitting forward, pink jowls quivering with indignation. "How dare you threaten me?"

"Threaten? What an ugly word. 'The truth shall make you free,' Mr. Chausson. I'm offering to *liberate* your guests with the truth, not threaten them."

For a moment, Chausson remained motionless. Then— slowly—he sank back into his chair. A minute passed, then two. "What is it you want?" he asked in a low voice.

"The sanatorium is the reason for my visit. I'm here to see any old files that might remain—in particular, those relating to a specific patient."

"And who might that patient be?"

"John James Audubon."

The general manager's forehead creased. And then he smacked his well-scrubbed hand on the desk in undisguised annoyance. "Not *again*!"

Pendergast looked at Chausson in surprise. "Excuse me?"

"Every time I think that wretched man is forgotten, somebody else comes along. And I suppose you'll be asking about that painting, as well."

Pendergast sat in silence.

"I'll tell you what I told the others. John James Audubon was a patient here nearly one hundred and eighty years ago. The, er, health care facility closed down more than a *century* ago. Any records—and certainly any painting—are long gone."

"And that's it?" Pendergast asked.

Chausson nodded with finality. "And that's it."

A look of sorrow came over Pendergast's face. "A pity. Well, good day, Mr. Chausson." And he rose from the chair.

"Wait a minute." The general manager also rose, in sudden alarm. "You're not going to tell the guests..." His voice trailed off.

Pendergast's sorrowful look deepened. "As I said—a pity."

Chausson put out a restraining hand. "Hold on. Just hold on." He took a handkerchief from his pocket, mopped his brow. "There may be a few files left. Come with me." And, fetching a deep, shuddering breath, he led the way out of the office.

Pendergast followed the little man through an elegant restaurant, past a food preparation area, and into an immense kitchen. The marble and gilt quickly gave way to white tile and rubberized floor mats. On the far side of the kitchen, Chausson opened a metal door. Old iron stairs led down into a chilly, damp, poorly lit basement corridor that seemed to tunnel forever into the Louisiana earth, its walls and ceiling of crumbling plaster, the floor of pitted brick.

At last, Chausson stopped before a banded iron door. With a groan of iron he pushed it open and stepped into blackness, the humid air heavy with the smell of fungus and rot. He twisted an old-fashioned light switch clockwise, and a vast empty space came into view, punctuated by the scurry and squeak of retreating vermin. The floor was littered with old asbestos-clad piping and various bric-a-brac, furred with age, mounded over with mold. "This was the old boiler room," he said as he picked his way through the rat droppings and detritus.

In the far corner sat several burst bundles of paper, damp, rodent-chewed, heavily foxed, and rotting with age. Rats had built a nest in one corner. "That's all that remains of the sanatorium paperwork," Chausson said, something of the old triumph creeping back into his voice. "I told you it was just scraps. Why it wasn't thrown out years ago, I have no idea—except that nobody ever comes in here anymore."

Pendergast knelt before the papers and, very carefully, began to go through them, turning each one over and examining it. Ten minutes passed, then twenty. Chausson looked at his watch several times, but Pendergast was completely insensible to the man's irritation. Finally, he rose, holding a thin sheath of papers. "May I borrow them?"

"Take them. Take the lot."

He slipped them into a manila envelope. "Earlier, you mentioned that others had expressed interest in Audubon and a certain painting."

Chausson nodded.

"Would that painting have been known as the Black Frame?"

Chausson nodded again.

"These others. Who were they and when did they come?"

"The first one came, let's see, about fifteen years ago. Shortly after I became general manager. The other one came maybe a year afterward."

"So I'm only the third to inquire," Pendergast said. "From your tone, I'd assumed there were more. Tell me about the first one."

Chausson sighed again. "He was an art dealer. Quite unsavory. In my business, you learn how to read a person from his manner, the things he says. This man almost scared me." He paused. "He was interested in the painting Audubon allegedly did while he was here. Implied that he'd make it well worth my time. He grew very angry when I could tell him nothing."

"Did he see the papers?" Pendergast asked.

"No. I didn't know they existed at the time."

"Do you remember his name?"

"Yes. It was Blast. You don't forget a name like that."

"I see. And the second person?"

"It was a woman. Young, reddish-brown hair, thin. Very pretty. She was much more pleasant—and persuasive. Still, there wasn't much more I could tell her than I told Blast. She looked through the papers."

"Did she take any?"

"I wouldn't let her; I thought they might be valuable. But now, I just want to get rid of them."

Pendergast nodded slowly. "This young woman—do you recall her name?"

"No. It was funny—she never gave it. I remember thinking about that after she left."

"Did she have an accent like mine?"

"No. She had a Yankee accent. Like the Kennedys." The manager shuddered.

"I see. Thank you for your time." Pendergast turned. "I'll see my own way out."

"Oh, no," Chausson said quickly. "I'll escort you to your car. I *insist*."

"Don't worry, Mr. Chausson. I won't say a word to your guests." And—with a small bow, and an even smaller, rather sad smile—Pendergast strode quickly to the long tunnel, toward the outside world.

20

D'Agosta pulled up in front of the whitewashed mansion, rising in airy formality from dead flower beds and bare-branched trees. The winter sky spat rain, puddles collecting on the blacktop. He sat in the rental car for a moment, listening to the last lousy lines of "Just You and I" on the radio, trying to overcome his annoyance at having been sent on what was hardly more than an errand. What the hell did he know about dead birds?

Finally, as the song faded away, he heaved himself from his seat, grabbed an umbrella, and stepped out of the car. He climbed the steps of Oakley Plantation House and entered the gallery: a porch with jalousie windows shut against the steady rain. Shoving his dripping umbrella into a stand, he shrugged off his raincoat, hung it on a rack, and entered the building.

"You must be Dr. D'Agosta," said a bright, bird-like

woman, rising from her desk and bustling toward him on stubby legs, sensible shoes rapping the boards. "We don't get many visitors this time of year. I'm Lola Marchant." She stuck out her hand.

D'Agosta took the hand and was given a surprisingly vigorous shake. The woman was all rouge and powder and lipstick, and she had to be at least sixty, stout and vigorous.

"Shame on you, bringing this bad weather!" She broke into a warbling laugh. "Even so, we always welcome Audubon researchers. Mostly we get tourists."

D'Agosta followed her into a reception hall, done up in white-painted wood and massive beams. He began to regret the cover he had given her over the phone. So little did he know about Audubon or birds, he felt sure he'd be busted on even the most minimal exchange of information. Best thing to do was keep his mouth shut.

"First things first!" Marchant went behind another desk and pushed an enormous logbook toward him. "Please sign your name and fill in the reason for your visit."

D'Agosta wrote down his name and the supposed reason.

"Thank you!" she said. "Now, let's get started. What, exactly, would you like to see?"

D'Agosta cleared his throat. "I'm an ornithologist"—he got the word out perfectly—"and I'd like to see some of Audubon's specimens."

"Wonderful! As you surely know, Audubon was only here for four months, working as a drawing master for Eliza Pirrie, the daughter of Mr. and Mrs. James Pirrie, owners of the Oakley Plantation. After a tiff with Mrs.

Pirrie he abruptly went back to New Orleans, taking with him all his specimens and drawings. But when we became a State Historic Site forty years ago, we were given a bequest of Audubon drawings, letters, and some of his actual bird specimens, which we've added to over the years—and now we have one of the finest Audubon collections in Louisiana!"

She smiled brightly at this recital, her bosom heaving slightly from the effort.

"Right," mumbled D'Agosta, removing a steno notebook from his brown suit coat, hoping it added verisimilitude.

"This way, Dr. D'Agosta, please."

Dr. D'Agosta. The lieutenant felt his apprehension increase.

The woman pounded her way across the painted pine floors to a set of stairs. They ascended to the second floor and walked through a large series of spacious rooms, furnished in period furniture, finally arriving at a locked door, which—when opened—revealed a set of attic stairs, steep and narrow. D'Agosta followed Marchant to the top. It was an attic in name only, being spotlessly clean and well kept, smelling of fresh paint. Old oaken cabinets with rippled glass lined three of the walls, with more modern, closed cabinets at the far end. The light came from a series of dormers with frosted windows, which let in a cool white light.

"We have about a hundred birds from Audubon's original collection," she said, walking briskly down the central corridor. "Unfortunately, Audubon was not much of a taxidermist. The specimens have been stabilized, of course. Here we are."

They stopped before a large, gray metal cabinet that looked almost like a safe. Marchant spun the center dial and turned the lever handle. With a sigh of air, the great door opened, revealing inner wooden cabinets with labels, stuck into brass label-holders, screwed to every drawer. A stench of mothballs washed over D'Agosta. Grasping one drawer, Marchant drew it out to display three rows of stuffed birds, yellowed tags around each claw, white cotton-wool poking out of their eyes.

"Those tags are Audubon's originals," said Marchant. "I'll handle the birds myself—please don't touch them without my permission. Now!" She smiled. "Which ones would you like to see?"

D'Agosta consulted his notebook. He had copied down some bird names from a website that listed all of Audubon's original specimens and their locations. Now he trotted them out. "I'd like to start with the Louisiana Water Thrush."

"Excellent!" The drawer slid in and another was pulled out. "Do you want to examine it on the table or in the drawer?"

"Drawer is fine." D'Agosta pushed a loupe into his eye and studied the bird closely with many grunts and mutterings. It was a ragged-looking thing, the feathers askew or missing, stuffing coming out. D'Agosta made what he hoped was a show of concentration, pausing to jot unintelligible notes.

He straightened. "Thank you. The American Goldfinch is the next on my list."

"Coming right up."

He made another show of examining the bird,

squinting at it through the loupe, taking notes, talking to himself.

"I hope you're finding what you're looking for," said Marchant, with a leading tone in her voice.

"Oh, yes. Thank you." This was already getting tiresome, and the smell of mothballs was making him sick.

"Now—" He pretended to consult his notebook. "—I'll look at the Carolina Parrot."

A sudden silence. D'Agosta was surprised to see Marchant's face reddening slightly. "I'm sorry, we don't have that specimen."

He felt an additional wash of annoyance: they didn't even have the specimen he'd come for. "But it's in all the reference books as being here," he said, more crossly than he intended. "In fact, it says you have two of them."

"We don't have them anymore."

"Where are they?" he said, with open exasperation.

There was a long silence. "I'm afraid they disappeared."

"Disappeared? Lost?"

"No, not lost. Stolen. Many years ago, when I was just an assistant. All that remain are a few feathers."

Suddenly D'Agosta was interested. His cop radar went off bigtime. He knew, right away, that this wasn't going to be a wild goose chase after all. "Was there an investigation?"

"Yes, but it was perfunctory. It's hard to get the police excited about two stolen birds, even if they are extinct."

"Do you have a copy of the old report?"

"We keep very good files here."

"I'd like to see it."

He found the woman looking at him curiously. "Excuse me, Dr. D'Agosta—but why? The birds have been gone for more than a dozen years."

D'Agosta thought fast. This changed the game. He made a quick decision, dipped into his pocket, and brought out his shield.

"Oh, my." She looked at him, her eyes widening. "You're a policeman. Not an ornithologist."

D'Agosta put it away. "That's right, I'm a lieutenant detective with NYPD homicide. Now be a dear and go get that file."

She nodded, hesitated. "What's it about?"

D'Agosta looked at her and noted a thrill in her eyes, a certain suppressed excitement. "Murder, of course," he said with a smile.

She nodded again, rose. A few minutes later she returned with a slender manila folder. D'Agosta opened it to find the most cursory of police reports, a single scribbled paragraph that told him nothing except that a routine check of the collection revealed the birds were missing. No sign of break-in, nothing else taken, no evidence collected at the scene, no fingerprints dusted, and no suspects named. The only useful thing was the time frame of the crime: it had to have occurred between September 1 and October 1, as the collection was inventoried once a month.

"Do you have logs of all the researchers who used the collections?"

"Yes. But we always check the collection after they leave, to make sure they haven't nicked something."

"Then we can narrow down the time frame even further. Bring me the logs, please."

"Right away." The woman bustled off, the eager clomping of her shoes echoing in the attic space as she descended the stairs.

Within a few minutes she returned, carrying a large buckram volume that she dropped on a central table with a thump. Turning the pages while D'Agosta watched, she finally arrived at the month in question. D'Agosta scanned the page. Three researchers had used the collection that month, the last one on September 22. The name was written in a generous, looping hand:

Matilda V. Jones
18 Agassiz Drive
Cooperstown, NY 27490

A fake name and address if ever there was one, thought D'Agosta. *Agassiz Drive my ass.* And New York State zip codes all began with a 1.

"Tell me," he asked, "do the researchers have to show you some kind of institutional affiliation, ID, or anything?"

"No, we trust them. Perhaps we shouldn't. But of course we supervise them closely. I just can't imagine how a researcher would manage to steal birds under our very noses!"

I can see a million ways, thought D'Agosta, but he didn't say anything out loud. The attic door was locked with an old-fashioned key, and the bird cabinet itself was a cheap model, with noisy tumblers that an experienced safecracker could defeat. Although, he mused, even that would hardly be necessary—he recalled seeing Marchant plucking a ring of keys off the wall of the reception hall as they set off upstairs. The door to the plantation house was unlocked—he had breezed right in. Anyone could wait until the curator on duty left the front desk on a bathroom break, pluck the keys off the nail, and go straight to the birds. Even worse, he'd been left alone with the unlocked bird cabinet himself when Marchant went to get the register. *If the birds had any value they'd all be gone by now*, he thought ruefully.

D'Agosta pointed to the name. "Did you meet this researcher?"

"As I said, I was just the assistant then. Mr. Hotchkiss was the curator, and he would have supervised the researcher."

"Where's he now?"

"He passed away a few years ago."

D'Agosta turned his attention back to the page. If Matilda V. Jones was indeed the thief—and he was fairly sure she was—then she was not a particularly sophisticated crook. Aside from the alias, the handwriting in her log entry did not have the appearance of having been disguised. He guessed the actual theft had taken place on or around September 23, the day after she had been shown the exact location of the birds by pretending to be a researcher. She probably stayed at a local inn for convenience. That could be confirmed by checking a hotel register.

"When ornithologists come here for research, where do they usually stay?"

"We recommend the Houma House, over in St. Francisville. It's the only decent place."

D'Agosta nodded.

"Well?" said Marchant. "Any clues?"

"Can you photocopy that page for me?"

"Oh, yes," she said, hefting and carting off the heavy volume, once again leaving D'Agosta alone. As soon as she was gone, he flicked open his cell phone and dialed.

"Pendergast," came the voice.

"Hello, it's Vinnie. Quick one: you ever heard the name Matilda V. Jones?"

There was a sudden silence, and then Pendergast's voice came back as chilly as an Arctic gust. "Where did you get that name, Vincent?"

"Too complicated to explain now. You know it?"

"Yes. It was the name of my wife's pet cat. A Russian Blue."

D'Agosta felt a shock. "Your wife's handwriting... was it large and loopy?"

"Yes. Now would you care to tell me what this is about?"

"Audubon's two stuffed Carolina Parakeets stored up at Oakley? Except for a few feathers, they're gone. And guess what: your wife stole them."

After a moment, a chillier response came: "I see."

D'Agosta heard the clomp of feet on the attic stairs. "Gotta go." He shut the cell phone just as Marchant rounded the corner with the photocopies.

"Well, Lieutenant," she said, laying them down. "Are you going to solve the crime for us?" She bestowed a vivid smile on him. D'Agosta noticed she had taken the occasion to re-rouge and touch up her lipstick. This was probably a lot more exciting, he thought, than back-to-back episodes of *Murder, She Wrote*.

D'Agosta shoved the papers in his briefcase and got up to leave. "No, I'm afraid the trail is too cold. *Way* too cold. But thanks for your help anyway."

21

Penumbra Plantation

Y ou're sure of this, Vincent? Absolutely sure?"

D'Agosta nodded. "I checked the local hotel, the Houma House. After examining the birds at Oakley Plantation—under the name of her cat—your wife spent the night there. She used her real name this time: they probably required identification, especially if she paid cash. No reason for her to spend a night unless she planned to return the next day, slip inside, and nab the birds." He passed a sheet of paper to Pendergast. "Here's the register from Oakley Plantation."

Pendergast examined it briefly. "That's my wife's handwriting." He put it aside, his face like a mask. "And you're sure of the date of the theft?"

"September twenty-third, give or take a few days."

"That puts it roughly six months after Helen and I were married."

An awkward silence descended on the second-floor

parlor. D'Agosta glanced away from Pendergast, looking uncomfortably around at the zebra rug and the mounted heads, his eye finally coming to rest on the large wooden gun case with its display of powerful, beautifully engraved rifles. He wondered which one had been Helen's.

Maurice leaned into the parlor. "More tea, gentlemen?"

D'Agosta shook his head. He found Maurice disconcerting; the old servant hovered about like a mother.

"Thank you, Maurice, we're fine for the moment," said Pendergast.

"Very good, sir."

"What have *you* come up with?" D'Agosta asked.

For a moment, Pendergast did not respond. Then, very slowly, he interlaced his fingers, placed his hands in his lap. "I visited the Bayou Grand Hotel, formerly the site of the Meuse St. Claire sanatorium, where Audubon painted the Black Frame. My wife had been there, asking about the painting. This was, perhaps, a few months after she first met me. Another man—an art collector or dealer, apparently of dubious repute—had also made inquiries about the painting, a year or so before Helen."

"So others were curious about the Black Frame."

"Very curious, it would seem. I also managed to find a few odd papers of interest in the basement of the sanatorium. Discussing the course of Audubon's illness, his treatment, that sort of thing." Pendergast reached for a leather portfolio, opened it, and pulled out an ancient sheet of paper enclosed in plastic, stained and yellow, missing its lower half to rot. "Here's a report on Audubon written by Dr. Arne Torgensson, his attending physician at the sanatorium. I'll read the relevant part."

The patient is much improved, both in the strength of his limbs and in his mental state. He is now ambulatory and has been amusing the other patients with stories of his adventures along the Frontier. Last week he sent out for paints, a stretcher and canvas, and began painting. And what a painting it is! The vigor of the brush strokes, the unusual palette, is quite remarkable. It depicts a most unusual . . .

Pendergast returned the sheet to the portfolio. "As you can see, the critical section is missing: a description of the painting. No one knows the subject."

D'Agosta took a sip of the tea, wishing it was a Bud. "Seems like a no-brainer to me. The painting was of the Carolina Parakeet."

"Your reasoning, Vincent?"

"That's why she stole the birds from Oakley Plantation. To trace—or, more likely, *identify*—the painting."

"The logic is faulty. Why *steal* the birds? Simply observing a specimen would be sufficient."

"Not if you're in competition, it wouldn't," D'Agosta said. "Others wanted the painting, too. In a high-stakes game, any edge you can give yourself—or deny others—you're gonna grab. In fact, that just might point to who mur—" But here he stopped abruptly, unwilling to voice this new speculation aloud.

Pendergast's penetrating glance showed he had divined his meaning. "With this painting, we just might have something that so far has escaped us." And here his voice dropped to almost a whisper. *"Motive."*

The room went quiet.

At last, Pendergast stirred. "Let us not get ahead of ourselves." He opened the portfolio again, withdrew another tattered scrap of paper. "I also recovered this, part of what is apparently Audubon's discharge report. Again, it is a mere fragment."

> …was discharged from care on the fourteenth day of November, 1821. On his departure he gave a painting, only just completed, to Dr. Torgensson, director of Meuse St. Claire, in gratitude for nursing him back to health. A small group of doctors and patients attended the discharge and many farewells were…

Pendergast dropped the fragment back into the portfolio and closed it with an air of finality.

"Any idea where the painting is now?" D'Agosta asked.

"The doctor retired to Port Royal, which will be my next stop." He paused. "There is one other item of at least tangential interest. Do you recall Helen's brother, Judson, mentioning that Helen once took a trip to New Madrid, Missouri?"

"Yes."

"New Madrid was the site of a very powerful earthquake in 1812, greater than eight point zero on the Richter scale—so powerful that it created a series of new lakes and changed the course of the Mississippi River. Approximately half the town was destroyed. There is one other salient fact."

"And that is—?"

"John James Audubon was in New Madrid at the time of the earthquake."

D'Agosta sat back in his chair. "Meaning?"

Pendergast spread his hands. "Coincidence? Perhaps."

"I've been trying to find out more about Audubon," said D'Agosta, "but to tell the truth I was never a good student. What do you know about him?"

"Now, a great deal. Let me give you a précis." Pendergast paused, composing his thoughts. "Audubon was the illegitimate son of a French sea captain and his mistress. Born in Haiti, he was raised in France by his stepmother and sent to America at the age of eighteen to escape conscription in Napoleon's army. He lived near Philadelphia, where he took an interest in studying and drawing birds and married a local girl, Lucy Bakewell. They moved to the Kentucky frontier where he set up a store, but he spent most of his time collecting, dissecting, stuffing, and mounting birds. He drew and painted them as a hobby, but his early work was weak and tentative, and his sketches—many of which survive—were as lifeless as the dead birds he was drawing.

"Audubon proved to be an indifferent businessman, and in 1820, when his shop went bankrupt, he moved his family to a shabby Creole cottage on Dauphine Street, New Orleans, where they lived in penury."

"Dauphine Street," murmured D'Agosta. "So that's how he got to know your family?"

"Yes. He was a charming fellow, dashing, handsome, a superb shot and expert swordsman. He and my great-great-grandfather Boethius became friends and often went shooting together. In early 1821, Audubon fell gravely ill—so ill he had to be taken by horse-drawn cart, comatose, to Meuse St. Claire. There he had a long convalescence. As you already know, during his recovery he painted the work called the Black Frame, subject unknown.

"When he recovered, still flat broke, Audubon suddenly conceived the idea to depict America's entire avifauna in life size—every bird species in the country—compiled into a grand work of natural history. While Lucy supported the family as a tutor, Audubon traipsed off with his gun and a box of artist's colors and paper. He hired an assistant and floated down the Mississippi. He painted hundreds of birds, creating brilliantly vibrant portraits of them in their native settings—something that had never been done before."

Pendergast took a sip of tea, then continued. "In 1826, he went to England, where he found a printer to make copper-plate engravings from his watercolors. Then he crisscrossed America and Europe, finding subscribers for the book that would ultimately become *The Birds of America*. The last print was struck in 1838, by which time Audubon had achieved great fame. A few years later, he began work on another highly ambitious project, *The Viviparous Quadrupeds of North America*. But his mind began to fail, and the book had to be completed by his sons. The poor man suffered a hideous mental decline and spent his last years in raving madness, dying at sixty-five in New York City."

D'Agosta gave a low whistle. "Interesting story."

"Indeed."

"And nobody has any idea what became of the Black Frame?"

Pendergast shook his head. "It's the Holy Grail of Audubon researchers, it seems. I'll visit Arne Torgensson's house tomorrow. It's an easy drive, a few miles west of Port Allen. I hope to pick up the trail of the painting from there."

"But based on the dates you've mentioned, you believe—" D'Agosta stopped, searching for the most tactful way to phrase the question. "You believe your wife's interest in Audubon and the Black Frame... started before she met you?"

Pendergast did not reply.

"If I'm going to help you," D'Agosta said, "you can't clam up every time I broach an awkward subject."

Pendergast sighed. "You are quite right. It does seem that Helen was fascinated—perhaps obsessed—by Audubon from early in life. This desire to learn more about Audubon, to be closer to his work, led—in part—to our meeting. It seems she was particularly interested in finding the Black Frame."

"Why keep her interest a secret from you?"

"I believe—" he paused, his voice hoarse, "—she did not wish me to know that our relationship was not founded on a happy accident, but rather a meeting that she had intentionally—perhaps even cynically—engineered." Pendergast's face was so dark, D'Agosta was almost sorry he'd asked the question.

"If she was racing someone else to find the Black Frame," D'Agosta said, "she might have felt herself in danger. In the weeks before her death, did her behavior change? Was she nervous, agitated?"

Pendergast answered slowly. "Yes. I always assumed it was some work-related complication, getting ready for the safari." He shook his head.

"Did she do anything out of the ordinary?"

"I wasn't around Penumbra much those last few weeks."

Over his shoulder, D'Agosta heard the clearing of a throat. Maurice again.

"I just wanted to inform you that I'm turning in for the night," the retainer said. "Will there be anything else?"

"Just one thing, Maurice," Pendergast said. "In the weeks leading up to my final trip with Helen, I was away a good deal of the time."

"In New York," Maurice said, nodding. "Making preparations for the safari."

"Did my wife say, or do, anything out of the ordinary while I was away? Get any mail or telephone calls that upset her, for example?"

The old manservant thought. "Not that I can remember, sir. Though she did seem rather agitated, especially after that trip."

"Trip?" Pendergast asked. "What trip?"

"One morning, her car woke me up as it headed down the drive—you recall how loud it was, sir. No note, no warning, nothing. It was around seven o'clock on a Sunday morning, I recall. Two nights later she came back. Not a word about where she'd been. But I recollect she wasn't herself. Upset about something, but wouldn't say a word about it."

"I see," Pendergast said, exchanging glances with D'Agosta. "Thank you, Maurice."

"Not at all, sir. Good night." And the old factotum turned and vanished down the hall on silent feet.

22

D'Agosta exited I-10 onto the Belle Chasse Highway, barreling along the nearly empty road. It was another warm February day, and he had the windows down and the radio set to a classic rock-and-roll station. He felt better than he had in days. As the car sang along the highway, he guzzled a Krispy Kreme coffee and snugged the cup back into the holder. The two pumpkin spice doughnuts had really hit the spot, calories be damned. Nothing could dampen his spirits.

The evening before he'd spent an hour talking to Laura Hayward. That started the upswing. Then he'd enjoyed a long, dreamless sleep. He woke up to find Pendergast already gone and Maurice waiting for him with a breakfast of bacon, eggs, and grits. Next, he'd driven into town, where he'd scored big with the Sixth District of the New Orleans Police Department. At first, on learning of his connection to the Pendergast family, they'd been suspicious, but when they found he was a regular guy, their attitude changed. He was given free use of their computer facilities, where it took less than ninety minutes to track down the dealer long interested in the Black Frame: John W. Blast, current residence Sarasota, Florida. He was an unsavory character indeed. Five arrests over the past ten years: suspicion of blackmail; suspicion of forgery; possession of stolen property; possession of prohibited wildlife products; assault and battery. Either he had money or good lawyers, or both, because he'd beaten the rap every time. D'Agosta had printed out the details, stuffed them into his jacket pocket, and—hungry again despite breakfast—hit the local Krispy Kreme before heading back to Penumbra.

Pendergast, he knew, would be eager to hear about this.

As he pulled up the drive of the old plantation, he saw that Pendergast had beaten him home: the Rolls-Royce sat in the shade of the cypress trees. Parking beside it, D'Agosta crunched his way across the gravel, then climbed the steps to the covered porch. He stepped into the entry hall, closing the front door behind him.

"Pendergast?" he called.

No reply.

He walked down the hallway, peering into the various public rooms. They were all dark and empty.

"Pendergast?" he called once more.

Perhaps he's gone out for a stroll, D'Agosta thought. *Nice enough day for it.*

He went briskly up the stairs, turned sharply at the landing, then stopped abruptly. Out of the corner of his eye he saw a familiar silhouette sitting silently in the parlor. It was Pendergast, occupying the same chair he'd sat in the previous night. The parlor lights were off, and the FBI agent was in darkness.

"Pendergast?" D'Agosta said. "I thought you were out, and—"

He stopped when he saw the agent's face. It carried an expression of blankness that gave him pause. He took the adjoining seat, his good mood snuffed out. "What's going on?" he asked.

Then Pendergast took a slow breath. "I went to Torgensson's house, Vincent. There's no painting."

"No painting?"

"The house is now a funeral home. The interior was gutted—right down to the structural studs and beams—to make way for the new business. There's nothing. *Nothing.*" Pendergast's lips tightened. "The trail simply ends."

"Well, what about the doctor? He must have moved someplace else; we can pick up the trail there."

Another pause, longer than before. "Dr. Arne Torgensson died in 1852. Destitute, driven mad by syphilis. But not before he'd sold off the contents of his house, piecemeal, to innumerable unknown buyers."

"If he sold the painting, there should be a record of it."

Pendergast fixed him with a baleful stare. "There *are* no records. He might have traded the painting to pay for coal. He might have torn it to shreds in his insanity. It might have outlived him and perished in the renovations. I've hit a brick wall."

And so he'd given up, D'Agosta thought. Come home, to sit in the dark parlor. In all the years he'd known Pendergast, he'd never seen the agent so low. And yet the facts didn't warrant this sort of despair.

"Helen was tracking the painting, too," D'Agosta said, rather more sharply than he intended. "You've been searching for it—what, a couple of days? She didn't give up for *years.*"

Pendergast did not respond.

"All right, let's take another approach. Instead of tracking the painting, we'll track your wife. This last trip she took, where she was gone for two or three days? Maybe it had something to do with the Black Frame."

"Even if you're right," Pendergast said. "That trip is a dozen years in the past."

"We can always try," D'Agosta said. "And then we can pay a visit to Mr. John W. Blast, retired art dealer, of Sarasota."

The faintest spark of interest flickered in Pendergast's eyes.

D'Agosta patted his jacket pocket. "That's right. He's the other guy who was chasing for the Black Frame. You're wrong when you say we've hit a wall."

"She could have gone anywhere in those three days," Pendergast said.

"What the hell? You're just giving up?" D'Agosta stared at Pendergast. Then he turned, stuck his head out into the hall. "Maurice? *Yo! Maurice!*" Where was the man when you finally needed him?

For a moment, silence. Then, a faint banging in the far spaces of the mansion. A minute later, feet sounded on the back stairway. Maurice appeared around the bend of the corridor. "I beg your pardon?" he panted as he approached, his eyes wide.

"That trip of Helen's you mentioned last evening.

When she left without warning, was gone for two nights?"

"Yes?" Maurice nodded.

"Isn't there anything more about it you can tell us? Gas station receipts, hotel bills?"

Maurice fell into a silent study, then said: "Nothing, sir."

"She didn't say anything at all after her return? Not a word?"

Maurice shook his head. "I'm sorry, sir."

Pendergast sat, utterly motionless, in his chair. A silent pall settled over the parlor.

"Come to think of it, there is one thing," Maurice said. "Although I don't think you'll find it of use."

D'Agosta pounced. "What was it?"

"Well..." The old servant hesitated. D'Agosta wanted to grab him by the lapels and shake him.

"It's just that...I recollect now that she called me, sir. That first morning, from the road."

Pendergast slowly rose. "Go on, Maurice," he said quietly.

"It was getting on toward nine. I was having coffee in the morning room. The phone rang, and it was Mrs. Pendergast on the line. She'd left her AAA card in her office. She'd had a flat tire and needed the member number." Maurice glanced at Pendergast. "You recall she never could do anything with cars, sir."

"That's it?"

Maurice nodded. "I got the card and read her the number. She thanked me."

"Nothing else?" D'Agosta pressed. "Any background noise? Conversation, maybe?"

"It was so long ago, sir." Maurice thought hard. "I believe there were traffic noises. Perhaps a honk. She must have been calling from an outdoor phone booth."

For a moment, nobody spoke. D'Agosta felt hugely deflated.

"What about her voice?" Pendergast asked. "Did she sound tense or nervous?"

"No, sir. In fact, now I do recollect—she said it was lucky, her getting the flat where she did."

"Lucky?" Pendergast repeated. "Why?"

"Because she could have an egg cream while she waited."

There was a moment of stasis. And then Pendergast exploded into action. Ducking past D'Agosta and Maurice, he ran to the landing without a word and went tearing down the stairs.

D'Agosta followed. The central hallway was empty, but he could hear sounds from the library. Stepping into the room, he saw the agent feverishly searching the shelves, throwing books to the floor with abandon. He seized a volume, strode to a nearby table, cleared the surface with a violent sweep of his arm, and flipped through the pages. D'Agosta noticed the book was a Louisiana road atlas. A ruler and pencil appeared in Pendergast's hand and he hunched over the atlas, taking measurements and marking them with a pencil.

"There it is," he whispered under his breath, stabbing a finger at the page. And without another word he raced out of the library.

D'Agosta followed the agent through the dining room, the kitchen, the larder, the butler's pantry, and the back kitchen, to the rear door of the plantation house. Pendergast took the back steps two at a time and charged through an expansive garden to a white-painted stable converted to a garage with half a dozen bays. He threw open the doors and disappeared into darkness.

D'Agosta followed. The vast, dim space smelled faintly of hay and motor oil. As his eyes adjusted, he made out three tarp-covered objects that could only be automobiles. Pendergast strode over to one and yanked off the tarp. Beneath lay a two-seat red convertible, low-slung and villainous. It gleamed in the indirect light of the converted barn.

"Wow." D'Agosta gave a whistle. "A vintage Porsche. What a beauty."

"A 1954 Porsche 550 Spyder. It was Helen's." Pendergast leapt in nimbly, felt under the mat for the key. As D'Agosta opened the door and got into the passenger seat, Pendergast found the key, fitted it to the ignition, turned. The engine came to life with an ear-shattering roar.

"Bless you, Maurice," Pendergast said over the growl. "You've kept it in top shape."

He let the car warm up for a few seconds, then eased it out of the barn. Once they were clear of the doors, he stomped on the accelerator. The vehicle shot forward, scattering a storm of gravel that peppered the outbuilding like so much buckshot. D'Agosta felt himself pressed into the seat like an astronaut on liftoff. As the car swept out of the driveway, D'Agosta could see Maurice's black-dressed form on the steps, watching them go.

"Where are we going?" he asked.

Pendergast looked at him. The despair was gone, replaced by a hard glitter in his eye, faint but noticeable: the gleam of the hunt. "Thanks to you, Vincent, we've located the haystack," he replied. "Now let's see if we can find the needle."

23

The sports car boomed along the sleepy byways of rural Louisiana. Mangrove swamps, bayous, stately plantations, and marshes passed in a blur. Now and then they slowed briefly to traverse a village, the loud, beastly engine eliciting curious stares. Pendergast had not bothered to put up the convertible's top, and D'Agosta felt increasingly windblown, his bald spot chapping in the blast of air. The car rode low to the ground, making him feel exposed and vulnerable. He wondered why Pendergast had taken this car instead of the far more comfortable Rolls.

"Mind telling me where we're going?" he yelled over the shriek of the wind.

"Picayune, Mississippi."

"Why there?"

"Because that's where Helen telephoned Maurice."

"You *know* that?"

"Within ninety-five percent certainty."

"How?"

Pendergast downshifted, negotiating a sharp bend in the road. "Helen was having an egg cream while she waited for the auto club."

"Yeah. So?"

"So: egg creams are a Yankee weakness I was never able to cure her of. You seldom find them outside of New York and parts of New England."

"Go on."

"There are—or were—only three places within driving distance of New Orleans that served egg creams. Helen sought them all out; she was always driving to one or another. Occasionally I went along. In any case, using the map just now, I inferred—based on the day of the week, the time of day, and Helen's proclivity for driving too fast—Picayune to be the obvious choice of the three."

D'Agosta nodded. It seemed simple, once explained. "So what's with the ninety-five percent?"

"It's just possible that she stopped earlier that morning, for some other reason. Or *was* stopped—she attracted speeding tickets by the bushel."

Picayune, Mississippi, was a neat town of low frame houses just over the Louisiana border. A sign at the town line proclaimed it a PRECIOUS COIN IN THE PURSE OF THE SOUTH, and another displayed pictures of the floats from the previous year's Krewe of Roses Parade. D'Agosta looked around curiously as they passed down the quiet, leafy streets. Pendergast slowed as they rumbled into the commercial district.

"Things have changed a bit," he said, glancing left and right. "That Internet café is of course new. So is that Creole restaurant. That little place offering crawfish po'boys, however, is familiar."

"You used to come here with Helen?"

"Not with Helen. I passed through the town several times in later years. There's an FBI training camp a few miles from here. Ah—this must be it."

Pendergast turned a corner onto a quiet street and pulled over to the curb. The street was residential except for the closest structure, a one-story cinder-block building set well back from the road and surrounded by a parking lot of cracked and heaving blacktop. A leaning sign on the building front advertised Jake's Yankee Chowhouse, but it was faded and peeling and the restaurant had obviously been closed for years. The windows in the rear section had muslin curtains, however, and a satellite dish was fixed to the cement wall: clearly the building served as residence as well.

"Let's see if we can't do this the easy way," Pendergast murmured. He pursed his lips, examining the street a moment longer. Then he began revving the Porsche with long jabs of his right foot. The big engine roared to life, louder and louder with each depression of the accelerator, leaves blowing out from beneath the car, until the vehicle's frame vibrated as violently as a passenger jet.

"My God!" D'Agosta yelled over the noise. "Do you want to wake the dead?"

The FBI agent kept it up another fifteen seconds, until at least a dozen heads were poking out of windows and doors up and down the street. "No," he replied, easing off at last and letting the engine rumble back into an idle. "I believe the living will suffice." He made a quick survey of the faces now staring at them. "Too young," he said of one, shaking his head, "and that one, poor fellow, is clearly too stupid...Ah: now *that* one is a possibility. Come on, Vincent." Getting out of the car, he strolled down the street to the third house on the left, where a man of about sixty wearing a yellowing T-shirt stood on the front steps, staring at them with a frown. He clutched a television remote in one meaty paw, a beer in the other.

D'Agosta suddenly understood why Pendergast had taken his wife's Porsche for this particular road trip.

"Excuse me, sir," Pendergast said as he approached the house. "I wonder if you'd mind telling me if, by chance, you recognize the vehicle we—"

"Blow it out your ass," the man said, turning and going back inside his house, slamming the door.

D'Agosta hoisted up his pants and licked his lips. "Want me to go drag the fat fuck back out?"

Pendergast shook his head. "No need, Vincent." He turned back, regarding the restaurant. An old, heavy-set woman in a flimsy housedress had come out of the kitchen and stood on the porch, flanked by a brace of plastic pink flamingos. She had a magazine in one hand and a cigarillo in the other, and she peered at them through old-fashioned teardrop glasses. "We may have flushed out just the partridge I was after."

They walked back to the old parking lot and the kitchen door of Jake's. The woman watched their approach with complete taciturnity, with no visible change of expression.

"Good afternoon, ma'am," Pendergast said with a slight bow.

"Afternoon yourself," she replied.

"Do you, by chance, own this fine establishment?"

"I might," she said, taking a deep drag on the cigarillo. D'Agosta noticed it had a white plastic holder.

Pendergast waved at the Spyder. "And is there any chance you recognize this vehicle?"

She looked away from them, peering at the car through her grimy glasses. Then she looked back. "I might," she repeated.

There was a silence. D'Agosta heard a window slam shut, and a door.

"Why, how remiss of me," Pendergast said suddenly. "Taking up your valuable time like this uncompensated." As if by magic, a twenty-dollar bill appeared in his hand. He held it out to the woman. To D'Agosta's surprise, she plucked it from his fingers and stuffed it down her withered but still ample cleavage.

"I saw that car three times," the woman said. "My son was crazy about them foreign sporty jobs. He worked the soda fountain. He passed away in a car crash on the outskirts of town a few years back. Anyhow, the first time it showed up he just about went nuts. Made everybody drop whatever they were doing and take a look."

"Do you remember the driver?"

"A young woman. Pretty thing, too."

"You don't recall what she ordered, do you?" Pendergast asked.

"I'm not likely to forget that. An egg cream. She said she'd come all the way from N'Orleans. Imagine, all that way for an egg cream."

There was another, briefer silence.

"You mentioned three times," Pendergast said. "What about the last time?"

The woman took another drag on the cigarillo, paused a moment to search her memory. "She showed up on foot that time. Had a flat tire."

"I commend you on your excellent memory, ma'am."

"Like I said, you don't forget a car—or a lady—like that any time soon. My Henry gave her the egg cream for free. She drove on back and let him get behind the wheel—wouldn't let him drive it, though. Said she was in a hurry."

"Ah. So she was going somewhere?"

"Said she'd been going in circles, couldn't find the turnoff for Caledonia."

"Caledonia? I'm not familiar with that town."

"It ain't a town—I'm talking about the Caledonia National Forest. Blame road wasn't marked then and it ain't marked now."

If Pendergast was growing excited, he didn't show it. To D'Agosta, the FBI agent's gestures—as he lit another cigarillo for the old woman—seemed almost languid.

"Is that where she was headed?" he asked, placing the lighter back into his pocket. "The national forest?"

The woman plucked the fresh cigarillo from her mouth, looked at it, masticated her gums a few times, then inserted the holder back between her lips as if she were driving home a screw. "Nope."

"May I ask where?"

The woman made a show of trying to remember. "Let me see now…That was a long time ago…" The excellent memory seemed to grow vague.

Another twenty appeared; once again, it was quickly shoved down into the same crevasse. "Sunflower," she said immediately.

"Sunflower?" Pendergast repeated.

The woman nodded. "Sunflower, Louisiana. Not two miles over the state line. Take the Bogalusa turnoff, just before the swamp." And she pointed the direction.

"I'm most obliged to you." Pendergast turned to D'Agosta. "Vincent, let us not waste any time."

As they strode back to the car, the woman yelled out, "When you pass the old mine shaft, take a right!"

24

Sunflower, Louisiana

K now what you'd like, sugar?" the waitress asked.
  D'Agosta let the menu drop to the table. "The catfish."

"Fried, oven-fried, baked, or broiled?"

"Broiled, I guess."

"Excellent choice." She made a notation on her pad, turned. "And you, sir?"

"Pine bark stew, please," said Pendergast. "Without the hush puppies."

"Right you are." She made another note, then turned away with a flourish, bouncing off on sensible white shoes.

D'Agosta watched as she wiggled toward the kitchen. Then he sighed, took a sip of his beer. It had been a long, wearisome afternoon. Sunflower, Louisiana, was a town of about three thousand people, surrounded on one side by liveoak forest, on the other by the vast cypress swamp known as Black Brake. It had proven utterly unremarkable: small shabby houses with picket fences, scuffed boardwalks in need of repair, redbone hounds dozing on front porches. It was a hardworking, hard-bitten, down-at-the-heels hamlet forgotten by the outside world.

They had registered at the town's only hotel, then split up and gone their separate ways, each trying to uncover why Helen Pendergast would have made a three-day pilgrimage to such a remote spot.

Their recent run of luck seemed to sputter out on the threshold of Sunflower. D'Agosta had spent five fruitless hours looking into blank faces and walking into dead ends. There were no art dealers, museums, private collections, or historical societies. Nobody remembered seeing Helen Pendergast—the photo he'd shown around triggered only blank looks. Not even the car produced a glimmer of recall. John James Audubon, their research showed, had never been anywhere near this region of Louisiana.

When D'Agosta finally met up with Pendergast in the hotel's small restaurant for dinner, he felt almost as dejected as the FBI agent had looked that morning. As if to match his mood, the sunny skies had boiled up into dark thunderheads that threatened a storm.

"Zilch," he said in answer to Pendergast's query, and described his discouraging morning. "Maybe that old lady remembered wrong. Or was just bullshitting us for another twenty. What about you?"

The food arrived, and the waitress laid their plates before them with a cheery "Here we are!" Pendergast eyed his in silence, dipping some stew out with his spoon to examine it more closely.

"Can I get you another beer?" she asked D'Agosta, beaming.

"Why not?"

"Club soda?" she asked Pendergast.

"No thank you, this will be sufficient."

The waitress bounced off again.

D'Agosta turned back. "Well? Any luck?"

"One moment." Pendergast plucked out his cell phone, dialed. "Maurice? We'll be spending the night here in Sunflower. That's right. Good night." He put away the phone. "My experience, I fear, was as discouraging as yours." However, his alleged disappointment was belied by a glimmer in his eye and a wry smile teasing the corners of his lips.

"How come I don't believe you?" D'Agosta finally asked.

"Watch, if you please, as I perform a little experiment on our waitress."

The waitress came back with a Bud and a fresh napkin. As she placed them before D'Agosta, Pendergast spoke in his most honeyed voice, laying the accent on thick. "My dear, I wonder if I might ask you a question."

She turned to him with a perky smile. "Ask away, hon."

Pendergast made a show of pulling a small notebook from his jacket pocket. "I'm a reporter up from New Orleans, and I'm doing research on a family that used to live here." He opened the notebook, looked up at the waitress expectantly.

"Sure, which family?"

"Doane."

If Pendergast had announced a holdup, the reaction

couldn't have been more dramatic. The woman's face immediately shut down, blank and expressionless, her eyes hooded. The perkiness vanished instantly.

"Don't know anything about that," she mumbled. "Can't help you." She turned and walked away, pushing through the door to the kitchen.

Pendergast slipped the notebook back into his jacket and turned to D'Agosta. "What do you think of my experiment?"

"How the hell did you know she'd react like that? She's obviously hiding something."

"That, my dear Vincent, is precisely the point." Pendergast took another sip of club soda. "I didn't single her out. Everyone in town reacts the same way. Haven't you noticed, during your inquiries this afternoon, a certain degree of hesitancy and suspicion?"

D'Agosta paused to consider. It was true that nobody had been particularly helpful, but he'd simply ascribed it to small-town truculence, local folk suspicious of some Yankee coming in and asking a lot of questions.

"As I made my own inquiries," Pendergast went on, "I ran into an increasingly suspicious level of obfuscation and denial. And then, when I pressed one elderly gentleman for information, he heatedly informed me that despite what I might have heard otherwise, the stories about the Doanes were nothing but hogwash. Naturally I began to ask about the Doane family. And that's when I started getting the reaction you just saw."

"And so?"

"I repaired to the local newspaper office and asked to see the back issues, dating from around the time of Helen's visit. They were unwilling to help, and it took this—" Pendergast pulled out his shield. "—to change their minds. I found that in the years surrounding Helen's visit, several pages had been carefully cut out of certain newspapers. I made a note of what the issues were, then made my way back down the road to the library at Kemp, the last town before Sunflower. Their copies of the newspapers had all the missing pages. And that's where I got the story."

"What story?" D'Agosta asked.

"The strange story of the Doane family. Mr. Doane was a novelist of independent means, and he brought his extended family to Sunflower to get away from it all, to write the great American novel far from the distractions of civilization. They bought one of the town's biggest and best houses, built by a small-time lumber baron in the years before the local mill shut down. Doane had two children. One of them, the son, won the highest honors ever awarded by the Sunflower High School, a clever fellow by all accounts. The daughter was a gifted poet whose works were occasionally published in the local papers. I read a few and they are, in fact, exceedingly well done. Mrs. Doane had grown into a noted landscape painter. The town became very proud of their talented, adopted family, and they were frequently in the papers, accepting awards, raising funds for one or another local charity, ribbon cutting, that sort of thing."

"Landscape painter," D'Agosta repeated. "How about birds?"

"Not that I could find out. Nor did they appear to have any particular interest in Audubon or natural history art. Then, a few months after Helen's visit, the steady stream of approving stories began to cease."

"Maybe the family got tired of the attention."

"I think not. There was one more article about the Doane family—one final article," he went on. "Half a year after that. It stated that William, the Doane son, had been captured by the police after an extended manhunt through the national forest, and that he was now in solitary confinement in the county jail, charged with two ax murders."

"The star student?" D'Agosta asked incredulously.

Pendergast nodded. "After reading this, I began asking around Kemp about the Doane family. The townspeople there felt none of the restraint I noticed here. I heard a veritable outpouring of rumor and innuendo. Homicidal maniacs that only came out at night. Madness and violence. Stalking and menace. It became difficult to sift fact from fiction, town gossip from reality. The only thing that I feel reasonably sure of is that all are now dead, each having died in a uniquely unpleasant way."

"All of them?"

"The mother was a suicide. The son died on death row while awaiting execution for the ax murders I spoke of. The daughter died in an insane asylum after refusing to sleep for two weeks. The last to die was the father, shot by the town sheriff of Sunflower."

"What happened?"

"He apparently took to wandering into town, accosting young women, threatening the townsfolk. There were reports of vandalism, destruction, babies gone missing. The people I spoke to hinted it might have been less of a killing and more of an execution—with the tacit approval of the Sunflower town fathers. The sheriff and his deputies shotgunned Mr. Doane in his house as he allegedly resisted arrest. There was no investigation."

"Jesus," D'Agosta replied. "That would explain the waitress's reaction. As well as all the hostility around here."

"Precisely."

"What the hell do you think happened to them? Something in the water?"

"I have no idea. But I will tell you this: I'm convinced they were the object of Helen's visit."

"That's a pretty big leap."

Pendergast nodded. "Consider this: they are the *only* unique element in an otherwise unremarkable town. There's nothing else here of interest. Somehow, they're the link we're searching for."

The waitress hustled up to their table, took away their plates, and went off, even as D'Agosta began to order coffee. "I wonder what it takes to get a cup of java around here," D'Agosta said, trying to attract her attention.

"Somehow, Vincent, I doubt you'll be getting your 'java' or anything more in this establishment."

D'Agosta sighed. "So who lives in the house now?"

"Nobody. It was abandoned and shut up since the shooting of Mr. Doane."

"We're going there," D'Agosta said, more as a statement than a question.

"Exactly."

"When?"

Pendergast raised his finger for the waitress. "As soon as we can get the check from our reticent but nevertheless most eloquent waitress."

25

The waitress did not arrive with the check. Instead, it was the manager of the hotel. He placed the check on the table and then, without even a show of apology, informed them they would not be able to stay the night after all.

"What do you mean?" D'Agosta said. "We booked the room; you took our credit card numbers."

"There's a large party coming in," the man replied. "They had prior reservations the front desk overlooked—and as you can see, this is a small hotel."

"Too bad for them," D'Agosta said. "We're already here."

"You haven't unpacked yet," the manager replied. "In fact, I'm told your luggage isn't even in your rooms yet. I've already torn up your credit card voucher. I'm sorry."

But he didn't sound sorry, and D'Agosta was about to rake the man over the coals when Pendergast laid a hand on his arm. "Very well," Pendergast said, reaching into his wallet and paying the dinner bill in cash. "Good evening, then."

The manager walked away, and D'Agosta turned to Pendergast. "You're gonna let that prick walk all over us? It's obvious he's kicking us out because of the questions you're asking—and the ancient history we're stirring up."

In response, Pendergast nodded out the window. Glancing through it, D'Agosta saw the hotel manager now crossing the street. As D'Agosta watched, the man walked past several store buildings, shuttered for the night, and then vanished into the sheriff's office.

"What the hell kind of town *is* this?" D'Agosta said. "Next thing you know, it'll be villagers with pitchforks."

"Our interest doesn't lie with the town," Pendergast said. "There's no point in complicating things. I suggest that we leave at once—before the local sheriff finds an excuse to run us out."

They exited the restaurant and made their way to the back parking lot of the hotel. The storm that had been threatening was fast approaching: the wind raked the treetops, and thunder could be heard rumbling in the distance. Pendergast put up the Porsche's top as D'Agosta climbed in. Pendergast slipped in himself, turned on the engine, nosed the car into a back alley, then made his way through town via back streets, avoiding main thoroughfares.

The Doane house was located about two miles past town, up an unpaved drive that had once been well tended but was now little more than a rutted track. He drove cautiously, careful not to bottom out the Spyder in the hard-packed dirt. Dense stands of trees crowded in on both sides of the road, their skeletal branches lacing the night sky above their heads. D'Agosta, flung around in his seat until his teeth rattled, decided that even the Zambian Land Rover would have been preferable in these conditions.

Pendergast rounded a final bend and the house itself came into view in the headlights, the sky roiling with clouds above. D'Agosta stared at it in surprise. He had expected a large, elegant structure, as ornate as the rest of the town was plain. What he saw was large, all right, but it was hardly elegant. In fact, it looked more like a fort left over from the days of the Louisiana Purchase. Built out of huge, rough-edged beams, it sported tall towers at either end and a long, squat central façade with innumerable small windows. Atop this façade was the bizarre anachronism of a widow's walk, surrounded by spiked iron railings. It stood alone on a small rise of land. Beyond to the east lay forest, dense and dark, leading to the vast Black Brake swamp. As D'Agosta stared at the structure, a tongue of lightning struck the woods behind, briefly silhouetting it in spectral yellow light.

"Looks like somebody tried to cross a castle with a log cabin," he said.

"The original owner was a timber baron, after all." Pendergast nodded at the widow's walk. "No doubt he used that to survey his domain. I read that he personally owned sixty thousand acres of land—including much of the cypress forests in the Black Brake—before the government acquired it for the national forest and a wilderness area."

He pulled up to the house and stopped. The agent glanced briefly in the rearview mirror before maneuvering the car around to the back and killing the engine.

"Expecting company?" D'Agosta asked.

"No point in attracting attention."

Now the rain started: fat drops that drummed against the windshield and the fabric top. Pendergast got out, and D'Agosta quickly followed suit. They trotted over to the shelter of a rear porch. D'Agosta glanced up a little uneasily at the rambling structure. It was exactly the kind of eccentric residence that might attract a novelist. Every tiny window was carefully shuttered, and the door itself was secured with a padlock and chain. A riot of vegetation had grown up around the house, softening the rough lines of its foundation, while moss and lichens draped some of the beams.

Pendergast took a final look around, then turned his attention to the padlock. He held it by the hasp, turning it this way and that, and then passed his other hand, holding a small tool, over the cylinder housing. A quick fiddle and it snapped open with a loud creak. Pendergast removed the chain and let it drop to the ground. The door itself was also locked; Pendergast bent over it and swiftly defeated the mechanism with the same tool. Then he rose again and turned the knob, pushing the door open with a squeal of protesting hinges. Pulling a flashlight from his jacket, he stepped inside. D'Agosta had long ago learned, when working with Pendergast, to never get caught without two things: a gun and a flashlight. Now he pulled out his own light and followed Pendergast into the house.

They found themselves in a large, old-fashioned

kitchen. In the center stood a wooden breakfast table, and an oven, refrigerator, and washing machine were arranged in a porcelain row along the far wall. Beyond that, any resemblance to a normal family kitchen ended. The cabinets were thrown open, and crockery and glassware, almost all of it broken, streamed out from the shelves and onto the countertops and floor. Remains of foodstuffs—grains, rice, beans—lay scattered here and there, desiccated, scattered by rats, and fringed with ancient mold. The chairs were overturned and splintered, and the walls were punctuated with holes made by a sledgehammer or—perhaps—a fist. Plaster had fallen from the ceiling in chunks, making miniature explosions of white powder here and there on the floor, in which vermin tracks and droppings could be clearly seen. D'Agosta played his beam around the room, taking in the whirlwind of destruction. His light stopped in one corner, where a large, long-dried accumulation of what seemed to be blood lay on the floor; on the wall above, at chest height, were several ragged holes made by blasts from a heavy-gauge shotgun with similar sprays of dried blood and offal.

"I'd guess this is where our Mr. Doane met his end," D'Agosta said, "courtesy of the local sheriff. Looks like one hell of a struggle took place."

"It would indeed appear to be the site of the shooting," Pendergast murmured in reply. "However, there was no struggle. This damage occurred before the time of death."

"What the hell happened, then?"

Pendergast glanced around the mess a moment longer before replying. "A descent into madness." He shone his light toward a door in the far wall. "Come on, Vincent—let us continue."

They walked slowly through the first floor, searching the dining room, parlor, pantry, living room, bathrooms, and other spaces of indeterminate use. Everywhere they found the same chaos: overturned furniture, broken glassware, books ripped into dozens of pieces and scattered mindlessly over the floor. The fireplace in the den held hundreds of small bones. Examining them carefully, Pendergast announced that they were squirrel remains, which—based on their relative positions—had been stuffed up the chimney, staying there until decay and putrefaction caused them to fall back down onto the firedogs. In another room they found a dark, greasy mattress, surrounded by the detritus of countless ancient meals: empty tins of Spam and sardines, candy bar wrappers, crushed beer cans. One corner of the room appeared to have been used as an open latrine, with no attempt at sanitation or concealment. There were no paintings on any of the walls of the rooms, black-framed or otherwise. In fact, the only decorative works the walls displayed were endless frantic doodles in purple Magic Marker: a storm of squiggles and manic jagged lines that was disquieting to look at.

"Jesus," D'Agosta said. "What could Helen possibly have wanted here?"

"It is exceedingly curious," Pendergast replied, "especially considering that at the time of her visit, the Doane family was the pride of Sunflower. This decline into criminal madness happened much later."

Thunder rumbled ominously outside, accompanied

by flashes of livid lightning through the shuttered windows. They descended into the basement, which, though less cluttered, showed signs of the same blizzard of lunatic destruction so evident on the first floor. After a thorough and fruitless search, they climbed to the second floor. Here the whirlwind of ruin was somewhat abated, although there were plenty of troubling signs. In what was clearly the son's bedroom, one wall was almost completely covered in awards for academic excellence and distinguished community service—based on their dates, taking place over a year or two around the time of Helen Pendergast's visit. The facing wall, however, was equally crowded with the desiccated heads of animals—pigs, dogs, rats—all hammered into the wood in the roughest manner possible, with no effort made to clean or even exsanguinate them: dried blood ran down in heavy streams from each mummified trophy onto those hammered in place below.

The daughter's room was even more creepy for showing a complete lack of personality: the only feature of note was a row of similarly bound red volumes in a bookshelf that was otherwise empty, save for an anthology of poetry.

They gradually walked through the empty rooms, D'Agosta trying to make sense of the senselessness of it.

At the very end of the hall, they came to a locked door.

Pendergast slid out his lockpicking tools, jimmied the lock, and attempted to open the door. It wouldn't budge.

"There's a first," said D'Agosta.

"If you will observe the upper doorjambs, my dear fellow, you'll see that the door, in addition to being locked, has been screwed shut." His hand fell from the knob. "We'll return to this. Let's take a look at the attic first."

The attics of the old house were a warren of tiny rooms packed under the eaves, full of moldy furniture and old luggage. They made a thorough inspection of the boxes and trunks, raising furious choking clouds of dust in the process, but found nothing more interesting than some musty old clothes, piles of newspapers sorted and stacked and tied with twine. Pendergast rummaged through an old toolbox and removed a screwdriver, slipping it into his pocket.

"Let's check the two towers," he said, brushing dust from his black suit with evident distaste. "Then we'll tackle the sealed room."

The towers were drafty columns of winding stairs and storage niches full of spiders, rat droppings, and piles of yellowing old books. Each tower staircase dead-ended into a tiny lookout room, with windows like the arrow slits of a castle, looking down over the lightning-troubled forest. D'Agosta found himself growing impatient. The house seemed to have little to offer them other than madness and riddles. Why had Helen Pendergast come here—if she'd come here at all?

Finding nothing of interest in the towers, they returned to the main house and the sealed door. As D'Agosta held the light, Pendergast drew out two long screws. He turned the knob, pushed the door open, and stepped inside. D'Agosta followed—and almost staggered backward in surprise.

It was like stepping into a Fabergé egg. It was not a

large room, but it seemed to D'Agosta jewel-like—filled
with treasures that glowed with internal brilliance. The
windows had been boarded over and nailed with canvas, leaving the interior almost hermetically preserved,
every surface so lovingly polished that even a decade of
abandonment could not dull the luster. Paintings covered every square inch of wall space, and the interior
was crowded with gorgeous handmade furniture and
sculptures, the floor spread with dazzling rugs, sparkling jewelry laid out on pieces of black velvet.

In the middle of the room stood a single divan, covered in richly tanned leather that had been tooled into
an astonishing cascade of abstract floral designs. The ebb
and flow of the hand-worked lines were so cunningly
wrought, so hypnotically beautiful, that D'Agosta could
scarcely take his eyes from them. And yet other objects
in the room cried out for his attention. At one end, several fantastical sculptures of elongated heads, carved in
an exotic wood, stood beside an array of exquisite jewelry in gold, gems, and lustrous black pearls.

D'Agosta walked through the room in an astonished
silence, hardly able to focus his attention on any one
thing before some fresh marvel drew it away. On one
table stood a collection of small, handmade books in
elegant leather bindings with gold tooling. D'Agosta
picked one up and thumbed through it, finding it full
of poems handwritten in a beautiful script, signed and
dated by Karen Doane. The loom-woven rugs formed
several layers on the floor, and they displayed geomet-
ric designs so colorful and striking that they dazzled
the eye. He flashed the light around the walls, marvel-
ing at the oil paintings, landscapes lustrous with life,

of the forest glades around the house, old cemeteries, vivid still lifes, and ever-more-fantastical landscapes and dreamscapes. D'Agosta approached the closest one and squinted, playing the light over it—observing that it was signed M. DOANE along the bottom margin.

Pendergast came up beside him, a silent presence. "Melissa Doane," he murmured. "The novelist's wife. It would appear that these paintings are hers."

"All of them?" D'Agosta played the beam over the other walls of the little room. There was no painting in a black frame, no painting, in fact, not signed M. DOANE.

"I'm afraid it's not here."

Slowly, D'Agosta let his flashlight drop to his side. He realized he was breathing fast, and that his heart was racing. It was bizarre—beyond bizarre. "What the hell is this place? And how has it stayed like this without being robbed?"

"The town protects its secrets well." Pendergast's silvery eyes darted about, taking everything in, an expression of intense concentration on his face. Slowly, once again, he paced the room, finally stopping at the table of handmade books. He quickly sorted through them, flipping the pages and putting them back. He left the room, and D'Agosta followed him down the hall as he entered the daughter's room. D'Agosta caught up as he was examining the shelf of identical red-bound volumes. His spidery hand reached out and plucked the last one down. He riffled through the pages; every one was blank. Pendergast put it back and drew out the penultimate volume. This one was full of nothing but horizontal lines, made apparently with a ruler, so densely drawn that each page was almost black with them.

Pendergast selected the next book, flipped through it, finding more dense lines and some crude, stick-like, childish sketches in the beginning. The next volume contained disjointed entries in a ragged hand that climbed up and down across the pages.

Pendergast began to read out loud, at random, prose written in poetic stanzas.

> *I cannot*
> *Sleep I must not*
> *Sleep. They come, they whisper*
> *Things. They show me*
> *Things. I can't tune it*
> *Out, I can't tune it*
> *Out. If I sleep again I will*
> *Die . . . Sleep = Death*
> *Dream = Death*
> *Death = I can't tune it*
> *Out*

Pendergast flipped a few pages. The ravings continued until they seemed to dissolve into disjointed words and illegible scratchings. More thoughtfully, he put the book back and drew out another, much earlier in the set, opening it in the middle. D'Agosta saw lines of strong and even writing, evidently that of a girl, with doodles of flowers and funny faces in the margins and *i*'s that were dotted with cheerful circles.

Pendergast read off the date.

D'Agosta did a quick mental calculation. "That would be about six months before Helen's visit," he said.

"Yes. When the Doanes were still new to Sunflower."

Pendergast paged through the entries, scanning them swiftly, pausing at one point to read out loud:

> Mattie Lee razzed me again about Jimmy. He may be cute but I can't stand the goth clothes and that thrash metal he's into. He slicks his hair back and smokes, holding the cigarette up close to the burning ash. He thinks it makes him look cool. I think it makes him look like a nerd trying to look cool. Even worse: it makes him look like a dweeb who looks like a nerd who's trying to be cool.

"Typical high-school girl," said D'Agosta, frowning.

"Perhaps a bit more incisive than most." The agent continued flipping forward through the volume. He stopped abruptly at an entry made some three months later. "Ah!" he exclaimed, sudden interest in his voice, and began to read.

> When I got home from school I saw Mom and Dad in the kitchen hovering over something on the counter. Guess what it was? A _parrot_! It was gray and fat, with a stumpy red tail and a big fat metal band around its leg with a number but no name. It was tame and would perch right on your arm. It kept cocking its head at me and peering into my eyes, like it was checking me out. Dad looked it up in the encyclopedia and said it was an African Grey. He said it had to be somebody's pet, it was too tame for anything else. It just showed up around noon, sitting in the peach tree next to the back door, making noise to announce its presence. I begged Dad to let

us keep it. He said we could until he found the real
owner. He says we have to run an ad. I told him to run
it in the <u>Timbuctoo Times</u> and he thought that was
pretty funny. I hope he never finds the real owner.
We made a little nest for it in an old box. Dad is going
to the pet store in Slidell tomorrow to get him a real
cage. While he was hopping around the counter he
found one of Mom's muffins, gave a squawk, and
started gorging on it, so I named him Muffin.

"A parrot," D'Agosta muttered. "Now, what are the
chances of that?"

Pendergast began flipping pages, more slowly now,
until he reached the end of the book. He took down
the next volume and began methodically examining the
dates of the entries—until he came to one. D'Agosta
heard a small intake of breath.

"Vincent, here is the entry she wrote on February
ninth—the day Helen paid them a visit."

The worst day <u>of my life</u>!!!
After lunch a lady came and knocked on our front
door. She was driving a red sports car and was all
dressed up with fashionable leather gloves. She said
she'd heard we had a parrot and wanted to know if
she could see it. Dad showed Muffin to her (still inside
her cage) and she asked how we got it. She asked a lot
of questions about the bird, when we got it, where it
came from, if it was tame, if it let us handle it, who
played with it the most. Stuff like that. She spent
all sorts of time looking at it and asking questions.
The woman wanted to see the band up close but my

father asked her first if she was the bird's owner.
She said yes and wanted the parrot back. My dad was
suspicious. He asked if she could name the number on
the parrot's bracelet. She couldn't. And she wasn't
able to show us any kind of proof that she owned it,
either, but told us a story that she was a scientist
and it had escaped from her lab. Dad looked like he
didn't believe a word of it and said firmly that when
she brought back some proof he'd be glad to give
up the bird, but until then Muffin would stay with
us. The lady didn't seem too surprised and then she
looked at me with a sad expression on her face. "Is
Muffin your pet?" I said yes. She seemed to think for
a while. Then she asked if Dad could recommend a
good hotel in town. He said there was only one, and
that he'd get her the number. He walked back into
the kitchen for the phone book. No sooner had he
gone than the woman grabbed Muffin's cage, stuffed
it into a black garbage bag she took from her purse,
ran out the door, threw the bag in her car, and took
off down the driveway! Muffin was screeching loudly
the whole time. I ran outside screaming and Dad
came running out and we got in the car and chased
her, but she was gone. Dad called the sheriff but he
didn't seem all that interested in finding a stolen bird,
especially since it might have been her bird to begin
with. Muffin was gone, just like that.

I went up to my room and I just couldn't stop
crying.

Pendergast closed the diary and slipped it into
his jacket pocket. As he did so, a flash of lightning

illuminated the black trees beyond the window and a rumble of thunder shook the house.

"Unbelievable," said D'Agosta. "Helen stole the parrot. Just like she stole those stuffed parrots of Audubon's. What in the world was she thinking?"

Pendergast said nothing.

"Did you ever see the parrot? Did she bring it back to Penumbra?"

Pendergast shook his head wordlessly.

"What about this scientific lab she talked about?"

"She had no lab, Vincent. She was employed by Doctors With Wings."

"Do you have *any* idea what the hell she was doing?"

"For the first time in my life I am completely and utterly at a loss."

The lightning flickered again, illuminating an expression on Pendergast's face of pure shock and incomprehension.

26

New York City

Captain Laura Hayward, NYPD Homicide, liked to keep the door of her office open to signal she hadn't forgotten her roots as a lowly TA cop patrolling the subways. She had risen far and fast in the department, and while she knew she was good and deserved the promotions, she was also uncomfortably aware that being a woman hadn't hurt at all, especially after the sex discrimination scandals of the previous decade.

But on this particular morning, when she arrived at six, she reluctantly shut the door even though no one else was in. The investigation into a string of Russian mafia drug killings on Coney Island had been dragging its ass around the department, generating huge amounts of paperwork and meetings. It had finally reached the point where someone—her—needed to sit down with the files and go through them all so at least one person could get on top of the case and move it forward.

Toward noon, her brain almost fried from the sense-less brutality of it all, she rose from her desk and decided to get some air by taking a stroll in the small park next to One Police Plaza. She opened her door and exited the outer office, running into a gaggle of cops hanging out in the hall.

They greeted her with a little more effusion than usual, with several sidelong, embarrassed glances.

Hayward returned the greetings and then paused. "All right, what is it?"

A telling silence.

"I've never seen a worse bunch of fakers," she said lightly. "Honestly, if you sat down to a game of Texas Hold 'Em, you'd all lose."

The joke fell flat, and after a moment's hesitation, a sergeant spoke up. "Captain, it's sort of about that, ah, FBI agent. Pendergast."

Hayward froze. Her disdain for Pendergast was well known in the department, as was her relationship with his sometime partner D'Agosta. Pendergast always managed to drag Vincent into deep shit, and she had a growing premonition that the present excursion to Louisiana would end as disastrously as the earlier ones. In fact, maybe it just had... As these thoughts flashed through her mind, Hayward tried to control her fea-tures, keep them neutral. "What about Special Agent Pendergast?" she asked coolly.

"It isn't Pendergast exactly," said the sergeant. "It's a relative of his. Woman named Constance Greene. She's down in central booking, gave Pendergast as her next-of-kin. Apparently she's his niece or something."

Another awkward silence.

"And?" Hayward prompted.

"She's been abroad. She booked passage on the *Queen Mary Two* from Southampton to New York, boarded with her baby."

"Baby?"

"Right. A couple months old at most. Born abroad. Anyway, after the ship docked she was held at passport control because the baby was missing. INS radioed NYPD and we've taken her into custody. They're booking her for homicide."

"Homicide?"

"That's right. Seems she threw her baby off the ship somewhere in the middle of the Atlantic Ocean."

27

Gulf of Mexico

The Delta 767 seemed almost to hover at thirty-four thousand feet, the sky serene and cloudless, the sea an unbroken expanse of blue far below, sparkling in the afternoon light.

"May I get you another beer, sir?" the stewardess asked, bending over D'Agosta solicitously.

"Sure," he replied.

The stewardess turned to D'Agosta's seatmate. "And you, sir? Is everything all right?"

"No," Pendergast said. He gestured dismissively toward the small dish of smoked salmon that sat on his seat-back tray. "I find this to be room temperature. Would you mind bringing me a chilled serving, please?"

"Not at all." The woman whisked the plate away with a professional gesture.

D'Agosta waited until she returned, then settled back in the wide, comfortable seat, stretching out his legs.

The only times he'd flown first-class were traveling with Pendergast, but it was something he could get used to.

A chime sounded over the PA system, and the captain announced that the plane would be landing at Sarasota Bradenton International Airport in twenty minutes.

D'Agosta took a sip of his beer. Sunflower, Louisiana, was already eighteen hours and hundreds of miles behind them, but the strange Doane house—with that single, jewel-like room of wonders surrounded by a storm of decay and furious ruin—had never been far from his mind. Pendergast, however, had seemed disinclined to discuss it, remaining thoughtful and silent.

D'Agosta tried once again. "I got a theory."

The agent glanced toward him.

"I think the Doane family is a red herring."

"Indeed?" Pendergast took a tentative bite of the salmon.

"Think about it. They went nuts many months after Helen's visit. How could the visit have anything to do with what happened later? Or a parrot?"

"Perhaps you're right," said Pendergast, vaguely. "What puzzles me is this sudden flowering of creative brilliance before...the end. For all of them."

"It's a well-known fact that madness runs in families—" D'Agosta thought better of concluding this observation. "Anyway, it's always the gifted ones that go crazy."

"*We poets in our youth begin in gladness; But thereof come in the end despondency and madness.*" Pendergast turned toward D'Agosta. "So you think their creativity led to madness?"

"It sure as hell happened to the Doane daughter."

"I see. And Helen's theft of the parrot had nothing to do with what happened to the family later, is that your hypothesis?"

"More or less. What do you think?" D'Agosta hoped to smoke out Pendergast's opinion.

"I think that coincidences do not please me, Vincent."

D'Agosta hesitated. "Look, another thing I've been wondering…was, or I mean did, Helen—sometimes act weird, or…odd?"

Pendergast's expression seemed to tighten. "I'm not sure I know what you mean."

"It's just these…" D'Agosta hesitated again. "These sudden trips to strange destinations. The secrets. This stealing of birds, first two dead ones from a museum, then a live one from a family. Is it possible Helen was under some kind of strain, maybe—or was, you know, suffering from some nervous condition? Because back in Rockland I heard rumors that her family was not exactly normal…"

He fell silent when the ambient temperature around their seats seemed to fall about ten degrees.

Pendergast's expression did not alter, but when he spoke there was a distant, formal edge to his voice. "Helen Esterhazy may have been unusual. But she was also one of the most rational, the most *sane* people I ever encountered."

"I'm sure she was. I wasn't implying—"

"And she was also the least likely to crack under pressure."

"Right," D'Agosta said hastily. Bringing this up was a bad idea.

"I think our time would be better spent discussing the subject at hand," Pendergast said, forcing the conversation onto a new track. "There are a few things you ought to know about *him*." He plucked a thin envelope from his jacket pocket, pulled out a sheet of paper. "John Woodhouse Blast. Age fifty-eight. Born in Florence, South Carolina. Current residence Forty-one Twelve Beach Road, Siesta Key. He's had several occupations: art dealer, gallery owner, import/export—and he was also an engraver and printer." He put back the sheet of paper. "His engravings were of a rather specialized kind."

"What kind is that?"

"The kind that features portraits of dead presidents."

"He was a *counterfeiter*?"

"The Secret Service investigated him. Nothing was ever proven. He was also investigated for smuggling elephant ivory and rhinoceros horn—both illegal since the 1989 Endangered Species Convention. Again, nothing was proven."

"This guy is slipperier than an eel."

"He is clearly resourceful, determined—and dangerous." Pendergast paused a moment. "There is one other relevant aspect...his name: John Woodhouse Blast."

"Yeah?"

"He's the direct descendant of John James Audubon through his son, John Woodhouse Audubon."

"No *shit*."

"John Woodhouse was an artist in his own right. He completed Audubon's final work, *Viviparous Quadrupeds of North America*, painting nearly half the plates himself after his father's sudden decline."

D'Agosta whistled. "So Blast probably feels the Black Frame is his birthright."

"That was my assumption. It would appear he spent much of his adult life searching for it, although in recent years he apparently gave up."

"So what's he doing now?"

"I've been unable to find out. He's keeping his present dealings close to his vest." Pendergast glanced out the window. "We shall have to be careful, Vincent. Very careful."

28

S iesta Key was a revelation to D'Agosta: narrow, palm-lined avenues; emerald lawns leading down to jewel-like azure inlets; sinuous canals on which plea-sure boats bobbed lazily. The beach itself was wide, its sand white and fine as sugar, and it stretched north and south into mist and haze. On one side rolled creamy ocean; on the other sat a procession of condos and lux-ury hotels, punctuated by swimming pools and hacien-das and restaurants. It was sunset. As he watched, the sunbathers and sand-castle builders and beachcombers all seemed to pause, as if at some invisible signal, to look west. Beach chairs were reoriented; video cameras were held up. D'Agosta followed the general gaze. The sun was sinking into the Gulf of Mexico, a semicircle of orange fire. He had never before seen a sunset unim-peded by cityscapes or New Jersey, and it surprised him: one minute the sun was there, falling, measurably falling behind the endless flat line of the horizon...and then it was gone, strewing pink bands of afterglow in its wake. He licked his lips, tasted the faint sea air. It wasn't much of a stretch to imagine himself and Laura moving to a place like this once he'd put in his twenty.

Blast's condo was on the top floor of a luxury high-rise overlooking the beach. They took the elevator up, and Pendergast rang the bell. There was a long delay, then a faint scratching sound as the peephole cover was swiveled aside. Another, briefer delay, followed by the unlocking and opening of the door. A man stood on the far side, short, slightly built, with a full head of brilliantined black hair combed straight back. "Yes?"

Pendergast offered his shield and D'Agosta did the same. "Mr. Blast?" Pendergast inquired.

The man looked from one shield to the other, then at Pendergast. There was no fear or anxiety in his eyes, D'Agosta noted—only mild curiosity.

"May we come in?"

The man considered this a moment. Then he opened the door wider.

They passed through a front hall into a living room that was opulently if gaudily decorated. Heavy gold curtains framed a picture window looking out over the ocean. Thick white shag carpeting covered the floor. A faint smell of incense hung in the air. Two Pomeranians, one white and one black, glared at them from a nearby ottoman.

D'Agosta turned his attention back to Blast. The man looked nothing like his ancestor Audubon. He was small and fussy, with a pencil mustache and—given the climate—a remarkable lack of tan. Yet his movements were quick and lithe, betraying none of the languid decadence of the surrounding decor.

"Would you care to sit down?" he said, motioning them toward a brace of massive armchairs upholstered in crimson velvet. He spoke with the faintest of southern drawls.

Pendergast took a seat, and D'Agosta did the same. Blast sank into a white leather sofa across from them. "I assume you're not here about my rental property on Shell Road?"

"Quite correct," Pendergast replied.

"Then how can I help you?"

Pendergast let the question hang in the air for a moment before answering. "We're here about the Black Frame."

Blast's surprise manifested itself only in a faint widening of the eyes. After a moment he smiled, displaying brilliant little white teeth. It was not a particularly friendly smile. The man reminded D'Agosta of a mink, sleek and ready to bite. "Are you offering to sell?"

Pendergast shook his head. "No. We wish to examine it."

"Always preferable to know one's competition," said Blast.

Pendergast threw one leg over the other. "Odd you should mention competition. Because that's another reason we're here."

Blast cocked his head to one side quizzically.

"Helen Esterhazy Pendergast." The FBI agent slowly enunciated each word.

This time Blast remained absolutely still. He looked from Pendergast to D'Agosta, then back. "I'm sorry, as long as we're on the subject of names: may I have yours, please?"

"Special Agent Pendergast," he said. "And this is my associate, Lieutenant D'Agosta."

"Helen Esterhazy Pendergast," Blast repeated. "A relative of yours?"

"She was my wife," said Pendergast coldly.

The little man spread his hands. "Never heard the name in my life. *Désolée*. Now, if that's all...?" He stood.

Pendergast rose abruptly as well. D'Agosta stiffened, but instead of physically confronting Blast, as he feared, the agent clasped his hands behind his back, walked over to the picture window, and gazed out of it. Then he turned and roamed about the room, examining the various paintings, one after the other, as if he were in a museum gallery. Blast remained where he was, motionless, only his eyes moving as they followed the agent. Pendergast moved into the front hall, paused a moment in front of a closet door. His hand suddenly dipped into his black suit, removed something, touched the closet door; and then quite suddenly he threw it open.

Blast started for him. "What the devil—?" he cried angrily.

Pendergast reached into the closet, shoved aside several items, and pulled out a long fur coat from the back; it bore the familiar yellow-and-black stripes of a tiger.

"How dare you invade my privacy!" Blast said, still advancing.

Pendergast shook out the coat, gazing up and down. "Fit for a princess," he said, turning to Blast with a smile. "Absolutely genuine." He reached in the closet again, pushing aside more coats while Blast stood there, red with anger. "Ocelot, margay...quite a gallery of endangered species. And they are new, certainly more recent than the CITES ban of 1989, not to mention the '72 ESA."

He returned the furs to the closet, closed the door. "The US Fish and Wildlife law enforcement office would no doubt take an interest in your collection. Shall we call them?"

Blast's response surprised D'Agosta. Instead of protesting further, he visibly relaxed. Baring his teeth in another smile, he looked Pendergast up and down with something like appreciation. "Please," he said with a gesture. "I see we have more to talk about. Sit down."

Pendergast returned to his seat and Blast resumed his own.

"If I am able to help you...what about the fate of my little collection?" Blast nodded toward the closet.

"It depends on how *well* the conversation goes."

Blast exhaled: a long, slow hissing sound.

"Allow me to repeat the name," said Pendergast. "Helen Esterhazy Pendergast."

"Yes, yes, I remember your wife well." He folded his manicured hands. "Please forgive my earlier dissembling. Long experience has taught me to be reticent."

"Proceed," Pendergast replied coldly.

Blast shrugged. "Your wife and I were competitors. I wasted the better part of twenty years looking for the Black Frame. I heard she was sniffing around, asking questions about it, too. I wasn't pleased, to say the least. As you are no doubt aware, I am Audubon's great-great-great-grandson. The painting was mine—by birthright. No one should have the right to profit from it—except me.

"Audubon painted the Black Frame at the sanatorium but did not take it with him. The most likely scenario, I postulated, was that he gave it to one of the three doctors who treated him. One of them disappeared completely. Another moved back to Berlin—if he'd had the painting, it was either destroyed by war or irretrievably lost. I focused my search on the third doctor, Torgensson—more out of hope than anything else." He spread his hands. "It was through this connection I ran into your wife. I met her only once."

"Where and when?"

"Fifteen years ago, maybe. No, not quite fifteen. At Torgensson's old estate on the outskirts of Port Allen."

"And what happened, exactly, at this meeting?" Pendergast's voice was taut.

"I told her exactly what I just told you: that the painting was mine by birthright, and I expressed my desire that she drop her search."

"And what did Helen say?" Pendergast's voice was even icier.

Blast took a deep breath. "That's the funny thing."

Pendergast waited. The air seemed to freeze.

"Remember what you said earlier about the Black Frame? 'We wish to examine it,' you said. That's exactly what she said. She told me she didn't want to *own* the painting. She didn't want to profit from it. She just wanted to *examine* it. As far as she was concerned, she said, the painting could be mine. I was delighted to hear it and we shook hands. We parted friends, you might say." Another thin smile.

"What was her exact wording?"

"She said to me, 'I understand you've been looking for this a long time. Please understand, I don't want to *own* it, I just want to *examine* it. I want to confirm something. If I find it I'll turn it over to you—but in return you have to promise that if you find it first, you'll give me free rein to study it.' I was delighted with the arrangement."

"*Bullshit!*" D'Agosta said, rising from his chair. He could contain himself no longer. "Helen spent years searching for the painting—just to *look* at it? No way. You're lying."

"So help me, it's the truth," Blast said. And he smiled his ferret-like smile.

"What happened next?" Pendergast asked.

"That was it. We went our separate ways. That was my one and only encounter with her. I never saw her again. And that is the God's truth."

"Never?" Pendergast asked.

"*Never.* And that's all I know."

"You know a great deal more," said Pendergast, suddenly smiling. "But before you speak further, Mr. Blast, let me offer *you* something that you apparently don't know—as a sign of trust."

First a stick, now a carrot, D'Agosta thought. He wondered where Pendergast was going with this.

"I have proof that Audubon gave the painting to Torgensson," said Pendergast.

Blast leaned forward, his face suddenly interested. "Proof, you say?"

"Yes."

A long silence ensued. Blast sat back. "Well then,

now I'm more convinced than ever that the painting is gone. Destroyed when his last residence burned down."

"You mean, his estate outside Port Allen?" Pendergast asked. "I wasn't aware there was a fire."

Blast gave him a long look. "There's a lot you don't know, Mr. Pendergast. Port Allen was *not* Dr. Torgensson's final residence."

Pendergast was unable to conceal a look of surprise. "Indeed?"

"In the final years of his life, Torgensson fell into considerable financial embarrassment. He was being hounded by creditors: banks, local merchants, even the town for back taxes. Ultimately he was evicted from his Port Allen house. He moved into a shotgun shack by the river."

"How do you know all this?" D'Agosta demanded.

In response, Blast stood up and walked out of the room. D'Agosta heard a door open, the rustling of drawers. A minute later he returned with a folder in one hand. He handed it to Pendergast. "Torgensson's credit records. Take a look at the letter on top."

Pendergast pulled a yellowed sheet of ledger paper, roughly torn along one edge, from the folder. It was a letter scrawled on Pinkerton Agency letterhead. He began to read. "*'He has it. The fellow has it. But we find ourselves unable to locate it. We've searched the shanty from basement to eaves. It's as empty as the Port Allen house. There's nothing left of value, and certainly no painting of Audubon's.'*"

Pendergast replaced the sheet, glanced through other documents, then closed the folder. "And you, ah, *purloined* this report so as to frustrate your competition, I presume."

"No point in helping one's enemies." Blast retrieved the folder, placed it on the sofa beside him. "But in the end it was all moot."

"And why is that?" Pendergast asked.

"Because a few months after he moved into the tenement, it was hit by lightning and burned down to its foundations—with Torgensson inside. If he hid the Black Frame elsewhere, the location is long forgotten. If he had it in the house somewhere, it burned up with everything else." Blast shrugged. "And that's when I finally gave up the search. No, Mr. Pendergast, I'm afraid the Black Frame no longer exists. I know: I wasted twenty years of my life proving it."

"I don't believe a word of it," D'Agosta said as they rode the elevator to the lobby. "He's just trying to make us believe Helen didn't want the painting to erase his motive for doing her harm. He's covering his ass, he doesn't want us to suspect him of her murder—it's as simple as that."

Pendergast didn't reply.

"The guy's obviously smart, you'd think he could come up with something a little less lame," D'Agosta went on. "They both wanted the painting and Helen was getting too close. Blast didn't want anybody else taking his rightful inheritance. Open and shut. And then there's the big-game connection, the ivory and fur smuggling. He's got contacts in Africa, he could have used them to set up the murder."

The elevator doors opened, and they walked through

the lobby into the sea-moist night. Waves were sighing onto the sand, and lights twinkled from a million windows, turning the dark beach to the color of reflected fire. Mariachi music echoed faintly from a nearby restaurant.

"How did you know about that stuff?" D'Agosta asked as they walked toward the road.

Pendergast seemed to rouse himself. "I'm sorry?"

"The stuff in the closet? The furs?"

"By the scent."

"Scent?"

"As anyone who has owned one will confirm, big-cat furs have a faint scent, not unpleasant, a sort of perfumed musk, quite unmistakable. I know it well: my brother and I as children used to hide in our mother's fur closet. I knew the fellow smuggled ivory and rhino horn; it wasn't a big leap to think he was also trading in illegal furs."

"I see."

"Come on, Vincent—Caramino's is only two blocks from here. The best stone crab claws on the Gulf Coast, I'm told: excellent when washed down with icy vodka. And I feel rather in need of a drink."

29

New York City

When Captain Hayward entered the shabby waiting area outside the interrogation rooms in the basement of One Police Plaza, the two witnesses she had called in leapt to their feet.

The homicide sergeant also rose, and Hayward frowned. "Okay, everyone sit down and relax. I'm not the president." She realized that all the gold on her shoulders probably was a bit intimidating, especially for someone who worked on a ship, but this was too much and it made her uncomfortable. "Sorry to call you out like this on a Sunday. Sergeant, I'll take one at a time, no particular order."

She passed into the interrogation room—one of the nicer ones, designed for questioning cooperative witnesses, not grilling uncooperative suspects. It had a coffee table, a desk, and a couple of chairs. The AV man was already there and he nodded, giving her a thumbs-up.

"Thanks," said Hayward. "Much appreciated, especially on such short notice." Her New Year's resolution had been to control her irritable temper with those below her on the totem pole. Those above still got the unvarnished treatment: *Kick up, kiss down*, that was her new motto.

She leaned her head out the door. "Send the first one in, please."

The sergeant brought in the first witness, who was still in uniform. She indicated a seat.

"I know you've already been questioned, but I hope you won't mind another round. I'll try to keep it short. Coffee, tea?"

"No thank you, Captain," the ship's officer said.

"You're the vessel's security director, is that correct?"

"Correct."

The security director was a harmless elderly gentleman with a shock of white hair and a pleasing British accent who looked like a retired police inspector from some small town in England. *And that's probably*, she thought, *exactly what he is.*

"So, what happened?" she asked. She always liked starting with general questions.

"Well, Captain, this first came to my attention shortly after sailaway. I had a report that one of the passengers, Constance Greene, was acting strangely."

"How so?"

"She'd brought on board her child, a baby of three months. This in itself was unusual—I can't recall a single case of a passenger ever bringing a baby quite that young aboard ship. Especially a single mother. I received a report that just after she boarded, a friendly passenger wanted to see her baby—and maybe got too close—and that Ms. Greene apparently threatened the passenger."

"What did you do?"

"I interviewed Ms. Greene in her cabin and concluded that she was nothing more than an overprotective mother—you know how some can be—and no real threat was intended. The passenger who complained was, I thought, a bit of a prying old busybody."

"How did she seem? Ms. Greene, I mean."

"Calm, collected, rather formal."

"And the baby?"

"There in the room with her, in a crib supplied by housekeeping. Asleep during my brief visit."

"And then?"

"Ms. Greene shut herself up in her cabin for three or four days. After that, she was seen about the ship for the rest of the voyage. There were no other incidents that I'm aware of—that is, until she couldn't produce her baby at passport control. The baby, you see, had been added to her passport, as is customary when a citizen gives birth abroad."

"Did she seem sane to you?"

"Quite sane, at least on my one interaction with her. And unusually poised for a young lady of her age."

The next witness was a purser who confirmed what the security director had said: that the passenger boarded with her baby, that she was fiercely protective of him, and that she had disappeared into her cabin for several days. Then, toward the middle of the crossing, she was seen taking meals in the restaurants and touring the ship without the baby. People assumed she had a nanny or was using the ship's babysitting service. She kept to herself, spoke to nobody, rebuffed all friendly gestures. "I thought," said the purser, "that she was one of these extremely rich eccentrics, you know, the kind who have so much money they can act as they please and there's no one to say otherwise. And..." He hesitated.

"Go on."

"Toward the end of the voyage, I began to think she was maybe just a little bit...mad."

Hayward paused at the door to the small holding cell. She had never met Constance Greene but had heard plenty from Vinnie. He had always spoken of her as if she were older, but when the door swung open Hayward was astonished to see a young woman of no more than twenty-two or twenty-three years of age, her dark hair cut in a stylish if old-fashioned bob, sitting primly on the fold-down bunk, still formally dressed from the ship.

"May I come in?"

Constance Greene looked at her. Hayward prided herself on being able to read a person's eyes, but these were unfathomable.

"Please do."

Hayward took a seat on the lone chair in the room. Could this woman really have thrown her own child into the Atlantic? "I'm Captain Hayward."

"Delighted to make your acquaintance, Captain."

Under the circumstances, the antique graciousness of the greeting gave Hayward the creeps. "I'm a friend of Lieutenant D'Agosta, whom you know, and I have also worked on occasion with your, ah, uncle, Special Agent Pendergast."

"Not uncle. Aloysius is my legal guardian. We're not related." She corrected Hayward primly, punctiliously.

"I see. Do you have any family?"

"No," came the quick, sharp reply. "They are long dead and gone."

"I'm sorry. First, I wonder if you could help me out with a detail here—we're having a little trouble locating your legal records. Do you happen to know your Social Security number?"

"I don't have a Social Security number."

"Where were you born?"

"Here in New York City. On Water Street."

"The name of the hospital?"

"I was born at home."

"I see." Hayward decided to give up this particular line; their legal department would eventually straighten it out, and, if the truth be admitted, she was just avoiding the difficult questions to come.

"Constance, I'm in the homicide division, but this isn't my case. I'm just here on a fact-finding mission. You're under no obligation to answer any of my questions and this is not official. Do you understand?"

"I understand perfectly, thank you."

Once again Hayward was struck by the old-fashioned cadence of her speech; something about the way she held herself; something in those eyes, so old and wise, that seemed out of place in such a young body.

She took a deep breath. "Did you really throw your baby into the ocean?"

"Yes."

"Why?"

"Because he was evil. Like his father."

"And the father is...?"

"Dead."

"What was his name?"

Silence fell in the room. The cool violet eyes never wavered from her own, and Hayward understood, better than from anything Greene might have said, that she would never, ever answer the question.

"Why did you come back? You were abroad—why come home now?"

"Because Aloysius will need my help."

"Help? What sort of help?"

Constance remained motionless. "He is unprepared to face the betrayal that awaits him."

30

Savannah, Georgia

Judson Esterhazy stood amid the antiques and over-stuffed furniture of his den, looking out one of the tall windows facing Whitfield Square, now deserted. A chill rain dripped from the palmettos and central cupola, collecting in puddles on the brick pavements of Habersham Street. To D'Agosta, standing beside him, Helen's brother seemed different on this visit. The easygoing, courtly manner had vanished. The handsome face appeared troubled, tense, its features drawn.

"And she never mentioned her interest in parrots, the Carolina Parakeet in particular?"

Esterhazy shook his head. "Never."

"And the Black Frame? You never heard her mention it, even in passing?"

Another shake of the head. "This is all new to me. I'm as much at a loss to explain it as you are."

"I know how painful this must be."

Esterhazy turned from the window. His jaw worked in what to D'Agosta seemed barely controlled rage. "Not nearly as painful as learning of this fellow Blast. You say he has a record?"

"Of arrests. No convictions."

"That doesn't mean he's innocent," Esterhazy said.

"Quite the opposite," said D'Agosta.

Esterhazy glanced his way. "And not just things like blackmail and forgery. You mentioned assault and battery."

D'Agosta nodded.

"And he was after this—this Black Frame, too?"

"As bad as anybody ever wanted anything," said D'Agosta.

Esterhazy's hands clenched; he turned back to the window.

"Judson," Pendergast said, "remember what I told you—"

"You lost a wife," Esterhazy said over his shoulder, "I lost a little sister. You never quite get over it but at least you can come to terms with it. But now, to learn *this*…" He drew in a long breath. "And not only that, but this *criminal* might have been involved in some way—"

"We don't know that for a fact," Pendergast said.

"But you can be damn sure we're going to find out," said D'Agosta.

Esterhazy did not respond. He merely continued looking out the window, his jaw working slowly, his gaze far away.

31

Three hundred and thirty miles to the south, another man was staring out another window.

John Woodhouse Blast looked down at the beach-combers and sunbathers ten stories below; at the long white lines of surf curling in toward the shore; at the beach that stretched almost to infinity. He turned away and walked across the living room, pausing briefly before a gilt mirror. The drawn face that stared back at him reflected the agitation of a sleepless night.

He'd been careful, so very careful. How could this be happening to him now? That pale death's-head of an avenging angel, appearing on his doorstep so unex-pectedly... He had always played a conservative game, never taking risks. And it had worked, until now...

The stillness of the room was broken by the ring of a telephone. Blast jumped at the sudden sound. He strode over to it, plucked the handset from the cradle.

From the ottoman, the two Pomeranians watched his every move.

"It's Victor. What's up?"

"Christ, Victor, it's about time you called back. Where the hell have you been?"

"Out," a rough, gravelly voice replied. "Is there a problem?"

"You bet there's a problem. A monstrous big fucking problem. An FBI agent came sniffing around last night."

"Anybody we know?"

"Name of Pendergast. Had an NYPD cop with him, too."

"What did they want?"

"What do you *think* they wanted? He knows too much, Victor—*way* too much. We're going to have to take care of this, and right away."

"You mean..." The gravelly voice hesitated.

"That's right. It's time to roll everything up."

"Everything?"

"Everything. You know what to do, Victor. See that it gets done. See that it gets done *right away*." Blast slammed down the phone and stared out the window at the endless blue horizon.

32

The dirt track wound through the piney forest and came out in a big meadow at the edge of a mangrove swamp. The shooter parked the Range Rover in the meadow and removed the gun case, portfolio, and backpack from the rear. He carried them to a small hillock in the center of the field, setting them down in the matted grass. He took a paper target from the portfolio and walked down the field to the swamp, counting his strides. The noonday sun pierced through the cypress trees, casting flecks of light across the green-brown water.

Selecting a smooth, broad trunk, the shooter pinned a target to the wood, tacking it down with an upholstery hammer. It was a warmish day for winter, in the low sixties, the smell of water and rotting wood drifting in from the swamp, a flock of noisy crows croaking and screeching in the branches. The nearest house was ten miles away. There wasn't a breath of wind.

He walked back up to where he had left his gear,

counting his steps again, satisfied that the target was about a hundred yards away.

He opened the hard Pelican case and removed the rifle from it: a Remington 40-XS tactical. At fifteen pounds, it was a heavy son of a bitch, but the trade-off was a better-than-0.75 MOA accuracy. The shooter hadn't fired the weapon in quite some time, but it was now cleaned and oiled and ready to go.

He knelt, laying it over his knee, and flipped down the bipod, adjusting and locking it in place. Then he lay down in the matted grass, set the rifle in front of him, moving it around until it was stable and solid. He closed one eye and peered through the Leupold scope at the target affixed to the tree. So far, so good. Reaching into his back pocket, he removed a box of .308 Winchester rounds and placed it in the grass to his right. Plucking out a round, he pushed it into the chamber, then another, until the four-round internal magazine was full. He closed the bolt and looked again through the scope.

He aimed at the target, breathing slowly, letting his heart rate subside. The faint trembling and movement of the weapon, as evident from the motion of the target in the crosshairs, subsided as he allowed his entire body to relax. He placed his finger on the trigger and tightened slightly, let his breath run out, counted the heartbeats, and then squeezed between them. A crack, a small kick. He ejected the shell, resumed breathing, relaxed again, and gave the trigger another slow squeeze. Another crack and kick, the sound rolling away quickly over the swampy flatlands. Two more shots finished the maga-zine. He rose to his feet, gathered the four shells, put them in his pocket, and walked down to inspect the target.

It was a fairly tight grouping, the rounds close enough to have cut an irregular hole to the left and slightly below the center of the target. Removing a plastic ruler from his pocket, he measured the offset, turned and walked back across the meadow, moving slowly to keep his exertion down. He lay down again, gathered the rifle into his hands, and adjusted the elevation and windage knobs on the scope to take his measurements into account.

Once again, with great deliberation, he fired four rounds at the target. This time the grouping lay dead center, all four rounds more or less placed in the same hole. Satisfied, he pulled the target off the tree trunk, balled it up, and stuffed it in his pocket.

He walked back to the center of the field and resumed firing position. It was now time for a little fun. When he first began firing, the flock of crows had risen in noisy flight and settled about three hundred yards away at the far edge of the field. Now he could see them on the ground under a tall yellow pine, strutting about in the needle duff and picking out seeds from a scattering of cones.

Peering through the scope, the man selected a crow and followed it in the crosshairs as it pecked and jabbed at a cone, shaking it with its beak. His forefinger tightened on the curved steel; the shot rang out; and the bird disappeared in a spray of black feathers, splattering the nearby tree trunk with bits of red flesh. The rest of the flock rose in an uproar, bursting into the blue and winging away across the treetops.

The man looked about for another target, this time aiming the scope down toward the swamp. Slowly, he swept the edge of the swamp until he found it: a massive bullfrog about 150 yards off, resting on a lily pad in a little patch of sun. Once again he aimed, relaxed, and fired; a pink cloud flew up, mingled with green water and bits of lily pad, arcing through the sunlight and gracefully falling back into the water. His third round clipped the head off a water moccasin, thrashing through the water in a frightened effort to get away.

One more round. He needed something really challenging. He cast about, looking around the swamp with a bare eye, but the shooting had disturbed the wildlife and there was nothing to be seen. He would have to wait.

He went back to the Range Rover and removed a soft-canvas shotgun case from the rear, unzipped it, and took out a CZ Bobwhite side-by-side 12-gauge with a custom-carved stock. It was the cheapest shotgun he owned, but it was still an excellent weapon and he hated what he was now about to do. He rummaged around in the Rover, removing a portable vise and a hacksaw with a brand-new blade.

He laid the shotgun over his knees and stroked the barrels, rubbed them down with a little gun oil, and laid a paper tape measure alongside. Marking off a spot with a nail, he put the hacksaw to it and went to work.

It was a long, tedious, exhausting business. When he was finished, he filed the burr off the end with a rattail, gave it a quick bevel, brushed it with steel wool, and then oiled it again. He broke the action and carefully cleaned out loose filings, then dunked in two shotgun shells. He strolled down to the swamp with the gun and the sawed-off barrels, flung the barrels as far out into the water as he could, braced the gun at his waist, and pulled the front trigger.

The blast was deafening and it kicked like a mule. Crude, vile—and devastatingly effective. The second barrel discharged perfectly as well. He broke the action again, put the shells in his pocket, wiped it clean, and reloaded. It worked smoothly a second time around. He was pained, but satisfied.

Back at the car, he slid the shotgun back in its case, put the case away, and removed a sandwich and thermos from his pack. He ate slowly, savoring the truffled fois gras sandwich while sipping a cup of hot tea with milk and sugar from the thermos. He made an effort to enjoy the fresh air and sun and not think about the problem at hand. As he was finishing, a female red-tailed hawk rose up from the swamp, no doubt from a nest, and began tracing lazy circles above the treetops. He estimated her distance at about two hundred fifty yards.

Now this, finally, was a challenge worthy of his skill.

He once more assumed a shooting position with the sniper rifle, aiming at the bird, but the scope's field of view was too narrow and he couldn't keep her in it. He would have to use his iron sights instead. He now peered at the hawk using those fixed sights, trying to follow her as she moved. Still no go: the rifle was too heavy and the bird too fast. She was tracing an ellipsis, and the way to hit her, he decided, was to pre-aim for a point on that ellipsis, wait until the hawk circled around toward it, and time the shot.

A moment later the hawk tumbled from the sky, a few feathers drifting along after her, carried off on the wind.

The shooter folded away the bipod, picked up and re-counted all the shells, put the gun back in its case, packed away his lunch and thermos, and hefted his pack. He gave the area one last look-over, but the only sign of his presence was a patch of matted grass.

He turned back toward the Range Rover with a deep feeling of satisfaction. Now, at least for a while, he could give free vent to his feelings, allow them to flow through his body, spiking his adrenaline, preparing him for the killing to come.

33

D'Agosta stood outside the visitors' center in brilliant afternoon sunlight, looking down Court Street toward the river. Besides the center itself—a fine old brick building, spotlessly renovated and updated—everything seemed brand new: the shops, the civic buildings, the scattering of homes along the riverbank. It was hard to believe that, somewhere in the immediate vicinity, John James Audubon's doctor had lived and died nearly 150 years before.

"Originally, this was known as St. Michel," Pendergast said at his side. "Port Allen was first laid out in 1809, but within fifty years more than half of it had been eaten away by the Mississippi. Shall we walk down to the riverfront promenade?"

He set off at a brisk pace, and D'Agosta followed in his wake, trying to keep up. He was exhausted and wondered how Pendergast maintained his energy after a week of nonstop traveling by car and plane, charging from one place to the next, rolling into bed at midnight and waking at dawn. Port Allen felt like one place too many.

First they had gone to see Dr. Torgensson's penultimate dwelling: an attractive old brick residence west of town, now a funeral home. They had rushed to the town hall where Pendergast had charmed a secretary, who allowed him to paw through some old plans and books. And now they were here, on the banks of the Mississippi itself, where Blast claimed Dr. Torgensson had spent his final unpleasant months in a shotgun shack, ruined, in a syphilitic and alcoholic stupor.

The riverfront promenade was broad and grand, and the view from the levee was spectacular: Baton Rouge spread out across the far bank, barges and tugs working their way up the wide flow of chocolate-colored water.

"That's the Port Allen Lock," Pendergast said, waving his hand toward a large break in the levee, ending in two huge yellow gates. "Largest free-floating structure of its kind. It connects the river to the Intracoastal Waterway."

They walked a few blocks along the promenade. D'Agosta felt himself reviving under the influence of the fresh breeze coming off the river. They stopped at an information booth, where Pendergast scanned the advertisements and notice boards. "How tragic—we've missed the Lagniappe Dulcimer Fête," he said.

D'Agosta shot a private glance toward Pendergast. Given how hard he'd taken the shock of his wife's murder, the agent had taken the news about Constance Greene—which Hayward had given them yesterday—with remarkably little emotion. No matter how long D'Agosta knew Pendergast, it seemed he never really *knew* him. The man obviously cared for Constance—and yet he seemed almost indifferent to the fact that she was now in custody, charged with infanticide.

Pendergast strolled back out of the booth and walked across the greensward toward the river itself, pausing at the remains of a ruined sluice gate, now half underwater. "In the early nineteenth century, the business district would have been two or three blocks out *there*," he said, pointing into the roiling mass of water. "Now it belongs to the river."

He led the way back across the promenade and Commerce Avenue, made a left on Court Street and a right on Atchafalaya. "By the time Dr. Torgensson was forced to move into his final dwelling," he said, "St. Michel had become West Baton Rouge. At the time, this neighborhood was a seedy, working-class community between the railroad depot and the ferry landing."

He turned down another street; consulted the map again; walked a little farther and halted. "I do believe," he drawled, "that we have arrived."

They had arrived at a small commercial mini-mall. Three buildings sat side by side: a McDonald's; a mobile phone store; and a squat, garishly colored structure named Pappy's Donette Hole—a crusty local chain D'Agosta had seen elsewhere. Two cars were parked in front of Pappy's, and the McDonald's drive-through was doing a brisk business.

"This is *it*?" he exclaimed.

Pendergast nodded, pointing at the cell phone store. "*That* is the precise location of Torgensson's shotgun shack."

D'Agosta looked at each of the buildings in turn.

His spirits, which had begun to rise during the brief walk, fell again. "It's like Blast said," he muttered. "Totally hopeless."

Pendergast put his hands in his pockets and strolled up to the mini-mall. He ducked into each of the buildings in turn. D'Agosta, who could not summon the energy to follow, merely stood in the adjoining parking lot and watched. Within five minutes the agent had returned. Saying nothing, he did a slow scan of the horizon, turning almost imperceptibly, until he had carefully scrutinized everything within a three-hundred-sixty-degree radius. Then he did it again, this time stopping about halfway through his scan.

"Take a look at that building, Vincent," he said.

D'Agosta followed the gesture with his eyes toward the visitor's center they had passed at the beginning of their loop.

"What about it?" D'Agosta asked.

"That was clearly once a water-pumping station. The Gothic Revival style indicates it probably dates back to the original town of St. Michel." He paused. "Yes," he murmured after a moment. "I'm sure it does."

D'Agosta waited.

Pendergast turned and pointed in the opposite direction. From this vantage point they had an unobstructed view down to the promenade, the ruined sluice gate, and the wide Mississippi beyond.

"How curious," Pendergast said. "This little mini-mall falls *on a direct line* between that old pumping station and the sluice gate at the river."

Pendergast broke into a swift walk toward the river again. D'Agosta swung in behind.

Stopping almost at the water's edge, Pendergast bent forward to examine the sluice gate. D'Agosta could see it led to a large stone pipe that was sealed with cement and partially backfilled.

Pendergast straightened up. "Just as I thought. There was an old aqueduct here."

"Yeah? So what's it mean?"

"That aqueduct was no doubt abandoned and sealed up when the eastern half of St. Michel crumbled into the river. Remarkable!"

D'Agosta did not share his friend's enthusiasm for historical detail.

"Surely you see it now, Vincent? Torgensson's shack must have been built *after this aqueduct was sealed up.*"

D'Agosta shrugged. For the life of him, he didn't see where Pendergast was going.

"In this part of the world it was common—for buildings constructed over the line of an old water pipe or aqueduct, anyway—to cut into an old aqueduct and use it as a basement. It saved a great deal of labor when basements were dug by hand."

"You think the pipe is still down there—?"

"Exactly. When the shack was built in 1855, they probably used a section of the capped and abandoned tunnel—now quite dry, of course—as the basement. Those old aqueducts were square, not round, and made of mortared stone. The builders merely had to shore up the foundations, construct two brick walls on the sides perpendicular to the existing aqueduct walls, and—voilà! Instant basement."

"And you think that's where we'll find the Black

Frame?" D'Agosta asked a little breathlessly. "In Torgensson's basement?"

"No. Not *in* the basement. Remember the creditor's note Blast showed us? *'We've searched the shack from basement to eaves. It has proven empty, nothing left of value, certainly no painting.'"*

"If it's not in the basement, then what's all the excitement about?" Pendergast's coyness could be so maddening sometimes.

"Think: a series of row houses, situated in a line above a preexisting tunnel, each with a basement fashioned from a segment of that tunnel. But, Vincent—think also of the spaces *between* the houses. Remember, the basements would be roughly the size of the houses *above* them."

"So...so you're saying there would be old spaces between the basements."

"Precisely. Sections of the old aqueduct *between* each basement, bricked off and unused. And that's where Torgensson might have hidden the Black Frame."

"Why hide it so well?"

"We can assume that if the painting was so precious to the doctor that he could not part with it even in the greatest penury, then it would be precious enough *that he would not want to ever be far from it*. And yet he had to hide it well from his creditors."

"But the house was struck by lightning. It burned to the ground."

"True. But if our logic is correct, the painting would likely have been safe in its niche, secure in the aqueduct tunnel between his basement and the next."

"So all we have to do is get into the basement of the wireless store."

Pendergast put a restraining hand on his arm. "Alas, that wireless store has no basement. I checked when I went inside. The basement of the structure that predated it must have been filled in after the fire."

Once again, D'Agosta felt a huge deflation. "Then what the hell are we going to do? We can't just get a bulldozer, raze the store, and dig a new basement."

"No. But we just might be able to make our way into the tunnel space from one of the *adjacent* basements, which I confirmed still exist. The question is: which one to try first?" Once again, that gleam that had been so often absent in recent days returned to Pendergast's eyes: the gleam of the hunt. "I'm in the mood for doughnuts," he said. "How about you?"

34

St. Francisville, Louisiana

Painstakingly, Morris Blackletter, PhD, fitted the servo mechanism to the rear wheel assembly. He checked it, checked it again, then plugged the USB cable from the guidance control unit into his laptop and ran a diagnostic. It checked out. He wrote a simple four-line program, downloaded it into the control unit, and gave the execute command. The little robot—a rather ugly confabulation of processors, motors, and sensory inputs, set atop fat rubber wheels—engaged its forward motor, rolled across the floor for exactly five seconds, then stopped abruptly.

Blackletter felt a flush of triumph all out of proportion with the achievement. Throughout his vacation—staring at English cathedrals, sitting in dimly lit pubs—he'd been anticipating this moment.

Years ago, Blackletter had read a study explaining how retired people frequently acquired interests diametrically different from the work that had occupied their professional lives. That, he thought ruefully, was certainly the case with him. All those years in the health profession—first at Doctors With Wings, later at a succession of pharmaceutical and medical research labs—he had been obsessed with the human body: how it worked, what made it fail, how to keep it healthy or cure its ills. And now here he was, toying with robots—the antithesis of flesh and blood. When they burned out, you just threw them away and ordered another. No grief, no death.

How different it was from those years he'd spent in Third World countries, parched and mosquito-bitten, threatened by guerrilla fighters and harassed by corruption, sometimes sick himself—working to contain epidemics. He had saved hundreds, maybe thousands of lives, but so many, many others had died. It hadn't been his fault, of course. But then there was the other thing, the thing he tried never to think about. That, more than anything, was what caused him to flee flesh and blood for the contentment of plastic and silicon...

Here he was, thinking about it again. He shook his head as if to rid himself of the terrible guilt of it and glanced back at the robot. Slowly, the guilt drained away—what was done was done, and his motives had always been pure. A smile settled over his features. He raised his hand and snapped his fingers.

The robot's audio sensor took note, and it swiveled toward the sound. "Robo want a cracker," it croaked in a metallic disembodied voice.

Feeling absurdly pleased, Blackletter rose to his feet and walked from his den to the kitchen for one last cup of tea before calling it a night. He suddenly paused, hand on the teapot, listening.

There it came again: the creak of a board.

Slowly, Blackletter set the pot back on the counter. Was it the wind? But no: it was a quiet, windless night.

Somebody in the street, perhaps? The sound was too close, too clear for that.

Perhaps it was all in his mind. Minds had a tendency to do that, he knew: the absence of real auditory stimuli frequently encouraged the brain to supply its own. He'd been puttering about in his den for hours, and...

Another creak. This time Blackletter knew for certain: the sound had come from inside the house.

"Who's that?" he called out. The creaking stopped.

Was it a burglar? Unlikely. There were far larger, grander houses on the street than his.

Who, then?

The creaking resumed, regular, deliberate. And now he could tell where it was coming from: the living room at the front of the house.

He glanced toward the phone, saw the empty cradle. *Damn these cordless phones.* Where had he left the handset? Of course—it was in the den, on the table by the laptop.

He walked quickly back into the room, plucked the telephone from the wooden surface. Then he froze. Somebody was in the hall just beyond. A tall man in a long trench coat stepped forward from the darkness.

"What are you doing in my house?" he demanded. "What do you want?"

The intruder did not speak. Instead, he pulled back his coat, revealing the twin barrels of a sawed-off shotgun. The butt-stock was of a heavy black wood, carved in paisley rosettes, and the bluing of the barrels gleamed faintly in the light of the den.

Blackletter found that he was unable to take his eyes from the weapon. He took a step back. "Wait," he began. "Don't. You're making a mistake…we can talk…"

The weapon swiveled upward. There was a tremendous boom-*boom* as both barrels fired almost simultaneously. Blackletter was flung backward, impacting the far wall with a shattering crash, then slumping to the ground. Framed pictures and knickknacks rained down around him from little wooden shelves.

The front door was already closing.

The robot, its audio sensors alerted, swiveled toward the motionless form of its builder. "Robo want a cracker," it said, the tinny voice muffled by the blood now coating its miniature speaker. "Robo want a cracker."

35

Port Allen, Louisiana

The following day was as dark and rainy as the previous day had been pleasant. That was just fine with D'Agosta—there would be fewer customers to deal with at the doughnut shop. He had deep misgivings about this whole scheme of Pendergast's.

Pendergast, behind the wheel of the Rolls, took the Port Allen exit from I-10, the wheels hissing on the wet asphalt. D'Agosta sat beside him, turning the pages of the *New Orleans Star-Picayune*. "I don't see why we couldn't do this at night," he said.

"The establishment has a burglar alarm. And the noise would be more apparent."

"You better do the talking. I have a feeling my Queens accent wouldn't go down well in these parts."

"An excellent point, Vincent."

D'Agosta noticed Pendergast glancing once again in the rearview mirror. "We got company?" he asked.

Pendergast merely smiled in return. Rather than his habitual black suit, he was wearing a plaid work shirt and denims. Instead of resembling an undertaker, he now looked like a gravedigger.

D'Agosta turned another page, paused at an article headlined *Retired Scientist Murdered in Home*. "Hey, Pendergast," he said after scanning the opening paragraphs. "Look at this: that guy you wanted to talk to, Morris Blackletter, Helen's old boss, was just found murdered in his house."

"Murdered? How?"

"Shotgunned."

"Do the police suspect a robbery gone wrong?"

"The article doesn't say."

"He must have just returned from his vacation. A great pity we didn't get to him earlier—he could have been rather useful."

"Somebody else got to him first. And I can guess who that somebody was." D'Agosta shook his head. "Maybe we should go back to Florida and sweat Blast."

Pendergast turned onto Court Street, heading for downtown and the river. "Perhaps. But I find Blast's motive to be obscure."

"Not at all. Helen might have told Blackletter about Blast threatening her." D'Agosta folded the paper, shoved it between the seat and the center pedestal. "We talk to Blast, and the following night Blackletter is killed. You're the one who doesn't buy coincidences."

Pendergast looked thoughtful. But instead of replying, he turned off Court Street and nosed the Rolls into a parking lot a block short of their destination. They stepped out into the drizzle, and Pendergast opened the trunk. He passed D'Agosta a yellow construction helmet and a large canvas workbag. He took out another helmet, which he fitted onto his head. Lastly, he pulled out a heavy tool belt—from which dangled an assortment of flashlights, measuring tapes, wire cutters, and other equipment—and buckled it around his waist.

"Shall we?" he said.

Pappy's Donette Hole was quiet: two plump girls stood behind the counter while a lone customer ordered a dozen double-chocolate FatOnes. Pendergast waited until the customer paid and left, then stepped forward, construction belt jangling.

"Manager around?" he said in a demanding voice, his southern accent sinking about five notches in refinement.

One of the girls wordlessly turned and went into the back. A minute later, she returned with a middle-aged man. His thick forearms were coated in blond hair, and he was sweating despite the cool of the day.

"Yeah?" he said, wiping flour onto an apron already heavy with grease and doughnut batter.

"You're the manager?"

"Yeah."

Pendergast reached into the back pocket of his denims, brought out an ID billfold. "We're from the Buildings Department, Code Enforcement Division. My name's Addison and my partner here is Steele."

The man scrutinized the ID Pendergast had doctored up the night before, then grunted. "So what do you want?"

Pendergast put away the billfold and pulled out a few stapled sheets of official-looking paper. "Our office has been conducting an audit of the construction and permits records of buildings in the general vicinity, and we've found several of them—including yours—that have problems. *Big* problems."

The man looked at the outstretched sheets, frowning. "What kind of problems?"

"Irregularities in the permitting process. Structural issues."

"That can't be," he said. "We get our inspections regular, just like the food and sanitation—"

"We're not *food inspectors*," Pendergast interrupted sarcastically. "The records show this structure was built without the proper permits."

"Hold on, now. We been here a dozen years—"

"Just why do you think the audit was ordered?" Pendergast said, still waving the sheets of paper in the man's sweaty face. "There've been irregularities. Allegations of *corruption*."

"Hey, I'm not the guy you need to talk to about that. The franchise office handles—"

"You're the guy who's here now." Pendergast leaned forward. "We need to get down into that basement and see just how bad the situation is." Pendergast stuffed the papers back into the pocket of his shirt. "And I mean *now*."

"You want to see the basement? Be my guest," the manager said, sweating profusely. "It ain't my fault if there's a problem. I just work here."

"Very well. Let's get going."

"Joanie here will take you down while Mary Kate attends to the customers—"

"Oh, no," Pendergast interrupted again. "Oh, no, no, no. No customers. Not until we're done."

"No customers?" the man repeated. "I'm trying to run a doughnut shop here."

Pendergast bent closer now. "This is a dangerous, maybe life-threatening situation. Our analysis shows the building is *unsound*. You are *required* to close your doors to the public until we have completed our check of the foundation and the load-bearing members."

"I don't know," the manager said, his frown deepening. "I'm gonna have to call the main office. We've never closed during business hours before, and my franchise contract states—"

"You don't *know*? We aren't going to waste time while you call up every Tom, Dick, and Harry you've a mind to." Pendergast leaned in even closer. "Why, exactly, are you stalling? Do you know what would happen if the floor collapsed under a customer while he was eating a box of—" here Pendergast paused to glance at the menu posted above the counter, "—chocolate-banana double-cream glazed FatOnes?"

Silently, the man shook his head.

"You'd be charged. Personally. Criminal negligence. Manslaughter in the second degree. Maybe even...in the *first* degree."

The manager took a step backward. He gulped for air, fresh sweat popping on his brow.

Pendergast let a strained silence build. "Tell you what I'll do," he said with sudden magnanimity. "While you put up the CLOSED sign, Mr. Steele and I will make a quick visual inspection downstairs. If the situation is less grave than we've been led to believe, business can resume while we complete our site report."

The man's face broke out in unexpected relief. He

turned to his employees. "Mary Kate, we're closing up for a few minutes. Joanie, show these men to the basement."

Pendergast and D'Agosta followed Joanie through the kitchen, past a pantry and restroom, to an unmarked door. Beyond, a steep concrete stairway led down into darkness. The girl switched on the light, revealing a graveyard of old equipment—professional stand mixers and industrial-strength deep-fat fryers, apparently all awaiting repair. The basement itself was clearly very old, with facing walls of undressed stone, roughly mortared. The other two walls were made of brick. These, though apparently even older, were much more carefully fitted together. A number of plastic garbage bins lined the floor by the stairway, and untidy heaps of tarps and plastic sheeting lay, apparently forgotten, in a corner.

Pendergast turned. "Thank you, Joanie. We'll work alone. Please shut the door on your way out."

The girl nodded and retreated up the stairs.

Pendergast walked over to one of the brick walls. "Vincent," he said, resuming his usual voice, "unless I am much mistaken, about twelve feet beyond this lies another wall: that of Arne Torgensson's basement. And in between we should find a section of the old aqueduct, in which, perhaps, the good doctor has hidden something."

D'Agosta dropped the tool sack on the ground with a thump. "I figure we got two minutes, tops, before that jackass upstairs calls his boss and the shit hits the fan."

"You employ such colorful expressions," Pendergast murmured, examining the brick wall with his loupe and rapping on it with a ball-peen hammer. "However, I think I can buy us some more time."

"Oh, yeah? How?"

"I'm afraid I must inform our managerial friend that the situation is even more dire than we first thought. Not only must the shop be closed to customers—the workers themselves must vacate the premises until we complete our inspection."

Pendergast's light tread up the stairs receded quickly into silence. D'Agosta waited in the cool, dry darkness. After a moment an irruption of noise sounded from above: a protest, raised voices. Almost as quickly as it started, the noise ceased. Pendergast reappeared on the landing. Carefully closing and locking the door behind him, he descended the stairs and walked over to the bag of tools. Reaching into it, he pulled out a short-handled sledgehammer and handed it to D'Agosta.

"Vincent," he said with a ghost of a smile, "I yield the floor to you."

36

As D'Agosta hefted the sledgehammer, Pendergast bent close to the ancient wall, rapping first on one stone, then another, all the while listening intently. The light was dim, and D'Agosta had to squint to see. After a few moments, the FBI agent gave a low grunt of satisfaction and straightened up.

"Here," he said, pointing to a brick near the middle of the wall.

D'Agosta came over, gave the sledgehammer a practice swing like a batter on deck.

"I've bought us five minutes," Pendergast said. "Ten at most. By then our managerial friend will undoubtedly be back. And this time he may bring company."

D'Agosta swung the sledgehammer at the wall. Though he missed the indicated spot by a few bricks, the iron impacted the wall with a blow that shivered its way through his hands and up his arms. A second blow struck truer, and a third. He set down the sledgehammer, wiped his hands on the back of his pants, got a better grip, and returned to work. Another dozen or so heavy blows and Pendergast gestured for him to stop. D'Agosta stepped back, panting.

The agent glided up, waving aside a pall of cement dust. Playing a flashlight over the wall, he rapped on the bricks again, one after another. "They're coming loose. Keep at it, Vincent."

D'Agosta stepped forward again and gave the wall another series of solid blows. With the last came a crumbling sound, and one of the bricks shattered. Pendergast darted forward again, cold chisel in one hand and hammer in the other. He felt briefly along the sagging wall, then raised the hammer and applied several carefully placed strikes to the surrounding matrix of mortar and ancient concrete. Several more bricks were jarred loose, and Pendergast pried away others with his hands. Dropping the chisel and hammer, he played his flashlight over the wall. A hole was now visible, roughly the size of a beach ball. Pendergast thrust his head through it, aiming his flashlight this way and that.

"What do you see?" asked D'Agosta.

In response, Pendergast stepped away. "A few more, if you please," he said, indicating the sledgehammer.

This time, D'Agosta aimed his blows all around the edges of the ragged hole, concentrating on its upper edge. Bricks, chips, and old plaster rained down. At last, Pendergast once again gave the signal to stop. D'Agosta did so gladly, heaving with the effort.

From beyond the closed door at the top of the stairwell came a noise. The manager was coming back into the building.

Pendergast again approached the yawning hole in

the wall, and D'Agosta crowded up behind. Through the billows of dust, the beams of their flashlights revealed a shallow space beyond the broken stones. It was a chamber perhaps twelve feet wide and four feet deep. Abruptly D'Agosta stopped breathing. His yellow beam had fallen on a flat wooden crate leaning against the far wall, reinforced on both sides by wooden struts. It was just about the size, D'Agosta thought, you'd expect a painting to be. There was nothing else visible through the pall of dust.

The doorknob above them rattled. "Hey!" came the voice of the manager. It had regained much of its original aggressive character. "What the heck are you doing down there?"

Pendergast glanced around rapidly. "Vincent," he said, turning and directing his beam to the pile of tarps and plastic sheets in the far corner. "Hurry."

Nothing more needed to be said. D'Agosta rushed over to the pile, rummaging through it for a tarp of sufficient size, while Pendergast ducked through the newly made hole in the wall.

"I'm coming down," the manager said, rattling the door. "Open this door!"

Pendergast dragged the crate from its hiding place. D'Agosta helped him maneuver it through the hole, and together they wrapped it in the plastic tarp.

"I've called the franchise office in New Orleans," came the manager's voice. "You can't just come in here and shut down the shop! This is the first time anyone's heard of these so-called inspections you're doing—"

D'Agosta grabbed one end of the crate, Pendergast the other, and they began ascending the stairs.

D'Agosta could hear a key going into the lock. "Make way!" Pendergast bellowed, emerging from the cloud of dust into the dim basement light. The wooden box was in their arms, shrouded by the tarp. "Make way, now!"

The door flung open and the red-faced manager stood blocking the door. "Just what the hell have you got there?" he demanded.

"Evidence in a possible criminal case." They gained the landing. "Things are looking even worse for you than before, Mr....." Pendergast peered at the manager's name tag. "Mr. Bona."

"Me? I've only been manager here for six months, I was transferred from—"

"You are the party of record. If there has been criminal activity here—and I am increasingly confident there has been—your name will be on the affidavit. Now, are you going to step aside or do I have to add impeding an active investigation to the list of potential charges?"

There was a brief moment of stasis. Then Bona stepped unwillingly to one side. Pendergast brushed past, cradling the tarp-covered crate, and D'Agosta followed quickly behind.

"We must hurry," Pendergast said under his breath as they charged out the door. Already, the manager was making his way down into the basement, punching a number into a cell phone as he went.

They ran down the street to the Rolls. Pendergast opened the trunk, and they put the crate inside, wrapped in its protective tarp. The hard hats followed, along with D'Agosta's workbag. They slammed the trunk and climbed hurriedly into the front seat, Pendergast not even bothering to remove his tool belt.

As Pendergast started the car, D'Agosta saw the manager emerging from the doughnut shop. The cell phone was still clamped in one hand. "Hey!" they heard him yelling from a block away. "Hey, you! Stop!"

Pendergast put the car in gear and jammed on the accelerator. The Rolls shrieked through a U-turn and tore down the road in the direction of Court Street and the freeway.

He glanced over at D'Agosta. "Well done, my dear Vincent." And this time, his smile wasn't ghostly—it was genuine.

37

They turned onto Alexander Drive, then took the on-ramp to I-10 and the Horace Wilkinson Bridge. D'Agosta sank back gratefully in his seat. The broad Mississippi rolled by beneath them, sullen-looking below the leaden sky.

"You think that's it?" D'Agosta asked. "The Black Frame?"

"Absolutely."

From the bridge, they crossed into Baton Rouge proper. It was midafternoon, and the traffic was moderate. Curtains of rain beat against the windshield and drummed on the vehicle roof. One after another the southbound cars fell smoothly behind them. They passed the I-12 interchange as D'Agosta stirred restlessly. He didn't want to get his hopes up. But maybe—just maybe—this meant he'd be seeing Laura Hayward sooner rather than later. He hadn't realized just how difficult this forced separation would be. Speaking to her every night helped, of course, but it was no substitute for…

"Vincent," Pendergast said. "Take a look in the rearview mirror, if you please."

D'Agosta complied. At first, he saw nothing unusual in the procession of cars behind them. But then, when Pendergast changed lanes, he saw another car—four, maybe five back—do the same. It was a late-model sedan, dark blue or black; it was hard to tell in the rain.

Pendergast accelerated slightly, passed a few cars, then returned to his original lane. A minute or two later, the dark sedan did the same.

"I see him," D'Agosta muttered.

They continued for several minutes. The car stayed with them, hanging back, careful not to be too obvious.

"You think that's the manager?" D'Agosta asked. "Bona?"

Pendergast shook his head. "That fellow behind us has been tailing us since this morning."

"What are we going to do?"

"I'm going to wait until we reach the outskirts of the city. Then, we shall see. Local roads might prove useful."

They passed the Mall of Louisiana, several parks and country clubs. The cityscape gave way to suburban sprawl, and then ultimately to patches of rural lowlands. D'Agosta drew out his Glock, racked a round into the chamber.

"Save that for a last resort," Pendergast said. "We can't risk damage to the painting."

What about damage to us? D'Agosta thought. He glanced in the rearview mirror, but it was impossible to see into the dark sedan. They were passing the Sorrento exit, the traffic thinning still further.

"Are we going to box him in?" D'Agosta said. "Force his hand?"

"My preference is to lose him," Pendergast said. "You'd be surprised what a vintage Rolls is capable of."

"Yeah, right—"

Pendergast floored the accelerator and turned the wheel sharply right. The Rolls shot forward, remarkably responsive for such a large vehicle, then sliced across two lanes of traffic and careered down the exit ramp without reducing speed.

D'Agosta lurched heavily into the passenger door. Glancing into the mirror again, he saw that their tail had followed suit and, cutting before a box truck, was now shooting down the ramp after them.

Reaching the bottom of the ramp, Pendergast blew past the stop sign and onto Route 22, tires squealing as the rear of the vehicle fishtailed through a one-hundred-twenty-degree arc. Expertly turning into the spin, Pendergast maneuvered into the proper lane and then stamped on the gas again. They tore down the state road, blowing past a painter's van, a Buick, and a crawfish transport truck. Angry horns sounded behind them.

D'Agosta glanced over his shoulder. The sedan was pacing them, abandoning any effort at concealment.

"He's still coming," he said.

Pendergast nodded.

Accelerating further, they sped through a small commercial area—three blocks of farm implement stores and hardware shops, moving past in a blur. Up ahead, a set of lights marked the intersection of Route 22 with the Airline Highway. Several vehicles were moving across it now, brake lights rippling in a serried stream. They shot over a railroad track, the Rolls briefly airborne at the rise, and neared the crossing. As they did so, the light turned yellow, then red.

"Christ," murmured D'Agosta, taking a tight grip on the handle of the passenger door.

Flashing his lights and leaning on the horn, Pendergast found a lane between the cars ahead and the oncoming traffic. A fresh volley of honks sounded as they hurtled through the rain-slick crossing, barely missing an eighteen-wheeler that was nosing into the intersection. Pendergast had not taken his foot from the accelerator, and the needle was now trembling past one hundred.

"Maybe we should just stop and confront the guy," said D'Agosta. "Ask him who he's working for."

"How dull. And we know who he's working for."

They whipped past one car, then another and another, the vehicles merely blurs of stationary color on the road. Now the traffic was all behind them and the road ahead was empty. Houses, commercial buildings, and the occasional sad-looking feed or supply store fell away as they entered the swamplands. A stand of crape trees, bleak sentinels under the gunmetal sky, whisked past in an instant. The windshield wipers beat their regular cadence against the glass. D'Agosta allowed his grip on the door handle to relax somewhat.

He glanced over his shoulder again. All clear.

No—no, it wasn't. From among the vague outlines of vehicles behind them, a single shape resolved itself. It was the dark sedan, far behind but coming up fast.

"Shit," D'Agosta said. "He got through that intersection. Tenacious bastard."

"We have what he wants," Pendergast said. "Another reason we mustn't let him catch up to us."

The road narrowed as they plunged deeper into the marshy lowlands. D'Agosta kept his gaze rearward while they negotiated a long, screaming turn. As the sedan dropped out of sight behind the curve and tall marsh grass, he felt the car decelerate.

"Now's our chance to—" he began.

All of a sudden the Rolls swerved violently to one side. Tumbled almost into the back of the car, D'Agosta fought to reseat himself. They had veered off the road onto a narrow dirt track that snaked into thick swamp. A dirty, dented sign read DESMIRAIL WILDLIFE AREA— SERVICE VEHICLES ONLY.

The car bucked fiercely from side to side as they tore down the muddy track. One moment D'Agosta felt himself thrown against the door; the next he was lifted bodily out of his seat, prevented from concussing himself against the roof only by the shoulder strap. *Another minute of this*, he thought grimly, *and we'll break both axles.* He ventured another look in the rearview mirror, but the path was too sinuous to see more than a hundred yards behind them.

Ahead, the service path narrowed and forked. A much narrower and rougher footpath diverged from it and ran straight ahead alongside a bayou, a chain of steel links stretched across it, marked by the sign WARN- ING: NO VEHICLES PAST THIS POINT.

Instead of slowing for the turn, Pendergast goosed the accelerator.

"Hey, whoa!" D'Agosta cried as they headed straight for the footpath. "Jesus—!"

They broke through the chain with a sound like a rifle shot. A profusion of egrets, vultures, and wood ducks rose from the surrounding yellowtop fields and bald cypresses, honking and shrieking in protest. The big car lurched left, then right, again and again, blurring D'Agosta's vision and making his teeth rattle in his skull. They plunged into a stand of umbrella grass, the big stems parting before them with a strange *whack, whack*.

D'Agosta had been in some hair-raising car chases in his day, but nothing like this. The swamp grass had grown so thick and tall they could see only a few car lengths ahead of them. Yet instead of reducing speed, Pendergast reached over and—still without decelerating—switched on the headlights.

D'Agosta hung on for dear life, afraid to tear his eyes from the view ahead even for a second. "Pendergast, slow down!" he yelled. "We've lost him! For chrissakes, *slow—*"

And then, quite suddenly, they were out of the grass. The car went over a rise of earth and they sailed, quite literally, into an open area on some high ground cut out of the deep swamp, a few gray outbuildings and fenced areas surrounded by pools. Only now, with the increased visibility and landmarks for orientation, did D'Agosta realize just how fast they'd been going. A large weather-beaten billboard to one side read:

GATORVILLE U.S.A.
100% farm-raised organic gators
Gator wrasslin, guided tours
Tannery on site—skins 8 feet & up, low low prices!
Gator meat by the pound
* CLOSED FOR THE SEASON *

The Rolls impacted the ground, bottoming out with a jarring force and hurtling forward; Pendergast suddenly braked, the car skidding across the dirt yard. D'Agosta's eyes swiveled from the sign to a rickety wooden building directly ahead, roofed in corrugated tin, its barn-like doors open. A sign in one window read PROCESSING PLANT. He realized there was no way they could stop in time.

The Rolls slewed into the barn; a violent deceleration and semi-crash followed that smacked D'Agosta back against the leather seats; and then they were at rest. A huge cloud of dust rolled over them. As his vision slowly cleared, he saw the Rolls had ploughed into a stack of oversize plastic meat containers, tearing a dozen of them wide open. Three brined, skinned alligator corpses were splayed across the hood and windshield, pale pink with long streaks of whitish fat.

There was a moment of peculiar stasis. Pendergast gazed out of the windshield—covered with rain, bits of swamp grass, Spanish moss, and reptile ordure—and then looked over at D'Agosta. "That reminds me," he said as the engine hissed and ticked. "One of these evenings we really must ask Maurice to make his alligator étouffée. His people come from the Atchafalaya Basin, you understand, and he has a wonderful recipe handed down in the family."

38

Sarasota, Florida

The sky began to clear with the coming of evening, and soon glimmers of moonlight lay coquettishly upon the Gulf of Mexico, hiding between the restless rolls of incoming waves. Clouds, still swollen with rain, passed by quickly overhead. Combers of surf fell ceaselessly upon the beach, falling back in long, withdrawing roars.

John Woodhouse Blast heeded none of it. He paced back and forth, restlessly, stopping now and then to check his watch.

Ten thirty already. What was the holdup? It should have been a simple job: get in, take care of business, get out. The earlier call had implied things were on track, even ahead of schedule—more, in fact, than he'd dared to expect. But that had been six hours ago. And now, with his hopes raised, the wait seemed even more excruciating.

He walked over to the wet bar, pawed down a crystal tumbler from its shelf, threw in a handful of ice cubes, and poured several fingers of scotch over them. He took a big gulp; exhaled; took a smaller, more measured sip. Then he walked over to his white leather sofa, put the glass onto an abalone coaster, prepared to sit down.

The sudden ringing of the phone broke the listening silence, and he started violently. He wheeled toward the sound, almost knocking over the drink in his eagerness, and grabbed the handset.

"Well?" he said, his voice high and breathless in his own ears. "Is it done?"

There was nothing but silence on the other end.

"Hello? You got shit in your ears, pal? I said, *is it done?*"

More silence. And then the line went dead.

Blast stared at the phone. Just what the hell was this? A hardball play for more money? Well, he knew how to play that game. Any wise guy trying to bend his ass over a barrel was going to wish he'd never been born.

He sat down on the sofa and took another drink. The greedy son of a bitch was waiting at the other end of the line, of course he was, just waiting for him to call back and offer more. Hell would freeze over first. Blast knew what jobs like these cost—and what's more, he knew how to hire *other* muscle, more experienced muscle, if certain sticky wheels needed regreasing...

The doorbell rang.

Blast allowed a smile to form on his face. He glanced at his watch again: two minutes. Only two minutes had passed since the phone call. So the son of a bitch wanted to talk. Thought he was a real wise guy. He took another sip of his drink, settled back into the couch.

The doorbell rang again.

Blast put the drink slowly back on the coaster. It was the son of a bitch's turn to sweat now. Maybe he could even get the price down a little. It had happened before.

The doorbell rang a third time. And now Blast pulled himself up, drew a finger across his narrow mustache, strode to the door, threw it open.

He stepped back quickly in surprise. Standing in the doorway was not the slimy son of a bitch he'd expected, but a tall man with dark eyes and movie-star looks. He wore a long black trench coat, its belt tied loosely around his waist. Blast realized he had made a serious mistake in opening the door. But before he could slam it shut, the man had stepped in and shut it himself.

"Mr. Blast?" he said.

"Who the hell are you?" Blast replied.

Instead of answering, the man stepped forward again. The movement was so sudden, so decisive, that Blast found himself forced to take another step backward. Whimpering, the Pomeranians ran for the safety of the bedroom.

The tall man looked him up and down, his eyes glittering with some strong emotion—anxiety? Rage?

Blast swallowed. He hadn't the faintest idea what this man wanted, but some inner sense of self-preservation, some sixth sense he'd gained operating for years on the narrowest edge of lawfulness, told him he was in danger.

"What do you want?" he asked.

"My name is Esterhazy," the man replied. "Does the name ring a bell?"

The name did ring a bell. A loud bell. That man Pendergast had mentioned it. Helen *Esterhazy* Pendergast.

"Never heard of it."

With a sudden movement, the man named Esterhazy jerked the belt of his trench coat free. The coat fell aside, revealing a sawed-off shotgun.

Blast fell back. Time slowed as adrenaline kicked in. He noticed, with a kind of horrifying clarity, that the butt-stock was black wood, ornately carved.

"Now, wait," he said. "Look, whatever it is, we can work it out. I'm a reasonable man. Tell me what you want."

"My sister. What did you do to her?"

"Nothing. Nothing. We just talked."

"Talked." The man smiled. "What did you talk about?"

"Nothing. Nothing important. Did that fellow Pendergast send you? I already told him all I know."

"And what *do* you know?"

"All she wanted to do was look at the painting. The Black Frame, I mean. She had a theory, she said."

"A theory?"

"I can't remember. Really, I can't. It was so long ago. Please believe me."

"No, I want to hear about the theory."

"I'd tell you if I could remember."

"Are you sure you don't recall anything more?"

"That's all I can remember. I *swear*, that's all."

"Thank you." With an ear-shattering roar, one of the barrels vomited smoke and flame. Blast felt himself physically lifted from the ground and thrown back, hitting the floor with a violent crash. A numbness crept across his chest, remarkable in the lack of pain, and for a moment he had a crazy hope the charge had missed... And then he looked down at his ruined chest.

As if from far away, he saw the man—now a little shadowy and indistinct—approach and stand over him. The snout-like shape of the shotgun barrels detached themselves from the form and hovered over his head. Blast tried to protest, but there was now another warmth, oddly comforting, filling his throat and he couldn't vocalize...

And then came another terrible confusion of flame and noise that this time brought oblivion.

39

New York City

It was seven fifteen in the morning, but already the Fifteenth homicide division was hard at work, logging in the several potential murders and manslaughters of the night before and assembling in breakout areas to discuss the progress of open cases. Captain Laura Hayward sat behind her desk, finishing an unusually comprehensive monthly report for the commissioner. The poor fellow was new on the job—having been hired up from Texas—and Hayward knew he would appreciate a bit of bureaucratic hand-holding.

She finished the report, saved it, then took a sip of her coffee. It was barely tepid: she had already been in the office more than an hour. As she put down the cup, her cell phone rang. It was her personal phone, not her official one, and only four people knew the number: her mother, her sister, her family lawyer—and Vincent D'Agosta.

She pulled the phone from her jacket pocket and looked at it. A stickler for protocol, she normally wouldn't answer it during working hours. This time, however, she closed the door to her office and flipped the phone open.

"Hello?" she spoke into it.

"Laura," came D'Agosta's voice. "It's me."

"Vinnie. Is everything okay? I was a little concerned when you didn't call last night."

"Everything's okay, and I'm sorry about that. It's just that things got a little...hectic."

She sat back down behind her desk. "Tell me about it."

There was a pause. "Well, we found the Black Frame."

"The painting you've been looking for?"

"Yes. At least, I think we did."

He didn't sound very excited about it. If anything, he sounded irritated. "How'd you find it?"

"It was hidden behind the basement wall of a doughnut shop, if you can believe it."

"So how did you get it?"

Another pause. "We, ah, broke in."

"Broke in?"

"Yeah."

Warning bells began to ring. "What'd you do, sneak in after hours?"

"No. We did it yesterday afternoon."

"Go on."

"Pendergast planned it. We went in pretending to be building code inspectors, and Pendergast—"

"I've changed my mind. I don't want to hear anything more about that. Skip to *after* you got the painting."

"Well, that's why I couldn't call like I normally do.

As we left Baton Rouge, we noticed we were being followed. We had quite a chase through the swamps and bayous of—"

"Whoa, Vinnie! Stop a moment. Please." This was exactly what she'd been afraid of. "I thought you promised me you'd take care of yourself, not get sucked into Pendergast's extracurricular crap."

"I know that, Laura. I haven't forgotten it." Another pause. "Once I knew we were close to the painting, *really* close, I felt like I'd do almost anything—if it helped solve the mystery, to get back to you."

She sighed, shook her head. "What happened next?"

"We shook the tail. It was midnight before we finally returned to Penumbra. We carried the wooden box we'd retrieved into the library and set it on a table. Pendergast was unbelievably fussy about it. Instead of opening the damn crate with a crowbar, we had to use these tiny tools that would have made a jeweler cross-eyed. It took hours. The painting must have been exposed to damp at some point, because its back was stuck to the wood, and that took even longer to tease loose."

"But it was the Black Frame?"

"It was *in* a black frame, all right. But the canvas was covered with mold and so dirty you couldn't make anything out. Pendergast got some swabs and brushes and a bunch of solvents and cleaning agents and began to remove the dirt—wouldn't let me touch it. After maybe fifteen minutes he got a small section of the painting clean, and then..."

"What?"

"The guy just suddenly went rigid. Before I knew it, he bundled me out of the library and locked the door."

"Just like that?"

"Just like that. I was standing there in the hallway. Never even got a glimpse of the painting."

"I keep telling you, the guy's not all there."

"I admit, he has his ways. This was about three in the morning so I thought, the hell with it, and crashed. Next thing I knew, it was morning. He's still in there, working away."

Hayward felt herself doing a slow burn. "Typical Pendergast. Vinnie, he's not your pal."

She heard D'Agosta sigh. "I've been reminding myself that it's his wife's death we're investigating here, that this all must be a huge shock to him...And he is my friend, even if he shows it in weird ways." He paused. "Anything new on Constance Greene?"

"She's under lock and key in the Bellevue Hospital prison ward. I interviewed her. She still maintains she threw her baby overboard."

"Did she say why?"

"Yes. She said it was evil. Just like its father."

"Jesus. I knew she was crazy, but not that crazy."

"How did Pendergast take the news?"

"Hard to tell—like everything with Pendergast. On the surface, it barely seemed to affect him."

There was a brief silence. Hayward wondered if she should try to pressure him to come home, but she realized she didn't want to add to his burdens.

"There's something else," D'Agosta said.

"What's that?"

"Remember the guy I told you about—Blackletter? Helen Pendergast's old boss at Doctors With Wings?"

"What about him?"

"He was murdered in his house the night before last. Two 12-gauge shells, point blank, blew his guts right through him."

"Good Lord."

"And that's not all. John Blast, the slimy guy we talked to in Sarasota? The other one interested in the Black Frame? I'd assumed he was the one tailing us. But I just heard it on the news—he was shot, too, just yesterday, not long after we snagged the painting. And guess what: once again, two 12-gauge rounds."

"Any idea what's going on?"

"When I heard about Blackletter being shot, I figured Blast was behind it. But now Blast's dead, too."

"You can thank Pendergast for that. Where he goes, trouble follows."

"Hold on a sec." There was a silence of perhaps twenty seconds before D'Agosta's voice returned. "That's Pendergast. He just knocked on my door. He says the painting is clean, and he wants my opinion. I love you, Laura. I'll call tonight."

And he was gone.

40

Penumbra Plantation

When D'Agosta opened the door, Pendergast was standing outside in the plushly carpeted corridor, hands behind his back. He was still dressed in the plaid work shirt and denim trousers of their foray to Port Allen.

"I'm very sorry, Vincent," he said. "Please forgive what must seem to you like the very height of rudeness and inconsideration on my part."

D'Agosta did not reply.

"Perhaps things will become clearer when you see the painting. If you don't mind—?" And he gestured toward the stairway.

D'Agosta stepped out and followed the agent down the hall toward the stairs. "Blast is dead," he said. "Shot with the same sort of weapon that killed Blackletter."

Pendergast paused in midstep. "Shot, you say?" Then he resumed walking—a little more slowly.

The library door stood open, yellow light from within

spilling out into the front hall. Silently, Pendergast led the way down the stairs and through the arched doorway. The painting stood in the center of the room, on an easel. It was covered with a heavy velvet shroud.

"Stand over there, in front of the painting," said Pendergast. "I need your candid reaction."

D'Agosta stood directly before it.

Pendergast stepped to one side, took hold of the shroud, and lifted it from the painting.

D'Agosta stared, flabbergasted. The painting was not of a Carolina Parakeet, or even of a bird or nature subject. Instead, it depicted a middle-aged woman, nude, gaunt, lying on a hospital bed. A shaft of cool light slanted in from a tiny window high up in the wall behind her. Her legs were crossed at the ankles, and her hands were folded over her breasts, almost in the attitude of a corpse. The outlines of her ribs protruded through skin the color of parchment, and she was clearly ill and, perhaps, not entirely sane. And yet there was something repugnantly inviting about her. A small deal table holding a water pitcher and some dressings sat beside the bed. Her black hair spread across a pillow of coarse linen. The painted plaster walls; the slack, dry flesh; the weave of the bed linens; even the motes in the dusty air were meticulously observed, rendered with pitiless clarity and confidence—spare, stark, and elegiac. Although D'Agosta was no expert, the painting struck him with an enormous visceral impact.

"Vincent?" Pendergast asked him quietly.

D'Agosta reached out, let the fingertips of one hand slide along the painting's black frame. "I don't know what to think," he said.

"Indeed." Pendergast hesitated. "When I began to clean the painting, *that* is the first thing that came to light." And he pointed at the woman's eyes, staring out of the plane of the painting toward the viewer. "After seeing that, I realized all our assumptions were wrong. I needed time, alone, to clean the rest of it. I didn't want you to see it exposed bit by bit: I wanted you to see the entire painting, all at once. I needed a fresh, immediate opinion. That is why I excluded you so abruptly. Once again, my apologies."

"It's amazing. But...are you sure it's even by Audubon?"

Pendergast pointed to one corner, where D'Agosta could just see a dim signature. Then he pointed silently to another, dark corner of the painted room—where a mouse was crouching, as if waiting. "The signature is genuine, but more to the point, nobody but Audubon could have painted that mouse. And I'm certain it was painted from life—at the sanatorium. It's too beautifully observed to be anything but real."

D'Agosta nodded slowly. "I thought for sure it was going to be a Carolina Parrot. What does a naked woman have to do with anything?"

Pendergast merely opened his white hands in a gesture of mystery, and D'Agosta could see the frustration in his eyes. Turning away from the easel, the agent said, "Glance over these, Vincent, if you please." A refectory table nearby was spread with a variety of prints, lithographs, and watercolors. On the left side were arranged various sketches of animals, birds, insects, still lifes, quick portraits of people. Lying on top was a watercolor of a mouse.

A gap separated the drawings laid out on the right side. They were a different matter entirely. These consisted almost entirely of birds, so life-like and detailed they seemed ready to strut off the paper, but there were also some mammals and woodland scenes.

"Do you note a difference?"

"Sure. The stuff on the left sucks. On the right—well, it's just beautiful."

"I took these from my great-great-grandfather's portfolios," Pendergast said. "These"—he gestured to the rude sketches on the left—"were given to my ancestor by Audubon when he was staying at the Dauphine Street cottage in 1821, just before he got sick. That is how Audubon painted before he entered the Meuse St. Claire sanatorium." He turned to the work that lay to the right. "And *this* is how he painted later in life. After he left the sanatorium. Do you see the conundrum?"

D'Agosta was still stunned by the image within the black frame. "He improved," he said. "That's what artists do. Why's that a conundrum?"

Pendergast shook his head. "Improved? No, Vincent, this is a *transformation*. Nobody improves that much. These early sketches are poor. They are workman-like, literal, awkward. There is nothing there, Vincent, *nothing* to indicate the slightest spark of artistic talent."

D'Agosta had to agree. "What happened?"

Pendergast raked the artwork with his pale eyes, then slowly walked back to an armchair he'd placed before the easel and sat down before the Black Frame. "This woman was clearly a patient at the sanatorium. Perhaps Dr. Torgensson grew enamored of her. Perhaps they had a relationship of some kind. That would explain why he clung to the painting so anxiously, even when sunk into deepest poverty. But that *still* doesn't explain why Helen would be so desperately interested in it."

D'Agosta glanced back at the woman, reclining—in an attitude almost of resignation—on the plain infirmary bed. "Do you suppose she might have been an ancestor of Helen's?" he asked. "An Esterhazy?"

"I thought of that," Pendergast replied. "But then, why her obsessive search?"

"Her family left Maine under a cloud," D'Agosta said. "Maybe there was some blemish in their family history this painting could help clear up."

"Yes, but what?" Pendergast gestured at the figure. "I would think such a controversial image would tarnish, rather than polish, the family name. At least we can now speculate why the subject of the painting was never mentioned in print—it is so very disturbing and provocative."

There was a brief silence.

"Why would Blast have wanted it so badly?" D'Agosta wondered aloud. "I mean, it's just a painting. Why search for so many years?"

"That, at any rate, is easily answered. He was an Audubon, he considered it his birthright. For him it became an idée fixe—in time, the chase became its own reward. I expect he would have been as astonished as we are at the subject." Pendergast tented his fingers, pressed them against his forehead.

Still, D'Agosta stared at the painting. There was something, a thought that wouldn't quite rise into consciousness. The painting was trying to tell him something. He stared at it.

Then, all of a sudden, he realized what it was.

"This painting," he said. "Look at it. It's like those watercolors on the table. The ones he did later in life."

Pendergast did not look up. "I'm afraid I don't follow you."

"You said it yourself. The mouse in the painting—it's clearly an Audubon mouse."

"Yes, very similar to the ones he painted in *Viviparous Quadrupeds of North America*."

"Okay. Now look at that mouse on that pile of early drawings."

Slowly, Pendergast raised his head. He looked at the painting and then the drawings. He glanced toward D'Agosta. "Your point, Vincent?"

D'Agosta gestured toward the refectory table. "That early mouse. I'd never have thought Audubon drew it. Same for all that early stuff, those still lifes and sketches. I'd *never* have thought those were by Audubon."

"That's precisely what I said earlier. Therein lies the conundrum."

"But I'm not so sure it's a problem."

Pendergast looked at him, curiosity kindling in his eyes. "Go on."

"Well, we have those early, mediocre sketches. And then we have this woman. What happened in between?"

The glimmer in Pendergast's eyes grew brighter. "The *illness* happened."

D'Agosta nodded. "Right. The illness changed him. What other answer is there?"

"Brilliant, my dear Vincent!" Pendergast smacked the arms of his chair and leapt to his feet, pacing about the room. "The brush with death, the sudden encounter with his own mortality, somehow changed him. It filled him with creative energy, it was the transformative moment of his artistic career."

"We'd always assumed Helen was interested in the *subject* of the painting," D'Agosta said.

"Precisely. But remember what Blast said? Helen didn't want to own the painting. She only wanted to *study* it. She wanted to confirm *when Audubon's artistic transformation took place.*" Pendergast fell silent and his pacing slowed and finally halted. He seemed stuck in a kind of stasis, his eyes turned within.

"Well," said D'Agosta. "Mystery solved."

The silvery eyes turned on him. "No."

"What do you mean?"

"Why would Helen hide all this from me?"

D'Agosta shrugged. "Maybe she was embarrassed by the way you met and the little white lie she told about it."

"One little white lie? I don't believe that. She kept this hidden for a far more significant reason than that." Pendergast sank back into the plush chair and stared at the painting again. "Cover it up."

D'Agosta draped the cloth over it. He was beginning to get worried. Pendergast did not look completely sane himself.

Pendergast's eyes closed. The silence in the library grew, along with the ticking of a grandfather clock in the corner. D'Agosta took a seat himself; sometimes it was best to let Pendergast be Pendergast.

The eyes slowly opened.

"We've been looking at this problem in entirely the wrong way from the very beginning."

"And how is that?"

"We've assumed Helen was interested in Audubon, the artist."

"Well? What else?"

"She was interested in Audubon, the *patient*."

"Patient?"

A slow nod. "That was Helen's passion. Medical research."

"Then why search for the painting?"

"Because he painted it right after his recovery. She wanted to confirm a theory she had."

"And what theory is that?"

"My dear Vincent, do we know what illness Audubon actually suffered from?"

"No."

"Correct. But that illness is the key to everything! It was the *illness* itself she wanted to know about. What it did to Audubon. Because it seems to have transformed a thoroughly mediocre artist into a genius. She knew something had changed him—that's why she went to New Madrid, where he'd experienced the earthquake: she was searching, far and wide, to understand that agent of change. And when she hit upon his illness, she knew her search was complete. She wanted to see the painting only to confirm her theory: that Audubon's illness did something to his mind. It had *neurological* effects. Marvelous neurological effects!"

"Whoa, you're losing me here."

Pendergast sprang to his feet. "And *that* is why she hid it from me. Because it was potentially an extremely valuable, proprietary pharmacological discovery. It had nothing to do with our personal relationship." With a sudden, impulsive movement he grasped D'Agosta by both arms. "And I would still be stumbling around in the dark, my dear Vincent—if not for your stroke of genius."

"Well, I wouldn't go so far as to say—"

Releasing his hold, Pendergast turned away and strode quickly toward the library door. "Come on— there's no time to lose."

"Where are we going?" D'Agosta asked, hurrying to follow, his mind still in a whirl of confusion, trying to piece together Pendergast's chain of logic.

"To confirm your suspicions—and to learn, once and for all, what it all must mean."

41

The shooter shifted position in the dappled shade, took a swig of water from the camouflaged canteen. He dabbed the sweatband around his wrist against each temple in turn. His movements were slow, methodical, completely hidden in the labyrinth of brush.

It wasn't really necessary to be so careful. There was no way the target would ever see him. However, years of hunting the other kind of prey—the four-legged variety, sometimes timid, sometimes preternaturally alert—had taught him to use exquisite caution.

It was a perfect blind, a large deadfall of oak, Spanish moss thrown across its face like spindrift, leaving only a few tiny chinks, through one of which he had poked the barrel of his Remington 40-XS tactical rifle. It was perfect because it was, in fact, natural: one of the results of Katrina still visible everywhere in the surrounding forests and swamps. You saw so many that you stopped noticing them.

That's what the shooter was counting on.

The barrel of his weapon protruded no more than an inch beyond the blind. He was in full shade, the barrel itself was sheathed in a special black nonreflective polymer, and his target would emerge into the glare of the morning sun. The gun would never be spotted even when fired: the flash hider on the muzzle would ensure that.

His vehicle, a rented Nissan four-by-four pickup with a covered bed, had been backed up to the blind; he was using the bed as a shooting platform, lying inside it with the tailgate down. The nose pointed down an old logging trail running east. Even if someone saw him and gave chase, it would be the work of thirty seconds to slide from the truck bed into the cab, start the engine, and accelerate down the trail. The highway, and safety, were just two miles away.

He wasn't sure how long he would have to wait—it could be ten minutes, it could be ten hours—but that didn't matter. He was motivated. Motivated, in fact, like he'd never been in his life. No, that wasn't quite true: there had been one other time.

The morning was hazy and dew-heavy, and in the darkness of the blind the air felt sluggish and dead. So much the better. He dabbed at his temples again. Insects droned sleepily, and he could hear the fretful squeaking and chattering of voles. They must have a nest nearby: it seemed the damn things were everywhere in the lowland swamps these days, ravenous as lab rabbits and almost as tame.

He took another swig of water, did another check of the 40-XS. The bipod was securely placed and locked. He eased the bolt open; made sure the .308 Winchester was seated well; snicked the bolt home again. Like most dedicated marksmen, he preferred the stability and accuracy of a bolt-action weapon; he had three extra rounds in the internal magazine, just in case, but the point of a Sniper Weapon System was to make the first shot count and he didn't plan on having to use them.

Most important was the Leupold Mark 4 long-range M1 scope. He looked through it now, targeting the dot reticule first on the front door of the plantation house, then the graveled path, then the Rolls-Royce itself.

Seven hundred, maybe seven hundred fifty yards. One shot, one kill.

As he stared at the big vehicle, he felt his heart accelerate slightly. He went over the plan once again in his mind. He'd wait until the target was behind the wheel, the engine started. The automobile would roll forward along the semicircular drive, pausing a moment before turning onto the main carriage road. That's where he would take the shot.

He lay absolutely still, willing his heart to slow once again. He could not allow himself to grow excited, or for that matter allow any emotion—impatience, anger, fear—to distract him. Utter calm was the answer. It had served him well before, in the veldt and the long grass, in circumstances more dangerous than these. He kept his eye glued to the scope, his finger resting lightly on the trigger guard. Once again, he reminded himself this was an assignment. That was the best way to look at it. Get this last job out of the way and he'd be done— and this time, once and for all...

As if to reward his self-discipline, the front door of the plantation house opened and a man stepped out.

He caught his breath. It was not his target, it was the other, the cop. Slowly—so slowly it seemed not to move—his finger drifted from the trigger guard to the trigger itself, its pull weight feather-light. The stocky man paused on the wide porch, looking around a little guardedly. The shooter did not flinch: he knew his cover was perfect. Now his target emerged from the gloom of the house, and together the two walked along the porch and down the steps to the gravel drive. The shooter followed them with the scope, the bead of his reticule centered on the target's skull. He willed himself not to shoot prematurely: he had a good plan, he should stick with it. The two were moving quickly, in a hurry to get somewhere. *Stick with the plan.*

Through the crosshairs of the scope, he watched as they approached the car, opened its doors, got in. The target seated himself behind the wheel, as expected; started the engine; turned to say a few words to his companion; then eased the car out into the drive. The shooter watched intently, letting his breath run out, willing his heart to slow still further. He would take the shot between its beats.

The Rolls took the gentle curve of the gravel drive at about fifteen miles per hour, then slowed as it approached the intersection with the carriage road. *This is it*, the shooter thought. All the preparation, discipline, and past experience fused together into this single moment of consummation. The target was in position. Ever so slightly, he applied pressure to the trigger: not squeezing it, but caressing it, more, a little more...

That was when—with a squeak of surprise followed

by a violent scrabbling—a gray-brown vole darted over the knuckles of his trigger hand. At the same time, a large ragged shadow, black against black, seemed to flit quickly over his blind.

The Remington went off with a bang, kicking slightly in his grasp. With a curse he brushed the scampering vole away and peered quickly through the scope, working the bolt as he did so. He could see the hole in the windshield, about six inches above and to the left of where he'd planned it. The Rolls was moving ahead fast now, escaping, the tires spinning as it sheared through the turn, gravel flying up behind in a storm of white, and being careful not to panic the shooter led it with his scope, waited for the heartbeat, once again applied pressure to the trigger.

. . . But even as he did so he saw furious activity inside the vehicle: the stocky man was darting forward, lunging for the wheel, filling the windshield with his bulk. At the same moment the rifle fired again. The Rolls slewed to a stop at a strange angle, cutting across the carriage path. A triangular corona of blood now covered the inside of the windshield, obscuring the view within.

Whom had he hit?

Even as he stared he saw a puff of smoke from the vehicle, followed by the crack of a gunshot. A millisecond later, a bullet snipped through the brush not three feet from where he was hidden. A second shot, and this one struck the Nissan with a clang of metal.

Instantly, the shooter kicked backward, tumbling from the truck bed and into the cab. As another bullet whined past, he started the engine and threw the rifle onto the passenger seat, where it fell atop another weapon: a shotgun, its double barrels sawn off short, sporting an ornately carved stock of black wood. With a grinding of gears and a screech of tires, he took off down the old logging path, trailing Spanish moss and dust.

He took one turn, then another, accelerating past sixty despite the washboard condition of the track. The weapons slid toward him and he pushed them back, throwing a red blanket over them. Another turn, another screech of tires, and he could see the state highway ahead of him. Only now, with safety clearly in sight, did he allow the frustration and disappointment to burst from him.

"*Damn* it!" Judson Esterhazy cried, slamming his fist against the dashboard again and again. "Goddamn it to hell!"

42

New York City

Dr. John Felder walked down the long, cool corridor in the secure ward at Bellevue, flanked by an escorting guard. Small, slender, and elegant, Felder was acutely aware of how much he stuck out in the general squalor and controlled chaos of the ward. This was his second interview with the patient. In the first he had covered all the usual bases, asked all the obligatory questions, taken all the proper notes. He had done enough to satisfy his legal responsibilities as a court-appointed psychiatrist and render an opinion. He had, in fact, reached a firm conclusion: the woman was incapable of distinguishing between right and wrong, and therefore not liable for her actions.

But he was still deeply unsatisfied. He had been involved in many unusual cases. He had seen things that very few doctors had seen; he had examined extraordinary presentations of criminal pathology. But he had never before seen anything quite like this. For perhaps the first time in his professional career, he felt he had not touched on the core mystery of this patient's psyche—not in the least.

Normally, that would make little difference in a bureaucracy such as this. Technically, his work was done. But still he had withheld his conclusion pending further evaluation, giving him the opportunity for another interview. And this time, he decided, he wanted to have a conversation. Just a normal conversation between two people—nothing more, nothing less.

He turned a corner, continued making his way down the endless corridors. The noises, the cries, the smells and sounds of the secure ward barely penetrated his consciousness as he mulled over the mysteries of the case. There was, first, the question of the young woman's identity. Despite a diligent search, court administrators had been unable to find a birth certificate, Social Security number, or any other documentary evidence of her existence beyond a few genteel and intentionally vague records from the Feversham Institute in Putnam County. The British passport found in her possession was real enough, but it had been obtained through an exceedingly clever fraud perpetrated on a minor British consular official in Boston. It was as if she had appeared on the earth fully formed, like Athena sprung from the forehead of Zeus.

As his footsteps echoed down the long corridors, Felder tried not to think too much about what he would ask. Where formal questioning had not penetrated her opacity, spontaneous conversation might.

He turned a last corner, arrived at the meeting room.

A guard on duty unlocked the gray metal door with a porthole window and ushered him into a small, spare, but not entirely unpleasant room with several chairs, a coffee table, some magazines, a lamp, and a one-way mirror covering a wall. The patient was already seated, next to a police officer. They both rose when he entered.

"Good afternoon, Constance," said Felder crisply. "Officer, you may remove her handcuffs, please."

"I'll need the release, Doctor."

Felder seated himself, opened his briefcase, removed the release, and handed it to the officer. The man looked it over, grunted his assent, then rose and removed the prisoner's handcuffs, hooking them to his belt.

"I'll be outside if you need me. Just press the button."

"Thank you."

The cop left and Felder turned his attention to the patient, Constance Greene. She stood primly before him, hands clasped in front, wearing a plain prison jumpsuit. He was struck again by her poise and striking looks.

"Constance, how are you? Please sit down."

She seated herself. "I'm very well, Doctor. How are you?"

"Fine." He smiled, leaning back and crossing one leg over the other. "I'm glad we've had a chance for another chat. There were just a few things I wanted to talk with you about. Nothing for the record, really. Is it all right if we speak for a few minutes?"

"Certainly."

"Very good. I hope I don't seem too curious. Perhaps you could call it a liability of my profession. I can't seem to turn it off—even when my work is done. You say you were born on Water Street?"

She nodded.

"At home?"

Another nod.

He consulted his notes. "Sister named Mary Greene. Brother named Joseph. Mother Chastity, father Horace. Am I right so far?"

"Quite."

Quite. Her diction was so...odd. "When were you born?"

"I don't recall."

"Well, of course you wouldn't *recall*, but surely you know the date of your birth?"

"I'm afraid I don't."

"It must have been, what, the late '80s?"

A ghost of a smile moved briefly across her face, passing almost before Felder realized it was there. "I believe it would have been more in the early '70s."

"But you say you're only twenty-three years old."

"More or less. As I mentioned before, I'm not sure of my exact age."

He cleared his throat lightly. "Constance, do you know that there's no record of your family residing at Water Street?"

"Perhaps your research hasn't been thorough enough."

He leaned forward. "Is there a reason why you're concealing the truth from me? Please remember: I'm only here to help you."

A silence. He looked into those violet eyes, that young, beautiful face so perfectly framed by auburn hair, with the unmistakable look he remembered from their first meeting: haughtiness, serene superiority, perhaps even disdain. She had all the air of...what? A queen? No, that wasn't quite it. Felder had seen nothing like it before.

He laid his notes aside, trying to assume an air of ease and informality. "How did you happen to become Mr. Pendergast's ward?"

"When my parents and sister died, I was orphaned and homeless. Mr. Pendergast's house at Eight Ninety-one Riverside Drive was..." A pause. "Was then owned by a man named Leng. Eventually it...became vacant. I lived there."

"Why there, in particular?"

"It was large, comfortable, and had many places to hide. And it had a good library. When Mr. Pendergast inherited the house, he discovered me there and became my legal guardian."

Pendergast. His name had been in the papers, briefly, in regard to Constance's crime. The man had refused all comment. "Why did he become your guardian?"

"Guilt."

A silence. Felder cleared his throat. "Guilt? Why do you say that?"

She did not answer.

"Was Mr. Pendergast perhaps the father of your child?"

Now an answer came, and it was preternaturally calm. "No."

"And what was your role in the Pendergast household?"

"I was his amanuensis. His researcher. He found my language abilities useful."

"Languages? How many do you speak?"

"None but English. I can read and write fluently in Latin, ancient Greek, French, Italian, Spanish, and German."

"Interesting. You must have been a clever student. Where did you go to school?"

"I learned on my own."

"You mean, you were self-educated?"

"I mean I learned on my own."

Could it be possible? Felder wondered. In this day and age, could a person be born and grow up in the city and yet remain completely and officially invisible? This informal approach was going nowhere. Time to get a little more direct, press her a little. "How did your sister die?"

"She was murdered by a serial killer."

Felder paused. "Is the case on file? Was the serial killer caught?"

"No and no."

"And your parents? What happened to them?"

"They both died of consumption."

Felder was suddenly encouraged. This would be easy to check, as tuberculosis deaths in New York City were meticulously documented. "In which hospital did they die?"

"None. I don't know where my father died. I know my mother died on the street and her body was buried in the potter's field on Hart Island."

She remained seated, hands folded in her lap. Felder felt a sense of increasing frustration. "Getting back to your birth: you don't even remember what year you were born?"

"No."

Felder sighed. "I'd like to ask you some questions about your baby."

She remained still.

"You say you threw your baby off the ship because it was evil. How did you know it was evil?"

"His father was evil."

"Are you ready to tell me who he was?"

No answer.

"Do you believe that evil is inheritable, then?"

"There are suites, aggregates, of genes in the human genome that clearly contribute to criminal behavior, and those aggregates are inheritable. Surely you have read about recent research on the Dark Triad of human behavior traits?"

Felder was familiar with the research and very surprised at the lucidity and erudition of the response.

"And so you felt it necessary to remove his genes from the gene pool by throwing your baby into the Atlantic Ocean?"

"That's correct."

"And the father? Is he still alive?"

"He's dead."

"How?"

"He was precipitated into a pyroclastic flow."

"He was . . . excuse me?"

"It's a geological term. He fell into a volcano."

It took him a moment to absorb this statement. "Was he a geologist?"

No answer. It was maddening, going around and around like this and getting nowhere.

"You say 'precipitated.' Are you implying he was pushed?"

Again, no answer. This was clearly a wild fantasy, not worth encouraging or pursuing.

Felder switched topics. "Constance, when you threw your baby off the boat, did you know you were committing a crime?"

"Naturally."

"Did you consider the consequences?"

"Yes."

"So you knew it was wrong to kill your baby."

"On the contrary. It was not only the right thing to do, it was the *only* thing to do."

"Why was it the only thing to do?"

The question was followed by silence. With a sigh, feeling once again like he'd been casting a net into the darkness, Dr. John Felder picked up his notebook and rose. "Thank you, Constance. Our time is up."

"You're most welcome, Dr. Felder."

He pressed the button. Immediately the door opened and the cop came in.

"I'm done here," he said. Then he turned to Constance Greene and heard himself say, almost against his will: "We'll have another session in a few days."

"It shall be my pleasure."

As Felder walked down the long corridor of the secure ward, he wondered if his initial conclusion was correct. She was mentally ill, of course, but was she truly insane—legally insane? If you removed from her all that was sane, all that was predictable, all that was normal in a person—what did it leave? Nothing.

Just like her identity. Nothing.

43

Baton Rouge

Laura Hayward strode along the second-floor corridor of Baton Rouge General, consciously keeping a measured pace. She had everything under control, her breathing, her facial expression, her body language. Everything. Before leaving New York, she had dressed carefully in jeans and a shirt, her hair loose, leaving her uniform behind. She was here as a private citizen: no more, and no less.

Doctors, nurses, and staff passed in a blur as she walked steadily on, toward the pair of double doors leading into surgery. She pushed through them, taking care to keep her pace slow and deliberate. The admissions kiosk was to her right but she passed by, ignoring the polite "May I help you?" from the nurse. She headed straight into the waiting room—and there saw a lone figure sitting at the far end, rising from his seat now and taking a step toward her, face grim, arm extended.

She walked up to him and in one smooth motion raised her right arm, drew it back, and cold-cocked him across the jaw. *"Bastard!"*

He staggered back but made no effort to defend himself. She hit him again.

"Selfish, arrogant bastard! It wasn't enough that you almost ruined his career. Now you've killed him, you son of a bitch!"

She drew back and swung at him a third time, but this time he caught her arm in a vise-like grip and drew her toward him, turning and gently—but firmly— pinning her. She struggled briefly. And then, as quickly as it had come, she felt all the anger, all the hatred, collapse inside her. She sagged in his grip, utterly drained. He helped her to a chair. Somewhere, she was dimly aware of a commotion, the sound of running footsteps, shouts. She looked up and found them surrounded by three security guards shouting various contradictory questions and commands, the receiving nurse standing behind them, hand over her mouth.

Pendergast stood up, removed his shield, and held it up at them. "I'll take care of this. No reason to be alarmed."

"But there's been an assault," said one of the security officers. "Sir, you're bleeding."

Pendergast took an aggressive step forward. "I will *handle* it, Officer. I thank you and these others for the swift response, and I bid you good evening."

After a few moments of confusion, the security officers departed, leaving one behind, who took a position at the waiting room door, hands clasped in front, staring hard and suspiciously at Hayward.

Pendergast sat down beside Hayward. "He's been in exploratory surgery for several hours. I understand it's very serious. I've asked to be briefed on his situation as soon as they've got anything to—ah, here's a surgeon now."

A doctor entered the waiting room, his face grave. He looked from Hayward to Pendergast, whose face was bleeding, but made no comment. "Special Agent Pendergast?"

"Yes. And this is Captain Hayward, NYPD, a close friend of the patient. You may speak freely with both of us."

"I see." The surgeon nodded, consulted a clipboard in his hand. "The bullet entered at an angle from behind and grazed the heart before lodging against the back of a rib."

"The heart?" Hayward asked, struggling to comprehend, even as she managed to collect herself, organize her thoughts.

"Among other things, it partially tore the aortic valve as well as blocking the blood supply to part of the heart. Right now we're trying to fix the valve and keep the heart going."

"What are his chances of…of survival?" she asked.

The surgeon hesitated. "Every case is different. The good news is that the patient did not lose too much blood. If the bullet had been even half a millimeter closer, it would have ruptured the aorta. It did, however, do significant damage to the heart. If the operation is successful, he has an excellent chance of a full recovery."

"Look," said Hayward, "I'm a cop. You don't have

to beat around the bush with me. I want to know what his chances are."

The surgeon looked at her with pale, faded eyes. "This is a difficult and complex procedure. We have a team of the best surgeons in Louisiana working on it as we speak. But even under the best of circumstances, a healthy patient, no complications...well, it's not often successful. It's like trying to rebuild a car engine— while it's running."

"Not often?" She felt suddenly sick. "What do you mean by that?"

"I don't know that any controlled studies have been done, but my best guess as a surgeon would put a successful outcome at five percent...or less."

This was followed by a long silence. *Five percent or less.*

"What about a heart transplant?"

"If we had a heart, all matched up and ready to go, it would be a possibility. But we don't."

Hayward felt around for the arm of the chair and sank down into it.

"Does Mr. D'Agosta have any relatives who should be notified?"

Hayward didn't answer for a moment. Then she said, "An ex-wife and a son...in Canada. There's no one else. And that's *Lieutenant* D'Agosta."

"My apologies. Now, forgive me, but I need to get back to the OR. The operation will continue for at least eight more hours—if all goes well. You're welcome to stay here, but I doubt there will be any more news until the end."

Hayward nodded vaguely. She couldn't wrap her

mind around it all. She seemed to have lost all power of ratiocination.

She felt the surgeon's light touch on her shoulder. "May I ask if the lieutenant is a religious man?"

She tried to focus on the question, finally nodding. "Catholic."

"Would you like me to ask the hospital priest to come?"

"The priest?" She glanced at Pendergast, unsure how to answer.

"Yes," said Pendergast, "we would very much like the priest to come. We would like to speak to him. And please tell him to be prepared to administer extreme unction, given the circumstances."

A soft beeping went off on the doctor's person and in an automatic motion he reached down, detached a pager from his belt, and looked at it. At the same time the public address system chimed and a smooth female voice sounded from a hidden speaker:

"*Code blue, OR two-one. Code blue, OR two-one. Code team to OR two-one.*"

"Excuse me," said the surgeon, a faint hurry in his voice, "but I have to go now."

44

The PA system chimed, then fell silent. Hayward sat where she was, suddenly frozen. Her mind reeled. She couldn't bring herself to look at Pendergast, at the nurses, anywhere but at the floor. All she could think of was the look in the surgeon's eyes as he had hurried away.

A few minutes later a priest arrived carrying a black bag, looking almost like a doctor himself, a small man with white hair and a neatly trimmed beard. He looked from her to Pendergast with bright bird-like eyes.

"I'm Father Bell." He set his bag down and extended a small hand. Hayward took it but instead of shaking her hand, he held it comfortingly. "And you are—?"

"Captain Hayward. Laura Hayward. I'm a . . . a close friend of Lieutenant D'Agosta."

His eyebrows rose slightly. "You're a police officer, then?"

"NYPD."

"Was this a line-of-duty injury?"

Hayward hesitated, and Pendergast smoothly picked up the flow. "In a way. I'm Special Agent Pendergast, FBI, the lieutenant's associate."

A crisp nod and a handshake. "I'm here to administer the sacraments to Lieutenant D'Agosta, specifically one that we call Anointing the Sick."

"Anointing the Sick," Hayward repeated.

"We used to call it the Last Rites, but that was always an awkward and inaccurate term. You see, it's a sacrament for the living, not the dying, and it's a healing sacrament." His voice was light and musical.

Hayward inclined her head, swallowed.

"I hope you don't mind me explaining these things in detail. My presence can sometimes be alarming. People think I'm only called in when someone's expected to die, which is not the case."

Even though she wasn't a Catholic, Hayward found his directness steadying. "That code we just heard." She paused. "Does that mean...?"

"There's a fine team of doctors working on the lieutenant. If there's a way to pull him out of this, they will find it. If not, then God's will be done. Now, does either of you think the lieutenant might have any reason to wish that I not administer the sacraments?"

"To tell you the truth, he was never a very observant Catholic..." Hayward hesitated. She couldn't remember the last time Vinnie had gone to church. But something about the idea of having the priest there seemed comforting, and she sensed that he'd appreciate it. "I would say yes. I think Vincent would approve."

"Very well." The priest squeezed her hand. "Is there anything I can do for either of you? Arrangements?

Phone calls?" He paused. "Confession? We have a chapel here in the hospital."

"No thank you," said Hayward. She glanced at Pendergast, but he said nothing.

Father Bell nodded at them in turn, then picked up his black bag and walked down the corridor toward the operating suites at a brisk and confident pace, perhaps even with a slight hurry in his step.

She put her face in her hands. *Five percent...or less.* One chance in twenty. The brief sense of comfort the priest had brought with him dissolved. She'd better get used to the idea that Vinnie wasn't going to make it. It was so useless, such a waste of a life. He wasn't even forty-five. Memories welled up in her mind, fragmented, torturous, the bad memories lacerating, the good memories even worse.

Somewhere in the background, she heard Pendergast speaking. "I want you to know, if things go badly, that Vincent did not throw his life away."

She stared through her fingers down the empty corridor where the priest had vanished, not responding.

"Captain. A police officer puts his life on the line every day. You can be killed anytime, anywhere, for anything. Breaking up a domestic quarrel, thwarting a terrorist attack. Any death in the line is honorable. And Vincent was engaged in the most honorable job there is: helping right a wrong. His effort has been vital, absolutely crucial to solving this murder."

Hayward said nothing. Her mind went back to the code. That had been a quarter hour ago. Perhaps, she thought, the priest was already too late.

45

South Mountain, Georgia

The trail broke free of the woods and came out atop the mountain. Judson Esterhazy halted at the edge of the open meadow just in time to see the sun set over the pine-clad hills, suffusing the misty evening with a ruddy glow, a distant lake shimmering white-gold in the dying light.

He paused, breathing lightly. The so-called mountain was one in name only, being more of a bump than anything else. The summit itself was long and narrow and ridge-like, covered with tall grass, with a granite bald spot on which stood the remains of a fire tower.

Esterhazy glanced around. The summit was empty. He made his way out of the yellow pines and walked along an overgrown fire road toward the tower, finally coming up beneath its looming form. He leaned on one of the rusted metal struts, fumbled in his pocket, removed his pipe and a tobacco pouch. Inserting the pipe into the pouch, he slowly packed it with tobacco, using his thumb, the scent of Latakia rising to his nostrils. When it was filled to his liking he removed it, cleaned a few stray bits from the rim, gave it a final pack, removed a lighter from the same pocket, flicked it on, and sucked flame into the bowl in a series of slow, even movements.

The blue smoke drifted off into the twilight. As he smoked, Esterhazy saw a figure emerge from the far end of the field at the top of the south trail. There were several trails to the top of South Mountain, each arriving from a different road in a different direction.

The fragrance of the expensive tobacco, the soothing effects of the nicotine, the comforting ritual, steadied his nerves. He did not watch the figure approach, but instead kept his eyes focused on the west, at the orange diffusion above the hills where the sun had been moments before. He kept his eyes there until he heard the sweep of boots through grass, the faint rasp of breathing. Then he turned toward the man—a man he hadn't seen in a decade. The man looked little different than he remembered: slightly jowlier, hair somewhat receded, but he was still strongly built and sinewy. He wore an expensive pair of swamp boots and a chambray shirt.

"Evening," the man said.

Esterhazy removed his pipe and gave it a lift by way of greeting. "Hello, Mike," he replied.

The man stood against the afterglow, and his features were indistinct. "So," he began, "sounds like you took it upon yourself to clean up a little mess, and instead it turned into a rather bigger mess."

Esterhazy wasn't going to be talked to like that—not by Michael Ventura. "Nothing involving this man Pendergast is a 'little mess,'" he said harshly. "This is precisely what I've been dreading all these years. Something had to be done and I did it. Nominally, the job belonged to you. But you would undoubtedly have made a bigger hash of it."

"Not likely. That's the kind of job I do best."

A long silence. Esterhazy took in a thin stream of smoke, let it leak out, trying to regain his equilibrium.

"It's been a long time," Ventura said. "Let's not get off on the wrong foot."

Esterhazy nodded. "It's just that... Well, I thought it was all long past. Buried."

"It'll never be long past. Not as long as there's Spanish Island to deal with."

A look of concern crossed Esterhazy's face. "Everything's all right, isn't it?"

"As well as could be expected."

Another silence.

"Look," Ventura said in a milder tone. "I know this can't be easy for you. You made the ultimate sacrifice; we're very grateful to you for that."

Esterhazy drew on his pipe. "Let's get down to it," he said.

"Okay. So just let me understand. Instead of killing Pendergast, you killed his partner."

"D'Agosta. A happy accident. He was a loose end. I also took care of a couple of other loose ends—Blast and Blackletter. Two people who should have been removed from circulation a long time ago."

Ventura spat into the grass by way of answer. "I don't

agree, and I never have. Blackletter was well paid for his silence. And Blast is only indirectly connected."

"Nevertheless, he was a loose end."

Ventura just shook his head.

"Now D'Agosta's girlfriend is down here. A girlfriend who just happens to be the youngest homicide captain in the NYPD."

"So?"

Esterhazy took the pipe from his mouth and spoke coldly. "Mike, you have no idea—and I mean *no* idea—how dangerous this man Pendergast is. I know him well. I needed to act immediately. Unfortunately, I failed to kill him on the first attempt. Which will make the second all that much more difficult. You do understand, don't you, that it's either him or us?"

"How much could he possibly know?"

"He's found the Black Frame, he knows about Audubon's illness, and somehow he knows about the Doane family."

A sharp intake of breath. "You're shitting me. How *much* about the Doane family?"

"Hard to say. He was in Sunflower. He visited the house. He's tenacious and clever. You can assume he knows—or will know—everything."

"Son of a bitch. How in the world did they find out?"

"No idea. Not only is Pendergast a brilliant investigator, but this time around he's motivated—*uniquely* motivated."

Ventura shook his head.

"And I've little doubt he's busy filling the ear of this homicide captain with his suspicions, just as he did with that partner of his, D'Agosta. I'm afraid it's only a matter of time before they pay our mutual friend a visit."

A pause. "You think this investigation's official?"

"It doesn't seem so. I think they're working out of school. I doubt others are involved."

Ventura thought for a moment before speaking again. "So now we finish the job."

"Exactly. Take out Pendergast and that captain. Do it now. Kill them all."

"The cop you hit, D'Agosta—are you sure he's dead?"

"I think so. He took a .308 round in the back." Judson frowned. "If he doesn't die of his own accord, we'll have to extend a helping hand. Leave that to me."

Ventura nodded. "I'll keep the rest in line."

"You do that. Need any help? Money?"

"Money's the last of our worries. You know that." And Ventura walked away across the field, toward the pink sky of evening, until his dark silhouette disappeared into the pines at the far end.

Judson Esterhazy spent the next fifteen minutes leaning against the fire tower, smoking his pipe and thinking. Finally he reamed it out and knocked the dottle onto the iron strut. Then he stuck the pipe back into his pocket, took one last look at the light dying away in the west, then turned and made his way down the trail toward the road on the other side of the hill.

46

Baton Rouge

Exactly how much time had passed—five hours or fifty—Laura Hayward wasn't sure. The slow succession of minutes blended with a strange fugue of loudspeaker announcements, rapid hushed voices, the bleating of instrumentation. At times, Pendergast was at her side. Other times she would find him gone. At first she willed the time to pass as quickly as possible. Then—as the wait grew longer—she only wanted time to slow down. Because the longer Vincent D'Agosta lay on that surgical table, she knew, the more his chances of survival dwindled.

Then—quite abruptly—the surgeon was standing before them. His scrub blues were creased and wrinkled, and his face looked pale and drawn. Behind him stood Father Bell.

At the sight of the priest, Hayward's heart gave a dreadful lurch. She had known this moment would come. And yet—now that it was here—she did not think that she could bear it. *Oh, no. Oh, no, no, no...* She felt Pendergast take her hand.

The surgeon cleared his throat. "I've come to let you know the operation was successful. We closed forty-five minutes ago and we've been monitoring closely since. The signs are **promising**."

"I'll take you to see him now," said Father Bell.

"Only for a moment," the surgeon added. "He's barely conscious and very weak."

For a moment, Hayward sat motionless, stunned, trying to take it in. Pendergast was speaking but she couldn't understand the words. Then she felt herself being raised—the FBI agent on one side, the priest on the other—and she was walking down the corridor. They turned left, then right, past closed doors and halls full of stretchers and empty wheelchairs. Through an open doorway they came to a small area enclosed by movable privacy screens. A nurse pulled one of the screens away and there was Vinnie. A dozen machines were attached to him, and his eyes were closed. Tubes snaked beneath the sheets: one containing plasma, another saline. Despite D'Agosta's hefty build, he looked fragile, papery almost.

She caught her breath. As she did so, his eyes fluttered open; closed; then opened again. He looked up at them silently in turn, his eyes at last looking into hers.

As Hayward stared down at him, she felt the last vestiges of her self-control—that commanding presence of mind she so prided herself on—crumble and fall away. Hot tears coursed down her cheeks.

"Oh, *Vinnie*," she sobbed.

D'Agosta's own eyes filled. And then he slowly closed them.

Pendergast put a steadying arm around her, and for a moment she turned her face to the fabric of his shirt, yielding to the emotion, letting sobs rack her frame. Only now—when she saw Vinnie alive—did she realize just how close she had come to losing him.

"I'm afraid you'll need to leave now," the surgeon said in a low voice.

She straightened up, dried her eyes, and took a long, shuddering, cleansing breath.

"He's not out of the woods yet. As it is, his heart has been severely damaged by the trauma. He's going to need an aortic valve replacement at the earliest opportunity."

Hayward nodded. She detached herself from Pendergast's arm, took one more look down at D'Agosta, then turned away.

"Laura," she heard him croak.

She glanced back. He was still lying there on the bed, eyes closed. Had it been her imagination?

Then he moved faintly and his eyes fluttered open again. His jaw worked but no sound came.

She stepped forward and bent over the bed.

"Make my work here count," he said in a voice that was barely a whisper.

47

Penumbra Plantation

A fire had been kindled in the great fireplace of the library, and Hayward watched the old manservant, Maurice, serving after-dinner coffee. He threaded his way between the furniture, an ancient figure with a curiously blank expression on his lined face. She noticed that he had been careful not to stare at the bruise on Pendergast's jaw. Perhaps, Hayward mused, over the years the old fellow had grown used to seeing his employer a little dinged up.

The mansion and grounds were exactly as she pictured they would be: ancient oaks draped with Spanish moss, white columned portico, faded antebellum furnishings. There was even an old family ghost, the ancient manservant had assured her, who haunted the nearby swamps—another predictable cliché. The only surprise, in fact, was Penumbra's general state of external disrepair. This was a little odd—Pendergast, she assumed, had plenty of money. She put these musings aside, telling herself she was completely uninterested in Pendergast and his family.

Before leaving the hospital the night before, Pendergast had asked her—in some detail—about her visit with Constance Greene. Following that, he offered her lodging at Penumbra. Hayward had refused, opting instead to stay at a hotel near the medical center. But another visit to D'Agosta the following morning had served to underline what the surgeon told her: his recovery would be slow and long. She could take time off from the job—that wasn't a problem, she'd accrued too much vacation time as it was—but the idea of cooling her heels in a depressing hotel room for days on end was unendurable. Especially because, at Pendergast's insistence, Vinnie was going to be moved to a secure location just as soon as medically possible, and—for the sake of security—she would be forbidden to visit. That morning, in a brief interlude of consciousness, Vinnie had once again implored her to pick up the case where he'd left off—to help see it through to the bitter end.

And so, when Pendergast sent his car round to pick her up after lunch, she'd checked out of the hotel and accepted his invitation to stay at Penumbra. She hadn't agreed to help, but she'd decided to hear the details. Some of it she knew already from Vinnie's phone calls. It had sounded like a typical Pendergast investigation, all hunches and blind alleys and conflicting evidence, strung together by highly questionable police work.

But back at Penumbra, as Pendergast had explained the case—starting at dinner, and then continuing over coffee—Hayward realized that the bizarre story had an internal logic. Pendergast explained his late wife's obsession with Audubon; how they had traced her interest in the Carolina Parakeet, the Black Frame, the lost parrot, and the strange fate of the Doane family. He read her passages from the Doane girl's diary: a chilling descent into madness. He described their encounter with Blast, another seeker of the Black Frame, himself recently murdered—as had been Helen Pendergast's former employer at Doctors With Wings, Morris Blackletter. And finally, he explained the series of deductions and discoveries that led to the unearthing of the Black Frame itself.

When Pendergast at last fell silent, Hayward leaned back in her chair, sipping her coffee, running over the bizarre information in her mind, looking for threads, logical connections, and finding precious little. A great deal more work would be necessary to fill in the blanks.

She glanced over at the painting known as the Black Frame. It was lit indirectly by the firelight, but she could nevertheless make out details: the woman on the bed, the stark room, the cold white nakedness of her body. Disturbing, to put it mildly.

She looked back at Pendergast, now attired in his signature black suit. "So you believe your wife was interested in Audubon's illness. An illness that somehow transformed him into a creative genius."

"Through some unknown neurological effect, yes. To someone with her interests, this would have been a very valuable pharmacological discovery."

"And all she wanted with the painting was confirmation for this theory."

Pendergast nodded. "That painting is the link between Audubon's early, indifferent work and his later brilliance. It's proof of the transition he underwent. But that doesn't quite get to the central mystery in this case: the birds."

Hayward frowned. "The birds?"

"The Carolina Parakeets. The Doane parrot."

Hayward herself had been puzzling over the connection to Audubon's illness, to no avail. "And?"

Pendergast sipped his coffee. "I believe we're dealing with a strain of avian flu."

"Avian flu? You mean, bird flu?"

"That, I believe, is the disease that laid Audubon low, that nearly killed him, and that was responsible for his creative flowering. His symptoms—high fever, headache, delirium, cough—are all consistent with flu. A flu he no doubt caught dissecting a Carolina Parakeet."

"Slow down. How do you know all this?"

In reply, Pendergast reached for a worn, leather-bound book. "This is the diary of my great-great-grandfather Boethius Pendergast. He befriended Audubon during the painter's younger days." Opening the journal to a page marked with a silken strand, he found the passage he was looking for and began to read aloud:

Aug. 21st. J. J. A. spent the evening with us again. He had amused himself throughout the afternoon in the dissection of two Carolina Parakeets—a curiously colored but otherwise unremarkable species. He then stuffed and mounted them on bits of cypress wood. We dined well and afterward took a turn around the

park. He took leave of us around half past ten. Next
week he plans to make a journey upriver, where he
professes to have business prospects.

Pendergast closed the journal. "Audubon never
made that journey upriver. Because within a week he
developed the symptoms that would eventually land
him in the Meuse St. Claire sanatorium."

Hayward nodded at the journal. "You think your
wife saw that passage?"

"I'm sure of it. Why else would she have stolen
those specimens of Carolina Parakeet—the very ones
Audubon dissected? She wanted to test them for avian
flu." He paused. "And do *more* than simply test them.
She hoped to extract from them a live sample of virus.
Vincent told me all that remained of the parrots my
wife stole were a few feathers. I'll head over to Oakley Plantation in the morning, retrieve those remaining
feathers—carefully—and have them tested to confirm
my suspicions."

"But all that still doesn't explain how those parakeets are linked to the Doane family."

"It's quite simple. The Doanes were sickened by the
same disease that struck Audubon."

"What makes you say that?"

"There are simply too many similarities, Captain,
for anything else to make sense. The sudden flowering
of creative brilliance. Followed by mental dissolution.
Too many similarities—and Helen knew it. *That's* why
she went to get the bird from them."

"But when she took the bird, the family was still
healthy. They didn't have the flu."

"One of the diaries in the Doane house records—in passing—the family coming down with the flu shortly after the bird arrived."

"Oh, my God."

"And then, rather quickly, they manifested signs of creative brilliance." He paused again. "Helen went there to get the bird away from the Doanes—I'm sure of that. To keep it from spreading the disease further, perhaps. And to test it, of course, to confirm her suspicions. Note what Karen Doane wrote in her diary about the day Helen took the bird. She wore leather gloves, and she stuffed the bird and its cage into a garbage bag. Why? Initially, I assumed the bag was simply for concealment. But it was to keep herself and her car from contamination."

"And the leather gloves?"

"Worn no doubt to conceal a pair of medical gloves beneath. Helen was trying to remove a viral vector from the human population. No doubt the bird, cage, and bag were all incinerated—after she'd taken the necessary samples, of course."

"*Incinerated?*" Hayward repeated.

"Standard procedure. Any samples taken would also have been ultimately incinerated."

"Why? If the Doane family was infected, they could just spread it to others. Burning the bird would be like shutting the barn door after the horse has escaped."

"Not quite. You see, avian flus jump easily from bird to human, but they have great difficulty passing from human to human. The neighbors would be safe. Of course, for the Doane family it was too late." Pendergast took a last sip of coffee, then put the cup aside.

"But this still leaves us with a central mystery: where did the Doanes' parrot escape from? And, even more importantly, *how* did it become a carrier?"

Despite her skepticism, Hayward felt herself intrigued. "Perhaps you're wrong. Maybe the virus lay dormant all this time. The parrot caught it naturally."

"Unlikely. Recall the parrot had been banded. No: the viral genome would have been painstakingly sequenced and rebuilt in a laboratory—using viral material from the stolen Carolina Parakeets. And then live birds were inoculated with it."

"So the bird escaped from a lab."

"Precisely." Pendergast stood up. "The biggest question of all remains: what does this have to do with Helen's murder and the recent killings and attacks on us—if anything?"

"Isn't there another question you're forgetting?" Hayward asked.

Pendergast looked at her.

"You say Helen stole the parrots Audubon studied—the ones that supposedly sickened him. Helen also visited the Doane family and stole their parrot—because, as you also say, she knew it was infected. By inference, Helen is the common thread that binds the two events. So aren't you curious what role *she* might have had in the sequencing and inoculation?"

Pendergast turned away, but not before a look of pain lanced across his face. Hayward almost regretted asking the question.

A long pause settled over the library. At last, Pendergast turned toward her again. "We must pick up where Vincent and I left off."

" 'We'?"

"You're going to grant Vincent's request, I assume. I need a competent partner. And as I recall, you're from this region originally. You'll do well, I assure you."

His assumptions, his patronizing attitude, were irritating in the extreme. She knew all too well of Pendergast's unorthodox investigative techniques, his breezy neglect for rules and procedures, his skirtings of the law. She would find that annoying, if not intolerable. It might even damage her career. She returned his steady gaze. If it weren't for this man, Vinnie wouldn't be in a hospital right now, critically wounded, in need of a new heart valve.

At the same time . . . Vinnie had asked her. Twice.

She realized she had already made the decision.

"All right. I'll help you see this thing through. For Vinnie's sake, not yours. But—" She hesitated. "I've got one condition. And it's non-negotiable."

"Of course, Captain."

"When—if—we find the person responsible for your wife's death, you must promise me *not* to kill him."

Pendergast went very still. "You realize this is the cold-blooded murderer of my wife we're discussing."

"I don't believe in vigilante justice. Too many of your perps end up dead before they even reach a courtroom. This time, we're going to let justice take its course."

There was a pause. "What you are asking—is difficult."

"It's the price of the dance," Hayward said simply.

Pendergast held her gaze for a long moment. And then—almost imperceptibly—he nodded.

48

In the dim garage, a man crouched behind a vehicle draped in a white canvas shroud. The time was seven in the evening, and the sun had set. The air smelled of car wax, motor oil, and mold. Sliding a 9mm Beretta semiautomatic pistol out of his belt, the man eased open the magazine, checked again that it was full. After snugging the gun back into his waistband, he opened and closed his hands three times, alternately stretching and clenching the fingers. The target would be arriving at any moment. The sweat crept down the nape of the man's neck and a tendon began to jump in his thigh, but he was unaware of either distraction, so concentrated was he on what was to come.

Frank Hudson had been scouting the grounds of Penumbra Plantation for the past two days, learning the movements and habits of the place. He had been surprised at how lax the security was: a single dotty, half-blind servant opening the house in the morning and shutting it up again at night on a schedule so regular you could set your watch by it. The entrance gates were left closed but unlocked during the day, and they were apparently unwatched. A diligent search had turned up no sign of security cameras, alarm systems, motion sensors, or infrared beams. The decrepit old plantation was so far off the beaten track that Hudson had little to fear from regular police patrols. There were few people at the plantation house besides the target and the servant: only a rather attractive woman with a great figure he'd seen a few times.

Hudson's target, the man named Pendergast, was the only irregularity in the timeless cycle of Penumbra Plantation. He came and went at the most unpredictable hours. But Hudson had observed long enough to see the beginning of a small pattern in his comings and goings, and it centered on wine. When the shuffling old servant began preparing dinner and uncorked a bottle of wine, Pendergast would be home no later than seven thirty in the evening to partake. If the servant did not uncork wine, it meant Pendergast would not be dining at home and would arrive much later in the evening, if at all.

This evening an uncorked bottle of wine stood on the sideboard, clearly visible through the dining room windows.

Hudson checked his watch. He rehearsed in his mind how it would go, what he would do. And then he froze: outside, he heard the sound of wheels crunching on gravel. This was it. Hudson waited, his breathing shallow. The car came to a halt outside the garage, the engine idling. A car door opened, followed by the sound of feet. The garage doors swung open, first one, then the other—they were not automatic—and the footsteps went back to the car. The engine revved slightly. The nose of the Rolls eased into the garage, the lights momentarily filling the space, blinding him. A moment later the lights went out, the engine died, and the garage was dark again.

He blinked, waiting for his eyes to readjust. His hand closed on the pistol grips and he eased the weapon from his belt, carefully thumbing off the safety.

He waited for the sound of the opening door, for his target to turn on the lights in the garage, but nothing happened. Pendergast seemed to be waiting in the car. What for? Feeling his heart accelerate in his chest, Hudson tried to control his breathing, maintain his lucidity. He knew he was well hidden, having adjusted the shroud on the vehicle so that it reached all the way to the ground, ensuring that even his feet were invisible.

Perhaps Pendergast was on his cell phone, finishing up a call. Or he was taking a rare opportunity to sit quietly, as people sometimes did, before getting out of the vehicle.

With infinite caution, Hudson raised his head ever so slightly to peer over the edge of the shroud; the dim form of the Rolls rested quietly in the dark, the only sound the ticking of the cooling engine. It was impossible to see inside the smoked windows.

He waited.

"Lose a button?" came a voice from right behind him.

With a grunt of surprise Hudson leapt up, his hand jerking instinctively, the gun going off with a loud crash in the enclosed space. As he tried to pivot he felt the gun wrenched from his hand and a wiry arm wrap around his neck. His body was spun around, then shoved up hard against the sheeted vehicle.

"In the great game of human life," the voice said, "one begins by being a dupe and ends up by being a rogue."

Hudson struggled ineffectually.

"Where are you, my friend, on that happy spectrum?"

"I don't know what the hell you're talking about," Hudson finally managed to gasp out.

"If you get a grip on yourself, I'll release you. Now: relax."

Hudson stopped fighting. As he did so, he felt the pressure release, his limbs freed. He turned to find himself face-to-face with his target, Pendergast: a tall man in black with a face and hair so pale they seemed to glow in the darkness, like a specter. He had Hudson's own Beretta in hand, pointed at him. "I'm sorry, we haven't been introduced. My name is Pendergast."

"Fuck you."

"I've always found that a curious expression when used pejoratively." Pendergast looked him up and down, then slid the gun into the waist of his own suit. "Shall we continue this conversation in the house?"

The man stared at him.

"Please." Pendergast gestured for him to walk toward the side door ahead of him. After a moment, Hudson complied. There might be a way to retrieve something out of this, after all.

He passed through the open garage door, Pendergast following, crossed the graveled drive, and mounted the steps to the shabby mansion. The servant held open the door.

"Is the gentleman to come in?" he asked, in a voice that made it clear he hoped not.

"Only for a few minutes, Maurice. We'll have a glass of sherry in the east parlor."

Pendergast gestured the man down the central hall and into a small sitting room. A fire was burning in the grate.

"Sit down."

Hudson gingerly took a seat on an old leather sofa. Pendergast seated himself opposite, checked his watch. "I have just a few minutes. Now once again: your name, please?"

Hudson struggled to collect himself, to adapt to this sudden and unexpected reversal. He could still pull this off. "Forget the name. I'm a private investigator, and I worked for Blast. That's all you need to know—and I'll bet it's more than enough."

Pendergast looked him up and down again.

"I know you have the painting," Hudson went on. "The Black Frame. And I know you killed Blast."

"How very clever of you."

"Blast owed me a lot of money. All I'm doing is collecting what's due. You pay me and I forget all I know about Blast's death. You understand?"

"I see. You're here on a sort of improvised blackmail scheme." The man's pale face broke into a ghastly grin, exposing white, even teeth.

"Just collecting what's owed me. And helping you out at the same time—if you get my meaning."

"Mr. Blast had poor judgment in personnel matters."

Uncertain what was meant by that, Hudson watched as Pendergast took the Beretta out of his black suit, checked the magazine, slapped it back in, and pointed the gun at him. At the same time, the servant arrived with a silver tray with two little glasses full of brown liquid, which he placed down, one after the other.

"Maurice, the sherry won't be necessary after all. I'm going to take this gentleman out into the swamp, shoot him in the back of the head with his own gun, and let the alligators dispose of the evidence. I'll be back in time for dinner."

"As you wish, sir," said the servant, taking up the drinks he had just set out.

"Don't bullshit me," said Hudson, feeling an uncomfortable twinge. Maybe he'd overplayed his hand.

Pendergast didn't seem to hear him. He rose, pointed the gun. "Let's go."

"Don't be a fool, you'll never get away with it. My people are expecting me. They know where I am."

"Your people?" The ghastly smile returned. "Come now, we both know you're strictly freelance and that you've told no one where you went tonight. To the swamp!"

"Wait." Hudson felt a sudden surge of panic. "You're making a mistake."

"Do you think that—having killed one man already—I wouldn't be eager to kill another who has learned about the crime and now wishes to extort money? On your feet!"

Hudson jumped up. "Listen to me, please. Forget about the money. I was just trying to explain."

"No explanations necessary. You haven't even told me your name, for which I thank you. It always gives me a twinge to remember the names of those I've killed."

"It's Hudson," he said quickly. "Frank Hudson. Please don't do this."

Pendergast pushed the barrel of the gun into his side and spun him toward the door with a hard shove. Like a zombie, Hudson stumbled out into the hall, through the front door, and onto the porch. The night rose before him, black and damp, filled with the croaking of frogs and the trilling of insects.

"No. God, no." Hudson knew now he'd made a terrible miscalculation.

"Keep moving, if you please."

Hudson felt his knees buckling and he sank down on the floorboards. "Please." The tears coursed down his face.

"I'll do it right here, then." Hudson felt the cold barrel of the gun touch the nape of his neck. "Maurice will just have to clean up."

"Don't do it," Hudson moaned. He heard Pendergast cock the Beretta.

"Why shouldn't I do it?"

"When I'm missing, the cops will find my car. It's close enough that they'll come knocking around here."

"I'll move your car."

"You'll leave your DNA in it, you can't avoid it."

"Maurice will move it. Besides, I can deal with a few cops."

"They'll search the swamp."

"As I said, the alligators will dispose of your corpse."

"If you think that, you don't know much about corpses. They have a way of turning up days, weeks later. Even in swamps."

"Not in *my* swamp, with *my* alligators."

"Alligators can't make human bones disappear—they go right through the gut, come out unchanged."

"Your knowledge of biology is impressive."

"Listen to me. The cops will find out I worked for Blast, connect Blast to you and me to you. I bought gas with a credit card just down the road. Believe me, they'll be all over this place."

"How will they connect me to Blast?"

"They will, you can count on it!" Hudson went on with true fervor. "I know the whole story, Blast told me. He told me about your visit. Right after you left, Blast ordered a rollup of his fur operation. He wasn't taking any chances, he was on the phone a minute after you left his place."

"What about the Black Frame? Was that you who chased us?"

"Yes, it was. Blast egged you on about the Black Frame. He wanted you to find it, figured you might be just smart enough to succeed where he'd failed. You impressed him. But the cops are going to know all about this if they don't already, all that bullshit you pulled at the Donette Hole. Believe me, if I disappear they'll be all over this place with hound dogs."

"They'll never connect me to Blast."

"Of course they will! Blast told me you accused him of killing your wife. You're up to your neck in the investigation already!"

"Did Blast kill my wife?"

"He said he didn't, had nothing to do with it."

"And you believed him?"

Hudson was talking as fast as he could, his heart

racing painfully in his chest. "Blast was no saint, but he wasn't a killer. He was a weasel, a con man, a manipulator. He didn't have the guts to kill someone."

"Unlike you. Hiding in my garage with a gun."

"No, no! This wasn't a hit, I was only looking to make a deal. I'm just a PI trying to make a living. You've *got* to believe me!" His voice cracked in panic.

"Must I?" Pendergast slid the gun away. "You may get up, Mr. Hudson."

He rose to his feet. His face was wet with tears and he was shaking all over, but he didn't care. He was overwhelmed with hope.

"You're slightly more intelligent than I had assumed. Instead of killing you, shall we go back inside, enjoy that sherry, and discuss the terms of your employment?"

Hudson sat in the sofa next to the hot fire, sweating all over. He felt drained, exhausted, and yet alive, tingling, as if he'd been born again and was walking the earth as a new man.

Pendergast sat back in his chair with a strange half smile. "Now, Mr. Hudson, if you're going to work for me, you've got to tell me everything. About Blast, about your assignment."

Hudson was only too grateful to talk. "Blast called me after you visited him. You really scared him, with your talk of illegal furs. He said he was putting his whole operation on ice, indefinitely. He also said you were on the track of the painting, the Black Frame, and he wanted me to follow you around so that if you found it, I could get it away from you."

Pendergast nodded over tented fingers.

"As I said, he hoped you'd lead him to the Black Frame. I followed you, I saw that business you pulled at Pappy's. I gave chase but you got away."

Another nod.

"So I went back to report to Blast, found him dead. Shotgun at close range, tore him up real nice. Owed me over five grand in time and expenses. I figured you killed him. And I figured to pay you a visit, take back what was owed me."

"Alas, I did not kill Blast. Someone else got to him."

Hudson nodded, not knowing whether to believe him or not.

"And what did you know of Mr. Blast's business?"

"Not much. Like I said, he was involved in the illegal wildlife trade—animal skins. But his big thing seemed to be that Black Frame. He was half crazy over it."

"And your own employment history, Mr. Hudson?"

"I used to be a cop, got put in the back office because of diabetes. Couldn't stand a desk job, so I became a PI. That was about five years ago. Did a lot of work for Mr. Blast, mostly looking into the backgrounds of his... business partners and suppliers. He was very careful who he dealt with. The wildlife market's crawling with undercover cops and sting operators. He mostly dealt with some guy named Victor."

"Victor who?"

"I never heard the last name."

Pendergast looked at his watch. "It is dinnertime, Mr. Hudson, and I'm sorry you can't stay."

Hudson felt sorry, too.

Pendergast reached into his suit and pulled out a

small sheaf of bills. "I can't speak for what Blast owes you," he said, "but this is for your first two days' employment. Five hundred a day plus expenses. From now on you work without a firearm and you work only for me. Understood?"

"Yes, sir."

"There's a small town called Sunflower, just west of the Black Brake swamp. I want you to get out a map, draw a circle with a fifty-mile radius around that town, and identify all the pharmaceutical companies and drug research facilities within that circle, going back fifteen years. I want you to drive to each one, in the guise of a lost motorist. Get as close as you can without trespassing. Don't take notes or pictures, keep it all in your head. Observe and report back to me in twenty-four hours. That will be the extent of your first assignment. Do you understand?"

Hudson understood. He heard the door open and voices in the hall; someone had arrived. "Yes. Thank you, sir." This was even more money than Blast had been paying him—and for the simplest of assignments. Just so long as he didn't have to go into the Black Brake swamp itself—he'd heard one too many rumors about that place as it was.

Pendergast saw him to the kitchen door. Hudson stepped out into the night, filled with a fierce gratitude and sense of loyalty toward the man who had spared his life.

49

St. Francisville, Louisiana

Laura Hayward followed the squad car out of town on a winding road that led south toward the Mississippi River. She felt conspicuous and more than a little awkward behind the wheel of Helen Pendergast's vintage Porsche convertible, but the FBI agent had offered his wife's car so courteously she simply hadn't had the heart to refuse. As she drove along the sloping road, overleafed with oaks and walnut trees, her mind drifted back to her first job with the New Orleans Police Department. She'd only been a substitute dispatcher then, but the experience had confirmed her desire to become a cop. That was before she'd headed north to New York City, to attend the John Jay College of Criminal Justice and later take her first job as a Transit Authority cop. In the almost fifteen years since, she'd lost most of her southern accent—and become a die-hard New Yorker, to boot.

The sight of St. Francisville—whitewashed houses with long porches and tin roofs, the heavy air redolent of magnolias—seemed to melt right through her New York carapace. She mused that her experience with the local police had, so far, gone better than the bureaucratic run-around she'd gotten in Florida trying to get information on the Blast homicide. There was still something to be said for the gentility of the Old South.

The squad car turned into a driveway and Hayward followed, parking next to it. She stepped out to see a modest ranch house, with tidy flower beds framed by two magnolias.

The two cops who had escorted her to the Blackletter house, a sergeant in the homicide division and a regular officer, climbed out of their car, hiking up their belts and walking toward her. The white one, Officer Field, had carrot hair and a red face and was sweating copiously. The other, Sergeant Detective Cring, had an almost excessive earnestness about him, a man who did his duty, dotted every *i* and crossed every *t* with close attention.

The house was whitewashed like its neighbors, neat and clean. Crime-scene tape, detached by the wind, fluttered over the lawn and coiled around the porch columns. The front door latch was sealed with orange evidence tape.

"Captain," said Cring, "do you want to examine the grounds or would you like to go inside?"

"Inside, please."

She followed them onto the porch. Her arrival at the St. Francisville police station unannounced had been a big event and, initially, not a positive one. They were not happy to see an NYPD captain—and a woman no less—arriving in a flashy car to check up on a local homicide without warning or peace officer status, or even a courtesy call from up north. But Hayward had been able to turn around their suspicion with friendly chatter about her days on the job in New Orleans, and pretty soon they were old buddies. Or at least, she hoped so.

"We'll do a walk-through," Cring went on as he approached the door. He took out a penknife and slit through the tape. Freed, the door swung open, its lock broken.

"What about those?" Hayward asked, pointing to a bootie box sitting by the door.

"The crime scene's already been thoroughly worked over," said Cring. "No need."

"Right."

"It was a pretty straightforward case," Cring said as they stepped inside, the house exhaling a breath of stale, faintly foul air.

"Straightforward how?" Hayward asked.

"Robbery gone bad."

"How do you know?"

"The house was tossed, a bunch of electronics taken—flat panel, couple of computers, stereo. You'll see for yourself."

"Thank you."

"It took place between nine and ten in the evening. The perp used a pry bar to get inside, as you probably noticed, and walked through this front hallway into the den, through there, where Blackletter was tinkering with his robots."

"Robots?"

"He was a robot enthusiast. Hobbyist stuff."

"So the perp went straight from here to the den?"

"It seems so. He apparently heard Blackletter in there, decided to eliminate him before robbing the house."

"Was Blackletter's car in the driveway?"

"Yes."

Hayward followed Cring into the den. A long table was covered with metal and plastic parts, wires, circuit boards, and all kinds of strange gizmos. The floor below sported a large black stain, and the cinder-block wall was sprayed with blood and peppered with buckshot. Evidence-marking cones and arrows were still positioned everywhere.

Shotgun, she thought. *Just like Blast.*

"It was a sawed-off," said Cring. "Twelve-gauge, based on the splatter analysis and the buckshot recovered. Double-ought buck."

Hayward nodded. She examined the door into the den: thick metal with a layer of hard soundproofing screwed into it on the inside. The walls and ceiling were also well soundproofed. She wondered if Blackletter had been working with the door open or shut. If he was a fastidious man—which seemed to be the case— he would have kept it shut to keep the dirt and dust out of the kitchen.

"After shooting the victim," continued Cring, "the perpetrator walked back into the kitchen—we found spots of secondary blood from footprints—and then back through the hallway to the living room."

Hayward was about to say something, but bit her tongue. This was no burglary, but it would do no good to point that out now. "Can we look at the living room?"

"Sure thing." Cring led her through the kitchen to the entry hall, then into the living room. Nothing had been touched; it was still a mess. A rolltop desk had been rifled, letters and pictures scattered about, books pulled off shelves, a sofa slit open with a knife. The wall sported a hole where the supports to the missing flatscreen had been affixed.

Hayward noticed an antique, sterling-silver letter opener with an opal inlaid in its handle lying on the floor, where it had been swept off the desk. Her eye roved about the living room, noting quite a few small, portable objects of silver and gold workmanship: ash-trays, small casks and boxes, teapots, teaspoons, salvers, candlesnuffers, inkstands, and figurines, all beautifully chased. Some had inlaid gemstones. They all seemed to have been unceremoniously swept to the floor.

"All these silver and gold objects," she asked. "Were any stolen?"

"Not that we know of."

"That seems odd."

"Things like that are very hard to fence, especially around here. Our burglar was most likely a drug addict just looking for some stuff to get a quick fix."

"All this silver looks like a collection."

"It was. Dr. Blackletter was involved with the local historical society and donated things from time to time. He specialized in antebellum American silver."

"Where'd he get his money?"

"He was a medical doctor."

"As I understand, he worked for Doctors With Wings, a nonprofit organization without a lot of money. This silver must be worth a small fortune."

"After Doctors With Wings, he did consulting work for various pharmaceutical companies. There are quite a few in this area; it's one of the mainstays of the local economy."

"Do you have a file on Dr. Blackletter? I'd like to see it."

"It's back at the station. I'll get you a copy when we're done here."

Hayward lingered in the living room. She had a vague feeling of dissatisfaction, as if there was more to extract from the crime scene. Her eye fell on a number of snapshots in silver frames that had apparently been swept from a bookshelf.

"May I?"

"Be my guest. The CSI people have been through here with a fine-tooth comb."

She knelt and picked up several of the frames. They showed what she presumed to be various family members and friends. Some were clearly of Blackletter himself: in Africa flying a plane, inoculating natives, standing before a bush clinic. There were several pictures showing Blackletter in company with an attractive blond woman some years his junior; in one he had his arm around her.

"Was Dr. Blackletter married?"

"Never," said Cring.

She turned this last picture over in her hands. The glass in the frame had cracked in its fall to the floor. Hayward slid the photo out of its frame and turned it over. Written on the back with a generous, looping hand was, TO MORRIS, IN MEMORY OF THAT FLIGHT OVER THE LAKE. LOVE, M.

"May I keep this? Just the photo, I mean."

A hesitation. "Well, we'll have to enter it in the chain-of-custody logs." Another hesitation. "May I ask the reason why?"

"It may be pertinent to my investigation." Hayward had been careful not to tell them exactly what her investigation was, and they, after making a few halfhearted attempts to find out, had tactfully dropped the subject.

But now Cring brought it up again. "If you don't mind me asking, we're sort of puzzled why an NYPD homicide captain would be interested in a fairly routine burglary and murder all the way down here. We don't mean to pry, but it would be useful to know what you're looking for—so we can help."

Hayward knew she couldn't keep dodging the question, so she opted for misdirection. "It involves a terrorism investigation."

A silence. "I see."

"Terrorism," Field repeated from behind her, speaking for the first time. He'd been following them so silently she'd almost forgotten he was there. "You got a lot of that up in New York, I hear."

"Yes," said Hayward. "You understand why we can't go into details."

"Absolutely."

"We're keeping a low profile on this one. Which is why I'm down here informally, if you know what I mean."

"Yes, of course," said Field. "If I may ask—anything to do with the robots?"

Hayward flashed him a quick smile. "The less said the better."

"Yes, ma'am," said the officer, flushing with pleasure at having guessed.

Hayward hated herself for telling lies like this. It was bad policy all around, and if it ever got out she could lose her job.

"Give the picture to me," said Cring, with a warning glance to his subordinate. "I'll see that it's logged and back in your hands right away." He slid the photograph into an evidence envelope, sealed it, and initialed it.

"I think we're done here," said Hayward, looking around, feeling guilty about her crude deception. She hoped Pendergast wasn't starting to rub off on her.

She stepped out of the dark house and into the humid sunlight. Glancing around, she noticed that the street dead-ended at the river not half a mile away. On impulse she turned back to Cring, who was securing the front door.

"Detective," she said.

He turned. "Ma'am?"

"You understand that you can't speak to anybody about what we just discussed."

"Yes, ma'am."

"But you probably also understand now why I believe this robbery to be a fake."

Cring rubbed his chin. "A fake?"

"Staged." She nodded down the street. "In fact, I'd bet that if you were to check, you just might find those missing electronics down there, beyond the end of the road, at the bottom of the Mississippi."

Cring looked from her, to the river, and back again. He nodded slowly.

"I'll swing by for that photo this afternoon," she said as she slipped into the Porsche.

50

Penumbra Plantation

The old servant, Maurice, opened the door for Hayward, and she entered the dim confines of the mansion house. It again struck her as exactly the kind of place she imagined Pendergast coming from, decaying antebellum gentry, from the dilapidated house down to the mournful old servant in formal clothes.

"This way, Captain Hayward," Maurice said, turning and gesturing toward the parlor with an upturned palm. She walked in to find Pendergast seated before a fire, a small glass by his right hand. He rose and indicated a seat for her.

"Sherry?"

She dropped her briefcase on the sofa and settled down beside it. "No thanks. Not my kind of drink."

"Anything else? Beer? Tea? A martini?"

She glanced at Maurice, not wanting to put him out

but exhausted by her travel. "Tea. Hot and strong, with milk and sugar, please."

With a decline of his head, the servant withdrew.

Pendergast settled back down, throwing one leg over the other. "How was your trip to Siesta Key and St. Francisville?" he asked.

"Productive. But first, how's Vinnie?"

"Doing quite well. The move to the private hospital was accomplished without incident. And the second operation, replacing the valve in his aorta with a pig valve, went beautifully and he is on the road to recovery."

She eased back, feeling a huge weight lifted. "Thank God. I want to see him."

"As I mentioned before, that would be unwise. Even calling him might be a bad idea. We seem to be dealing with a very clever killer—who, I believe, has some inside source of information about us." Pendergast took a sip of his sherry. "In any case, I just received the lab report about the feathers I purloined from Oakley Plantation. The birds were indeed infected with an avian influenza virus, but the very small sample I was able to obtain was simply too degraded to cultivate. Nevertheless, the researcher I employed made an important observation. The virus is neuroinvasive."

Hayward sighed. "You're going to have to explain that."

"It hides in the human nervous system. It's highly *neurovirulent*. And that, Captain, is the final piece of the puzzle."

The tea came and Maurice poured out a cup. "Go on."

Pendergast rose and paced before the fire. "The parrot virus makes you sick, just like any flu virus. And like many viruses, it hides in the nervous system as a way of avoiding the bloodstream and thus the human immune system. But that's where the similarities end. Because this virus also *has an effect* on the nervous system. And that effect is most unusual: it enhances brain activity, triggers a flowering of the intellect. My researcher—an exceedingly clever fellow—tells me that this could be caused by a simple loosening of neural pathways. You see, the virus makes the nerve endings slightly more sensitive—making them fire more quickly, more easily, with less stimuli. Trigger-happy nerves, as it were. But the virus also inhibits production of acetylcholine in the brain. And it seems this combination of effects ultimately unbalances the system, eventually overwhelming the victim with sensory input."

Hayward frowned. This seemed like a reach, even for Pendergast. "Are you sure about this?"

"Additional research would be needed to confirm the theory, but it's the only answer that fits." He paused. "Think of yourself for a moment, Captain Hayward. You are sitting on a couch. You are aware of the pressure of the leather against your back. You are aware of the warmth of the teacup in your hand. You can smell the roast saddle of lamb that we will be having for dinner. You can hear a variety of sounds: crickets, songbirds in the trees, the fire in the fireplace, Maurice in the kitchen."

"Of course," Hayward said. "What's your point?"

"You are aware of those sensations and probably a hundred more, if you were to stop and take note of them. But that's the point: you *don't* take note. A part of your brain—the thalamus, to be exact—is acting as a traffic cop, making sure you are only aware of the sensations that are important at the moment. Imagine what it would be like if there were no traffic cop? You would be continually bombarded by sensation, unable to ignore any of it. While it might in the short run enhance cognitive function and creativity, in the long run it would drive you mad. Literally. *That* is what happened to Audubon. And it happened to the Doane family—only much more rapidly and powerfully. We already suspected the madness shared by Audubon and the Doanes was more than coincidence—we just didn't have the link. Until now."

"The Doanes' parrot," Hayward said. "It had the virus, too. Just like the parrots stolen from Oakley Plantation."

"Correct. My wife must have discovered this extraordinary effect by accident. She realized that Audubon's illness seemed to have profoundly changed him, and as an epidemiologist she had the tools to figure out why. Her leap of genius was in realizing it wasn't just a psychic change caused by a brush with death; it was a *physical* change. You asked what her role in all this was: I have reason to believe she might, through the best of intentions, have taken her discovery to a pharmaceutical company, which tried to develop a drug from it. A mind-enhancement drug, or what I believe today is called a 'smart' drug."

"So what happened to that drug? Why wasn't it developed?"

"When we learn that, I think we will be much closer to understanding why my wife was killed."

Hayward spoke again, slowly. "I learned today that Blackletter was a consultant for several pharmaceutical companies after leaving Doctors With Wings."

"Excellent." Pendergast resumed pacing. "I'm ready for your report."

Hayward briefly summarized her visits to Florida and St. Francisville. "Both Blast and Blackletter were killed by a professional wielding a 12-gauge sawed-off shotgun loaded with double-ought buckshot. He entered the premises, killed the victims, then tossed the place and took a few things to make it look like a robbery."

"Which pharmaceutical companies did Blackletter consult for?"

Hayward opened her briefcase, slid out a manila envelope, extracted a sheet, and handed it to him.

Pendergast walked over and took it. "Did you dig up any of Blackletter's former contacts or associates?"

"Just one—a snapshot of an old flame."

"An excellent start."

"Speaking of Blast, there's something I don't understand."

Pendergast put the photo aside. "Yes?"

"Well—it's pretty obvious the person who killed Blackletter also killed him. But why? He didn't have anything to do with this avian flu—did he?"

Pendergast shook his head. "No, he didn't. And that is a very good question. I believe it must concern the conversation Helen once had with Blast. Blast told me that, when he confronted her about the Black Frame and her reasons for wanting it, she said: 'I don't want to own it, I just want to examine it.' We now know Blast was telling the truth about this. But of course, whoever arranged for my wife's murder cannot have known what transpired in that conversation. She might have told him more—perhaps much more. About Audubon and the avian flu, for example. And so, for safety's sake, Blast had to die. He wasn't a big loose end—but he was a loose end nonetheless."

Hayward shook her head. "That's cold."

"Cold indeed."

At that moment Maurice came in, a look of distaste on his face. "Mr. Hudson is here to see you, sir."

"Send him in."

Hayward watched as a short, stocky, obsequious-looking fellow came into the room, all trench coat, fedora, pinstripes, and wingtips. He looked every inch the film noir caricature of a private investigator, which is what he evidently thought he was. She was amazed that Pendergast would have any truck with such a person.

"Hope I'm not interrupting," he said, ducking his head and removing his hat.

"Not at all, Mr. Hudson." She noticed Pendergast didn't introduce her. "You have the list of pharmaceutical companies I asked for?"

"Yes, sir. And I visited each one—"

"Thank you." Pendergast took the list. "Please wait in the east parlor, where I will take your report in good time." He nodded to Maurice. "Make sure Mr. Hudson is comfortable with a nonalcoholic beverage." The old servant led the man back out into the hallway.

"What in the world did you do to make him so . . ." Hayward searched for the right word. "Meek?"

"A variant of the Stockholm syndrome. First you threaten his life, then with great magnanimity you spare him. The poor fellow made the mistake of hiding in my garage with a loaded gun, in a rather ill-considered blackmail attempt."

Hayward shuddered, remembering afresh why she found Pendergast's methods so distasteful.

"Anyway, he's working for us now. And the first assignment I gave him was to compile a list of all the pharmaceutical companies within fifty miles of the Doane house—reasoning fifty miles to be the outside limit of how far an escaped parrot would fly. All that remains is to compare it to your list of the companies Blackletter consulted for." Pendergast held up the two sheets of paper, glancing back and forth between them. His face suddenly hardened. He lowered the sheets and his eyes met hers.

"We have a match," he said. "Longitude Pharmaceuticals."

51

Baton Rouge

The house, of cheerful yellow stucco with white trim, stood in a gentrified neighborhood at the fringes of Spanish Town in Baton Rouge, with a tiny front garden overflowing with tulips. Laura Hayward followed Pendergast up the brick walk to the front door. She eyed the large sign that read NO SOLICITING. That did not seem like a good omen, and she was miffed that Pendergast had turned down her suggestion they call ahead to set up an appointment.

A small man with wispy hair opened the door, peering at them through round glasses. "May I help you?"

"Is Mary Ann Roblet at home?" Pendergast asked in his most mellifluous southern accent, irritating Hayward further. She reminded herself again that she was doing this not for him, but for Vinnie.

The man hesitated. "Whom may I say is calling?"

"Aloysius Pendergast and Laura Hayward."

Another hesitation. "Are you, ah, religious folk?"

"No, sir," said Pendergast. "Nor are we selling any-thing." He waited, with a pleasant smile on his face.

The man, after a moment of further hesitation, called over his shoulder. "Mary Ann? Two people to see you." He waited at the door, not inviting them in.

A moment later a vivacious woman bustled to the door, plump, ample-breasted, her silver hair coiffed, makeup tastefully applied. "Yes?"

Pendergast introduced themselves once again while at the same time removing the FBI shield from his suit, opening it in front of her with a smooth motion, and then closing it and restoring it somewhere inside the black material. Hayward noticed with a start that tucked inside the shield was the snapshot she had retrieved in Blackletter's house.

A blush crept up on Mary Ann Roblet's face.

"May we speak with you in private, Mrs. Roblet?"

She was flustered, unable to reply, her blush growing deeper.

The man, evidently her husband, hovered suspi-ciously in the background. "What is it?" he asked. "Who are these people?"

"They're FBI."

"FBI? *FBI*? What the heck is this about?" He turned to them. "What do you want?"

Pendergast spoke up. "Mr. Roblet, it's purely rou-tine, nothing to be concerned about. But it is confiden-tial. We need to speak with your wife for a few minutes, that's all. Now, Mrs. Roblet, may we come in?"

She backed away from the door, her face now entirely red.

"Is there a place inside where we can talk in private?" asked Pendergast. "If you don't mind."

Mrs. Roblet recovered her voice. "We can go into the den."

They followed Mrs. Roblet into a small television room, with two overstuffed chairs and a sofa, white wall-to-wall carpeting, and a huge plasma television at one end. Pendergast firmly shut the door as Mr. Roblet hung about in the hall, frowning. Mrs. Roblet seated herself primly on the sofa, adjusting the hem of her dress. Instead of taking one of the chairs, Pendergast sat down beside her on the sofa.

"My apologies for disturbing you," said Pendergast in a low, pleasant voice. "We hope to take up only a few minutes of your time."

After a silence, Mrs. Roblet said, "I assume you're looking into the... death of Morris Blackletter."

"That's correct. How did you know?"

"I read about it in the papers." Her carefully constructed face already looked like it was beginning to fall apart.

"I'm very sorry," said Pendergast, extracting a small packet of tissues from his suit and offering her one. She took one, dabbed her eyes. She was making a heroic effort to hold herself together.

"We're not here to pry into your past life or disturb your marriage," Pendergast went on in a kindly voice. "I imagine it must be difficult to grieve secretly for someone you once cared about a great deal. Nothing we say in here will get back to your husband."

She nodded, dabbing again. "Yes. Morris was... was a wonderful man," she said quietly, then her voice changed, hardened. "Let's just get this over with."

Hayward shifted uncomfortably. *Damn Pendergast*

and his methods, she thought. This kind of an interview should take place in a formal setting: a police station with recording devices.

"Of course. You met Dr. Blackletter in Africa?"

"Yes," she said.

"Under what circumstances?"

"I was a nurse with the Libreville Baptist Mission in Gabon. That's in West Africa."

"And your husband?"

"He was the mission's senior pastor," she said in a low voice.

"How did you meet Dr. Blackletter?"

"Is this really necessary?" she whispered.

"Yes."

"He ran a small clinic next to the mission for Doctors With Wings. Whenever there was an outbreak of disease in the western part of the country, he used to fly into the bush to inoculate the villagers. It was very, very dangerous work, and when he needed help, sometimes I would go with him."

Pendergast laid a kindly hand on hers. "When did your relationship with him begin?"

"Around the middle of our first year there. That would be twenty-two years ago."

"And when did it end?"

A long silence. "It didn't." Her voice faltered.

"Tell us about his work back here in the States, after he left Doctors With Wings."

"Morris was an epidemiologist. A very good one. He worked for a number of pharmaceutical companies as a consultant, helping them design and develop vaccines and other drugs."

"Was one of them Longitude Pharmaceuticals?"

"Yes."

"Did he ever tell you anything about his work with them?"

"He kept quiet about most of his consulting work. It was pretty hush-hush, industrial secrets and all that. But it's funny you should mention that company, because he did talk about it a few times. More than most of them."

"And?"

"He worked there for about a year."

"When was that?"

"Maybe eleven years ago. He quit abruptly. Something happened there he didn't like. He was angry and frightened—and believe me, Morris was not an easily frightened man. I remember one evening he talked about the company CEO. Slade was his name. Charles J. Slade. I remember him saying the man was evil, and that the sign of a truly evil man was his ability to draw good people into his maelstrom. That was the word he used, *maelstrom*. I remember having to look it up. Morris abruptly stopped talking about Longitude shortly after he quit, and I never heard him speak of it again."

"He never worked for them again?"

"Never. The company went into bankruptcy almost immediately after Morris left. Fortunately, he had been paid by then."

Hayward leaned forward. "Excuse me for interrupting, but how do you know he was paid?"

Mary Ann Roblet turned gray eyes on her, damp and red. "He loved fine silverwork. Antiques. He went out and spent a fortune on a private collection, and when I asked him how he afforded it he told me he'd received a large bonus from Longitude."

"A large bonus. After a year of work." Pendergast thought a moment. "What else did he say about this man, Slade?"

She thought for a moment. "He said he'd brought down a good company. Wrecked it with his own thoughtlessness and arrogance."

"Did you ever meet Slade?"

"Oh, no. Never. Morris and I never had any kind of public relationship. It was always…private. I did hear that everyone was in deathly fear of Slade. Except for June, that is."

"June?"

"June Brodie. Slade's executive secretary."

Pendergast thought about this for a moment. Then he turned to Hayward. "Do you have any further questions?"

"Did Dr. Blackletter ever indicate what he was working on at Longitude or whom he worked with?"

"He never talked about the confidential research. But from time to time he did mention a few of the people he worked with. He liked to tell funny stories about people. Let's see…My memory isn't what it used to be. There was June, of course."

"Why 'of course'?" Pendergast asked.

"Because June was so important to Slade." She paused, opened her mouth to speak again, then colored slightly.

"Yes?" Pendergast pressed.

Roblet shook her head.

After a brief silence, Hayward continued. "Who else did Dr. Blackletter work with at Longitude?"

"Let me think. The senior VP of science, Dr. Gordon Groebel, whom Morris reported to directly."

Hayward quickly jotted down the name. "Anything about this Dr. Groebel in particular?"

"Let me think...Morris called him misguided a few times. Misguided and greedy, if I remember." She paused. "There was someone else. A Mr. Phillips. Denison Phillips, I believe. He was the firm's general counsel."

A silence fell in the little sitting room. Mary Ann Roblet dried her eyes, took out a compact case and touched up her face, plumped her hair, and added a touch of lipstick.

"Life goes on, as they say," she said. "Will that be all?"

"Yes," said Pendergast, rising. "Thank you, Mrs. Roblet."

She didn't answer. They followed her out the door and into the hall. Her husband was in the kitchen, drinking coffee. He jumped up and came to the front hall as they prepared to leave.

"Are you all right, dear?" he asked, looking at her with concern.

"Quite all right. You remember that nice Dr. Blackletter who used to work at the mission years ago?"

"Blackletter, the flying doctor? Of course I remember him. Fine fellow."

"He was killed in St. Francisville in a burglary a few days ago. These FBI agents are investigating."

"Good heavens," said Roblet, looking more relieved than anything else. "That's terrible. I didn't even know he lived in Louisiana. Hadn't thought of him in years."

"Neither had I."

As they climbed into the Rolls, Hayward turned to Pendergast. "That was exceptionally well done," she said.

Pendergast turned, inclined his head. "Coming from you, I accept that as a very great compliment, Captain Hayward."

52

Frank Hudson paused in the shade of a tree on the walkway in front of the Vital Records Building. The air-conditioning inside had been cranked to Siberian temperatures, and coming out into the unseasonable heat and humidity made him feel like an ice cube dropped into warm soup.

Setting down his briefcase, he pulled a handkerchief out of the breast pocket of his pin-striped suit and mopped his bald crown. *Nothing like a Baton Rouge winter*, he thought irritably. Stuffing the hankie back into his pocket, patting it in place to leave a rakish corner exposed, he squinted in the bright sunlight toward the parking lot and located his vintage Ford Falcon. Near it, a stout woman in plaid was getting out of a beaten-to-hell Nova, all in a huff, and he watched her slam the door once, twice, trying to get it to latch.

"Bastard," he heard the woman mutter to the car, trying to slam the door again. "Son of a bitch."

He mopped again, replaced the fedora on his head.

He'd rest here a moment longer in the shade before getting into his car. The assignment Pendergast had given him had been a piece of cake. June Brodie, thirty-five. Secretary, married, no kids, a good looker. It was all there in the files. Husband a nurse-practitioner. She'd been trained as a nurse herself, but ended up working for Longitude. Fast-forward fourteen years. Longitude goes bankrupt, she loses her job, and a week after that she climbs into her Tahoe. Drives to Archer Bridge a few miles out of town. Disappears. The handwritten suicide note left in the car says, *Can't take it anymore. All my fault. Forgive me.* They drag the river for a week, nothing. It's a favorite spot for jumpers, the river is swift and deep, lots of bodies are never found. End of story.

It had taken Hudson only a few hours to pull the information together, go through the files. He was worried he hadn't done enough to justify his five-hundred-dollar-a-day salary. Maybe he shouldn't mention it only took him two hours.

The file was complete, right down to a photocopy of the suicide note; the FBI agent ought to be pleased with it. As far as the pay went, he'd play it by ear. This was too lucrative a connection to take chances by gaming the man or trying to squeeze out a few pennies more.

Hudson picked up the briefcase and stepped out of the shade into the baking parking lot.

With a final curse, Nancy Milligan slammed the car door and it stayed shut. She was sweating, exasperated, and mad: mad at the unusual heat, mad at the old clunker of a car, and particularly mad at her husband.

Why did the blame fool make her run his errands instead of getting up off his fat ass and doing them himself? Why the city of Baton Rouge needed a copy of his birth certificate at *his* age . . . it made no sense.

She straightened up and was embarrassed to see a man standing across the parking lot, fedora pushed back on his head, mopping his brow, looking in her direction.

In that very moment his hat flew into the air and the entire side of his head went blurry, coalescing into a jet of dark fluid. At the same time a sharp *crack!* rolled through the spreading oaks. The man slowly toppled to the ground, straight as a tree, landing so heavily his body rolled like a log before coming to rest, arms wrapped around in a crazy self-hug. The hat hit the ground at the same time, rolling a few yards and then, with a wobble, coming to rest on its crown.

For a moment, the woman just stood beside her car, frozen. Then she took out her cell phone and dialed 911 with numb fingers. "A man," she said, surprised by the calmness of her voice, "has just been shot in the parking lot of the Vital Records Building, Louisiana Avenue."

In answer to a question she replied, "Yes, he is most certainly dead."

53

The parking lot and part of the nearby street had been marked off with crime-scene tape. A crowd of reporters, news teams, and cameras seethed behind blue police barricades, along with a smattering of rubberneckers and disgruntled people who couldn't get their cars out of the lot.

Hayward stood next to Pendergast behind the barriers, watching the investigators do their work. Pendergast had persuaded her, against her will, that they should remain civilians and not involve themselves in the investigation. Nor should they reveal that the PI had been working for them. Hayward reluctantly agreed: to admit their connection to Hudson would involve them in endless paperwork, interviews, and difficulties; it would hamper their work and expose them to press reports and public scrutiny. Bottom line, it would almost guarantee they would never find Vinnie's attacker and this man's killer—evidently the same person.

"I don't get it," Hayward said. "Why go after Hudson? Here we are, interviewing everyone, blundering about, stirring the pot—and all he was doing was pulling some public files on June Brodie."

Pendergast squinted into the sun, his eyes narrowed, and said nothing.

Hayward **tightened** her lips and watched the forensic team do **their work**, crouching over the hot asphalt. They looked **like crabs** moving slowly over the bottom of the sea. So far they had done everything right. Meticulous, by the book, not a single misstep that she could identify. They were professionals. And perhaps that was no surprise; the very public assassination of a man in broad daylight in front of a government building was not an everyday event in Baton Rouge.

"Let us stroll over this way," Pendergast murmured. She followed him as he slipped through the crowd, moving across the large lawn, circling the parking lot, heading toward the far corner of the Vital Records Building. They stopped before a cluster of yews, severely clipped into oblong shapes, like squashed bowling pins.

Hayward, suddenly suspicious, watched Pendergast approach the bushes.

"This is where the shooter fired from," he said.

"How do you know?"

He pointed to the tilled ground around the yews, covered with raked bark chips. "He lay down here, and the marks of his bipod are there."

Hayward peered without getting too close and, with some effort, finally made out the two almost invisible indents in the ground where the bark had been pushed aside.

"Pendergast, you've got an admirable imagination. How do you know he shot from over here in the first place? The police seem to think it came from another direction." Most of the police activity had been focusing along the street.

"By the position of the fedora. The force of the round kicked the victim's head to one side, but it was the rebound of the neck muscles that jerked the hat off."

Hayward rolled her eyes. "That's pretty thin."

But Pendergast wasn't listening. Once again he was moving across the lawn, this time more rapidly. Hayward took off, struggling to catch up.

He crossed the four hundred yards of open ground, closing in on the parking lot. Expertly slipping his way through the crowd, he came up to the barricades. Again his silver eyes, squinting against the bright sun, peered into the sea of parked cars. A small pair of binoculars made their appearance, and he looked around.

He slipped the binoculars back into his suit. "Excuse me—Officers?" He leaned over the barricade, trying to get the attention of two detectives conferring over a clipboard.

They studiously ignored him.

"Officers? Hello, excuse me."

One of the detectives looked over with obvious reluctance. "Yes?"

"Come here, please." Pendergast gestured with a white hand.

"Sir, we're very busy here."

"Please. It's important. I have *information*."

Hayward was surprised and irritated by Pendergast's

whining, which seemed almost calculated to provoke skepticism. She'd taken pains to curry favor with the local cops—the last thing she wanted was for Pendergast to queer that now.

The detective approached. "Did you see it happen?"

"No. But I see *that*." Pendergast pointed into the parking lot.

"What?" The detective followed his pointing finger.

"That white Subaru. In the front right door, just below the window trim, is a bullet hole."

The detective squinted, and then shuffled off, threaded his way among the cars to the Subaru. He bent over. A moment later his head shot back up. He shouted at the team and waved.

"George? *George!* Get the team over here. There's a round in this door panel!"

The forensic team hustled to the car, while the detective came striding back to Pendergast, suddenly interested, his eyes narrowed. "How'd you see that?"

Pendergast smiled. "I have excellent eyesight." He leaned in. "And if you'll excuse the speculation of an ignorant bystander, I would say that—given the position of the bullet hole and the placement of the victim—it might be worth examining the shrubbery at the southeast corner of the building as a likely place from which the shot originated."

The detective's eyes flickered to the building and along the trajectory, immediately comprehending the geometry of the situation. "Right." He waved two detectives over and spoke to them in a low voice.

Immediately Pendergast began moving away.

"Sir? Just a minute, sir."

But Pendergast was already out of hearing, mingling with the general hubbub of the crowd. He drifted toward the building, Hayward in tow, keeping with the moving masses of people. But instead of heading toward their parked car, he turned and entered the Vital Records Building.

"That was an interesting exchange," Hayward said.

"It seemed prudent to furnish them with any available assistance. We need every possible edge we can obtain in this case. However, I believe"—Pendergast continued as they approached the receptionist—"that our adversary might just have made his second false move."

"Which is?"

Instead of answering, Pendergast turned to the clerk. "We're interested in seeing your files on a June Brodie. They may still be out of the stacks—a gentleman, I believe, was looking at them earlier today."

As the woman was retrieving the file from a sorting cart, Hayward turned to Pendergast. "Okay. I'll bite this one time. What was the first false move?"

"Missing me at Penumbra and hitting Vincent instead."

54

New York City

Dr. John Felder stepped down from the witness stand at the involuntary-commitment hearing and took his seat. He avoided looking in the direction of Constance Greene, the accused; there was something profoundly unsettling about the steady gaze from those violet eyes. Felder had said what he had to say and what his professional belief was: that she was profoundly mentally ill and should be involuntarily committed. It was moot, because she was already charged with first-degree murder with bail denied, but it was still a necessary stage in the legal process. And, Felder had to admit, in this particular case it was an eminently valid determination. Because despite her self-possession, despite her high intelligence and apparent lucidity, Felder was now convinced she was deeply insane—unable to tell right from wrong.

There was some shuffling of papers and clearing of

throats as the judge wrapped up the hearing. "I note for the record," he intoned, "that the alleged mentally ill person has not availed herself of legal counsel."

"That's correct, Your Honor," said Greene primly, hands folded on her prison-garb skirt.

"You have a right to speak at this proceeding," the judge said. "Is there anything you wish to say?"

"Not at present, Your Honor."

"You have heard the testimony of Dr. Felder, who says he believes you are a danger to yourself and to others and should be involuntarily committed to an institution for the mentally ill. Do you have any comment on that testimony?"

"I would not wish to dispute an expert."

"Very well." The judge handed a sheaf of papers to a court officer, and received another in return. "And now I have a question of my own." He pulled his glasses down his nose and looked at her.

Felder was mildly surprised. He had attended dozens of involuntary-commitment hearings, but rarely, if ever, had a judge asked questions directly of the accused. Usually the judge concluded with a pontification of some kind, replete with moral urgings and pop-psychology observations.

"Ms. Greene, no one seems to be able to establish your identity or even verify your existence. The same is true of your baby. Despite a diligent search, there appears to be no evidence that you gave birth. The latter point is a problem for your trial judge. But I also face significant legal issues in committing you involuntarily without a Social Security number or evidence that you are an American citizen. In short, we do not know who you really are."

He paused. Greene looked at him attentively, hands still folded.

"I wonder if you're ready to tell this court the truth about your past," the judge said in a stern but not unkindly tone. "Who you really are, and where you are from."

"Your Honor, I've already told the truth," said Constance.

"In this transcript you indicate that you were born on Water Street in the 1970s. But the record shows this cannot be true."

"It *isn't* true."

Felder felt a certain weariness creep in. The judge should know better; this was fruitless, a waste of the court's time. Felder had patients to attend to—paying patients.

"You say it right here, in this transcript I have in my hand."

"I do not say it."

The judge, exasperated, began to read from the transcript:

Question: *When were you born?*
Answer: *I don't recall.*
Question: *Well, of course you wouldn't recall, but surely you know the date of your birth?*
Answer: *I'm afraid I don't.*
Question: *It must have been, what, the late '80s?*
Answer: *I believe it would have been more in the early '70s.*

The judge looked up. "Did you or did you not say these things?"

"I did."

"Well, then. You claim to have been born in the early 1970s on Water Street. But the court's research has proven this to be untrue beyond any doubt. And in any case you look far too young to have been born more than thirty years ago."

Greene said nothing.

Felder started to rise. "Your Honor, may I interject?"

The judge turned to him. "Yes, Dr. Felder?"

"I've already thoroughly explored this line of questioning with the patient. With respect, Your Honor, I would remind the court that we are not dealing with a rational mind. I hope I won't offend the court by saying that in my professional opinion, there will be no useful result from this line of questioning."

The judge tapped the folder with his glasses. "Perhaps you're right, Doctor. And am I to understand that the nominative next-of-kin, Aloysius Pendergast, defers to the court in this matter?"

"He declined any invitation to be heard, Your Honor."

"Very well." The judge gathered up another sheaf of papers, took a deep breath, and looked out over the small, empty courtroom. He put his glasses back in place and bent over the papers. "This court finds—" he began.

Constance Greene rose to her feet, her face suddenly flushed. For the first time, she looked like she was experiencing emotion; in fact, to Felder she looked almost angry. "On second thought, I believe I *shall* speak," she said, her voice suddenly possessing an edge. "If I may, Your Honor?"

The judge sat back and folded his hands. "I will allow a statement."

"I was indeed born on Water Street in the '70s—the *1870s*. You will find all you need to know in the city archives on Centre Street, and more in the New York Public Library. About me; about my sister, Mary, who was sent to the Five Points Mission and later killed by a mass murderer; about my brother, Joseph; about my parents, who died of tuberculosis—there's a fair amount of information there. I know, because I have seen the records myself."

The silence stretched out in the court. Finally the judge said, "Thank you, Ms. Greene. You may be seated."

She sat down.

The judge cleared his throat. "The court finds that Ms. Constance Greene, age unknown, address unknown, is of unsound mind and represents a clear and present danger to herself and others. Therefore, we order that Ms. Constance Greene be committed involuntarily to the Bedford Hills Correctional Facility for appropriate observation and treatment. The term of this commitment shall be indefinite."

He gave a tap with the gavel for emphasis. "Court dismissed."

Felder rose, feeling oddly dispirited. He threw a glance toward the unknown woman, who had risen again and was now flanked by two muscular guards. Standing between them, she looked small and almost frail. The color had left her face, which was once again expressionless. She knew what had just occurred—she *had* to know—and yet she showed not the slightest hint of emotion.

Felder turned away and walked out of the courtroom.

55

Sulphur, Louisiana

The rental Buick hummed along the diamond-cut concrete of Interstate 10. Hayward had set the cruise control at seventy-five miles an hour, despite Pendergast's murmured observation that, at seventy-nine miles per hour, they would arrive in town five minutes earlier.

They had already logged two hundred miles on the Buick that day, and she had noted that Pendergast was becoming uncharacteristically irritable. He made no secret of his dislike of the Buick and had suggested more than once they switch to the Rolls-Royce—its windshield freshly repaired—but Hayward had refused to get into it. She couldn't imagine conducting an effective investigation while tooling around in a Rolls, and she wondered why Pendergast would even consider using such a flamboyant car for work. Driving his wife's vintage sports car had been bad enough; after twenty-four hours of that, Hayward had returned it to its garage and insisted on renting a much less exciting but infinitely more anonymous vehicle.

Pendergast seemed particularly annoyed that the first two names on Mary Ann Roblet's list hadn't panned out: one was long dead, the other non compos mentis and, on top of that, in a hospital on life support. They were now on their way to the third and last. He was Denison Phillips IV, former general counsel of Longitude, retired and living a quiet life on Bonvie Drive in the Bayou Glades Country Club area of Sulphur. The name and address had already created a picture in Hayward's mind of a member of a certain minor southern gentry: pompous, self-important, alcoholic, cunning, and above all uncooperative. From her days at LSU she knew the type all too well.

She saw the exit sign for Sulphur and slowed, moving into the right lane.

"I'm glad we ran a file on our Mr. Phillips," Pendergast said.

"He came up clean."

"Indeed," came the curt reply. "I'm referring to the file on Mr. Denison Phillips the Fifth."

"His son? You mean, that drug conviction on his rap sheet?"

"It's rather serious: possession of more than five grams of cocaine with intent to sell. I also noted in the file that he's pre-law at LSU."

"Yeah. I'd like to see him get into law school with that on his record. You can't qualify for the bar with a felony."

"One would assume," Pendergast drawled, "that

the family is connected and has reason to believe the record will be expunged when Denison the Fifth attains twenty-one. At least, I feel confident that's their *intention*."

Hayward took her eyes off the road long enough to glance at Pendergast. There was a hard gleam in his eyes as he spoke these last words. She could just imagine how he was planning to handle this. He'd put the screws on, threaten to obstruct any attempt to expunge the conviction, perhaps even threaten to call the press, and in every way make it impossible for Denison Phillips V to join his father's law firm . . . unless the old man talked, and talked effusively. More than ever, she wished Vinnie were here instead of recuperating in Caltrop Hospital. Handling Pendergast was exhausting work. For the hundredth time, she wondered exactly why Vinnie—an old-school cop like herself—held Pendergast and his supreme unorthodoxy in such high regard.

She took a deep breath. "Say, Pendergast, I wonder if you'd do me a favor."

"Of course, Captain."

"Let me take first crack at this particular interview." She felt the FBI agent's eyes on her.

"I know his type well," she went on. "And I've got an idea for how best to handle him."

There was a brief and to Hayward's mind somewhat frosty silence before Pendergast replied, "I shall observe with interest."

Denison Phillips IV met them at the door of his spacious golf-club development home, old enough that the trees planted around had attained quasi-stately proportions.

He was so exactly what Hayward had imagined, so exquisitely the type, that she was instantly disgusted. The seersucker jacket with the paisley handkerchief tucked into the breast pocket, the monogrammed pale yellow shirt unbuttoned at the top, green golfing slacks, and afternoon martini in hand completed the picture.

"May I ask what this is in reference to?" he drawled, in a faux-genteel accent in which all traces of servile ancestry had been carefully removed several generations before.

"I am Captain Hayward of the New York City Police Department, formerly of the New Orleans Police Department," she said, switching into the bland, neutral tone she used when dealing with potential informants. "And this is my associate, Special Agent Pendergast of the FBI." As she spoke, she removed her shield, swept it past Phillips. Pendergast didn't bother doing the same.

Phillips glanced from one to the other. "You are aware this is Sunday?"

"Yes, sir. May we come in?"

"Perhaps I need to speak to my attorney first," said Phillips.

"Naturally," Hayward replied, "that would be your right, sir, and we'd wait as long as it took for him to arrive. But we're here informally with only a few quick questions. You're not in any way a target of our investigation. All we need is ten minutes of your time."

Phillips hesitated and then stepped aside. "In that case, come in."

Hayward followed Phillips into the house, all white carpeting, white brick, white leather, gold and glass. Pendergast silently brought up the rear. They came into a living room with picture windows overlooking a fairway.

"Please sit down." Phillips took a seat, setting his martini on a leather coaster on a side table. He did not offer them one.

Hayward cleared her throat. "You were a partner in the law firm of Marston, Phillips, and Lowe, is that right?"

"If this is about my law firm, I really can't answer any questions."

"And you were the general counsel to the Longitude corporation, up to and through the period of its bankruptcy some eleven years ago?"

A long silence. Phillips smiled and placed his hands on his knees, rising. "I'm sorry, but we're already beyond where I'm comfortable going without legal representation. I would suggest you return with a subpoena. I will gladly answer questions with counsel present."

Hayward rose. "As you wish. Sorry to bother you, Mr. Phillips." She paused. "Give our regards to your son."

"You know my son?" came the easy reply, with no hint of anxiety.

"No," said Hayward. They moved toward the front hall.

As her hand touched the doorknob, Phillips finally asked, his voice very calm, "Then why did you mention him just now?"

Hayward turned. "I can see, Mr. Phillips, that you are a gentleman of the Old South. A forthright man of old-fashioned values who appreciates directness."

Phillips greeted this with a certain wariness.

Hayward went on, subtly modulating her voice into the southern inflections that she usually suppressed. "Which is why I'll be straight with you. I'm here on a special errand. We need information. And we're in a position to help your son. About that matter of the drug conviction, I mean."

This was greeted with a dead silence. "All that's been taken care of," Phillips said at last.

"Well, you see—that depends."

"Depends on what?"

"On just how forthright you prove to be."

Phillips frowned. "I don't understand."

"You're in possession of information that's very important to us. Now, my associate here, Agent Pendergast— let's just say that the two of us are in disagreement on how best to elicit that information. He, and the Bureau, are in a position to make sure that your son's record is *not* expunged. And he's of the opinion that this is the easiest way to guarantee your help. By keeping your son's record dirty, by preventing him from attending law school—or at least *threatening* to prevent him from attending—he believes he can force your hand."

Hayward paused. Phillips looked at them in turn. A vein in his temple throbbed.

"I, on the other hand, would prefer to cooperate. See, I'm in with the local constabulary. I used to be one of them myself. I'm in a position to *help* clear your son's record. Help make sure he gets into law school, passes the bar, joins your firm. Seems to me that would be good for everyone. What do you think?"

"I see: the classic good-cop, bad-cop routine," said Phillips.

"A tried-and-true approach."

"What do you want to know?" Phillips asked, voice thin.

"We're working on an old case, and we have reason to believe you can help us. As I mentioned, it involves Longitude Pharmaceuticals."

A veiled expression came over Phillips's face. "I'm not at liberty to discuss the company."

"That's really a shame. And I'll tell you why. Because hearing this obstructionist attitude—and hearing it from your own lips—is just going to reinforce my associate's notion that *his* way of handling this is the right way to go. I'll be embarrassed—and your son will never, ever get a law degree."

Phillips did not reply.

"It's also a shame because Agent Pendergast here is in a position to help, as well as to hurt." Hayward paused briefly to let this sink in. "You see, you'll need the FBI's help if you want to correct your son's record. With a drug conviction like that...well, as you might imagine, there will be a federal file to take care of, in addition to the local paperwork."

Phillips swallowed. "We're talking about a small-time drug conviction. The FBI would have no interest in that."

"Possession *with intent to sell*. That automatically generates a federal file." She nodded slowly. "Being a corporate lawyer, perhaps you didn't know that. Trust me, that file is sitting in a cabinet somewhere, a time bomb waiting to blow up your son's future."

Pendergast stood beside her, motionless. He hadn't said a word during the entire exchange.

Phillips licked his lips, wet them with the martini, exhaled. "What is it you want to know, exactly?"

"Tell us about the avian flu experiments at Longitude."

The ice chips in the martini tinkled as Phillips's hand shook.

"Mr. Phillips?" Hayward prompted.

"Captain, if I spoke to you of that, and the fact got out, it would result in my death."

"Nothing's going to get out. Nothing will come back to haunt you. You have my word."

Phillips nodded.

"But you have to tell us the whole truth. That's the deal."

A silence ensued.

"And you'll help him?" Phillips asked at last. "Clear his record, on both the local and federal level?"

Hayward nodded. "I'll see to it personally."

"Very well. I'll tell you what I know. Which isn't much, I'm afraid. I wasn't part of the avian group. Apparently they—"

"'They'?"

"It was a secret cell within Longitude. Formed thirteen or fourteen years ago. The names were kept secret—the only one I knew was Dr. Slade. Charles J. Slade, the CEO. He headed it. They were trying to develop a new drug."

"What kind of drug?"

"A mind-enhancement drug or treatment of some sort, developed from a strain of avian flu. Very hush-hush. They poured a huge amount of money and time into it. Then everything fell apart. The company got into financial trouble, began to cut corners, safety protocols weren't observed. There were accidents. The project was shut down. Then, just when it looked like the worst had passed, a fire broke out that destroyed Complex Six and killed Slade, and—"

"Just a minute," Pendergast interrupted, speaking for the first time. "You mean Dr. Slade is dead?"

The man looked at him and nodded. "And that was only the beginning. Not long after, his secretary committed suicide and the company went bankrupt. Chapter Eleven. It was a disaster."

There was a brief silence. Glancing at Pendergast, Hayward noticed a look of surprise and—what, disappointment?—on the normally expressionless face. Clearly, this was an unexpected development.

"Was Slade a medical doctor?" Pendergast asked.

"He had a PhD."

"Do you have a picture of him?"

Phillips hesitated. "It would be in my old annual report file."

"Please get it."

The man rose, disappeared through a door leading to a library. A few moments later he returned with an annual report, which he opened and handed to Pendergast. The agent gazed at the picture printed in the front, above the CEO's message, and passed it to Hayward. She found herself gazing at a strikingly handsome man: chiseled face, a shock of white hair over a pair of intense brown eyes, jutting brow, and cleft chin, looking more like a movie star than a CEO.

After a moment, Hayward laid the report aside and resumed. "If the project was hush-hush, why'd they bring you in?"

A hesitation. "I mentioned the accident. They were using parrots at the lab to culture and test the virus. One of the parrots escaped."

"And flew across the Black Brake swamp to infect a family in Sunflower. The Doanes."

Phillips looked at her sharply. "You seem to know a lot."

"Keep going, please."

He took another gulp of his drink, his hands still shaking. "Slade and the group decided...to let the, ah, *spontaneous* experiment take its course. By the time they tracked down the bird, you see, it was too late anyway—the family was infected. So they let it play out, to see if the new strain of virus they had developed would work."

"And it didn't."

Phillips nodded. "The family died. Not right away, of course. That was when they brought me in, after the fact, to advise on the legal ramifications. I was horrified. They were guilty of egregious violations of the law, multiple felonies up to and including negligent homicide. The legal and criminal exposure was catastrophic. I told them there wasn't any viable legal avenue for them to take that would end up in a place they'd like. So they buried it."

"You never reported it?"

"It all fell under attorney–client privilege."

Pendergast spoke again. "How did the fire start? The one Slade died in?"

Phillips turned toward him. "The insurance company did a thorough investigation. It was an accident, improper storage of chemicals. As I said, at the time the company was cutting corners to save money any way they could."

"And the others in the avian group?"

"I didn't know their names, but I've heard they're dead, too."

"And yet someone threatened your life."

He nodded. "It was a phone call, just days ago. The caller didn't identify himself. It seems your investigation has stirred the pot." He took a deep breath. "That's all I know. I've told you everything. I was never part of the experiment or the death of the Doane family. I was brought in after the fact to clean up—that's all."

"What can you tell us of June Brodie?" Hayward asked.

"She was Slade's executive secretary."

"How would you characterize her?"

"Youngish. Attractive. Motivated."

"Good at her job?"

"She was Slade's right hand. She seemed to have a finger in every pie."

"What does that mean?"

"She was heavily involved in running the day-to-day business of the company."

"Does that mean she knew about the secret project?"

"As I said, it was highly confidential."

"But she was Slade's executive secretary," Pendergast interjected. "Heavily motivated. She'd see everything that went across his desk."

Phillips didn't reply.

"What kind of a relationship did she have with her employer?"

Phillips hesitated. "Slade never discussed that with me."

"But you heard rumors," Pendergast continued. "Was the relationship more than just professional?"

"I couldn't say."

"What kind of a man was Slade?" Hayward asked after a moment.

At first, it appeared as if Phillips wouldn't answer. Then the defiant look on his face softened and he fetched a sigh of resignation. "Charles Slade was an amazing combination of visionary brilliance and extraordinary caring—mingled with unbelievable greed, even cruelty. He seemed to embody both the best and the worst—as many CEOs do. One minute he could be weeping over the bed of a dying boy...the next minute, slashing ten million from the budget and thus orphaning the development of a drug that would have saved thousands."

There was a brief silence.

Pendergast was looking steadily at the lawyer. "Does the name Helen Pendergast or Helen Esterhazy ring a bell?"

The lawyer looked back, not the slightest glimmer of recognition in his eyes. "No. I've never heard either of those names before. At least, not until you showed up at my door, Agent Pendergast."

Pendergast held the door of the Buick open for Hayward. She paused before getting in. "See how smoothly that went?"

"Indeed." He closed the door, walked around the vehicle, and slipped in himself. The irritation she had noted earlier seemed to have disappeared. "And yet I'm rather curious."

"What about?"

"About your representations about me to our friend Phillips. Telling the man I would have threatened him, used his son's criminal record against him. How do you know I wouldn't have handled him as you did?"

Hayward started the car. "I know you. You would've hammered the poor man down to within an inch of his life. I've seen you do it before. Instead of a hammer, I used a carrot."

"Why?"

"Because it works, especially with a man like that. And it'll help me sleep better at night."

"I hope you don't find the beds at Penumbra disagreeable, Captain?"

"Not in the least."

"Good. Personally, I find them most satisfactory." And as he turned his face forward, Hayward thought she saw the ghost of a smile flit across it. All of a sudden she realized she might have been mistaken in assuming how he'd have handled Denison Phillips IV. But, she mused, now she never would know.

56

Itta Bena, Mississippi

The road ran flat through the swamp outside the
small town, cypress trees on either side, a weak
morning sun filtering through their branches. A faded
sign, almost lost in the landscape, announced:

> Longitude Pharmaceuticals, Inc.
> Established 1966
> "Greeting the Future with Better Drugs"

The Buick bumped and vibrated on the poor road,
the tires slapping the asphalt. In the rearview mirror,
Hayward could see a dot approaching that soon resolved
itself into Pendergast's Rolls-Royce. He had insisted
they take two cars that morning, claiming to have various research errands of his own, but she was pretty sure
he was just looking for an excuse to get out of her rented
Buick and back into his more comfortable Rolls.

The Rolls rapidly approached, exceeding the speed limit by a generous margin, moved into the left lane, and flashed past her, rattling the Buick as it went. She got just a glimpse of a black-cuffed, pale hand raised in greeting as it passed.

The road went into a long curve and Hayward soon caught up to the Rolls again, idling at the gate to the plant, Pendergast speaking with the guard inside the adjoining guardhouse. After a lengthy exchange in which the guard went back and forth to the telephone several times, both cars were waved through.

She drove past a sign reading LONGITUDE PHARMA-CEUTICALS, INC, ITTA BENA FACILITY and into the parking lot in time to see Pendergast checking his Les Baer .45. "You're not expecting trouble?" she asked.

"One never knows," said Pendergast, returning the gun to its holster and patting his suit.

A crabgrass lawn led to a complex of low, yellow brick buildings surrounded on three sides by the fingers of a marshy lake, full of swamp lilies and floating duck-weed. Through a screen of trees, Hayward could see more buildings, some of which looked to be overgrown with ivy and in ruins. And beyond everything lay the steamy fastness of Black Brake swamp. Staring toward the wetland, dark even in the bright light of day, Hayward shivered slightly. She had heard plenty of legends about the place, growing up: legends of pirates, ghosts, and things even stranger. She slapped away a mosquito.

She followed Pendergast into the main building. The receptionist had already laid out two badges, one for MR. PENDERGAST and the other for MS. HAYWARD. Hayward plucked her badge and attached it to her lapel.

"Take the elevator to the second floor, last door on your right," said the gray-haired receptionist with a big smile.

As they got into the elevator, Hayward said: "You didn't tell them we were cops. Again."

"It is sometimes useful to see the reaction before that information is known."

Hayward shrugged. "Anyway, doesn't this seem just a little too easy to you?"

"Indeed it does."

"Who'll do the talking?"

"You did so well last time, would you care to do the honors again?"

"Delighted. Only this time I might not be so nice." She could feel the reassuring weight of her own service piece, snugged tight under her arm.

The elevator creaked up a single floor, and they emerged to find themselves in a long linoleum hallway. They strolled down to the far end and came to a door, open, beyond which a secretary worked in a spacious office. A faded but still-elegant oak door stood closed at the far end.

Hayward entered first. The secretary, who was quite young and pretty, with a ponytail and red lipstick, looked up. "Please take a seat."

They sat on a taupe sofa, beside a glass table piled with dog-eared trade magazines. The woman spoke from her desk in a brisk manner. "I'm Joan Farmer, Mr. Dalquist's personal secretary. He's going to be tied up all day and asked me to find out how we can help you."

Hayward leaned toward her. "I'm afraid you can't help us, Ms. Farmer. Only Mr. Dalquist can."

"As I said, he's busy. Perhaps if you explained to me what you needed?" Her tone had dropped a few degrees.

"Is he in there?" Hayward nodded toward the shut door.

"Ms. Hayward, I hope I've made myself clear that he is not to be disturbed. Now: one more time, how can we assist you?"

"We've come about the avian flu project."

"I'm not familiar with that project."

Hayward finally reached into her pocket, removed the shield billfold, laid it on the table, and opened it. The secretary started momentarily, leaned forward, looked at it, and then examined Pendergast's shield, which he had removed as well, following Hayward's lead.

"Police—and FBI? Why didn't you say so up front?" Her startled look was quickly replaced by undisguised annoyance. "Please wait here." She stood up and knocked softly on the closed door before opening it and disappearing, shutting it firmly behind her.

Hayward glanced over at Pendergast. They both rose simultaneously, walked over to the doorway, and pushed through.

They found themselves in a pleasant, although somewhat spartan, office. A man who looked more like a professor than a CEO, with glasses, a tweed jacket, and khaki pants, was conferring with the secretary in front of a large desk. His white hair was carefully combed, and a white brush mustache sat above lips pursed in irritation as he watched them enter.

"This is a private office!" the secretary said.

"I understand you people are police officers," said

Dalquist. "Now, if you have a warrant, I'd like to see it."

"We don't have a warrant," said Hayward. "We were hoping to speak to you informally. However, if we need a warrant, we'll go get one."

A hesitation. "If I knew what this was all about, that might not be necessary."

Hayward turned to Pendergast. "Special Agent Pendergast, perhaps Mr. Dalquist is right and we should get a warrant after all. By the book, I always say."

"It might be advisable at that, Captain Hayward. Of course, word of the warrant might get out."

Dalquist sighed. "Please sit down. Miss Farmer, I'll handle it from here, thank you. Please close the door on your way out."

The secretary left, but neither Hayward nor Pendergast sat down.

"Now, what's this business about avian flu?" asked Dalquist, his face flushing. Hayward stared but could see no glimmer of knowledge in his hostile blue eyes.

"We don't work on flu here at all," Dalquist went on, stepping back behind his desk. "We're a small pharmaceutical research company with a few products to treat certain collagen diseases—and that's it."

"About thirteen years ago," Hayward said, "Longitude conducted an illegal research project here into avian flu."

"Illegal? How so?"

"Safety procedures weren't observed. A diseased bird escaped the facility, infected a local family. They all died, and Longitude covered it up. And are still covering it up—as certain recent homicides would suggest."

A long silence. "That's a monstrous charge. I know nothing about it. Longitude went through a bankruptcy about a decade ago. A complete Chapter Eleven reorganization. There's nobody here from those days. The old management team is gone; we downsized, and we now concentrate on a few core products."

"Core products? Such as?"

"Treatments for dermatomyositis and polymyositis, primarily. We're small and focused. I've never heard of any work being done here on avian flu."

"Nobody is left from a decade ago?"

"None as far as I know. We had a disastrous fire that killed the former CEO, and the entire facility was shut down for months. When we restarted, we were essentially a different company."

Hayward pulled an envelope from her jacket. "It's our understanding that, at the time of your bankruptcy, Longitude closed down research lines on several important orphan drugs and vaccines. Just like that. You were the only facility working on those lines. It left millions of sick people in the Third World without hope."

"We were *bankrupt*."

"So you shut them down."

"The new board shut them down. Personally, I wasn't involved with the company until two years after that period. Is there a crime in that?"

Hayward found herself breathing hard. This wasn't good. They were getting nowhere. "Mr. Dalquist, your corporate filings indicate you make almost eight million dollars a year in salary and benefits. Your few drugs are very profitable. What are you doing with all that money?"

"Just what every other corporation does. Salaries, taxes, dividends, overhead, R and D."

"Forgive my saying so, but considering those profits, your research facility looks decidedly run-down."

"Don't let appearances fool you. We've got state-of-the-art equipment here. We're isolated, so we don't have to run a beauty contest." He spread his hands. "Apparently you don't like the way we do business. Maybe you don't like me. You may not like that I make eight million a year, and that we're now quite a profitable company. Fine. But we're innocent of these accusations. Totally innocent. Do I look like the kind of man involved in murder?"

"Prove it."

Dalquist came around his desk. "My first impulse is to stop you cold, make you get a warrant, fight this thing tooth and nail in the courts, use our highly paid attorneys to delay and harass you for weeks or months. Even if you prevailed, you'd end up with a limited search warrant and a mountain of paperwork. But you know what? I'm not going to do that. I'm going to give you a free pass, right here and now. You can go anywhere you like, look into anything, and have access to any documents. We've got nothing to hide. Will that satisfy you?"

Hayward glanced at Pendergast. His face was unreadable, his silvery eyes hooded.

"That would certainly be a start," she said.

He leaned over his desk and pressed a button. "Miss Farmer, please draft a letter for my signature giving these two people complete, total, and unlimited access to the entire facilities of Longitude Pharmaceuticals, with instructions that employees are to answer all questions fully and truthfully and provide access to even the most sensitive areas and documents."

He punched the button and looked up. "I just hope to see you off the premises as soon as possible."

Pendergast broke a long silence. "We shall see."

57

By the time they reached the far end of the Longitude Pharmaceuticals compound, Hayward felt exhausted. Dalquist had kept his word: they had been granted access to everything—labs, offices, archives. They had even been allowed to wander through the long-shuttered buildings that littered the sprawling campus. Nobody had accompanied them, no security harassed them; they were given free rein.

And they had found absolutely nothing. Beyond a few low-level service employees, nobody at the facility remained from the pre-bankruptcy days. The company records, which went back decades, made no reference to an avian flu project. Everything appeared to be on the up-and-up.

Which made Hayward suspicious. In her experience, everyone—even honest people—had something to hide.

She glanced at Pendergast as they walked down the corridor of the last shuttered building. She could discern nothing about his thoughts from his cool, ala-baster face.

They exited the far door, a fire exit crash door that groaned as they opened it. It gave out onto a broken cement stoop and patchy lawn. To the right lay a nar-row muddy lake, a stranded bayou, surrounded by bald cypress trees hung with Spanish moss. Straight ahead, through a tangle of vegetation, Hayward could see the remains of a brick wall covered with vines, and behind it a jutting, burned-out ruin tucked away at the far edge of the campus, surrounded on three sides by the dark fastness of Black Brake swamp. Beyond the ruin, an old pier, burned and ruined, hardly more than a series of pilings, fell away into the dark waters of the swamp.

A fine rain had begun to fall, bedewing the grass, and ominous clouds rolled low in the sky.

"I forgot my umbrella," Hayward said, looking into the wet, dismal trees.

Pendergast, who had been staring off in the direc-tion of the pier and the swamp, reached into his suit. *Oh, no*, she thought, *don't tell me he's got an umbrella in there*. But instead he removed a small packet contain-ing clear plastic rain covers, one for her and another for himself.

In a few minutes, they were squishing across the lawn toward the tangled remains of an old chain-link secu-rity fence, topped with concertina wire. A gate lay on the ground, sprawled and broken, and they entered through a narrow gap. Beyond lay the remains of the burned building. It was of yellow brick like the rest, but the roof had collapsed, great charred beams sticking into the sky, the windows and door frames black holes with scorched streaks above. Massive carpets of kudzu crept up the walls and lay in heavy mats over everything.

Hayward followed Pendergast through a shattered doorway. The detective paused to examine the door lying on the ground and the frame itself, and then he knelt and began fiddling with the door lock with some lock-picking tools.

"Curious," he said, rising.

The entryway was strewn with charred pieces of wood, and the ceiling above had partially caved in, allowing a dim light to penetrate the interior. A flock of swallows burst out of the darkness and flew away, wheeling and crying at the disturbance. The odor of dampness clung faintly to everything. Water dripped from the black timbers, making pools on the once-tiled floor.

Pendergast slipped a penlight out of his pocket and shone it around. They moved into the interior, stepping over debris, the thin beam of Pendergast's light playing this way and that. Passing through a broken archway, they walked down an old corridor, burned-out rooms on either side. In places melted glass and aluminum had puddled on the floor, along with scorched plastic and the wire skeletons of furniture.

Hayward watched as Pendergast silently flitted through the dark rooms, probing and peering. At one point, he stopped at the remains of a filing cabinet and poked among a sodden mass of burned papers in the bottom of a drawer, pushing them apart. The very center remained unburned, and he plucked out a few pieces, examining them. "*'Delivery completed to Nova G.,'*" he read aloud from one of the papers. "This is just a bunch of old shipping manifests."

"Anything of interest?"

More poking. "Unlikely." Removing several charred fragments, he slipped them into a ziplock bag, which in turn disappeared into his suit jacket.

They arrived in a large central room where the fire appeared to have been fiercest. The ceiling was gone and mats of kudzu had risen over the debris, leaving humps and nodding growths. Pendergast glanced around, then walked over to one and reached into it, grabbing the vine and yanking it aside, exposing the skeleton of an old machine thick with wires and gears whose purpose Hayward couldn't begin to guess. He moved through the room, pulling aside more vines, exposing more melted, skeletal instrumentation.

"Any idea what this stuff was?" Hayward asked.

"An autoclave—incubators—and I would guess *that* was once a centrifuge." He flashed the light toward a large half-melted mass. "And here we have the remains of a laminar flow cabinet. This was once a first-class microbiology lab."

He kicked aside some debris, bent down, picked something up. It glinted dully in the light, and he slipped it into his pocket.

"The report of Slade's death," said Hayward, "indicated that his body was found in a laboratory. That must be this room."

"Yes." Pendergast's light flashed over a row of heavy, melted cabinets under a hood. "And there is where the fire started. Chemical storage."

"You think it was deliberately set?"

"Certainly. The fire was necessary to destroy the evidence."

"How do you know?"

Pendergast reached into his pocket and showed the thing he had picked up to Hayward. It was a strip of aluminum, about three-quarters of an inch long, that had evidently escaped the fire. A number was stamped into it.

"What is it?"

"An unused bird leg-band." He examined it closely, then handed it to Hayward. "And no ordinary leg-band, either." He pointed to its inner edge, where a band of silicon could be clearly seen. "Take a look. It's been chipped with what is no doubt a homing transmitter. Now we know how Helen tracked the parrot. I was wondering how she was able to locate the Doanes before they presented any symptoms of avian flu."

Hayward handed it back. "If you don't mind me asking, what makes you think the fire was deliberately set? The reports were pretty clear that they found no evidence of accelerants or foul play."

"The person who started this fire was a top-notch chemist who knew what he was doing. It is asking far too much of coincidence to believe this building burned accidentally, right after the avian flu project was shut down."

"So who burned it?"

"I would direct your attention to the high security, the once-formidable perimeter fence, the special, almost unpickable locks on the doors, the windows that were once barred and covered with frosted glass. The building was set apart from the others as well, almost into the swamp, protected on all sides. This fire was surely set by someone on the inside. Someone with high-level access."

"Slade?"

"The arsonist burned up in his own fire is not an uncommon phenomenon."

"On the other hand," said Hayward, "the fire might have been murder. Slade, as head of the project, knew too much."

Pendergast's pale eyes turned on her slowly. "My thoughts exactly, Captain."

They stood in silence, the rain dripping through the ruins.

"Seems like we're at a dead end," said Hayward.

Silently, Pendergast removed the ziplock bag with the charred paper and handed it to Hayward. She examined it. One of the fragments was a requisition for a shipment of petri dishes, with a handwritten note at the bottom upping the number "as per the direction of CJS." And it was signed with a single initial, *J*.

"CJS? That must be Charles J. Slade."

"Correct. And this *is* of definite interest."

She handed it back. "I don't see the significance."

"The handwriting evidently belongs to June Brodie, Slade's secretary. The one who committed suicide on the Archer Bridge a week after Slade died. Except that this note scribbled on the requisition would suggest she did not commit suicide after all."

"How in the world can you tell?"

"I happen to have a photocopy of the suicide note from her file at the Vital Records office, left in her car just before she threw herself off the Archer span." Pendergast removed a piece of paper from his suit jacket, and Hayward unfolded it. "Compare the handwriting with that of the fragment I just discovered: a purely routine notation jotted down in her office. Very curious."

Hayward stared at one and then the other, looking back and forth. "But the handwriting's exactly the same."

"That, my dear Captain, is what's so very curious." And he placed the papers back within his suit jacket.

58

The sun had already set in a scrim of muddy clouds by the time Laura Hayward reached the small highway leading out of Itta Bena, heading east toward the interstate. According to the GPS, it was a four-and-a-half-hour drive back to Penumbra; she'd be there before midnight. Pendergast had told her he wouldn't be home until even later; he was off to see what else he could dig up on June Brodie.

It was a long, lonely, empty highway. She felt drowsy and opened the window, letting in a blast of humid air. The car filled with the smell of the night and damp earth. At the next town, she'd grab a coffee and sandwich. Or maybe she could find a rib joint. She hadn't eaten since breakfast.

Her cell phone rang, and she fumbled it out of her pocket one-handed. "Hello?"

"Captain Hayward? This is Dr. Foerman at the Caltrop Hospital."

Hayward was instantly chilled by the serious tone of his voice.

"I'm sorry to disturb you in the evening but I'm afraid I had to call. Mr. D'Agosta has taken a sudden turn for the worse."

She swallowed. "What do you mean?"

"We're doing tests, but it appears he might be suffering from a rare kind of anaphylactic shock related to the pig valve in his heart." He paused. "To be frank, it looks very grave. We...we felt you should be notified."

Hayward couldn't speak for a moment. She slowed, pulled to the side of the highway, the car slewing into the soft shoulder.

"Captain Hayward?"

"I'm here." She punched *Caltrop, LA* into her GPS with shaking fingers. "Just a moment." The GPS ran a calculation displaying the time from her location to Caltrop. "I'll be there in two hours. Maybe less."

"We'll be waiting."

She closed the phone and dropped it on the passenger seat. She took in a long, shuddering breath. And then—quite abruptly—she gunned the Buick and swung the wheel violently into a U-turn, propelling gravel behind the car, the rear end swinging back onto the highway with a screech of rubber.

Judson Esterhazy strolled through the double glass doors into the warm night air, hands shoved into the pockets of his doctor's whites, and breathed deeply. From his vantage point in the covered entryway of the hospital's main entrance, he surveyed the parking lot. Brightly lit by sodium lamps, it wrapped around the main entrance and ran down one side of the small hospital; it was three-quarters empty. A quiet, uneventful March evening at Caltrop Hospital.

He turned his attention to the layout of the grounds. Beyond the parking lot, a smooth lawn ran down to a small lake. At the far end of the hospital stood a park with a scattering of tupelo trees, carefully planted and tended. A path wound through them, granite benches placed at strategic points.

Esterhazy strolled across the lot to the edge of the little park and sat down on a bench, to all appearances simply a resident or internist out for a breath of fresh air. Idly, he read the names carved into the bench as some fund-raising gimmick.

So far, everything was going to plan. True, it had been very difficult finding D'Agosta: somehow Pendergast had created a new identity for him, along with fake medical records, birth certificate, the works. If it hadn't been for Judson's access to private pharmaceutical records, he might never have found the lieutenant. Ultimately it had been the pig-heart valve that furnished the necessary clue. He knew D'Agosta had been moved to a cardiac care facility because of his injured heart. D'Agosta's prelims indicated he had a severely damaged aortic valve. The bastard should have died, but when he held on despite all odds, Judson realized he'd require a pig-heart valve.

There weren't many orders for pig valves floating through the system. *Trace the pig valve, find the man.* And that's what he'd done.

It was then he realized there was a way to kill two birds with one stone. After all, D'Agosta wasn't the primary target—but, comatose and dying, he could still make very effective bait.

He glanced at his watch. He knew that Pendergast and Hayward were still operating out of Penumbra; they couldn't be more than a few hours away. And of course they'd have been alerted to D'Agosta's condition by now and would be driving like maniacs to the hospital. The timing was perfect. D'Agosta was now dying from the dose of Pavulon he'd administered, the dosage being well into the fatal range but carefully calibrated so as not to kill immediately. That was the beauty of Pavulon—the dosage could be adjusted to draw out the drama of death. It mimicked many of the symptoms of anaphylactic shock and had a half-life in the body of less than three hours. Pendergast and Hayward would arrive just in time for the deathbed rattle—but then, of course, they wouldn't get as far as the deathbed.

Esterhazy rose and strolled along the brick path leading through the little park. The glow from the parking lot did not penetrate far, leaving most of the area in darkness. This would have made a good place to shoot from—if he'd been using the sniper rifle. But of course that would not work. When the two arrived, they would park as close to the main entrance as possible, jump out, and run into the building—a continually moving target. After his failure with Pendergast outside Penumbra, Esterhazy did not care to repeat the challenge. He would take no risks this time.

Hence the sawed-off shotgun.

He walked back toward the hospital entrance. It offered a far more straightforward opportunity. He would position himself on the right-hand side of the walkway, between the area lights. No matter where Pendergast and Hayward parked, they'd have to pass right by him. He would meet them there in his doctor's uniform, clipboard in hand, head bowed over it. They would be worried, rushing, and he'd be a doctor—there would be no suspicion. What could be more natural? He'd let them approach, get out of the line of sight of anyone inside the double glass doors. Then he'd swing up the sawed-off from under his lab coat and fire from the hip at point-blank range. The double-ought buck would literally blow their guts and spinal cords out through their backs. Then all he had to do was walk the twenty feet to his own car, get in, and drive away.

With his eyes closed he ran through the sequence, counting off the time. Fifteen seconds, more or less, beginning to end. By the time the security guard at the reception desk called for backup and screwed up the courage to get his fat ass outside, Judson would be gone.

This was a good plan. Simple. Foolproof. His targets would be off guard, exposed. Even the legendarily cool Pendergast would be flustered. No doubt the man blamed himself for D'Agosta's condition—and now his good friend was dying.

The only danger, and it was a slight one, would be if someone accosted or challenged him in the hospital before he had time to act. But that didn't seem likely. It was an expensive private hospital, big enough that no one had looked twice at him when he walked in and flashed his credentials. He had gone straight to D'Agosta's room and found him drugged up with pain-killers, sound asleep after the operation. They hadn't posted a guard, evidently because they felt they'd disguised his identity well enough. And he had to admit they'd done a brilliant job at that, all the paperwork in order, everyone in the hospital thinking he was Tony Spada from Flushing, Queens...

Except that he was the only patient in the entire region needing a forty-thousand-dollar porcine aortic valve xenograft.

He'd injected the Pavulon high up in the IV drip. By the time the code came through, he was in another part of the hospital. No one questioned him or even looked askance at his presence. Being a doctor himself, he knew exactly how to look, how to behave, what to say.

He checked his watch. Then he strolled over to his car and got in. The shotgun gleamed faintly from the floor of the passenger seat. He'd stay here, in the darkness, for a little while. Then he'd hide the shotgun under his coat, exit the vehicle, get into position between the lights... and wait for the birds to fly in.

Hayward could see the hospital at the end of the long, straight access drive, a three-story building glowing in the night, set amid a broad rising lawn, its many windows reflecting on the waters of a nearby pond. She accelerated, the road dipping down to cross a stream, then rising up again. As she approached the entrance she braked hard, making an effort to get her excessive speed under control, came into the final curve before the parking lot, the tires squealing softly on the dew-laden asphalt.

She came to a short, screeching halt in the closest parking space, threw open the door, and jumped out.

She trotted across the lot and entered the covered walk-way to the front doors. Immediately she saw a doctor standing to one side of the walkway, between the pools of light, holding a clipboard. A surgical mask was still in position on his face—he must have just come from the OR.

"Captain Hayward?" the doctor asked.

She veered toward him, alarmed at the thought he was waiting for her. "Yes, how is he?"

"He's going to be just fine," came the slightly muf-fled response. The doctor let the clipboard drop casu-ally in one hand while he reached under his white coat with the other.

"Thank God—" she began, and then she saw the shotgun.

59

New York City

Dr. John Felder mounted the broad stone steps of the main branch of the New York Public Library. Behind him, the evening traffic on Fifth Avenue was a staccato chorus of horns and grinding diesels. He paused a moment between the large stone lions, Patience and Fortitude, to check his watch and rearrange the thin manila folder that was tucked beneath one arm. Then he made his way to the brass doors at the top of the stairs.

"I'm sorry, sir," said the guard standing before them. "The library is closed for the day."

Felder took out his city credentials and showed them to the man.

"Very good, sir," said the guard, stepping deferentially away from the doors.

"I put in a request for some research materials," Felder said. "I was told they were ready for examination."

"You can inquire in the General Research Division," the guard replied. "Room Three Fifteen."

"Thank you."

His shoes rang out against the floor as he walked through the vast and echoing entrance hall. It was almost eight in the evening and the cavernous space was deserted save for a second guard at a receiving station, who again examined his credentials and pointed the way up the sweeping staircase. Felder mounted the marble stairs slowly and thoughtfully. Arriving at the third floor, he walked down the corridor to the entrance of Room 315.

Room 315 did not do the space justice. Nearly two city blocks long, the Main Reading Room rose fifty feet to a rococo coffered ceiling busy with murals. Elegant chandeliers hung over seemingly endless rows of long oaken reading tables, still appointed with their original bronze lamps. Here and there, other researchers with after-hours access sat at the tables, poring over books or tapping quietly on laptops. While many books lined the walls, they were merely a drop in the library's bucket: in the subterranean levels beneath his feet, and the others below the green surface of adjoining Bryant Park, six million more volumes were stored.

But Felder had not come here to look at books. He had come for the library's equally vast collection of genealogical research materials.

He walked to the research assistance station that bisected the room, itself made of ornately carved wood, as large as a suburban house. After a brief whispered exchange, a library cart full of ledgers and folders was presented to him. He wheeled it to the nearest table, then took a seat and began placing the materials on the polished wooden surface. They were darkened and foxed with age but nevertheless impeccably clean. The various documents and sets of records had one thing in common: they dated from 1870 to 1880, and they documented the area of Manhattan in which Constance Greene claimed to have grown up.

Ever since the commitment proceedings, Felder had been thinking about the young woman's story. It was nonsense, of course—the ravings of someone who had completely lost touch with reality. A classic case of circumscribed delusion: psychotic disorder, unspecified.

And yet Constance Greene did not present like the typical person totally out of touch with reality. There was something about her that puzzled—no, *intrigued*—him.

I was indeed born on Water Street in the '70s—the 1870s. You will find all you need to know in the city archives on Centre Street, and more in the New York Public Library… I know, because I have seen the records myself.

Was this some clue she was offering them: some morsel of information that might clear up the mystery? Was it perhaps a cry for help? Only a careful examination of the records could provide an answer. He briefly wondered why he was doing this: his involvement in the case was over, and he was a very busy man with a successful private practice. And yet… he found himself damnably curious.

An hour later, Felder sat back in his chair and took a deep breath. Among the reams of yellowing documents was a Manhattan subcensus entry that indeed listed the family in question as dwelling at 16 Water Street.

Leaving the papers on the table, he rose and made his way down the stairs to the Genealogical Research Division on the first floor. His search of the Land Records and Military Service Records came up empty, and the 1880 US census showed nothing, but the 1870 census listed a Horace Greene as living in Putnam County, New York. An examination of Putnam County tax records from the years prior provided a few additional crumbs.

Felder walked slowly back upstairs and sat down at the table. Now he carefully opened the manila folder he had brought and arranged its meager contents—obtained from the Public Records Office—on its surface.

What, exactly, had he learned so far?

In 1870, Horace Greene had been a farmer in Carmel, New York. Wife, Chastity Greene; one daughter, Mary, aged eight.

In 1874, Horace Greene was living at 16 Water Street in Lower Manhattan, occupation stevedore. He now had three children: Mary, twelve; Joseph, three; Constance, one.

In 1878, New York City Department of Health death certificates had been issued for both Horace and Chastity Greene. Death in each case was listed as tuberculosis. This would have left the three children—now aged sixteen, seven, and five—orphans.

An 1878 police ledger listed Mary Greene as being charged with "streetwalking"—prostitution. Court records indicated she had testified that she had tried to find work as a laundress and seamstress, but that the pay had been insufficient to provide for herself and her siblings. Social welfare records from the same year listed Mary Greene as being confined to the Five Points

Mission for an indefinite period. There were no other records; she seemed to have disappeared.

Another police ledger, from 1880, recorded one Castor McGillicutty as having beaten Joseph Greene, ten, to death upon catching the boy picking his pocket. Sentence: ten dollars and sixty days of hard labor in The Tombs, later commuted.

And that was it. The last—and indeed only— mention of a Constance Greene was the 1874 census.

Felder returned the documents to the folder and closed it with a sigh. It was a depressing enough story. It seemed clear that the woman calling herself Constance Greene had seized upon this particular family—and this lone bit of information—and made it the subject of her own delusional fantasies. But why? Of all the countless thousands, millions, of families in New York City— many with more extensive and colorful histories—why had she chosen this one? Could they have been her ancestors? But the records for the family seemed to end with this generation: there was nothing he could find to foster any belief that even a single member of the Greene family had survived beyond 1880.

Rising from his seat with another sigh, he went to the research desk and requested a few dozen local Manhattan newspapers from the late 1870s. He paged through them at random, glancing listlessly at the articles, notices, and advertisements. It was of course hopeless: he didn't know what he was looking for, exactly—in fact he didn't know why he was looking in the first place. What was it about Constance Greene and her condition that puzzled him so? It wasn't as if...

Suddenly—while leafing through an 1879 issue of

the Five Points tabloid *New-York Daily Inquirer*—he paused. On an inside page was a copperplate engraving titled *Guttersnipes at Play*. The illustration depicted a row of tenements, squalid, rough-and-tumble. Dirty-faced urchins were playing stickball in the street. But off to one side stood a single thin girl, looking on, broom in one hand. She was thin to the point of emaciation, and in contrast with the other children her expression was downcast, almost frightened. But what had stopped Felder dead was her face. In every line and detail, it was the spitting image of Constance Greene.

Felder stared at the engraving for a long moment. Then, very slowly, he closed the newspaper, a thoughtful, sober expression on his face.

60

Caltrop, Louisiana

A rapid series of shots rang out as Hayward threw herself sideways, instantly followed by the roar of the shotgun. She landed hard on the ground, feeling the backwash from the cloud of buckshot that blasted by her. She rolled, yanking out her piece. But the phony doctor had already wheeled about and was flying toward the parking lot, white coat flapping behind him. She heard more shots and a screeching of wheels as a vintage Rolls-Royce came careering across the parking lot, tires smoking. She saw Pendergast was leaning out the driver's window, firing his pistol like a cowboy firing from a galloping horse.

With a scream of rubber the Rolls went into a power slide. Even before it came to a stop, Pendergast flung the door open and ran up to her.

"I'm fine!" she said, struggling to rise. "I'm *fine*, damn it! Look—he's getting away!"

Even as she spoke she heard an unseen engine roar to life in the lot. A car went screeching away, a flash of red taillights disappearing out the access drive.

He hauled her to her feet. "No time. Follow me."

He pushed through the double doors and they ran past a scene of growing panic and alarm, a security guard crouching behind his desk yelling into the phone, the receptionist and several employees lying prone on the floor. Ignoring them, Pendergast charged through another set of double doors and grabbed the first doctor he encountered.

"The code in Three Twenty-three," he said, showing his badge. "It's attempted murder. The patient has been injected with a drug of some kind."

The doctor, almost without blinking, said: "Got it. Let's go."

The three ran up a staircase to D'Agosta's room. Hayward was confronted with a buzz of activity: a group of nurses and doctors working purposefully and almost silently next to a bank of machines. Lights blinked and alarms softly sounded. D'Agosta was lying in the bed, unmoving.

The doctor calmly stepped into the room. "Everyone listen. This patient was injected with a drug intended to kill him."

A nurse raised her head. "How in the world—?"

The doctor cut her off with a gesture. "The question is: *Which drug are these symptoms consistent with?*"

A rising hubbub followed, a furious discussion, a review of charts and data sheets. The doctor turned to Pendergast and Hayward. "There's nothing more you can do now. Please wait outside."

"I want to wait here," Hayward said.

"Absolutely not. I'm sorry."

As Hayward turned, another alarm went off and she saw the EKG monitor flatlining. "Oh, my God," she burst out. "Let me wait here, please, *please*—"

The door shut firmly and Pendergast gently led her away.

The waiting room was small and sterile, with plastic chairs and a single window that looked out into the night. Hayward stood by it, staring unseeing into the black rectangle. Her mind was working furiously but going nowhere, like a broken engine. Her mouth was dry, and her hands were trembling. A single tear trickled down her cheek—a tear of frustration and unfocused rage.

She felt Pendergast's hand on her shoulder. She brushed it off and took a step away.

"Captain?" came the low voice. "May I remind you there's been an attempted homicide—against Lieutenant D'Agosta. And against you."

The cool voice penetrated the fog of her fury. She shook her head. "Just get the hell away from me."

"You need to start thinking about this problem like a police officer. I need your help, and I need it now."

"I'm not interested in your problem anymore."

"Unfortunately, it isn't my problem anymore."

She swallowed, staring into the darkness, fists clenched. "If he dies…"

The cool, almost mesmerizing voice went on. "That's out of our hands. I want you to listen to me carefully. I want you to be Captain Hayward, not Laura Hayward, for a moment. There is something important we must discuss. Now."

She closed her eyes, feeling numb to the core. She didn't even have the energy to rebuff him.

"It would seem," said Pendergast, "we're dealing with a killer who is also a doctor."

She closed her eyes. She was tired of this, tired of it all, tired of life. If Vinnie died...She forced the thought out of her mind.

"Extraordinary measures were taken to keep Vincent's location a secret. Clearly the would-be killer had special access to patient charts, medical supply and pharmaceutical records. There are only two possibilities. The first is that he or she was a member of the team that is actually treating Vincent, but that would be both extremely coincidental and extremely unlikely: they have all been carefully vetted. The other possibility—and the one I believe to be the case—is that Vincent was found by tracing the pig valve used in his recent operation. His assailant might even be a cardiac surgeon."

When she said nothing, he went on. "Do you realize what this means? It means Vincent was used as bait. The perpetrator deliberately induced a deadly coma, knowing it would lure us to the bedside. Naturally he anticipated we would arrive together. The fact we didn't is the only thing that saved us."

She remained with her back turned, hiding her face. *Bait*. Vinnie, used as bait. After a brief silence, Pendergast continued.

"There's nothing more we can do about that for the present. Meanwhile, I believe I have made a critical discovery. While we were separated, I looked into

June Brodie's suicide and found some interesting coincidences. As we know, the suicide occurred only a week after Slade's death in the fire. About a month afterward, June's husband told his neighbors he was going on a trip abroad and left, never to be seen again. The house was shut up and eventually sold. I tried to trace him but found the trail completely cold—except I could find no evidence he had left the country."

Despite herself, Hayward turned slowly around.

"June was an attractive woman. And it appears she'd been having a long-term affair with Slade."

Hayward spoke at last. "There you have it," she snapped. "It wasn't a suicide. The husband murdered her and took off."

"There are two pieces of evidence against that supposition. The first is the suicide note."

"He forced her to write it."

"As you know, there's no sign of stress in the handwriting. And there's something else. Not long before her suicide, June Brodie was diagnosed with a particularly fast-acting form of amyotrophic lateral sclerosis: Lou Gehrig's disease. It would have killed her fairly quickly anyway."

Hayward thought. "The disease would argue for suicide."

"Murder," murmured Pendergast. "Suicide. Perhaps it was neither."

Hayward ignored this typically Pendergastian comment. "Your PI, Hudson, was killed while investigating Brodie. In all likelihood, that means whoever's behind all this doesn't want us on her trail. That makes June Brodie a person of key importance for us."

Pendergast nodded. "Indeed."

"What else do you know about her?"

"Her family background is unremarkable enough. The Brodies were once quite wealthy—oil money— but in the 1960s the oil ran out, and they fell on hard times. June grew up in reduced circumstances, went to a local community college, graduated with a nursing degree, but only practiced for a few years. Perhaps the profession didn't agree with her, or perhaps she simply wanted the higher salary of a personal secretary to a CEO. In any case, she took the job at Longitude, where she worked for the rest of her life. She married her high-school sweetheart but, it seems, soon found a more exciting diversion in Charles Slade."

"And the husband?"

"Either he didn't know or he put up with it." Pendergast had slipped a manila folder out of his suit coat and handed it to her. "Now, please take a look at these."

She opened it to find a number of yellowed newspaper clippings in plastic sleeves, along with a map. "What's all this?"

"You just said June Brodie was of key importance. And I agree. But I rather think there's something else of key importance here—*geography*."

"Geography?"

"Black Brake swamp, to be precise." Pendergast nodded toward the clippings.

She leafed through them quickly. They were mostly local newspaper stories of legends and superstitions about Black Brake: mysterious lights seen at night, a frogger who disappeared, stories of buried treasure and ghosts. She'd heard many such rumors growing up. The swamp, one of the largest in the South, was notorious.

"Consider," said Pendergast, running his finger along the map. "On one side of the Black Brake you have Longitude Pharmaceuticals. On the other, Sunflower and the Doane family house. You have the Brodie family, who lived outside Malfourche, a small town on the lake at the eastern end of the swamp."

"And?"

Pendergast tapped the map lightly. "And right here in the middle of the Black Brake, you have Spanish Island."

"What's that?"

"The Brodie family owned a hunting camp in the middle of the swamp, called Spanish Island. No doubt it's an island in the delta sense: an area of higher, firmer mud. The camp itself would have been built on piers and creosote pylons. It went bankrupt in the 1970s. The camp was shuttered and never reopened."

Hayward glanced at him. "So?"

"Look at these stories. All from local papers in the small towns bordering the swamp: Sunflower, Itta Bena, and particularly Malfourche. I first noticed these stories when I was going through the newspaper archives of Sunflower, but thought nothing of them at the time. If you *map* these stories, though, you find they're all vaguely oriented toward one place—Spanish Island, in the deepest heart of the swamp."

"But...but they're all just legends. Colorful legends."

"Where there's smoke, there's fire."

She shut the file and handed it back. "This isn't

police work; this is guesswork. You don't have a single hard fact pointing to Spanish Island as a place of interest in this case."

A faint flicker passed through Pendergast's eyes. "Five years ago, an environmental group did a cleanup of an old illegal dumping ground in the swamp beyond Malfourche. You see these dumps all over the South, where people junked old cars, refrigerators, anything that would sink. One of the things they hauled out of the muck was a car. Naturally, they went after the registered owner to fine him. But they never found him."

"Who'd it belong to?"

"The car was registered to Carlton Brodie, June's husband. It was the last car he owned. I would presume it was the car he drove off with when he told everyone he was going...*abroad.*"

Hayward frowned, opened her mouth to speak, shut it again.

"And there's something else—something that's been bothering me ever since I saw it this morning. Remember that burned-out pier we saw at Longitude? The one behind Complex Six?"

"What about it?"

"Why on earth would Longitude Pharmaceuticals need a pier on Black Brake swamp?"

Hayward thought a moment. "It could have predated Longitude."

"Perhaps. But it looked to me as if it dates to the same period as the corporation. No, Captain: everything—especially that dock—points to Spanish Island as our next port of call."

The door of the waiting room opened, and the

doctor came striding in. Even before Hayward could speak, he was talking.

"He's going to make it," the man said, almost unable to control his own elation. "We figured it out just in time. Pavulon, a powerful muscle relaxant. That was the drug he was injected with. Some was missing from medical stores."

Hayward felt momentarily dizzy. She grasped the side of a chair and eased herself down. "Thank God."

The doctor turned to Pendergast. "I don't know how you figured out it was an injection, exactly, but that deduction saved his life."

Hayward glanced at the FBI agent. This hadn't occurred to her.

"We've called the local authorities, of course," the doctor went on. "They'll be here any moment."

Pendergast slipped the file into his suit. "Excellent. I'm afraid we have to leave, Doctor. It's extremely urgent. Here's my card; have the police contact me. And have them immediately arrange round-the-clock protection for the patient. I doubt the killer will make another attempt, but one never knows."

"Yes, Mr. Pendergast," said the doctor, taking the card emblazoned with the FBI seal.

"We have no time to waste," said Pendergast, turning and striding toward the door.

"But . . . what are we doing now?" Hayward asked.

"We're going to Spanish Island, of course."

61

Penumbra Plantation

Darkness cloaked the old Greek Revival mansion. Heavy clouds obscured the swollen moon, and a blanket of unseasonable heat lay over the late-winter landscape. Even the swamp insects seemed somnolent, too lazy to call out.

Maurice made his way quietly through the first floor of the plantation house, peering into the various rooms, making sure the windows were locked, the lights off, and everything in order. Sliding the deadbolt of the front door and turning the key, he took another look around, grunted in satisfaction, and then moved toward the stairway.

The ring of a telephone on the hall table shattered the silence.

Maurice looked toward it, startled. As it continued to ring he made his way toward it, one veined and knotted hand plucking the handset from its cradle.

"Yes?" he said.

"Maurice?" It was Pendergast's voice. There was a

faint but steady background noise, a thrumming like the rush of wind.

"Yes?" Maurice said again.

"I wanted to let you know that we won't be home this evening, after all. You may secure the deadbolt on the kitchen door."

"Very good, sir."

"You can expect us sometime tomorrow evening. If we are delayed further, I'll let you know."

"I understand." Maurice paused a moment. "Where are you going, sir?"

"Malfourche. A tiny town on Black Brake swamp."

"Very good, sir. Have a safe trip."

"Thank you, Maurice. We'll see you tomorrow."

The line went dead, and Maurice replaced the receiver. He paused a moment, staring at it, thinking. Then he picked it up again and dialed.

The phone rang several times before a man's voice answered.

"Hello?" Maurice said. "Mr. Judson, sir?"

The voice on the other end answered in the affirmative.

"This is Maurice at Penumbra Plantation. I'm fine, thank you. Yes. Yes, I just heard from him. They're heading to Black Brake swamp. A town called Malfourche. Given your concern for him, I thought you'd want to know. No, he didn't say why. Yes. Very well, sir. You're welcome. Good night."

He hung up the phone again, then walked to the back of the house and secured the kitchen door as ordered. After a final look around, he returned to the main hallway and climbed the stairs to the second floor. There were no further interruptions.

62

Malfourche, Mississippi

Mike Ventura pulled up to the rotting docks outside Tiny's Bait 'n' Bar. It was a crooked, ramshackle wooden building perched on pilings, and Ventura could hear the sounds of country music, whoops, and raucous laughter drifting across the water.

He brought his shallow-draft bass boat into one of the few empty slips, cut the engine, hopped out, and tied up. It was midnight and Tiny's was rocking, the docks packed with boats, from loaded BassCats to crappy plywood skiffs. Malfourche, he thought, might be a hard-luck town, but they still knew what a good time was. He licked his lips, thinking that a frosty one and a shot of JD would be the first order of business—before the real business began.

Pushing through the doors, he was assaulted by the sounds and smells of Tiny's: the loud music, the beer, neon, sawdust, humidity, and the scent of the swamp lapping on the pilings below. The bait shop on the left and the bar on the right were all part of the same barn-like space. Given the late hour, the lights were off in the bait-shop area, where large refrigerators and tubs contained the assortment of the live bait that Tiny's was so famous for: nightcrawlers, crawfish, leeches, wax-worms, Georgia jumpers, spawn, and mousees.

Ventura bellied up to the bar and right away Tiny himself, the bartender and proprietor—an immense, jiggling, adipose mountain of a man—smacked down a can of Coors, ice chips adhering to its sides, followed immediately by a double shot of JD.

Ventura nodded his thanks and raised the Jack Daniel's, downed it, and chased it with a pull of Coors.

Damn if that wasn't just what the doctor ordered. He'd been in the swamp too long. As he drank his beer, he looked around the old joint with a welling feeling of affection. It was one of the last places where you didn't have to look at jigaboos or faggots or Yankees. It was all white and nobody had to say anything, everyone around knew it, and that's the way it was and always would be, amen.

The wall behind the bar was festooned with hundreds of cards, photos of loggers with axes, more recent photos of prize fish and boats, mounted fish, signed dollar bills, an aerial view of Malfourche from the days when it was a thriving center for everything from cypress loggers to gator hunters. Back when everyone had a decent boat and a pickup truck and house that was actually worth something. Before they turned half the swamp into a wilderness area.

Fucking wilderness area.

Ventura polished off the beer and even before he

could ask, another was plunked down in front of him, along with a single shot of JD. Tiny knew him well. But instead of going for it right away, Ventura considered the pressing business at hand. He was going to enjoy this, and he was going to make some big money from it—while at the same time keeping his own hands clean. His eye strayed to the many anti-environmental slogans tacked to the wall, SIERRA CLUB GO HIKE TO HELL, and SUPPORT WILDLIFE—FEED AN ENVIRONMENTALIST TO THE GATORS, and so on. For sure, this was a good plan.

He leaned over the bar, gestured to the proprietor. "Tiny, I got an important announcement to make. Mind cutting the music?"

"Sure thing, Mike." Tiny went over to the sound system and turned it down. Almost immediately the place fell silent, everyone's attention turning to the bar.

Ventura slid off his stool and sauntered into the middle of the bar, his cowboy boots thumping on the worn boards.

"Yo Mike!" someone yelled, and there was some drunken clapping and whistling. Ventura took no notice. He was a well-known personage, former county sheriff, a man of means but never uppity. On the other hand, he'd always made a point not to mix too much with the crackers and rednecks, kept up a certain formality. They respected that.

He hooked his thumbs into his belt and gave a slow look around the place. Everyone was waiting. It wasn't every day that Mike Ventura spoke to the people. Amazing how the place had quieted down. It gave him a certain satisfaction, a feeling that he had reached a point in his life of respect and accomplishment.

"We got a problem," he said. He let that sink in for a few seconds, then went on. "A problem in the shape of two people. Environmentalists. They're coming down here *undercover* to take a gander at this end of Black Brake. Looking to expand that wilderness area over the rest of Black Brake *and* the Lake End."

He glared around at the crowd. There were murmurs, hisses, inarticulate shouts of disapproval. "The Lake End?" someone shouted. "The hell with that!"

"That's right. No more bass fishing. No more hunting. Nothing. Just a wilderness area so those Wilderness Society sons of bitches can come down here with their *kayaks* looking at the *birds*." He spat the words out.

A loud chorus of boos and catcalls, and Ventura held up his hand for silence. "First they took the logging. Then they took half the Brake. Now they're talking about taking the rest, along with the lake. There won't be *nothing* left. You remember last time, when we did things their way? We went to the hearings, we protested, we wrote letters? Remember all that? What happened?"

Another clamor of disapproval.

"That's right. They bent us over and *you know what*!"

A roar. People were up off their stools. Ventura held up his hands again. "Now, listen up. They're gonna be here tomorrow. Not sure when, but probably early. A tall, skinny fellow in a black suit—and a woman. They're going into the swamp on a reconnaissance."

"Reconnay-sance?" somebody echoed.

"A look-see. Real scientific-like. Just the two of them. But they're coming undercover—those cowardly sons of bitches know they don't dare show their real faces around here."

This time there was an ugly silence.

"That's right. I don't know about you folks, but I'm done writing letters. I'm done going to hearings. I'm *done* listening to those Yankee peckerwoods tell me what to do with my own fish and timber and land."

A sudden, fresh crescendo of shouts. They could see where he was going. Ventura dipped into his back pocket, pulled out a wad of money, and shook it. "I don't never expect nobody to work for free." He slapped the wad on a greasy table. "Here's a down payment, and there'll be more where that came from. Y'all know the saying: what sinks in the swamp never rises. I want y'all to *solve* this problem. Do it for yourselves. Because if you don't, nobody else will, and you might as well kiss what's left of Malfourche good-bye, sell your guns, give your houses away, pack your Chevys, and move in with the faggots in Boston and San Francisco. Is that what you want?"

A roar of disapproval, more people lurching to their feet. A table crashed to the floor.

"You be ready for those environmentalists, hear? You take care of them. Take care of them good. *What sinks in the swamp never rises.*" He glared around, then held up a hand, bowing his head. "Thank you, my friends, and good night."

The place erupted in a fury, just as Ventura knew it would. He ignored it, striding to the door, banging through it, and walking out into the humid night onto the dock. He could hear the pandemonium inside, the angry voices, the cursing, the sound of the music coming back up. He knew that, by the time those two arrived, at least some of the boys would have sobered up enough to do what needed doing. Tiny would see to it.

He flipped open his cell phone and dialed. "Judson? I just solved our little problem."

63

Hayward emerged into the bright sun and stepped onto the motel balcony to see Pendergast below in the courtyard, loading his suitcase into the trunk of the Rolls. It was unreasonably hot for the beginning of March, the sun like a heat lamp on the back of her neck, and Hayward wondered if all those years living in the North had made her soft. She lugged her overnight bag down the concrete steps and threw it into the trunk beside Pendergast's.

The interior of the Rolls was cool and fresh, the creamy leather chilly. Malfourche lay ten more miles down the road, but there were no motels left in the dying town; this had been the closest one.

"I've done some research into the Black Brake swamp," Pendergast said as he pulled out onto the narrow highway. "It's one of the largest and wildest swamps in the South. It covers almost seventy thousand acres, and is bounded by a lake to the east known as Lake End and a series of bayous and channels to the west."

Hayward found it hard to pay attention. She already knew more about the swamp than she wanted to, and the horrors of the previous evening clouded her mind.

"Our destination, Malfourche, lies on the eastern side on a small peninsula. *Malfourche* means 'Bad Fork' in French, after the bayou it sits on: a dead-end slack-water branch-lake that to early French settlers looked like the mouth of a river. The swamp once contained one of the largest cypress forests in the country. About sixty percent of it was timbered before 1975, when the western half of the swamp was declared a wildlife refuge and, later, a wilderness area, in which no motorized boats are allowed."

"Where did you pick up all this?" Hayward asked.

"I find it remarkable that even the worst motels have Wi-Fi these days."

"I see." *Doesn't he ever sleep?*

"Malfourche is a dying town," he went on. "The loss of the timbering industry hit it hard, and the creation of the wilderness area cut deeply into the hunting and fishing businesses. They're hanging on by the skin of their teeth."

"Then perhaps arriving by Rolls-Royce might not be the best idea—if we want to encourage people to talk."

"On the contrary," murmured Pendergast.

There was no sign at a crossroads and they had to stop and ask for directions. Soon after, they passed a few dilapidated wooden houses, roofs sagging, yards full of old cars and junk. A whitewashed church flashed by, followed by more shacks, and then the road opened into a ramshackle main street, drenched in sunlight, running down to a set of docks on a weedy lake. Virtually all the storefronts were shuttered, the flyspecked glass windows covered with paper or whitewashed, faded FOR RENT signs in many of them.

"Pendergast," she said suddenly, "there's something I just don't understand."

"What's that?"

"This whole thing is crazy. I mean, shooting Vinnie, trying to shoot me. Killing Blackletter and Blast and the Lord only knows who else. I've been a cop for a long time, and I know—I *know*—there are easier ways to do this. This is just too extreme. The whole thing is a dozen years old. By trying to kill cops, they're bringing more attention to themselves—not less."

"You're right," Pendergast said. "It is extreme. Vincent made a similar point about the lion. It implies a great deal. And I find it rather suggestive... don't you?"

He parked in a small lot up the street from the docks. They stepped out into the ferocious sun and looked about. A group of slovenly dressed men were hanging out down by the boat slips, and all had turned and were now staring at them hard. Hayward felt acutely aware of the Rolls-Royce and once again questioned Pendergast's insistence on driving such a car for his investigations. Still, it had made no sense to drive two cars here, and she'd left her rental at the hospital.

Pendergast buttoned his black suit and looked about, cool as ever. "Shall we stroll down to the boat slips and chat up those gentlemen?"

Hayward shrugged. "They don't exactly look talkative."

"Talkative, no. Communicative, possibly." Pendergast

headed down the street, his tall frame moving easily. The men watched their approach with narrowed eyes.

"Good day, gentlemen," said Pendergast, in his most honeyed, upper-class New Orleans accent, giving them a slight bow.

Silence. Hayward's apprehension increased. This seemed like the worst possible way to go about getting information. The hostility was so thick you could cut it with a knife.

"My associate and I are here for a little sightseeing. We are birders."

"Birders," said a man. He turned and said it again to the group. *"Birders."*

The crowd laughed.

Hayward winced. This was going to be a total loss. She saw movement out of the corner of her eye and glanced over. Another group of people was filing silently out of a barn-like building on creosote pilings adjacent to the docks. A hand-painted sign identified it as TINY'S BAIT 'N' BAR.

An enormously fat man was the last to exit. His bullet-shaped head was shaved and he wore a tank top stretched to the limit by a huge belly, his arms hanging down like smoked hams, and—thanks to the sun— about the same color. He muscled through the crowd and came striding down the dock, clearly the authority figure of the group, pulling to a halt in front of Pendergast.

"To whom do I have the pleasure?" Pendergast asked.

"Name's Tiny," he said, looking Pendergast and Hayward up and down with piss-hole eyes. He didn't offer his hand.

Tiny, thought Hayward. *It figures.*

"My name is Pendergast, and this is my associate Hayward. Now, Tiny, as I was saying to these gentlemen here, we wish to go birding. We're looking for the rare Botolph's Red-bellied Fisher to round out our life lists. We understand it can be found deep in the swamp."

"That so?"

"And we were hoping to speak to someone who knows the swamp and might be able to advise us."

Tiny stepped forward, leaned over, and deposited a stream of tobacco juice at Pendergast's feet, so close that some of it splattered on Pendergast's wingtips.

"Oh, dear, I believe you've soiled my shoes," said Pendergast.

Hayward wanted to cringe. Any idiot could see they'd already lost the crowd, that they would get nothing of value from them. And now there might be a confrontation.

"Looks that way," drawled Tiny.

"Perhaps you, Mr. Tiny, can help us?"

"Nope," came the response. He leaned over, puckered his thick lips, and deposited another stream of tobacco, this time directly on Pendergast's shoes.

"I believe you did that on purpose," Pendergast said, his voice high and cracking in ineffectual protest.

"You believe right."

"Well," he said, turning to Hayward, "I get the distinct feeling we're not wanted here. I think we should take our business elsewhere." To her utter astonishment, he hurried off down the street toward the Rolls, and she had to jog to catch up. Raucous laughter echoed behind him.

"You're going to walk off like that?" she asked.

Pendergast paused at the car. Someone had keyed a message in the paint of the hood: FUCK ENVIROS. He got in the car with an enigmatic smile.

Hayward opened the driver's-side door but didn't get in. "What the hell do you think you're doing? We haven't even begun to get the information we need!"

"On the contrary, they were most eloquent."

"They vandalized your car, spat on your shoes!"

"Get in," he said firmly.

She slid in. Pendergast turned and screeched off in a cloud of dust, and they started out of town.

"That's it? We're running?"

"My dear Captain, have you ever known me to run?"

She shut up. Soon the Rolls slowed and, to her surprise, swung into the driveway of the church they had passed earlier. Pendergast parked in front of the house beside the church and stepped out. Wiping his shoe on the grass, he glided onto the porch and rang the bell. A man soon opened the door. He was tall and rail-thin, with heavy features, a white beard, and no mustache. He reminded Hayward a bit of Abraham Lincoln.

"Pastor Gregg?" said Pendergast, seizing his hand. "I'm Al Pendergast, pastor of the Hemhoibshun Parish Southern Baptist Church. Delighted to make your acquaintance!" He shook the bewildered minister's hand with great enthusiasm. "And this is my sister Laura. May we speak with you?"

"Well, I...certainly," said Gregg, slowly recovering from his surprise. "Come in."

They entered the cool confines of a tidy house.

"Please, sit down." Gregg still seemed rather bewildered; Pendergast, on the other hand, ensconced himself in the most comfortable chair and threw one leg over the other, looking completely at home.

"Laura and I are not here on church business," he said, removing a steno pad and a pen from his suit. "But I had heard of your church and your reputation for hospitality, and so here we are."

"I see," said Gregg, obviously not seeing at all.

"Pastor Gregg, in my spare time from my pastoral duties, I have an avocation: I am an amateur historian, a collector of myths and legends, a rummager in the dusty corners of forgotten southern history. In fact I'm writing a book. *Myths and Legends of the Southern Swamps.* And that is why I am here." Pendergast said this last triumphantly, then sat back.

"How interesting," Gregg replied.

"When I travel, I always look up the local pastor first. He never fails me, never."

"Glad to hear it."

"Because the local pastor knows the folks. He knows the legends. But as a man of God, he is not superstitious. He isn't swayed by such things. Am I right?"

"Well, it's true one hears stories. But they are just that, Pastor Pendergast: stories. I don't pay much attention to them."

"Exactly. Now this swamp, the Black Brake, is one of the biggest and most legendary in the South. Are you familiar with it?"

"Naturally."

"Have you heard of a place in the swamp called Spanish Island?"

"Oh, yes. It's not really an island, of course—more an area of mudflats and shallow water where the cypress trees were never cut. It's out in the middle of the swamp, virgin forest. I've never seen it."

Pendergast began to scribble. "They say there was an old fishing and hunting camp there."

"Quite right. Belonged to the Brodie family, but it was closed up thirty years ago. I believe it's just rotted back into the swamp. That's what happens to abandoned buildings, you know."

"Are there any stories about Spanish Island?"

He smiled. "Of course. The usual ghost stories, rumors that the place is occupied by squatters and used for drug smuggling—that sort of thing."

"Ghost stories?"

"The locals are full of talk about the heart of the swamp, where Spanish Island is located: strange lights at night, odd noises, that sort of thing. A few years ago, a frogger disappeared in the swamp. They found his rented airboat drifting in a bayou not far from Spanish Island. I expect he got drunk and fell off into the water, but the local folk all say he was murdered or went swamp crazy."

"Swamp crazy?"

"If you spend too much time in the swamp, it gets to you and you go crazy. So people say. While I don't exactly believe that, I must say it is an...intimidating place. Easy to get lost in."

Pendergast wrote this all down with expressions of interest. "What about the lights?"

"The froggers go out at night, you know, and sometimes come back with stories of strange lights moving through the swamp. They're just seeing each other, in my opinion. You need a light, you see, to frog. Or it might be a natural phenomenon, glowing swamp gas or something like that."

"Excellent," said Pendergast, taking a moment to scribble. "This is just the sort of thing I'm looking for. Anything else?"

Encouraged, Gregg went on. "There's always talk of a giant alligator in the swamp. Most of the southern swamps have similar legends, as I'm sure you know. And sometimes they turn out to be true—there was an alligator shot in Lake Conroe over in Texas a few years back that was over twenty-three feet long. It was eating a full-grown deer when it was killed."

"Amazing," said Pendergast. "So if one wanted to visit Spanish Island, how would one go about it?"

"It's marked on the older maps. Problem is, getting there's a whole different deal, with all the mazes of channels and mud bars. And the cypresses are thick as thieves deep in there. During low water, there's a growth of ferns and brambles shooting up that are wellnigh impassable. You just can't go straight through to Spanish Island. Frankly, I don't think anyone's been out there in years. It's deep in the refuge, no fishing or hunting allowed, and it's hell getting in and out of there. I would strongly advise against it."

Pendergast shut the steno book and rose. "Thank you very much, Pastor. This is all very helpful. May I contact you again if necessary?"

"Certainly."

"Very good. I'd give you one of my cards but I'm fresh out. Here's my telephone number, if you need to call. I'll be sure to send you the book when it's published."

Getting back into the Rolls, Hayward asked, "What now?"

"Back to our friends in Malfourche. We have unfinished business there."

64

They arrived in the same parking lot, and parked in the same dusty spot. The same group of men were still down at the docks, and once again they all turned and stared. As he and Hayward got out of the car, Pendergast murmured, "Continue to allow me to handle the situation, if you please, Captain."

Hayward nodded, slightly disappointed. She had been half hoping that one of the good old boys would step over the line so she could bust his ass and haul him in.

"Gentlemen!" said Pendergast, striding toward the group. "We are back."

Hayward felt a fresh cringe.

The fat one—Tiny—stepped forward and waited, arms crossed.

"Mr. Tiny, my associate and I would like to rent an airboat to explore the swamp. Are any available?"

To Hayward's surprise, Tiny smiled. A number of glances were exchanged in the crowd.

"Sure, I can rent you an airboat," said Tiny.

"Excellent! And a guide?"

Another exchange of glances. "Can't spare a guide," Tiny said slowly, "but I'd be right glad to show you where to go on a map. Got 'em for sale inside."

"Specifically, we're hoping to visit Spanish Island."

A long silence. "No problem," said Tiny. "Come on round to the private dock on the other side, where we keep the boats, and we'll set you up."

They followed the immense man around behind the structure to the commercial dock on the other side. Half a dozen sad-looking airboats and bass boats sat in their slips. Pendergast, pursing his lips, looked them over briefly, selecting the newest-looking airboat.

Half an hour later, they were in the fourteen-foot airboat, Pendergast at the wheel, moving into Lake End. As they came into open water, Pendergast throttled up, the propeller making a roaring sound, the boat skimming across the water. The town of Malfourche, with its shabby docks and sad, crooked buildings, slowly vanished into a light mist that clung to the surface of the lake. The FBI agent, in his black suit and brilliant white shirt, looked ludicrously out of place in the cockpit of the airboat.

"That was easy," Hayward said.

"Indeed," Pendergast replied, glancing across the surface of the water. Then he looked at her. "You realize, Captain, that they had prior news of our arrival?"

"What makes you think that?"

"One might expect a certain hostility to wealthy customers arriving in a Rolls-Royce. But the level of hostility was so specific, and so immediate, that one must conclude they were expecting us. Judging from the message gouged into my car, they believed we were environmentalists."

"You did say we were birders."

"They get birders here all the time. No, Captain: I'm convinced they thought we were environmental bureaucrats, or perhaps government scientists, masquerading as birders."

"A case of mistaken identity?"

"Possibly."

The boat skimmed the brown waters of the lake. As soon as the town had vanished completely, Pendergast turned the boat ninety degrees.

"Spanish Island is west," said Hayward. "Why are we heading north?"

Pendergast pulled out the map Tiny had sold him. The fat man's scribblings and dirty thumbprints were all over it. "I asked Tiny to indicate every route into Spanish Island that he knew. Clearly, those fellows know the swamp better than anyone else. This map should prove most useful."

"Please don't tell me you're going to trust that man."

Pendergast smiled mirthlessly. "I trust him implicitly—to lie. We can safely discount all these routes he has marked. Which leaves us a northern approach. That way we can evade the ambush here, in the bayous west of Spanish Island."

"Ambush?"

Pendergast's eyebrows shot up. "Captain, surely you realize the only reason we were able to rent this boat at all was because they planned to surprise us in the swamp. Not only did someone notify them we would be coming, but it seems he or she also fed them some sort of story designed to arouse their ire, with instructions to intimidate or perhaps even kill us if we try to go into the swamp."

"It might just be a coincidence," said Hayward. "Maybe the real environmental official is just now arriving in Malfourche."

"I might be concerned about that if we'd arrived in your Buick. But there can be little doubt they were expecting two people *fitting our descriptions*. Because the look on their faces as soon as we stepped out was one of absolute certainty."

"How could anyone have possibly known where we were going?"

"An excellent question, one for which I have no answer. Yet."

Hayward thought for a minute. "So why did you antagonize them like that? Act like a whiny city slicker?"

"Because I had to be absolutely sure of their enmity. I needed to be completely certain they would mismark the map. This way I'm confident of the route we must take. On a more general level, an aroused, angry, and suspicious crowd is far more revealing in its actions than one that is mixed or partially friendly. Think back to our little encounter, and I think you will agree that we learned a great deal more from that angry crowd than we would have otherwise. I find the Rolls to be most useful in that regard."

Unconvinced, Hayward was disinclined to argue the point and said nothing.

Taking one hand from the wheel, Pendergast removed a manila folder from his jacket and passed it to Hayward. "Here I have some Google Earth images of the swamp. Not altogether helpful, because so much is obscured by trees and other growth, but it does seem to reinforce the notion that the northern approach to Spanish Island is the most promising."

The lake curved around and—in the distance ahead, emerging from the mists—Hayward could see the low, dark line of cypress trees that marked the edge of the swamp. A few minutes later the trees loomed up before them, draped in moss, like the robed guardians to some awful netherworld, and the airboat was swallowed up by the hot, dead, enveloping air of the swamp.

65

Black Brake Swamp

Parker Wooten had anchored his skiff about twenty yards into a dead-end bayou at the northern tip of Lake End, over a deep channel cut where the bayou met the main body of the lake. He was fishing slowly over a tangle of sunken timber with a Texas-rigged fire-tail worm, casting in a radial pattern in between sips from a quart bottle of Woodford Reserve. It was a perfect time to fish the back bayous: while everyone else was off chasing the environmentalists. In this very spot last year he had landed an eleven-pound, three-ounce largemouth bass, the Lake End record. Ever since then it had been almost impossible to fish Lemonhead Bayou without competition lashing the water on every side. Despite the frenzy, Wooten was pretty sure there were some wise old big ones still lurking down there, if only you could fish them at a quiet moment. The others all used live bait from Tiny's, the party line being that wise old bass knew all about plastic worms. But Wooten had always taken a contrarian view to fishing. He figured that a wise old bass, aggressive and irritable, would be more likely to strike at something that looked different—to hell with the mousees and nightcrawlers the others used.

His walkie-talkie—obligatory when in the swamp—was tuned to channel 5, and every few seconds he'd hear an exchange among members of Tiny's posse as they positioned themselves in the west bayous, waiting for the enviros to show up. Parker Wooten would have none of it. He'd spent five years in Rumbaugh State Prison and there was no way in hell he was ever going back. Let the rest of the yahoos take the rap. He'd take the bass instead.

He cast again, let the bait sink, and then gave it a little tug, bumping it off a sunken log, and started reeling in, twitching the tip. The fish weren't biting. It was too hot and maybe they'd gone to deeper water. Or maybe what was needed here was a firecracker with a blue tail. He was still reeling in when he heard the faint roar of an airboat. Shoving the rod into a holder, he picked up his binoculars and scanned the lake beyond. Pretty soon, the boat came into view, skimming along the surface, its lower section lost in the low haze drifting over the water, the vessel's flat bottom making a rapid slapping sound. And then it was gone.

Parker sat back in his skiff. He took a small sip of Woodford to help him think. It was those two enviros, all right, but they weren't anywhere near where they were supposed to be. Everyone was in the west bayous but here they were, far to the north.

Another sip and he removed his walkie-talkie. "Hey, Tiny. Parker here."

"Parker?" came Tiny's voice after a moment. "I thought you weren't going to join us."

"I ain't joined you. I'm at the north end, fishing Lemonhead Bayou. And you know what? I just saw one a your airboats come on by, them two in it."

"No way. They're coming in through the west bayous."

"The hell they are. I just saw them go by."

"You see them yourself, or is that the Woodford Reserve seeing them?"

"Look here," Wooten said, "you don't want to listen to me, fine. You can wait in the west bayous till they're skating on Lake Pontchartrain. I'm telling you they're going in from the north and what you do with that is your business."

Wooten snapped off the walkie-talkie with annoyance and shoved it in his gear box. Tiny was getting too big for his own britches, figuratively and for real. He took a sip from the Woodford, nestled the precious bottle back down in its box, then tore the plastic worm from the hook and rigged another, throwing it up-bayou. As he cranked and twitched it in, he felt a certain sudden heaviness on his line. Slowly, carefully, he kept the line almost slack for a moment, letting the fish swim off with it—and then, with a sharp but not hard jerk, set the hook. The line tightened, the tip bent double, and Parker Wooten's annoyance immediately vanished as he realized he had hooked a really big one.

66

The channel tightened, and Pendergast shut down the airboat engine. The silence that ensued seemed even louder than the roar of the boat had been.

Hayward glanced over at him. "What now?"

Pendergast removed his suit jacket, draped it over his seat, and slid a pole out of its rack. "Too tight to run the engine—we wouldn't want to snag a branch at three thousand RPMs. I'm afraid we have to pole."

Pendergast took up a position in the stern and began poling the boat forward along an abandoned logging "pull" channel, overhung with cypress branches and tangled stands of water tupelo. It was late afternoon, but the swamp was already in deep shadow. Overhead there was no hint of sun, just enveloping blankets of green and brown, layer upon layer. Now the sound of insects and birds swelled to fill the void left by the engine: strange calls, cries, twitters, drones, and whoops.

"I'll take over whenever you need a break," Hayward said.

"Thank you, Captain." The boat glided forward.

She consulted the two maps, laid out side by side: Tiny's map and the Google Earth printout. After two hours they had made it perhaps halfway to Spanish Island, but the densest, most maze-like part of the swamp lay ahead, past a small stretch of open water marked on the map as Little Bayou.

"What's your plan once we're past the bayou?" Hayward pointed at the printout. "Looks pretty tight in there. And there are no more logging channels."

"You'll take over the poling and I shall navigate."

"And just how do you intend to navigate?"

"The currents flow east to west, toward the Mississippi River. As long as we keep in the west-flowing current, we'll never get dead-ended."

"I haven't seen the slightest indication of a current since we began."

"It's there."

Hayward slapped at a whining mosquito. Irritated, she squeezed some more insect repellent into her hands and slathered it on her neck and face. Ahead now she could see, through the ribbed tree trunks, a glow of sunlight.

"The bayou," she said.

Pendergast poled the boat forward, and the trees thinned. Suddenly they were out on open water, startling a family of coots that quickly took off, flapping low on the water. He racked the pole and fired up the engine, the airboat once again skimming over the mirror-like surface of the bayou, heading for the heavy tangle of green and brown at its western end. Hayward leaned back, savoring the cooling rush of air, the relative openness after the cloying and claustrophobic swamp.

When the bayou narrowed again—too soon— Pendergast slowed the boat. Minutes later, they stopped at a complicated series of inlets that seemed to go every which way, obscured by stickweed and water hyacinths.

Hayward peered at the map, then the printout, and then shrugged. "Which one?" she asked.

Pendergast didn't answer. The engine was still idling. Suddenly he swung the boat a hundred eighty degrees and throttled it up; at the same time Hayward heard a rumble coming from all around them.

"What the *hell*?" she said.

The airboat leapt forward with a great roar, back in the direction of the open bayou, but it was too late: a dozen bass boats with powerful outboards came growling out of the dark swamp from both sides of the narrow channel, blocking their retreat.

Pulling his gun, Pendergast fired at the closest boat; its engine cover flew off. Hayward pulled her own weapon as answering fire tore into the propeller of their airboat; with a great *whack* the propeller flew apart, shattering the oversize cage; their boat slowed and swung sideways, dead in the water.

Hayward took cover behind a seat, but—as she quickly reconnoitered—she realized the situation was hopeless. They had driven into an ambush and were now surrounded by bass boats and skiffs, manned by at least thirty people, all armed, all with guns aimed at them. And there in the lead boat stood Tiny, a TEC-9 in his fat paws.

"Stand up, both of you!" he said. "Hands over your

heads, nice and slow!" This was punctuated by a warning spray of gunfire over their heads.

Hayward glanced at Pendergast, also crouched behind the seat. Blood was trickling from a nasty cut on his forehead. He gave a curt nod, then rose, hands over his head, his handgun dangling by his thumb. Hayward did the same.

With a growl, Tiny brought his boat up alongside, a skinny man in its bow holding a big handgun. Tiny hopped out onto their boat, the airboat yawing with his weight. He reached up and took the guns from their hands. Examining Pendergast's Les Baer, he grunted in approval and shoved it in his belt. He took Hayward's Glock and tossed it onto the floor of his boat.

"Well, well." He grinned, deposited a stream of tobacco juice into the water. "I didn't know you enviros believed in guns."

Hayward stared at him. "You're making a serious mistake," she said evenly. "I'm a captain of homicide with the New York Police Department. And I am going to ask you to put down your weapon or face the consequences."

An oleaginous smile bloomed on Tiny's face. "That so?"

"I'm going to lower one hand to show you my identification," said Hayward.

Tiny took a step forward. "No, I think I'll find it myself." Holding the TEC-9 to her head, he groped in her shirt pockets, first one, then the other, helping himself to a couple of generous feels in the process.

"Tits are real," he said, to a burst of raucous laughter. "Fucking monsters, too."

He moved down to her pant pocket, fishing about, at last removing her shield wallet. He flipped it open. "Well, lookee here!"

He held it up, showing it around. Then he examined it himself, pursing his wet lips. "Captain L. Hayward, says here. Homicide division. And there's even a picture! You send away for this from the back of a comic book?"

Hayward stared back. Could he really be so stupid? It made her afraid.

Tiny closed the wallet, reached behind himself, made a wiping motion over his enormous derriere, and tossed it into the water with a splash. "That's what I think of your badge," he said. "Larry, get up here and search this one."

The lean man climbed onto the airboat and approached Pendergast.

"Any bullshit and I let loose with this here," he said, gesturing with the gun. "Simple as that."

The man began searching Pendergast. He removed a second gun, some tools, papers, and his shield.

"Lemme see that," Tiny said.

The man named Larry handed it over. Tiny examined it, spat tobacco juice on it, shut it, and tossed it in the water. "More comic-book tin. You folks are something else, you know that?"

Hayward felt the barrel of the gun digging into her side.

"You really are," Tiny said, his voice getting louder. "You come down here, feed us a bunch of birder bullshit, and then you think some fake badges are gonna save your sorry asses. Is that what they told you to do in case of emergency? Let me tell you something: we know who you are and why you're here. You ain't gonna take one more inch of our swamp away from us. This is our land, how we make a living. This is how my granddaddy fed my daddy, and it's how I'm feeding my kids. It ain't some Disneyland for jackoff Yankee kayakers. It's *our* swamp."

Approving sounds rose up from the surrounding boats.

"Excuse me for interrupting your little speech," said Hayward, "but I am in fact a police officer and he's an FBI agent, and for your information you are all under arrest. *All* of you."

"Oooooh!" said Tiny, shoving his fat face into hers. "I'm *soooo* scared." The smell of whiskey and rotting onions washed over Hayward.

He looked around. "Hey! Maybe we should have ourselves a little striptease here, what say?" Tiny hooked a thumb under one of his own immense man-boobs and gave it a jiggle.

A roar of approval, catcalls, hoots.

"Let's see some *real* hooters!"

Hayward looked at Pendergast. His face was completely unreadable. The skinny man named Larry was holding a gun to his head, and two dozen other weapons were pointed in their direction.

Tiny reached out and grabbed the collar of Hayward's blouse, giving it a jerk and trying to rip it open; she twisted away, buttons popping off.

"Feisty!" said Tiny, then hauled off and smacked her hard across the face, sending her sprawling in the bottom of the boat.

"Get up," he said, to the sound of laughter. Tiny wasn't laughing. She rose, face burning, and he jammed the gun in her ear. "All right, bitch. Take off your own shirt. For the boys."

"Go to hell," Hayward said.

"Do it," Tiny murmured, pushing the muzzle into her ear. She felt the blood begin to well up. Her blouse was already halfway ripped open.

"Do it!"

She placed a shaking hand on a button, began to undo it.

"Yeah!" came the yells. "Oh, *yeah*!"

Another sideways glance at Pendergast. He remained motionless, expressionless. What was going through his head?

"Unbutton and give 'em air!" screamed Tiny, jabbing with the gun.

She undid the button to another roar, started on the next.

67

Suddenly Pendergast spoke. "This is no way to treat a lady."

Tiny swiveled toward him. "No way to treat a lady? I think it's a fucking *great* way!"

A chorus of agreement. Hayward looked at the sea of red, sweating, eager faces.

"Would you care to know what I think?" Pendergast said. "I think you are an embonpoint swine."

Tiny blinked. "Huh?"

"A fat pig," said Pendergast.

Tiny drew back a meaty fist and smacked Pendergast in the solar plexus. The agent gasped and bent forward. Tiny hit him again in the same spot and Pendergast sank to his knees, the wind knocked out of him.

Tiny looked down at Pendergast and spat on him disdainfully. "This is taking *way* too long," he said. Then he grasped Hayward's shirt and—with a powerful tug—tore the remaining buttons away.

There was a roar of approval from the surrounding

boats. Pulling a huge skinning knife from a pocket of his overalls, Tiny opened it, then pulled Hayward's ruined shirt aside with its blade, exposing her brassiere.

"Holy *shit*!" somebody said.

Tiny gazed hungrily at Hayward's generous breasts. She swallowed painfully and made a move to cover herself with her buttonless shirt but Tiny shook his head, pushed her hands away, and traced the blade of his knife teasingly along the topline of her bra. Then—very slowly—he inserted the tip of the blade under the fabric between the cups. With a jerk, he brought the knife toward him, slitting the bra into two pieces. Hayward's breasts swung free to a hugely appreciative roar.

Hayward saw Pendergast rise, stumbling. Tiny was too preoccupied to notice.

Pendergast steadied himself, leaning heavily to one side. Then—with a sudden, almost imperceptible movement—he shifted his weight to the other side. The boat rocked, throwing Tiny and Larry off balance.

"Hey, easy now—"

Hayward saw a blur, a flash of steel; with a groan Larry doubled over, his clenched hand firing the gun blindly downward; there was a sudden gush of blood into the bottom of the boat.

Tiny twisted around to protect himself, sweeping the TEC-9 through the air, letting loose a long burst of fire, but the agent moved so fast the spray of bullets missed him. A sinuous arm whipped around Tiny's fat neck and jerked his head back, a stiletto at his throat; at the same time Hayward smashed the man's forearm, jarring the TEC-9 loose.

"Don't move," Pendergast said, sinking the knife

partway into the man's neck. With his other hand he neatly extracted his Les Baer from the man's waistband.

Tiny roared, twisting his huge bulk, pawing to get at Pendergast; the knife sank deeper, twisted, flashing; there was a small splatter of blood, and then a fresh stillness.

"Move and die," said Pendergast.

Hayward stared, horrified, her own exposed condition momentarily forgotten: Pendergast had somehow managed to work the stiletto into the man's neck, exposing the jugular; the knife blade had already slipped underneath it, stretching it from the wound.

"Shoot me and it's cut," Pendergast said. "I fall, it's cut. He moves, it's cut. She's touched again—it's cut."

"What the fuck!" Tiny screamed in terror, his eyes rolling. "What's he done? Am I bleeding to death?"

A dead silence. All guns were still trained on them.

"Shoot him!" Tiny cried. "Shoot the girl! What are you doing?"

Nobody moved. Hayward stared, transfixed in horror, at the sight of the bulging, pulsing vein, slick over the gleam of the bloodied blade.

Pendergast nodded toward one of the big side mirrors mounted on the gunwale of the boat. "Captain, fetch that mirror for me, please."

Hayward forced herself to move, covering herself as best she could and wrenching the mirror off.

"Hold it up for Tiny's benefit."

She complied. Tiny stared into it, at himself, his eyes widening in terror. "What are you doing…Oh, my God, please, don't…" His voice trailed off into a quaver, his bloodshot eyes wide, his huge body immobilized with terror.

"All weapons in Mr. Tiny's boat, there," said Pendergast quietly, nodding at the empty vessel next to theirs. "Everything. Now."

No one moved.

Pendergast pulled the vein away from the bleeding wound with the flat of his knife. "Do what I say or I cut."

"You heard him!" Tiny said in a kind of terrified, squeaking whisper. "Guns in the boat! *Do what he says!*"

Hayward continued to hold up the mirror. The men, murmuring, began passing their guns forward and tossing them into the boat. Pretty soon the flat bottom of the boat was filled with an arsenal.

"Knives, Mace, everything."

More things were tossed in.

Pendergast turned toward the skinny man, Larry, lying in the bottom of the boat. He was bleeding from a knife wound in his arm and a self-administered gunshot to his foot. "Remove your shirt, please."

After a brief hesitation, the man did as ordered.

"Pass it over to Captain Hayward."

Hayward took the damp, odorous garment. Turning away from the surrounding boats as much as was possible, she removed her torn blouse and ruined bra and shrugged into the bloody shirt.

Pendergast turned toward her. "Captain, would you care to arm yourself?"

"This TEC-9 looks suitable," Hayward said, picking up the handgun from the pile of weapons. She looked it over, removed the magazine, examined it, slapped it back in. "Converted to fully automatic. Fifty-round magazine, too. Plenty of rounds left to smoke everyone right here, right now."

"An effective, if inelegant, choice," said Pendergast.

Hayward pointed the TEC-9 at the group. "Who still wants to see the floor show?"

Silence. The only sound was Tiny's choked sobbing. The tears streamed down his face, but he remained as immobile as a statue.

"I'm afraid," Pendergast said, "that you folks have made a serious error. This lady is indeed a homicide captain of the NYPD, and I am truly a special agent with the Federal Bureau of Investigation. We're here on a murder investigation that has nothing to do with you or your town. Whoever told you we were environmentalists lied to you. Now: I'm going to ask a question, just once, and if I get an answer that isn't satisfactory, I'm going to cut Tiny's jugular and my colleague, Captain Hayward, is going to shoot you down like dogs. Self-defense, of course. Being law enforcement, who's to contradict us?"

A silence.

"The question is this: Mr. Tiny, *who called you to say we were coming?*"

Tiny couldn't get the answer out fast enough. "It was Ventura, Mike Ventura, Mike Ventura..." He choked out the words in between stifled sobs, his voice reduced to a babble.

"And who is Mike Ventura?"

"A guy who lives over in Itta Bena, but he comes down here a lot, big sportsman, lots of money, spends a lot of time in the swamp. It was him, he came into my place, told us all you was environmentalists, you was looking to turn the rest of Black Brake into a refuge, take away all the work from us swampers—"

"Thank you," said Pendergast, "that's sufficient. Here's what's going to happen. My colleague and I are going to continue on our way in Mr. Tiny's excellently equipped and fully loaded bass boat. With all the guns. You all go on home. Understand?"

Nothing.

He tightened the knife beneath the vein. "May I have a response, please?"

Murmurs, nods.

"Excellent. You can see we are now heavily armed. And I can assure you that both of us know how to use these weapons. Captain, would you care to demonstrate?"

Hayward pointed the TEC-9 at a nearby stand of saplings and opened fire. Three short bursts. The trees toppled slowly into the water.

Pendergast slipped the knife out from under the vein. "You're going to need a few stitches, Mr. Tiny."

The fat man merely blubbered.

"I'd advise you all to discuss it among yourselves and come up with a nice, believable story as to how Mr. Tiny here cut his neck and how old Larry there shot himself in the foot. Because the captain and I have bigger fish to fry, and we don't want any more disruptions. Assuming you don't annoy us further—and assuming you leave my rather expensive car alone—we don't see the need to bring charges or arrest anyone—do we, Captain?"

She shook her head. Funny how Pendergast's way

of doing things began to make sense—out here in the middle of nowhere, without backup, in front of a crowd who wanted nothing better than to serially rape her and murder them both and sink their bodies in the swamp.

Pendergast stepped into the bass boat, Hayward following, picking her way among the assorted weaponry. Firing up the engine, Pendergast eased the boat forward; the surrounding boats unwillingly parted to give him passage. "We'll see you all again," he called out. "I regret to say that when we do, there might be more unpleasantness."

Then he throttled up and the bass boat headed into the widest inlet at the end of the bayou, heading south into the thick braid of vegetation under a dying evening light.

68

Mike Ventura watched from his parked Escalade, A/C going full blast, as the boats straggled back into the slips beyond Tiny's. The sun had just set over the water, the sky a dirty orange. He began to feel uneasy; this did not look like a war party returning from a successful raid. It had more the sullen, dispirited, bedraggled appearance of a rout. When one of the last boats brought in Tiny—who staggered out onto the dock with a bloody, wadded handkerchief tied around his neck, blood caking one side of his shirt—he knew for certain something had gone wrong.

A couple of men supported Tiny, one beneath each meaty arm, as he shuffled into his establishment and disappeared. Meanwhile, others in the crowd had seen Ventura and were talking and gesturing—and then began moving his way. They did not look happy.

Ventura reached over and pressed the automatic

locks on the doors, which shot down with a click. The men circled his car in silence, their faces red and streaked with sweat.

Ventura cracked the window an inch. "What happened?"

Nobody answered. After a tense moment, a man raised a fist and brought it down on the hood with a loud bang.

"What the hell?" Ventura cried.

"What the hell?" the man screamed. *"What the hell?"*

Another fist came down and then, suddenly, they were pummeling the car, kicking the sides, swearing and spitting. Astonished and horrified, Ventura snugged the window tight and threw the car into reverse, backing up so fast those standing behind had to throw themselves to one side to avoid being run over.

"Son of a bitch!" the mob screamed with one voice. "Liar!"

"They were feds, asshole!"

"Lying bastard!"

Giving the wheel a frantic twist, Ventura threw the car into drive and gunned the engine, spraying dirt and gravel in a one-hundred-eighty-degree arc. As he accelerated, a rock smacked the back window with a dull thud, turning it into a spiderweb of cracks.

When he pulled onto the small highway, his cell phone rang. He picked it up: Judson. *Shit.*

"I'm almost there," came Judson's voice. "How'd it go?"

"Something messed up. And I mean *messed up.*"

*   *   *

By the time Ventura arrived at his neatly kept compound at the edge of the swamp, Esterhazy's pickup was already there. The tall man stood next to the bed of the truck, dressed in khaki, unloading guns. Ventura pulled up and got out. Esterhazy turned toward him, his face dark.

"What happened to your car?" he asked.

"The swampers attacked it. Over in Malfourche."

"Didn't they take care of things?"

"No. Tiny came back with a neck wound and nobody had their guns. They wanted to string me up. I've got a big problem on my hands."

Esterhazy stared at him. "So those two are still heading to Spanish Island?"

"It seems so."

Esterhazy looked past Ventura's rambling white-washed house and wide, billiard-table lawn to the private dock, where Ventura's three boats were tied up: a Lafitte skiff, a brand-new bass boat with a hydraulic jack plate and a Humminbird console, and a powerful airboat. His jaw tightened. He reached into the pickup bed and removed the last gun case. "It would appear," he said slowly, "that we're going to have to handle the problem ourselves."

"And right away. Because if they reach Spanish Island, it's *over*."

"We won't let it get that far." Esterhazy squinted toward the sunset. "Depending on how fast they're moving, they might be getting close already."

"They're moving slowly. They don't know the swamp."

Esterhazy looked at the bass boat. "With that two

fifty Yamaha, we might just be able to intercept them when they cross that old logging pullboat canal near Ronquille Island. You know what I'm talking about?"

"Of course," said Ventura, irritated that Esterhazy might even question his knowledge of the swamp.

"Then put these guns in the boat and let's get moving," said Judson. "I've got an idea."

69

Black Brake Swamp

A buttery moon rose among the massive trunks of the bald cypresses, spreading a faint light through the night-darkened swamp. The boat's spotlight cast a beam into the tangle of trees and other vegetation ahead, now and then illuminating pairs of glowing eyes. Hayward knew most of the eyes belonged to frogs and toads, but nevertheless felt herself growing seriously spooked. Even if the strange stories she'd heard as a child about Black Brake were legends, she knew the place was nevertheless infested with very real alligators and venomous snakes. She poled the bass boat forward, drenched in sweat, walking the pole from the middle backward. Larry's shirt felt coarse and itchy against her bare skin. Pendergast lay on the front deck, maps spread out, examining them intently with the aid of his flashlight. It had been a long, slow journey, full of dead ends, false leads, and painstaking navigation.

Pendergast shone his light into the water and dropped a pinch of dirt from a cup overboard, testing the current. "A mile or less," he murmured, going back to the maps.

She poled, walked back to the stern, pulled the pole up, walked forward, stuck it into the muddy bottom again. She felt as if she were drowning in the greenish black jungle that surrounded them. "What if the camp's gone?"

No answer. The moon rose higher, and Hayward breathed the deep, moist, fragrant air. A mosquito flew into her ear, buzzing frantically. She smacked it, flicked it away.

"Up ahead is the last logging channel," Pendergast said. "Beyond that lies the final stretch of swamp before Spanish Island."

The boat nosed through a patch of rotting water hyacinth, the sour vegetative smell rising from the water and enveloping them.

"Turn off the spotlight and running lights, please," Pendergast said. "We don't want to alert them to our approach."

Hayward switched off the lights. "You really think there's a 'them' there?"

"I'm quite sure *something* is there. Why go to such lengths to stop us?"

As her eyes adjusted, Hayward found herself surprised at just how much light there was in the swamp under the full moon. Ahead, through the tree trunks, she could see a lane of shimmering water. In a moment the boat had slipped into the logging channel, now half overgrown with duckweed and hyacinth. The branches of the cypresses knitted together overhead, forming a tunnel.

Suddenly the boat stopped dead. Hayward lurched forward, using the pole to keep herself steady.

"We've snagged something beneath the surface," Pendergast said. "Probably a root or a fallen tree branch. See if you can't pole around it."

Hayward pushed herself against the pole. The stern of the boat swung around, impacting heavily against a cypress trunk. The vessel shuddered and swayed, then came loose from the obstruction. As Hayward leaned into the pole, preparing to launch them back into the logging channel, she saw something long, glistening, and black slip from the branches overhead and fall across her shoulders. It slithered around the skin of her neck, cool and dry, and it was all she could do to keep from crying out in surprise and revulsion.

"Don't move," said Pendergast. "Not a muscle."

She waited, willing herself to stay still, as Pendergast took a slow step toward her, then stopped and balanced himself carefully on the arsenal that lay in the boat's bottom. And then one hand shot forward, grabbed the thick coiling presence from her shoulders, and flung it away with a vicious snap. Hayward turned to watch the snake writhing through the air, easily more than a yard long, before landing in the water astern.

"*Agkistrodon piscivorus,*" Pendergast said grimly. "Cottonmouth water moccasin."

Her skin tingled, and the nasty slithering sensation refused to go away. Taking a deep breath, she shuddered and grasped the pole. They moved back into the channel and continued deeper into the overgrown fastness. Pendergast took a look around, then returned to his maps and charts. As she poled, Hayward kept a cautious eye on the braiding of tree trunks above her. Mosquitoes, frogs, snakes—the only thing she hadn't yet encountered was an alligator.

"We may have to get out and travel on foot soon," Pendergast murmured. "There would appear to be obstructions ahead." He glanced up from the map, looked around once again.

Hayward thought about the alligators. *On foot. Great.*

She placed the pole, gave the boat another shove. Suddenly, in a silent flash of black, Pendergast lunged at her, tackling her at the waist, and they both tumbled over the gunwale of the boat into the black water. She righted herself underwater, too surprised to struggle, her feet sinking into the muck below. As she pushed off and her head broke the surface, she heard a fusillade of shots.

A *clang* sounded as a round struck the engine, and a gout of flame erupted. *Clang! Clang!* The shots were coming from the darkness to her right.

"Get a weapon," Pendergast whispered in her ear.

She grasped the gunwale and, waiting for a lull in the shooting, hoisted herself up, grabbed the closest gun—a heavy rifle—and slid back down. Another fusillade of shots tore into the boat, several striking the engine. A trickle of flame ran down the bottom of the boat: the gas line had been hit.

"Don't return fire!" Pendergast whispered, giving her a push. "Get to the other side of the boat, head for the far side of the channel, and take cover."

She half swam, half waded through the water, keeping

her head as low as possible. The burning boat erupted into flames behind them, casting a yellow glow over the water. There was a muffled *crump!* and she felt the pressure-wave of the explosion wash over her, a ball of fire rising orange and black into the night. A series of smaller explosions crackled from the burning pile of firearms.

Suddenly shots were striking all around, sending up gouts of water.

"We're spotted," Pendergast said urgently. "Immerse and swim!"

Hayward took a deep breath, ducked below the water, and, rifle awkwardly gripped in one hand, began to propel herself forward in the watery darkness. As her feet sank into the muck, she could feel hard—and sometimes not-so-hard—objects and the occasional slimy wriggle of a fish. She tried not to think about the water moccasins, or about the nutrias and eight-inch leeches and everything else that infested the swamp. She could hear the *zip zip* of bullets entering the water around her. With her lungs almost bursting she rose, gasped in another breath, and submerged again.

The water seemed to be alive with the buzzing sound of bullets. She had no idea where Pendergast was but she kept going, rising every minute or so to gulp air. The mud under her feet began to rise. Soon she was crawling in ever-shallower water, the trees on the far side of the canal looming up. The shooter was still firing to her right, the bullets striking the tree trunks above her. The shots were more intermittent now. He had evidently lost her and was simply shooting into her general vicinity.

She dragged herself onto the slippery bank, rolling

onto her back amid the hyacinths and fighting to catch her breath. She was completely covered with mud. It had happened so fast she hadn't had time to think— but now she thought. Furiously. It wasn't the swampers this time, she was sure of that. It appeared to be a lone shooter. Someone who knew they were coming and had time to prepare.

She ventured a look around but saw no sign of Pendergast. Cradling the rifle with one hand, she half crawled, half swam up a shallow rivulet into the cover of the trees. She grasped an old, rotting cypress stump and settled herself behind it. As she did so, she heard a faint splashing sound. She almost called out, thinking it was Pendergast, when a spotlight abruptly went on in the channel, illuminating the swamp to her left.

She ducked down, trying to make herself as small as possible behind the stump. Slowly, with great deliberation, she shifted the rifle in front of her. It was covered with mud. Immersing it in the water of the rivulet, she agitated it slightly, letting the mud dissolve away, then brought the weapon up and felt along its length, trying to figure out what it was. Lever-action, heavy, octagon barrel, big caliber. It seemed to be a .45-70, a modern replica of an Old West rifle, maybe a Winchester reproduction of an old Browning—which meant it would probably still fire despite the immersion. The magazine would hold between four and nine rounds.

The spotlight lanced through the trees, scanning the swamp. The shooting had stopped, but the light was moving closer.

She should shoot out the light. That was, in fact, her only target, as everything else was invisible in the glare.

Moving slowly and silently, she raised the gun, shaking out the last of the water. With infinite care she cocked the lever, feeling a round slip into the chamber. So far, so good. The light was now very visible, moving slowly along the canal. She raised the gun to take aim—and suddenly felt a hand on her shoulder.

Stifling a cry, she ducked back down.

"Do not fire," came Pendergast's almost inaudible voice. "It might be a trap."

Swallowing her surprise, she nodded.

"Follow me." Pendergast turned and crawled up the rivulet, and Hayward did the same. The moon was temporarily hidden behind clouds, but the dying glow from the burning boat gave them just enough light to see by. The little channel narrowed, and soon they were crossing a mudflat covered with about a foot of water. The beam shot across the flat, moving toward them. Pendergast stopped and took a deep breath, sinking into the water as deeply as possible. He looked as mud-encrusted as she was. Hayward followed suit, almost burying her face in the muck. The light passed directly over them. She tensed, waiting for a shot, but there was none.

When the light had passed, she rose. Beyond the flat she could see a massive grouping of dead cypress stumps and rotting trunks. Pendergast was heading directly for it. Hayward followed suit, and within a minute they had taken up a position.

Hayward quickly rinsed and recleaned her gun. Pendergast plucked his Les Baer from its holster and did the same. They worked quickly and silently. The light came back, this time closer, moving directly toward them.

"How do you know it's a trap?" Hayward whispered.

"Too obvious. There's more than one gunman there, and they're waiting for us to fire at the light."

"So what do we do?"

"We wait. In silence. Unmoving."

The light snapped off and darkness reigned. Pendergast crouched, immovable, unreadable, behind the great tangle of stumps.

She listened intently. There were splashes and rustles in the night, seemingly everywhere. Animals moving, frogs jumping. Or was it people?

The burning boat finally sank, the slick of burning gasoline rapidly dying out, leaving the swamp in a cool quasi-darkness. Still they waited. The light came on again, drawing ever closer.

70

Judson Esterhazy, wearing shoulder waders, moved with infinite caution through the thick vegetation, a Winchester .30-30 in his hands. It was much lighter than the sniper rifle, far more maneuverable, and a gun he'd used for hunting deer since he was a teenager. Powerful but sleek, it was almost like an extension of himself.

Through the trees he could see Ventura's light, shining about, steadily approaching the area where Pendergast and the woman must have gone to ground. Esterhazy was positioned about a hundred yards behind where they had been driven. Little did they know they were being squeezed in a pincer movement, as he worked up behind their position among the fallen trees while Ventura approached from the front. The two were sitting ducks. All he needed was for them to shoot once—a single shot—and then he could pinpoint their position and kill them both. And eventually they would be forced to shoot out the light.

The plan was working perfectly, and Ventura had

played his part well. The light—on a long pole—moved slowly, haltingly, ever closer to their position. He could see its beam fitfully illuminating a tangle of cypress roots and a massive, rotting trunk—an old blowdown. That was where they were: there was no other decent cover anywhere nearby.

He maneuvered himself slowly to acquire a line of sight to the blowdown. The moon was higher in the sky and now it emerged from behind the clouds, casting a pale light into the darkest recesses of the swamp. He had a glimpse of the two of them, crouched behind the log, focused entirely on the light in front of them— and fully exposed to his flanking maneuver. He didn't even need them to shoot the light after all.

Slowly, Judson raised the rifle to his cheek, peering through the Trident Pro 2.5x night-vision scope. The scene leapt into sharp relief. He couldn't get a line on both at once, but if he took down Pendergast first, the woman would not present much of a challenge.

Shifting slightly, he maneuvered the scope so that Pendergast's back was centered on the crosshairs, and readied himself for the shot.

Hayward crouched behind the rotting trunk as the light swung back and forth in the darkness, moving erratically.

Pendergast whispered in her ear. "I think that light's on a pole."

"A pole?"

"Yes. Look at the curious way it's bobbing. It's a ruse. And that confirms there's a second shooter." Suddenly he grabbed her and shoved her down into the shallow water, her face in the muck. Half a second later she heard a shot just overhead, the dull thud of a bullet hitting wood.

With desperate movements, she followed Pendergast as he crawled through the muck and then wedged himself up behind a tangle of roots, pulling her next to him. More shots came, this time from both forward and behind, tearing through the roots in two directions.

"This cover's no good," gasped Hayward.

"No, it isn't. We can't stay here—it's only a matter of time until one of those bullets finds its mark."

"But what can we do?"

"I'm going to take out the shooter behind us. When I leave, I want you to count ninety seconds, fire, count another ninety, then fire again. Don't bother aiming—it's the noise I require. Take care your muzzle flash is concealed . . . and then, *only* then, after the first two fake shots, shoot out the light. And then charge him—and kill."

"Got it."

With a flash Pendergast disappeared into the swamp. A fresh burst of gunfire rang out in response.

Hayward counted to ninety and then, keeping the rifle muzzle low, fired. The .45-70 roared and kicked back, surprising her with its noise, the sound echoing and scattering through the swamp. In answer, a fusillade of bullets tore through the roots just above her head and she burrowed down in the muck, and then she heard Pendergast's answering fire to her left, his .45 blasting into the night. The fire shifted away from her. The light bobbed but did not advance.

She counted again, pulled the trigger, and a second roar from the heavy-caliber rifle split the air.

Once again, the fire came her way and was answered by a rapid tattoo of shots from Pendergast, this time from a different place. The light had still not moved.

Hayward turned, crouched in the muck, and took aim at the light with exquisite care. Slowly, she squeezed the trigger, the gun roared, and the light dissolved in a shower of sparks.

Immediately she was up and moving as fast as she could through the heavy, sucking mud toward where the light had been. She could hear Pendergast firing furiously behind her, pinning down the rearward shooter.

A pair of shots clipped through a stand of ferns next to her; she charged ahead, rifle at the ready, and then burst through the ferns to find the shooter crouching in a shallow-draft boat. He turned toward her in surprise and she threw herself into the water, aiming and firing as she did so. The man fired simultaneously and she felt a sharp blow to her leg, followed by a sudden numbness. She gasped and tried to rise to her feet, but her leg refused to move.

She worked the action frantically, expecting at any moment to be hit by a second, fatal shot. But none came and she realized she must have hit the shooter. With a supreme effort she half crawled, half stumbled into the shallow water and grabbed the gunwale, aiming the rifle within.

The shooter lay on the floor of the boat, blood streaming from a wound in his shoulder. His rifle lay in two pieces—the round had evidently struck it—and he was fumbling with one hand trying to pull out a handgun. He was not one of the swampers—in fact, she had never seen him before.

"Don't move!" she barked, aiming the rifle at him and trying not to gasp with pain. She reached over, snatched away the handgun, pointed it at him. "Stand up, nice and slow. Keep your hands in sight."

The man groaned, raised one hand. The other hung uselessly at his side.

Remembering the second shooter, Hayward kept as low as possible. She checked the handgun, saw it had a full magazine, took it and tossed the heavy rifle into the water.

The man groaned, a patch of moonlight draping his torso, the dark stain of blood slowly spreading downward from his shoulder. "I'm hit," he groaned. "I need help."

"It's not fatal," said Hayward. Her own wound was throbbing, her leg felt like a piece of lead. She hoped she wasn't bleeding to death. Because she was half immersed in water, the shooter didn't know she'd been shot. She could feel the slither and bump of things against her wounded leg—probably fish, attracted to the blood.

More shots rang out behind her, the massive sound of Pendergast's .45 interspersed with the sharper crack of the second shooter's rifle. The firing became sporadic, and then there was silence. A long silence.

"What's your name?" Hayward asked.

"Ventura," the man said. "Mike—"

A single crack. The man named Ventura jerked backward and, with a single grunt, collapsed heavily into the bottom of the boat, twitched, and was still.

Hayward, in sudden panic, dropped down low into the water, clinging to the gunwale with one hand. Vile water creatures were worrying at her wound, and she could feel the wriggling of countless leeches.

She heard a splash, swung around with the gun—only to see Pendergast moving toward her through the water, low and slow. He gestured at her to remain silent, then grasped the gunwale, looked around intently for a moment, and in one swift movement swung himself into the boat. She heard him moving about, then he was back over the side, sinking back into the water next to her.

"You all right?" he whispered.

"No. I'm hit."

"Where?"

"Leg."

"We've got to get you out of the water." The agent grasped her arm and began to tow her to shore. The silence was profound; the shooting had frightened all life in the swamp into a standstill. There were no splashes, no croaks or chirps and rustlings.

She felt a faint current, and then something hard and scaly brushed her underwater. She stifled a scream. The surface of the water dimpled in the moonlight, and two reptilian eyes rose, along with a pair of scaly nostrils. With a terrifying explosion of water it lunged at her; Pendergast simultaneously fired his gun; she felt something sharp and massive and inexorable clamp down on her injured leg and she was yanked underwater, the pain spiking excruciatingly.

Struggling, Pendergast still gripping her arm, she tried to twist away, but the huge alligator was pulling her down into the mud at the bed of the channel. She tried to scream, her mouth filling with stagnant water.

She heard the thud of his shots above the surface. She twisted again, jammed the handgun into the thing gripping her leg, and fired.

A huge report; the concussion of the shot and the violent, spastic reaction of the alligator combining into a single huge explosion. The terrible biting pressure was released and she clawed her way out of the muck, gasping.

With an almost violent motion Pendergast hauled her to shore, pulling her into the shallow water and onto a bed of ferns. She felt him tear up her pant leg, rinse the wounds as best he could, and bind them with the strips of cloth.

"The other shooter," she said, feeling dizzy. "Did you get him?"

"No. It's possible I winged him—I routed him from his hiding place and saw his shadow flitting back into the swamp."

"Why hasn't he started shooting again?"

"He may be looking for a new spot from which to improve his fire discipline. The fellow in the boat was killed by a .30-30 round. Not one of ours."

"An accident?" she gasped, trying to keep her mind off the pain.

"Probably not."

He slung her arm around his shoulders and hauled her to her feet. "There's only one thing we can do—get you to Spanish Island. Now."

"But the other shooter. He's still out there, somewhere."

"I know." Pendergast nodded at her leg. "But that wound can't wait."

71

Her arm around Pendergast's neck, Hayward stumbled through the sucking mud, slipping constantly, at times almost dragging him into the muck with her. With every step, pain shot through her leg as if a red-hot rod of iron had been embedded from shin to thigh, and she had to stifle a cry. She was keenly aware that the shooter was still out there, in the dark. The very quietness of the swamp unsettled her, made her fear he was waiting. Despite the stifling heat of the night and the tepid swamp water, she felt shivery and light-headed, as if all this were happening to someone else.

"You must get up, Captain," came Pendergast's soothing voice. She realized that she had fallen yet again.

The curious emphasis on her title roused her somewhat and she struggled to her feet, managed a step or two, and then felt herself crumpling again. Pendergast continued to half hold, half drag her along, his arms like steel cables, his voice soft and soothing. But then the mud grew deeper, sucking at her legs almost like quicksand, and with the effort of staggering she felt herself merely sinking forward into the mire.

He steadied her and with a great effort she managed to free one leg, but the wounded leg was now deep in the muck and throbbed unbearably at every effort to move it. She fell back into the swamp, sinking almost to her thighs. "I can't," she said, gasping with pain. "I just can't do it." The night whirled crazily about, her head buzzed painfully, and she could feel him holding her upright.

Pendergast glanced around quietly, carefully. "All right," he whispered. He was silent for a moment, and then she heard him softly tearing something up—his suit jacket. The dark swamp, the trees, the moon were all turning around, and around...Mosquitoes swarmed her, in her nostrils and her ears, roaring like lions. She sank back into the watery muck, wishing with all her might that the clinging mud was her bed back home, and that she was safe and warm in Manhattan, Vinnie breathing quietly beside her...

She came to as Pendergast was tying some sort of crudely contrived harness around her upper arms. She struggled for a moment, confused, but he put his hand on hers to reassure her. "I'm going to pull you along. Just stay relaxed."

She nodded, comprehension slowly dawning.

He slung the two strips of the harness over his shoulders and began to pull. At first, she didn't move. Then the swamp slowly released its sucking embrace and she found herself sliding forward over the water-covered muck, half bobbing, half slipping. The trees loomed

overhead, black and silver in the moonlight, their inter-
locking branches and leaves above forming a speckled
pattern of dark and light. Weakly, Hayward wondered
where the shooter was hiding; why they had heard
no further shots. Five minutes might have passed, or
thirty; she lost all sense of time.

Suddenly Pendergast paused.

"What is it?" Hayward groaned.

"I see a light through the trees."

72

Pendergast leaned over Hayward, examining her closely. She was in shock. Given the sloppy, mud-drenched state of her person, it was difficult to tell how much blood she had lost. The moonlight slanted across her face, ghostly white where it wasn't smeared with dirt. Gently, he pulled her up to a sitting position, loosened the harness, and propped her back against a tree trunk, camouflaging her position with a few fern leaves. Rinsing a rag in the murky water, he tried to clean some of the mud from her wound, pulling off numerous leeches in the process.

"How are you doing, Captain?"

Hayward swallowed, her mouth working. Her eyes blinked, unable to focus. He felt her pulse; shallow and rapid. Bending over to her ear, he whispered, "I have to leave you. Just for a while."

For a moment, her eyes widened in fear. Then she nodded and managed to speak, her voice hoarse. "I understand."

"Whoever is living at Spanish Island knows we're here; they undoubtedly heard the shots. Indeed, the remaining shooter may well have come from Spanish Island and is awaiting us there—hence the silence. I must approach with great care. Let me see your weapon."

He took the handgun—a .32—examined the magazine, then slapped it back in place and pressed it into her hands. "You've got four rounds left. If I don't come back...you may need them." He placed the flashlight in her lap. "Don't use it unless you have to. Watch for the gleam of eyes in the moonlight. Look at the distance between them. More than two inches, it's either a gator or our shooter. Do you understand?"

Again she nodded, clasping the gun.

"This is a good blind. You won't be seen until you want to be seen. But listen to me carefully, now: you *must* stay awake. To lose consciousness is to die."

"You'd better get going," she murmured.

Pendergast peered into the darkness. A faint yellow glow was just barely visible through the ranks of tree trunks. He took out a knife and, reaching up, scored a large X on opposite sides of the biggest tree trunk. Leaving Hayward, he set off southward, approaching the distant lights in a tightening, spiral-like trajectory.

He moved slowly, extracting his feet from the muck with care so as to make as little noise as possible. There was no sign of activity, no sounds from the distant light that flickered and disappeared among the dark trunks. As he tightened the spiral, the trees thinned and a dull yellow rectangle came into view: a curtained window, floating in the blackness, amid a cluster of vague buildings with pitched roofs.

In another ten minutes, he had maneuvered close enough to have a clear view of the old hunting camp on Spanish Island.

It was a vast, rambling place, built just above the waterline on creosote pilings: at least a dozen large, shingled buildings wedged in among a massive stand of ancient bald cypresses heavily draped in curtains of Spanish moss. It lay right on the edge of a small slack-water bayou. The camp was built on marginally higher ground, surrounded by a screen of ferns, bushes, and tall grass. The heavy fringe of vegetation, combined with the almost impenetrable skeins of hanging moss, gave the place a hidden, cocooned feeling.

Pendergast moved laterally, still circling the place, checking for guards and getting a feel for the layout. At one end, a large wooden platform led to a pier with a floating dock projecting into the bayou. Tied to it was an unusual boat, which Pendergast recognized as a small, Vietnam-era brownwater navy utility boat. It was a hybrid species of swampcraft with a draft of only three inches and a quiet, underwater jet drive—ideal for creeping around a swamp. Although some of the outbuildings were in ruins, their roofs sagging inward, the central camp was in good condition and clearly inhabited. A large outbuilding was also in impeccable shape. Heavy curtains were drawn over the windows, diffusing the faintest yellow glow from inside.

As he completed his circle, Pendergast was surprised: nobody seemed to be on watch. It was quiet as a tomb. If the shooter was here, he was exceptionally well hidden. He waited, listening. And then he heard something: a faint, desolate cry, thin and birdlike, just on the threshold of audibility, such as from one that has lost all hope, soon dying away. When that, too, ended, a profound stillness fell on the swamp.

Pendergast removed his Les Baer and circled up behind the camp, wriggling into a dense clump of ferns at the edge of the supporting pilings. Again he listened but could hear nothing more; no footfalls on the wooden planks above, no flash of a light, no voices.

Affixed to one of the pilings was a crude wooden ladder made from slippery, rotting slats. After a few more minutes he half crawled, half swam toward it, grasped the lower rung, and pulled himself up, one rung at a time, testing each in turn for solidity. In a moment his head had reached the level of the platform. Peering over, he could still see nothing in the moonlight, no sign of anyone on guard.

Easing himself onto the platform, he rolled over the rough wooden boards and lay there, sidearm at the ready. Straining to listen, he thought now that he could hear a voice, exceptionally faint even to his preternatural hearing, murmuring slowly and monotonously, as if reciting the rosary. The moon was now directly overhead and the camp, deep in the cluster of trees, was speckled with moonlight. He waited one moment more. Then he rose to his feet and darted into the shadow of the nearest outbuilding, flattening himself against the wall. A single window, shades drawn, cast a faint light across the platform.

He inched forward, around the corner, and ducked to pass below second window. Pivoting around another corner, he reached a door. It was old and dilapidated, with rusted hinges, the paint peeling off in strips. With exquisite care he tried the handle, found it locked; a moment's effort unlocked it. He waited, crouching.

No sound.

He slowly turned the knob, eased the door open, then ducked quietly through and covered the room with his weapon.

What greeted his eye was a large, elegant sitting room, somewhat dilapidated. A massive stone fireplace loomed over one end, dominated by a moldering stuffed alligator on a plaque, with a rack of briar pipes and a bulbous gasogene set on the huge timbered mantel. Empty gun cases lined one wall, other cases filled with decaying fly and spinning rods, display cases exhibiting flies and lures. Burgundy leather furniture, much patched and cracked with age, was grouped around the dead fireplace. The room appeared dusty, little used. For such a large space it seemed remarkably empty.

The faintest tread of a foot sounded directly above his head, the murmur of a voice.

The room was illuminated with several hanging kerosene lanterns, their light set at the dimmest possible setting. Pendergast unhooked one, turned the wick to brighten it, and moved across the room to a narrow enclosed staircase, heavily carpeted, on the far end. Slowly, he ascended the stairs.

The difference between the second and first floors was remarkable. There was none of the heavy scattering of objects here, the confusion of colors and shapes and patterns. As he reached the top of the stairs, a long hallway greeted his eye, lined on either side with bedrooms, evidently from the days when the camp had paying guests. But the usual decorations, the chairs and the paintings and the bookcases, were completely missing. The doors were open, displaying barren rooms. Each window had been covered with gauze, apparently to filter out light. Everything was in muted pastel, almost black and white. Even the knotholes had been carefully filled in.

At the end of the hall, a larger door stood ajar, light illuminating its edges. Pendergast moved down the hall like a cat. The last set of bedrooms he passed were evidently still in use, one very large and elegant although still quite spartan, with a freshly made bed, adjoining bathroom and dressing room—and a one-way mirror, looking into a second, adjoining bedroom, smaller and more austere, with no furniture other than a large double bed.

Pendergast crept up to the door at the end of the hall and listened. He could hear, for the first time, the faint throb of a generator. No sound came from the room: all was silent.

He positioned himself to one side, and then in a swift motion pivoted around and kicked the door in with one powerful blow. It flew open and Pendergast simultaneously dropped to the floor.

An enormous blast from a shotgun ripped through the door frame above him, taking out a chunk the size of a basketball, showering him with splinters, but before the shooter could unload another round of buckshot Pendergast had used his momentum to roll and rise; the second blast obliterated a side table by the door but by then Pendergast was on top of the shooter, arm sliding around her neck. He wrenched the shotgun from her hands and spun her around—and found himself grasping a tall, strikingly beautiful woman.

"You can unhand me now," she said calmly.

Pendergast released her and stepped back, covering her with the .45. "Don't move," he said. "Keep your hands in sight." He rapidly scouted the room and was astonished at what he saw: a state-of-the-art critical care facility, filled with gleaming new medical equipment—a physiologic monitoring system, pulse oximeter, apnea monitor, ventilator, infusion pump, crash cart, mobile X-ray unit, half a dozen digital diagnostic devices. All powered by electricity.

"Who are you?" the woman asked. Her voice was frosty, her composure recovered. She was dressed simply and elegantly in a pale cream dress without pattern, no jewelry, and yet she was carefully made up, her hair recently done. Most of all, Pendergast was impressed by the fierce intelligence behind her steely blue eyes. He recognized her almost immediately from the photographs in the Vital Records file in Baton Rouge.

"June Brodie," he said.

Her face paled, but only slightly. In the tense silence that ensued, a faint cry, of pain or perhaps despair, came muffled through a door at the far end of the room. Pendergast turned; stared.

When June Brodie spoke again, her voice was cool. "I'm afraid your unexpected arrival has disturbed my patient. And that is really most unfortunate."

73

P atient?" Pendergast asked.

Brodie said nothing.

"We can discuss the matter later," Pendergast said. "Meanwhile, I have an injured colleague in the swamp. I require your boat. And these facilities."

When nothing happened, he waved his gun. "Anything less than full haste and cooperation will be seriously detrimental to your health."

"There's no need to threaten me."

"I'm afraid there is. May I remind you who fired first?"

"You came bursting in here like the Seventh Cavalry—what did you expect?"

"Shall we bandy civilities later?" Pendergast said coldly. "My colleague is badly hurt."

Still remarkably composed, June Brodie turned, pressed the tab on a wall intercom, and spoke into it with a voice of command. "We have visitors. Prepare to receive an emergency patient—and meet us with a stretcher down on the dock."

Brodie walked through the room and exited the door without looking over her shoulder. Pendergast followed her back down the hallway, gun at the ready. She descended the stairs, crossed the main parlor of the lodge, exited the building, and walked across the platform to the pier to the floating dock. She stepped gracefully into the back and fired up the engine. "Untie the boat," she said. "And please put away that gun."

Pendergast tucked the gun in his belt and untied the boat. She revved the engine, backing it out.

"She's about a thousand yards east-southeast," said Pendergast, pointing into the darkness. "That way," he added. "There's a gunman in the swamp. But of course, you probably know all about that. He may be wounded—he may not."

Brodie looked at him. "Do you want to retrieve your colleague, or not?"

Pendergast indicated the boat's control panel.

Saying nothing else, the woman accelerated the boat and they sped along the muddy shores of the bayou. After a few minutes she slowed to enter a tiny channel, which wound this way and that, dividing and braiding into a labyrinth of waterways. Brodie managed to penetrate the swamp in a way that Pendergast was surprised was possible, always keeping to a sinuous channel that, even in bright moonlight, was almost invisible.

"More to the right," he said, peering into the trees. They were using no lights; it was easier to see farther in the moonlight—and it was safer as well.

The boat wound among the channels, now and then threatening to ground in the shallow muck but always sliding across when the jet drive was gunned.

"There," said Pendergast, pointing to the mark on the tree trunk.

The boat grounded sluggishly on a mud bar. "This is as far as we can go," Brodie murmured.

Pendergast turned to her, searched her quickly and expertly for concealed weapons, and then spoke in a low voice. "Stay here. I'll go retrieve my colleague. Continue to cooperate and you'll survive this night."

"I repeat: you don't need to threaten me," she said.

"It's not a threat; it's clarification." Pendergast climbed over the side of the boat and began making his way through the muck.

"Captain Hayward?" he called.

No answer.

"Laura?"

Still nothing but silence.

In a moment he was at Hayward's side. She was still in shock, semi-conscious, her head lolling against the rotten stump. He glanced back and forth briefly, listening for a rustle or the crack of a twig; looking for any glint of light off metal that might indicate the presence of the shooter. Seeing nothing, he gripped Hayward under the arms and dragged her through the muck back to the boat. He lifted her over the side, and Brodie grasped the limp body and helped set it in the bottom.

Without a word she turned and fired up the engine; they backed out of the channel and then returned at high speed to the camp. As they approached, a small, silent man wearing hospital whites came into view, standing at the dock with a stretcher. Pendergast and Brodie lifted Hayward out of the boat and placed her on the stretcher; the man then rolled her along the platform and into the main parlor of the lodge. He and Pendergast carried the stretcher up the stairs, down the hall, and into the bizarrely high-tech emergency room, positioning it beside a bank of critical care equipment.

As they moved her from the stretcher onto a surgical bed, June Brodie turned to the little man in white. "Intubate her," she said sharply. "Orotracheal. And oxygen."

The man leapt into action, passing a tube into Hayward's mouth and delivering oxygen, both of them working with a swift economy of action that clearly attested to years of experience.

"What happened?" she asked Pendergast as she cut away a mud-heavy sleeve with a pair of medical scissors.

"Gunshot wound and alligator bite."

June Brodie nodded, then listened to Hayward's pulse and took her blood pressure, examining the pupils with a light. The movements were practiced and highly professional. "Hang a bag of dextran," she told the man in scrub whites, "and run a 14g IV."

While he worked, she readied a needle and took a blood sample, filling a syringe and transferring it to vacuum tubes. She plucked a scalpel from a nearby sterile tray and, with several deft cuts, removed the rest of the pant leg.

"Irrigation."

The man handed her a large saline-filled syringe, and she washed the mud and filth away, plucking off numerous leeches as she did so and tossing everything into a red-bag disposer. Injecting a local around the ugly lacerations and the bullet wound, she worked diligently but calmly, cleaning everything with saline and antiseptic. Lastly, she administered an antibiotic and dressed the wound.

She looked up at Pendergast. "She'll be fine."

As if on cue, Hayward's eyes opened and she made a sound in the endotracheal tube. She shifted on the surgical bed, raised a hand, and gestured at the tube.

After briefly examining her, June ordered the tube removed. "I felt it was better to be safe than sorry," she said.

Hayward swallowed painfully, then looked around, her eyes coming into focus. "What's going on?"

"You've been saved by a ghost," said Pendergast. "The ghost of June Brodie."

74

Hayward looked at the vague figures in turn, then tried to sit up. Her head was still swimming.

"Allow me." Brodie reached over and raised the backrest of the surgical bed. "You were in light shock," she said. "But you'll soon be back to normal. Or as close as possible, given the conditions."

"My leg..."

"No permanent damage. A flesh wound and a nasty bite from a gator. I've numbed it with a local, but when that wears off it's going to hurt. You're going to need a further series of antibiotic injections, too—lots of unpleasant bacteria live in an alligator's mouth. How do you feel?"

"Out of it," said Hayward, sitting up. "What is this place?" She peered at June. "June... June Brodie?" She looked around. What kind of hunting camp would contain a place like this—an emergency room with state-of-the-art equipment? And yet it was like no emergency room she had ever seen. The lighting was too dim, and except for the medical equipment the space was utterly bare: no books, paintings, posters, even chairs.

She swallowed and shook her head, trying to clear it. "Why did you fake your suicide?"

Brodie stepped back and gazed at her. "I imagine you must be the two officers investigating Longitude Pharmaceuticals. Captain Hayward of the NYPD and Special Agent Pendergast of the FBI."

"We are," said Pendergast. "I'd show you my badge, but I fear the swamp has claimed it."

"That won't be necessary," she said coolly. "Perhaps I shouldn't answer any questions until I call an attorney."

Pendergast gave her a long, steady look. "I am not in any mood for obstructionism," he said in a low, menacing voice. "You *will* answer any questions I put to you, attorney and Miranda be damned." He turned to the man in surgical whites. "Stand over there next to her."

The short man hastily complied.

"Is that the patient?" Pendergast asked Brodie. "The one you mentioned earlier?"

She shook her head. "Is this any way to treat us, after we helped your partner?"

"Don't irritate me."

Brodie fell silent.

Pendergast looked at her, a terrible expression on his face. His Les Baer still hung ominously by his side. "You will answer my questions completely, starting now. Understood?"

The woman nodded.

"Now: why this extensive medical setup? Who is your 'patient'?"

"I am the patient," came a cracked, whispery voice, to the accompaniment of a door opening in the far wall. "All this largesse is for me." A figure stood in the darkness outside the door, tall and still and gaunt, a scarecrow silhouette barely visible in the darkness beyond the emergency room. He laughed: a papery laugh, more breath than anything else. After a moment the shadow stepped very slowly from the darkness into the half-light and raised his voice only slightly.

"Here's Charles J. Slade!"

75

Judson Esterhazy had gunned the 250 Merc and aimed the bass boat south, accelerating to a dangerous speed down the old logging pullboat channel. With a supreme effort of will, he drew back a little on the throttle, quieted the turmoil in his mind. There was no question it had been time to cut his losses and run. He had left Pendergast and the injured woman back in the swamp, without a boat, a mile from Spanish Island. Whether they made it there or not was not his most pressing concern; he was safe and it was time to beat a strategic retreat. He would have to act decisively, and soon, but for now the wise course was to go to ground, lick his wounds—and reemerge refreshed and stronger.

Yet somehow he felt uncomfortably certain Pendergast would reach Spanish Island. And—even given all that had happened between him and its occupant—he was finding it hard to leave Slade behind, and unprotected; harder, so much harder, than he'd steeled himself to ever expect.

In a curious way, deep down, he had known this would be the result as soon as Pendergast had shown up in Savannah with his accursed revelation. The man was preternatural. Twelve years of meticulous deception, blown up in a matter of two weeks. All because one barrel of a bloody rifle had not been cleaned. Unbelievable how such a small oversight could lead to such enormous consequences. And he hadn't helped matters any, blurting out about Audubon and New Madrid in his surprise at seeing Pendergast.

At least, Esterhazy thought, he had not made the mistake of underestimating the man . . . as so many others had done, to their great sorrow. Pendergast had no idea of his involvement. Nor did he know of the trump card he held in reserve. Those secrets Judson knew—without the slightest doubt—Slade would take with him, to the grave or elsewhere.

The night air breezed by his boat, the stars shimmered in the sky above, the trees stood blackly against the moonlit sky. The pullboat channel narrowed and grew shallow. Esterhazy began to calm further. There was always the possibility—a distinct one—Pendergast and the woman would die in the swamp before making it to the camp. After all, the woman had taken one of his rounds. She could easily be bleeding to death. Even if the wound wasn't immediately fatal, it would be sheer hell dragging her through that last section of swamp, infested with alligators and water moccasins, the water thick with leeches, the air choking with mosquitoes.

He slowed as the boat came to the silted-over end of the channel. Esterhazy shut off the engine, swiveled it up out of the water, and began poling. The very mosquitoes he had just been thinking about now arrived in swarms, clustering about his head and landing on his neck and ears. He slapped and cursed.

The silty channel divided, and he poled into the left one; he knew the swamp well. He continued, checking the fish finder to monitor the depth of the water. The moon was now high in the sky, and the swamp was almost as clear as day. Midnight: six hours to dawn.

He tried to imagine the scene at Spanish Island when they arrived, but it was depressing and frustrating. He spat into the water and put it out of his head. It didn't concern him anymore. Ventura had allowed himself to be captured by Hayward, the damn fool, but he'd said nothing before Judson put a bullet through his brain. Blackletter was dead; all those who could connect him to Project Aves were dead. There was no way to put the Project Aves genii back in the bottle. If Pendergast lived, it would all come out, *they* might ultimately get wind of it, there was no help for that; but what was now critical was erasing his own role from it.

The events of the past week had made one thing crystal clear: Pendergast would figure it out. It was only a matter of time. That meant even Judson's own carefully concealed role would come to light. And because of that, Pendergast had to die.

But this time, the man would die on Esterhazy's terms, in his own good time, and when the FBI agent least expected it. Because Esterhazy retained one critical advantage: the advantage of surprise. The man was not invulnerable, and Esterhazy knew now exactly where his weakness lay and how to exploit it. Stupid of him not to have seen it before. A plan began to form in his mind. Simple, clean, effective.

The channel deepened enough to drop his engine. He lowered it and fired up, motoring slowly through the channels, working his way westward, constantly monitoring the depth below the keel. He would be at the Mississippi well before dawn; he could scuttle the boat in some backwater bayou and emerge from the swamp a new man. A line from *The Art of War* surfaced in his mind, unbidden:

Forestall your opponent by seizing what he holds dear, and contrive to strike him at the time and on the ground of your choosing.

So perfectly apposite to his situation.

76

The specter that presented itself in the doorway froze Hayward with shock. The man was at least six and a half feet tall, gaunt, his face hollow with sunken cheeks, his dark eyes large and liquid under heavy brows, chin and neck bristling with half-shaven swipes of bristle. His hair was long and white, brushed back, curling behind the ears and tumbling to his shoulders. He wore a charcoal-gray Brooks Brothers suit jacket pulled over a hospital gown, and he carried a short stock-whip in one hand. With the other he wheeled an IV rack, which doubled as a kind of support.

It seemed to Hayward that he had almost materialized out of thin air, so quiet and stealthy had been his approach. His eyes—so bloodshot, they looked almost purple—didn't dart around the room as one would expect from a lunatic; rather, they moved very slowly from one person to the other, staring at—almost through—everyone in turn. When his eyes reached her, he winced visibly and closed his eyes.

"No, no, no," he murmured, his voice as whispery as the wind.

Turning away, June Brodie retrieved a spare lab coat and draped it over Larry's muddy shirt. "No bright colors," she whispered to Hayward. "Keep your movements slow."

Sluggishly, Slade opened his eyes again. The look of pain eased somewhat. Releasing his hold on the rack, he slowly raised a large, massively veined hand in a gesture of almost biblical gravitas. The hand unfolded, the long fingers shaking slightly, the index finger pointing at Pendergast. The huge dark eyes rested on the FBI agent. "You're the man looking to find out who killed his wife." His voice was thin as rice paper, and yet it somehow projected an arrogant self-assurance.

Pendergast said nothing. He seemed dazed, his torn suit still dripping with mud, his pale hair smeared and tangled.

Slowly, Slade let his arm fall to his side. "*I* killed your wife."

Pendergast raised his .45. "Tell me."

"No, *wait*—" June began.

"Silence," said Pendergast with quiet menace.

"That's right," breathed Slade, "*silence*. I ordered her killed. Helen—Esterhazy—Pendergast."

"Charles, the man has a gun," said June, her voice low but imploring. "He's going to kill you."

"Poppycock." He raised a finger and twirled it. "We all lost somebody. He lost a wife. I lost a son. So it goes." Then he repeated, with sudden intensity, in the same faint voice, *"I lost a son."*

June Brodie turned toward Pendergast, speaking

sotto voce. "You mustn't get him talking about his son. That would set him back—and we'd made such progress!" A sob, immediately stifled, escaped her throat.

"I *had* to have her killed. She was going to expose us. Terribly dangerous...for *all* of us..." Slade's eyes suddenly focused on nothing, widening as if in terror, staring at a blank wall. "Why are you here?" he murmured at nothing. "It isn't time!" He slowly raised the whip up over his head and brought it down with a terrific smack on his own back, once, twice, three times, each blow causing him to stagger forward, the tatters of the torn suit jacket fluttering to the ground.

The blow seemed to snap him back to reality. He straightened, refocused his eyes. The room became very still.

"You see?" the woman said to Pendergast. "Don't provoke him, for God's sake. He'll hurt himself."

"Provoke? I intend to do far more than that."

Pendergast's menacing tone chilled Hayward. She felt trapped, helpless, vulnerable, stuck in the bed with IVs. She grasped the tubes, pressed down on her arm, and yanked them out. She swung up and out of bed, momentarily dizzy.

"I will handle this," Pendergast told her.

"Remember," Hayward replied, "you promised you wouldn't kill him."

Pendergast ignored her, facing the man.

Slade's eyes suddenly went far away again, as if seeing something that wasn't there; his mouth worked strangely, the dry lips twitching and stretching in unvoiced speech, of which Hayward gradually made out a rapid susurrus of words. "Go away, go away, go away, go away…" He brought the whip down again on his back, which again seemed to shock him into lucidity. Trembling, he fumbled—moving as if underwater, yet with evident eagerness—for the IV rack, located a bulb hanging from a tube, and gave it a decided press.

Drugs, she thought. *He's an addict.*

The old man's eyes rolled up white for a moment before he recovered, the eyes popping open again. "The story is easily told," he went on in his low, hoarse voice. "Helen…Brilliant woman. A juicy piece of ass, too…I imagine you had some rollicking good times, eh?"

Hayward could see the gun in Pendergast's hand shaking ever so slightly under the fierceness of his grip.

"She made a discovery…" Another gasp and Slade's eyes defocused, staring into an empty corner, his lips trembling and whispering, unintelligible words tumbling out. His whip hand fluttered uselessly.

With a brisk step forward Pendergast slapped him across the face with shocking force. "Keep going."

Slade came back. "What do they say in the movies? *Thanks, I needed that!*" The old man shook briefly with silent mirth. "Yes, Helen…Her discovery was quite remarkable. I imagine you could tell me most of the story already, Mr. Pendergast. Right?"

Pendergast nodded.

A cough erupted from the wizened chest, silent spasms racking his frame. Slade wheezed, stumbled, pressed the bulb again. After a moment he resumed. "She brought the discovery to us, the avian flu, through an intermediary, and Project Aves was born. She hoped a miracle drug might be the result, a *creativity* treatment.

After all, it worked for Audubon—for a while. Mind enhancement. The ultimate drug..."

"Why did you give it up?" Pendergast asked. The neutral tone did not fool Hayward—the gun was still shaking in his hand. Hayward had never seen him so close to losing control.

"The research was expensive. Hideously expensive. We began to run out of money—despite all the corners we cut." And he raised his hand and—slowly, slowly—waved it around the room.

"And so this is where you did the work," Pendergast said. "Spanish Island was your laboratory."

"Bingo. Why build an expensive level-4 biocontainment facility, with negative pressure and biosuits and all the rest? We could just do it out here in the swamp, save ourselves a pot of money. We could keep the live cultures out here, do the really dangerous work where nobody was going to see, where there were no annoying government regulators poking their noses in."

So that's why Longitude had a dock facing the swamp, Hayward thought.

"And the parrots?" Pendergast asked.

"They were kept back at Longitude. Complex Six. But as I said, mistakes were made. One of our birds escaped, infected a family. A disaster? Not when I pointed out to everyone: *Here's a way to save millions in experimental protocols; let's sit tight and just see what happens!*"

He burst into another fit of silent mirth, his unshaven Adam's apple bobbing grotesquely. Bubbles of snot blew out of his nose and flecked his suit. He hacked up a huge gobbet of phlegm and bent over, allowing it to slide off his lips to the floor. Then he resumed.

"Helen objected to our way of doing business. The lady was a crusader. Once she found out about the Doane family—right before your little safari, by the way—she was going to expose us, go to the authorities no matter what. Just as soon as she got back." He spread his hands. "What else could we do but kill her?"

Pendergast spoke quietly. "Who is 'we'?"

"A few of us in the Aves Group. Dear June, here, had no idea—back then, at least. I kept her in the dark until just before the fire. Neither did poor old Carlton." He flapped at the silent man.

"The names, please."

"You have all the names. Blackletter. Ventura. By the way, where is Mike?"

Pendergast did not reply.

"Probably rotting in the swamp, thanks to you. Damn you to hell, Pendergast. He was not only the best security director a CEO could ask for, but he was our one link to civilization. Well, you may have killed Ventura, but you couldn't have killed *him*." Here Slade's low tone became almost proud. "And *his* name you shall not have. I want to save that—to keep a little surprise for your future, maybe pay you back for Mike Ventura." He sniggered. "I'm sure he'll pop up when you least expect him."

Pendergast raised the gun again. "The name."

"No!" cried June.

Slade winced once more. "Your voice, my dear—*please*."

Brodie turned to Pendergast, clasping her hands together as if in supplication. "Don't hurt him," she whispered fiercely. "He's a good man, a *very* good man!

You have to understand, Mr. Pendergast, he's also a victim."

Pendergast's eyes went toward her.

"You see," she went on, "there was another accident at Project Aves. Charles got the disease himself."

If Pendergast was surprised by this, he showed no sign. "He made the decision to kill my wife *before* he got sick," he replied in a flat tone.

"That's all in the past," she said. "Nothing will bring her back. Can't you let it go?"

Pendergast stared at her, his eyes glittering.

"Charles almost died," she continued. "And then he...he had the idea for us to come out here. My husband," she nodded at the silent man standing to one side, "joined us later."

"You and Slade were lovers," Pendergast said.

"Yes." Not even a blush. She straightened up. "We *are* lovers."

"And you came out here—to hide?" said Pendergast. "Why?"

She said nothing.

Pendergast turned back to Slade. "It makes no sense. You had recovered from the illness before you retreated to the swamp. The mental deterioration hadn't begun. It was too early. *Why did you retreat to the swamp?*"

"Carlton and I are taking care of him," Brodie went on hastily. "Keeping him alive...It's very difficult to keep the ravages of the disease at bay...Don't question him further, you're disturbing him—"

"This disease," Pendergast said, cutting her off with a flick of his wrist. "Tell me about it."

"It affects the inhibitory and excitatory circuits of

the brain," Brodie whispered eagerly, as if to distract him. "Overwhelms the brain with physical sensations—sight, smell, touch. It's a mutant form of flavivirus. At first it presents almost as acute encephalitis. Assuming he lives, the patient appears to recover."

"Just like the Doanes." Slade giggled. "Oh, dear me, yes—*just* like the Doanes. We kept a very close eye on *them*."

"But the virus has a predilection for the thalamus," Brodie continued. "Especially the LGB."

"Lateral geniculate body," Slade said, slapping himself viciously with the whip.

"Not unlike herpes zoster," Brodie went on rapidly, "which takes up residence in the dorsal root ganglion and years, or decades, later resurfaces to cause shingles. But it eventually kills its host neurons."

"End result—insanity," Slade whispered. His eyes began to defocus and his lips began moving silently, faster and faster.

"And all this—" Pendergast gestured with the gun. "The morphine drip, the flail—are distractions from the continuous barrage of sensation?"

Brodie nodded eagerly. "So you see, he's not responsible for what he's saying. We might just be able to get him back to where he was before. We've been trying—trying for years. There's still hope. He's a good man, a healer, who's done good works."

Pendergast raised the gun higher. His face was as pale as marble, his torn suit hanging off his frame like rags. "I have no interest in this man's good works. I want only one thing: the name of the final person on Project Aves."

But Slade had slid off again into his own world, jabbering softly at the blank wall, his fingers twitching. He gripped the IV stand and his whole body began to tremble, the stand shaking. A double press of the bulb brought him back under control.

"You're torturing him!" Brodie whispered.

Pendergast ignored her, faced Slade. "The decision to kill her: it was yours?"

"Yes. At first the others objected. But then they saw we had no choice. She wouldn't be appeased, she wouldn't be bought off. So we killed her, and most ingeniously! Eaten by a trained lion." He broke into another carefully contained spasm of silent laughter.

The gun began to shake more visibly in Pendergast's hands.

"Crunch, crunch!" Slade whispered, his eyes wide with glee. "Ah, Pendergast, you have no idea what sort of Pandora's box you've opened up with this investigation of yours. You've roused the sleeping dog with a kick in the ass."

Pendergast took aim.

"You promised," Hayward said in a low, insistent voice.

"He must die," whispered Pendergast, almost to himself. *"This man must die."*

"The man must die," Slade said mockingly, his voice rising briefly above a whisper before falling again. "Kill me, please. Put me out of my misery!"

"You *promised*," Hayward repeated.

Abruptly, almost as if overcoming an invisible opponent in a physical struggle, Pendergast lowered the pistol with a jerk of his hand. Then he took a step toward

Slade, twirled the gun around, and offered him the grip.

Slade seized it, yanked it from Pendergast's grasp.

"Oh, my God," Brodie cried. "What are you doing? He'll kill you for sure!"

Slade, with an expert motion, retracted the slide, snapped it back, then slowly raised the gun at Pendergast. A crooked smile disfigured his gaunt face. "I'm going to send you to the same place I sent your bitch of a wife." His finger curled around the trigger and began to tighten.

77

Just a moment," Pendergast said. "Before you shoot, I'd like to speak to you a minute. In private."

Slade looked at him. The big handgun looked almost like a toy in his gnarled fist. He steadied himself against the IV rack. "Why?"

"There's something you need to know."

Slade looked at him a moment. "What a poor host I've been. Come into my office."

June Brodie made a move to protest, but Slade, with a flick of the gun, gestured Pendergast through the doorway. "Guests first," he said.

Pendergast shot a warning glance at Hayward, then disappeared through the dark rectangle.

The hallway was paneled with cedar, painted over in gray. Recessed lights in the ceiling cast low, regular pools of light onto neutral carpeting, its weave tight and plush. Slade walked slowly behind Pendergast, the wheels of his IV making no noise as they turned. "Last door on the left," he said.

The room that served as Slade's office had once been the game room of the lodge. A dartboard hung on the wall, and there were a couple of chairs and two tables shoved up against the walls, tops inlaid for backgammon and chess. A snooker table near the back apparently served as Slade's desk: its felt surface was empty save for carefully folded tissues, a crossword magazine, a book on advanced calculus, and several additional flails, their tips tattered from constant use. A few ancient snooker balls, crazed with craquelure, still lay forlornly in one pocket. There was little other furniture: the big room was remarkably bare. Gauzy curtains were drawn tightly over the windows. The space had the stillness of a tomb.

Slade closed the door with exquisite care. "Sit down."

Pendergast dragged a cane chair out and set it on the thick carpet before the table. Slade wheeled his IV rack behind the table and sat down very slowly and carefully in the lone easy chair. He pressed the bulb on the IV line, eyes fluttering as the morphine hit his bloodstream, sighed, then trained the gun again on Pendergast. "Okey-dokey," he said, his voice remaining whispery and slow. "Say what you have to say so that I can get on with shooting you." He smiled faintly. "It'll make a mess, of course. But June will clean it up. She's good at cleaning up my messes."

"Actually," Pendergast said, "you're not going to shoot me."

Slade emitted a careful little cough. "No?"

"That's what I wanted to speak to you about. You're going to shoot yourself."

"Now, why would I want to do that?"

Instead of replying, Pendergast stood up and walked over to a cuckoo clock that stood on a side wall. He pulled up the counterweights, set the time to ten minutes before twelve, then gave the pendulum a flick with his fingernail to start it.

"Eleven fifty?" Slade said. "That's not the correct time."

Pendergast sat down again. Slade waited. The tick of the now-active cuckoo clock began to fill the silence. Slade seemed to stiffen slightly. His lips began to move.

"You are going to kill yourself because justice demands it," Pendergast said.

"To satisfy you, I suppose."

"No. To *thwart* me."

"I *won't* kill myself," Slade said out loud, the first words he had spoken above a papery whisper.

"I hope you won't," Pendergast said, plucking two snooker balls from the corner pocket. "You see, I want you to live."

Slade said, "You're making no sense. Even to a madman."

Pendergast began rolling the pool balls back and forth in one hand, Queeg-like, clacking them together.

"Stop that," Slade hissed, wincing. "I don't like it."

Pendergast clacked the balls together a little more loudly. "I *had* planned to kill you. But now that I've seen the condition you're in, I realize the cruelest thing I could do would be to let you live. There's no cure. Your suffering will go on, only increasing with old age and infirmity, your mind sinking ever deeper into misery and ruin. Death would be a release."

Slade shook his head slowly, his lips twitching, the muttered sounds of broken words tumbling from his lips. He groaned with something very much like physical pain, and then gave the morphine drip another pump.

Pendergast reached into his pocket, took out a small test tube half full of black granules. He tipped out a small line of the granules along the edge of the pool table.

The action seemed to bring Slade back around. "What are you doing?"

"I always carry a little activated charcoal. It's useful in so many field tests—as a scientist, you must know that. But it has its own aesthetic properties, as well." From another pocket Pendergast pulled out a lighter, swiftly lit one end of the granules. "For example, the smoke it emits tends to curl upward in such beautiful gossamer patterns. And the smell is far from unpleasant."

Slade leaned backward sharply. He trained the gun, which had sagged to the floor, toward Pendergast again. "You put that out."

Pendergast ignored him. Smoke curled up in the still air, looping and coiling. He leaned back in his chair, forcing it to rock slightly, the old canework creaking. He rolled the pool balls together as he went on. "You see, I knew—or at least guessed at—the nature of your affliction. But I never stopped to think just how awful it would be to endure. Every creak, click, tap, and squeak intruding itself into your brain. The chirping of the birds, the brightness of the sun, the smell of smoke... To be tormented by every little thing carried into your brain by the five senses, to live at the edge of being overwhelmed every minute of every hour of every day. To know that nothing can be done, *nothing at all*. Even your, ah, unique relationship with June Brodie can provide nothing but temporary diversion."

"Her husband lost his apparatus in Desert Storm," Slade said. "Blown off by an IED. I've stepped in to fill the breach, so to speak."

"How nice for you," said Pendergast.

"Go stuff your conventional morality. I don't need it. Anyway, you heard June." The mad sheen to his eyes seemed to fade somewhat, and he looked almost serious. "We're working on a cure."

"You saw what happened to the Doanes. You're a biologist. You know as well as I do there's no hope for a cure. Brain cells cannot be replaced or regrown. The damage is permanent. You *know* this."

Slade seemed to go off again, his lips moving faster and faster, the hiss of air from his lungs like a punctured tire, repeating the same word, "No! No, no, no, no, no!"

Pendergast watched him, rocking, the snooker balls moving more quickly in his hand, their clacking filling the air. The clock ticked, the smoke curled.

"I couldn't help but notice," Pendergast said, "how everything here was arranged to remove any extraneous sensory trigger. Carpeted floor, insulated walls, neutral colors, plain furnishings, the air cool, dry, and scentless, probably HEPA-filtered."

Slade whimpered, his lips fairly blurring with maniacal, and virtually silent, speech. He lifted the flail, smacked himself.

"And yet even with all that, even with the counter-irritant of that flail and the medicines and the constant dosings of morphine, it isn't enough. You are still in constant agony. You feel your feet upon the floor, you feel your back against the chair, you see everything in this room. You hear my voice. You are assaulted by a thousand other things I can't begin to enumerate—because my mind unconsciously filters them out. You, on the other hand, cannot tune it out. *Any* of it. Listen to the snooker balls! Examine the curling smoke! Hear the relentless passage of time."

Slade began to shake in his chair. *"Nonononono-nonoooo!"* spilled off his lips, a single never-ending word. A loop of drool descended from one corner of his mouth, and he shook it away with a savage jerk of his head.

"I wonder—what must it be like to eat?" Pendergast went on. "I imagine it's horrible, the strong taste of the food, the sticky texture, the smell and shape of it in your mouth, the slide of it down your gullet...Isn't that why you're so thin? No doubt you haven't enjoyed a meal or a drink—*really* enjoyed—for a decade. Taste is just another unwanted sense you can't rid yourself of. I'll wager that IV drip isn't only for the morphine—it's for intravenous feeding as well, isn't it?"

"Nononononononono..." Slade reached spastically for the flail, dropped it back on the desk. The gun trembled in his hand.

"The taste of food—mellow ripe Camembert, beluga caviar, smoked sturgeon, even the humblest eggs and toast and jam—would be unbearable. Perhaps baby food of the most banal sort, without sugar or spice or texture of any kind, served precisely at body temperature, would only just be bearable. On special occasions, naturally." Pendergast shook his head sympathetically. "And you can't sleep—can you? Not with all those raging sensations crowding in on you. I can imagine it: lying on the bed, hearing the least of noises: the woodworms gnawing between the lathe and plaster, the beat of your heart in your eardrums, the ticking of the house, the scurry of mice. Even with your eyes closed your sight betrays you, because darkness is its own color. The blacker the room, the more things you see crawling within the fluid of your vision. And everything—*everything*—pressing in on you at once, always and forever."

Slade shrieked, covering his ears with claw-like hands and shaking his entire body violently, the IV drip line flailing back and forth. The sound ripped through the stillness, shockingly loud, and Slade's entire body seemed to convulse.

"That is why you will kill yourself, Mr. Slade," Pendergast said. "Because *you can*. I've provided you with the means to do it. In your hand."

"Yaaahhhhhhhhh!" Slade screamed, writhing, the tortured movements of his body a kind of feedback from his own screams.

Pendergast rocked more quickly, the chair creaking, rolling the balls ceaselessly in his hand, faster and faster.

"I could have done it anytime!" Slade cried. "Why should I do it now? Now, now, now, now, *now*?"

"You couldn't have done it before," Pendergast said.

"June has a gun," Slade said. "A lovely gun, gun, gun."

"No doubt she is careful to keep it locked up."

"I could overdose on morphine! Just go to sleep, *sleep*!" His voice subsided into a rapid gibbering, almost like the humming of a machine.

Pendergast shook his head. "I'm sure June is equally careful to regulate the amount of morphine you have access to. I would guess the nights are hardest—like about now, as you're quickly using up your allotted dose without recourse for the endless, *endless* night ahead."

"*Eeeyaaahhhhhhhhhh!*" Slade screamed again—a wild, ululating scream.

"In fact, I'm sure she and her husband are careful to limit your life in countless ways. You're not her patient—you're her *prisoner*."

Slade shook his head, his mouth working frantically, soundlessly.

"And with all her ministrations," Pendergast went on, "all her medication, her perhaps more exotic means of holding your attention—she can't stop all those sensations from creeping in. Can she?"

Slade didn't respond. He pressed the morphine button once, twice, three times, but apparently nothing more was coming through. Then he slumped forward, head hitting the felt of the desk with a loud crack, jerked it back up, his lips contracting spastically.

"Usually I consider suicide a cowardly way out," Pendergast said. "But in your case it's the only sensible solution. Because for you, life really is so much infinitely worse than death."

Still, Slade didn't respond. He banged his head again and again onto the felt.

"Even the least amount of sensory input is exquisitely

painful," Pendergast went on. "That's why this environment of yours is so controlled, so minimalist. Yet I have introduced new elements. My voice, the smell of the charcoal, the curls and colors of its smoke, the squeaking of the chair, the sound of the billiard balls, the ticking of the clock. I would estimate you are now a vessel that is, so to speak, full to bursting."

He continued, his voice low and mesmerizing. "In less than half a minute now, the cuckoo of that clock is going to sound—twelve times. The vessel will burst. I don't know exactly how many of the cuckoo calls you'll be able to withstand before you use that gun on yourself. Perhaps four, perhaps five, perhaps even six. But I know that you *will* use it—because the sound of that gun firing, that final sound, is the *only* answer. The *only* release. Consider it my gift to you."

Slade looked up. His forehead was red from where it had impacted the table, and his eyes wheeled in his head as if set free of each other. He raised his gun hand toward Pendergast, let it fall back, raised it again.

"Good-bye, Dr. Slade," Pendergast said. "Just a few seconds now. Let me help count them down for you. Five, four, three, two, one..."

78

Hayward waited, perched on a gurney, in the gleaming room full of medical equipment. The other occupants of the large space—June Brodie and her silent husband—stood like statues by the far wall, listening, waiting. Occasionally a voice would sound—a cry of rage or despair, a strange gibbering laugh—but they drifted only faintly through the thick, apparently soundproofed walls.

From her vantage point, she could see both exits—the one that led to Slade's office, and the one that led down the stairs and out into the night. She was all too aware that a second shooter was still out there somewhere—and that at any moment he might come bursting in from the stairwell. She lifted her weapon, checked it.

Once again, her eye drifted to the doorway through which Pendergast and Slade had disappeared. What was going on? She had rarely felt worse in her life—utterly exhausted, covered with caked mud, her leg throbbing viciously as the painkiller began to wear off. It had been at least ten minutes, maybe a quarter of an hour since they had left, but some sixth sense told her to heed Pendergast's urgent instruction to remain where she was. He had promised not to kill Slade—and she had to believe that, whatever else he was, Pendergast was a gentleman who kept his word.

At that moment, a handgun fired, a single shot, the muffled boom shuddering the room. Hayward raised her weapon, and with a cry June Brodie ran to the doorway.

"Wait!" Hayward said. "Stay where you are."

There was no further sound. A minute passed, then two. And then—quiet, but distinct—came the sound of a closing door. A moment later the faintest of treads sounded in the carpeted hallway. Hayward sat up straight on the gurney, heart racing.

Agent Pendergast stepped through the doorway.

Hayward stared at him. Under the thick encrustation of mud he was paler than usual, but otherwise he appeared unhurt. He glanced at the three of them in turn.

"Slade—?" Hayward asked.

"Dead," came the reply.

"You killed him!" June Brodie shrieked, running past Pendergast and into the corridor. He did nothing to stop her.

Hayward slid off the gurney, ignoring the pain shooting through her leg. "You son of a bitch, you promised—"

"He died by his own hand," Pendergast said.

Hayward stopped.

"Suicide?" Mr. Brodie said, speaking for the first time. "That's not possible."

Hayward stared at Pendergast. "I don't believe it. You told Vinnie you would kill him—and you did."

"Correct," Pendergast replied. "I did vow to do that. Nevertheless, all I did was talk to him. He committed the deed."

Hayward opened her mouth to continue, then shut it again. Suddenly she didn't want to know any more. What did that mean—*talk* to him? She shuddered.

Pendergast was watching her closely. "Recall, Captain, that Slade *ordered* the killing. He did not carry it out. There is still work to be done."

A moment later June Brodie reappeared. She was sobbing quietly. Her husband walked over and tried to put a comforting arm over her shoulder. She shrugged it away.

"There's nothing to keep us here any longer," Pendergast told Hayward. He turned to June. "I'm afraid we'll have to borrow your utility boat. We'll see it's returned to you tomorrow."

"By a dozen cops armed to the teeth, I suppose?" the woman replied bitterly.

Pendergast shook his head. "There's no reason anyone else need know about this. In fact, I think it's in all of our best interests that no one ever does. I suggest you burn this place to the ground and then leave it, never to return. You tended a madman in his final sufferings—and as far as I'm concerned, that's where the story begins and ends. No need to report the suicide of a man who is already officially dead. You and your husband will want to work out an appropriate cover story to minimize any official interest in yourselves—or in Spanish Island—"

"*Madman*," June Brodie interrupted. She almost spat out the word. "That's what you call him. But he was more than that—*much* more. He was a good man. He did good work—wonderful work. If I could have cured him, he would have done it again. I tried to tell you, but you wouldn't listen. *You wouldn't listen...*" Her voice broke, and she struggled to master herself.

"His condition was incurable," Pendergast said, not unkindly. "And I'm afraid there's no way his experimental putterings could make up for cold-blooded murder."

"Putterings! *Putterings?* He did *this!*" And she stabbed her own breast with a finger.

"This?" Pendergast said. A look of surprise came over his mud-smeared face. Then, suddenly, the surprise disappeared.

"If you know so much about me, you must have known of my condition," she said.

Pendergast nodded. "Amyotrophic lateral sclerosis. Now I understand. That clarifies the last question in my mind—why you moved into the swamp *before* Slade went mad."

"I don't understand," said Hayward.

"Lou Gehrig's disease." Pendergast turned toward Mrs. Brodie. "You don't appear to be suffering any symptoms at present."

"I have no symptoms because I no longer have the disease. After his recovery, Charles had a period of... genius. Amazing genius. That's what it does to you, the avian flu. He had ideas... wonderful ideas. Ideas to help me... and others, as well. He created a treatment for

ALS, utilizing complex proteins grown in vats of living cells. The first of the so-called biologics. Charles developed them first, *by himself*, ten years ahead of his time. He had to retreat from the world to do his work. He did it—*all* of it—right here."

"I see now why this room appears to be far more than a clinic," Pendergast said. "It's an experimental laboratory."

"It is. Or was. Before...before he changed."

Hayward turned to her. "This is extraordinary. Why haven't you shared this with the world?"

"Impossible," Mrs. Brodie said, almost in a whisper. "It was all in his head. We begged him but he never wrote it down. He grew worse, and then it was too late. That's why I wanted to restore him to his old self. He loved me. He cured me. And now the secret of that cure has died with him."

Heavy clouds veiled the moon as they pulled away from Spanish Island. There was little light—either for a sniper, or for a pilot—and Pendergast kept the boat to a crawl, the engine barely audible as they nosed through the thick vegetation. Hayward sat in the bow, a pair of crutches appropriated from the lodge at her side. She was thinking quietly.

For perhaps half an hour, not a word was exchanged. Finally, Hayward roused herself and glanced back at Pendergast, piloting from the rear console.

"Why did Slade do it?" she asked.

Pendergast's eyes shone faintly as he glanced at her.

"Disappear, I mean," she went on. "Hide himself away in this swamp."

"He must have known he was infected," Pendergast replied after a moment. "He'd seen what had happened to the others; he realized he was going to go mad... or worse. He wanted to make sure he could exercise some kind of control over his care. Spanish Island was the perfect choice. If it hadn't been discovered yet, it never would be. And because it had been used as a lab, they already had much of the equipment he'd need. No doubt he harbored hopes for a cure. Perhaps it was while trying to discover one that he managed to cure June Brodie."

"Yes, but why such an elaborate setup? Stage his own death, stage Mrs. Brodie's death. I mean, he wasn't on the run from the law or anything like that."

"No, not from the law. It does seem like an extreme reaction. But then a man isn't likely to be thinking clearly under those circumstances."

"Anyway, he's dead now," she went on. "So can you find some peace? Some resolution?"

For a moment, the agent did not respond. When at last he spoke, his voice was flat, uninflected. "No."

"Why not? You've solved the mystery, avenged your wife's murder."

"Remember what Slade said: there's a surprise in my future. He could only have meant the second shooter—the one who's still out there, somewhere. As long as he is loose, he remains a danger to you, to Vincent, and to me. And..." He paused a moment. "There's something else."

"Go on."

"As long as there is even one more person out there who bears responsibility for Helen's death, I cannot rest."

She looked at him, but his gaze had suddenly shifted.

Pendergast appeared to be strangely transfixed by the full moon—which had emerged from the clouds and was finally setting into the swamp. His face was briefly illuminated by slivers of light as the orb sank through the dense vegetation, and then, as the moon finally disappeared below the horizon, the glow was snuffed out, the swamp plunged again into darkness.

79

The navy utility boat, with Pendergast at the wheel, slid into an unoccupied boat slip across the inlet from the docks beyond Tiny's Bait 'n' Bar. The sun, rising toward noon, was pouring unseasonable heat and humidity into every corner of the muddy waterfront.

Hopping out, Pendergast tied up and helped Hayward onto the dock, then handed her the pair of crutches.

Though it was only late morning, the twang of country-and-western music came from the ramshackle Bait 'n' Bar on the far side of the docks. Pendergast removed June Brodie's 12-gauge pump-action shotgun and raised it over his head.

"What are you doing?" Hayward asked, balancing on the crutches.

"Getting everyone's attention. As I alluded to before, we have unfinished business here." An enormous boom sounded as Pendergast fired the shotgun into the air.

A moment later people came spilling out of the Bait 'n' Bar like hornets from a hive, many with beers in their hands. Tiny and Larry were nowhere to be seen, but the rest of the crew, Hayward noticed, were there in force. Hayward remembered their leering, sweating faces with a trace of nausea. The large group stared silently at the two figures. They had washed up before leaving Spanish Island, and June Brodie had given Hayward a clean blouse, but she knew they must both be muddy sights.

"Come on down, boys, and watch the action!" Pendergast called out, walking across the landing toward Tiny's and the second set of docks.

Haltingly, warily, the crowd worked its way down toward them. Finally one man, more courageous than the rest, stepped forward. He was large and mean looking, with a small, ferret-like face atop a large amorphous body. He stared at them with squinty blue eyes. "What the hell you want now?" he said, advancing while tossing his can of beer into the water. Hayward recognized him as one of the ones cheering the loudest when her brassiere was cut in two.

"You said you were gonna leave us alone," someone else called out.

"I said I wouldn't *arrest* you. I didn't say I wouldn't come back to *bother* you."

The man hitched up his pants. "You already bothering me."

"Excellent!" Pendergast stepped onto the docks behind Tiny's, crowded with boats of various descriptions. Hayward recognized most of them from the previous day's ambush. "And now: which of these fine vessels belongs to Larry?"

"None of your business."

Pendergast casually tilted the shotgun down, pointing it into a nearby boat, and pulled the trigger. A massive boom echoed across the lake, the boat shuddering with the discharge, a gout of water shooting up, leaving a twelve-inch hole ripped out of its welded aluminum hull. Muddy water came swirling in, the nose of the boat tipping downward.

"What the *hell*?" a man in the crowd yelled. "That's my boat!"

"Sorry, I thought it was Larry's. Now, which is Larry's? This one?" Pendergast aimed the gun at the next boat, discharged it. Another geyser of water rose up, showering the crowd, and the boat jumped and began to settle immediately.

"Son of a bitch!" another man screamed. "Larry's is the 2000 Legend! That one over there!" He gestured to a bass boat at the far end of the slip.

Pendergast strolled over and inspected it. "Nice. Tell Larry this is for tossing my badge into the swamp." Another blast from the shotgun, which punched through the outboard engine, the cover flying off. "And this one's because he's such a low fellow." A second shot holed the boat at the transom, kicking up a geyser. The stern filled with water, the boat tilted up by the nose, the engine sinking.

"Christ! This bastard's crazy!"

"Indeed." Pendergast strolled down the dock, racked a fresh round into the shotgun, and casually aimed at the next boat. "This one's for giving us incorrect directions." *Boom.*

Another casual step. "This is for the double punch to the solar plexus."

Boom.

"And this is for expectorating on me."

Boom. Boom. Two more boats went down.

Removing his .45, Pendergast handed it to Hayward. "Keep an eye on them while I reload." He pulled a handful of shells from his pocket and inserted them.

"And this is *most especially* for humiliating and exposing my esteemed colleague to your vulgar, lascivious gaze. As I said before, that was no way to treat a lady." As he strolled down the dock, he fired into the bottom of each remaining boat, one after the other, pausing only to reload. The crowd stared, shocked into absolute silence.

Pendergast halted before the group of sweating, shaking, beery men. "Anybody else in the bar?"

Nobody spoke.

"You can't do this," a man said, his voice cracking. "This ain't legal."

"Perhaps somebody should call the FBI," said Pendergast. He strolled toward the door into the Bait 'n' Bar, cracked it open, glanced inside. "Ma'am?" he said. "Please step out."

A flustered woman with bleached-blond hair and enormous red fingernails came bustling out and broke into a run toward the parking lot.

"You've lost a heel!" Pendergast called after her, but she kept going, hobbling like a lame horse.

Pendergast disappeared inside the bar. Hayward, pistol in hand, could hear him opening and closing doors and calling out. He emerged. "Nobody home."

He walked around to the front and faced the crowd. "Everyone, please withdraw to the parking lot and take cover behind those parked cars."

Nobody moved.

Boom! Pendergast unloaded the shotgun over their heads and they hastily shuffled to the dirt parking lot. Pendergast backed away from the building, racked a fresh round into the shotgun, and aimed at the large propane tank snugged up against the side of the bait shop. He turned to Hayward.

"Captain, we might need the penetrative power of that .45 ACP, so let us both fire on the count of three."

Hayward took a stance with the .45. *I could get used to the Pendergast "method,"* she thought, aiming at the big white tank.

"One..."

"Holy shit, no!" wailed a voice.

"Two...

"Three!"

They fired simultaneously, the .45 kicking hard. A gigantic explosion erupted, and a massive wave of heat and overpressure swept over them. The entire building disappeared, engulfed in a boiling fireball. Soaring out of the fireball, trailing streamers of smoke, came thousands of bits and pieces of debris that rained down around them—writhing nightcrawlers, bugs, burning maggots, pieces of wood, reels, streamers of fishing line, shattered fishing rods, broken liquor bottles, pigs' trotters, pickles, lime wedges, coasters, and exploded beer cans.

The fireball rose in a miniature mushroom cloud while the debris continued to patter down. Gradually, as the smoke cleared, the burning stub of the building came into view. There was virtually nothing left.

Pendergast slung the shotgun over his shoulder and strolled down the dock toward Hayward. "Captain, shall we go? I think it's time we paid a visit to Vincent. Police guard or not, I'll feel better once we've moved him to new quarters—perhaps a place more private, not far from New York City, where we can keep an eye on him ourselves."

"Amen to that." And with a certain relief, Hayward thought that it was a good thing she wouldn't be working with Pendergast much longer. She had enjoyed that just a little too much.

80

New York City

Dr. John Felder sat in his consulting office in the Lower Manhattan building of the New York City Department of Health. It was on the seventh floor, where the Division of Mental Hygiene was located. He glanced around the small, tidy space, mentally assuring himself that everything was in order: the medical references in the bookshelves lined up and dusted, the impersonal paintings on the wall all perfectly level, the chairs before his desk set at just the right angle, the surface of his desk free of any unnecessary items.

Dr. Felder did not normally receive many guests in his office. He did most of his work—so to speak—in the field: in locked wards and police holding tanks and hospital emergency rooms, and he carried out his small private practice in a consulting room on lower Park Avenue. But this appointment was different. For one thing, Felder had asked the gentleman to see him, not the other way around. The psychiatrist had done a background check on the man—and what he learned was rather disconcerting. Perhaps the invitation would prove to be a mistake. Even so, this man seemed to be the key, the *only* key, to the mystery of Constance Greene.

A quiet double tap sounded at the door. Felder glanced at his watch: ten thirty precisely. Punctual. He rose and opened the door.

The apparition that stood in the doorway did little to relieve Felder's misgivings. He was tall, thin, and immaculately dressed, his pallid skin a shocking contrast to the black suit. His eyes were as pale as his skin, and they seemed to regard Felder with a combination of keen discernment, mild curiosity, and—perhaps— just a little amusement.

Felder realized he was staring. "Come in, please," he said quickly. "You're Mr. Pendergast?"

"I am."

Felder showed the man to one of the consultation seats and then took his place behind the desk. "I'm sorry, but it's actually Dr. Pendergast, isn't it? I took the liberty of looking into your background."

Pendergast inclined his head. "I have two PhDs, but, frankly, I prefer my law enforcement title of special agent."

"I see." Felder had interviewed his share of cops, but never an FBI agent, and he wasn't quite sure how to begin. The straightforward approach seemed as good as any.

"Constance Greene is your ward?"

"She is."

Felder leaned back in his chair, casually throwing one leg over the other. He wanted to make sure he gave the impression of relaxation and informality. "I wondered if you could tell me a little more about her. Where she was born, what her early life was like . . . that sort of thing."

Pendergast continued to regard him with the same neutral expression. For some reason Felder began to find it irritating.

"You are the committing psychiatrist in the case, are you not?" Pendergast asked.

"My evaluation was submitted as evidence at the involuntary-commitment hearing."

"And you recommended commitment."

Felder smiled ruefully. "Yes. You were invited to the court hearing, but I understand that you declined to—"

"What, precisely, was your diagnosis?"

"It's rather technical—"

"Indulge me."

Felder hesitated a second. "Very well. Axis One: schizophrenia of the paranoid type, continuous, with a possible premorbid Axis Two state of schizotypal personality disorder, along with psyphoria and indications of dissociative fugue."

Pendergast nodded slowly. "And you base this finding on what evidence?"

"Simply put, on the delusion that she is Constance Greene: a girl who was born almost a century and a half ago."

"Let me ask you something, Doctor. Within the context of her, ah, *delusion*, have you noticed any discontinuity or nonconformity?"

Felder frowned. "I'm not sure what you mean."

"Are her delusions internally consistent?"

"Beyond the belief that her child was evil, of course, her delusions have been remarkably consistent. That's one of the things that interests me."

"What has she told you, exactly?"

"That her family moved from an upstate farm to Water Street, where she was born in the early 1870s, that her parents died of tuberculosis and her sister was killed by a serial murderer. That she, an orphan, was taken in by a former resident of 891 Riverside Drive, about whom we have no record. That you ultimately inherited that house and, by extension, the responsibility for her well-being." Felder hesitated.

Pendergast seemed to pick up on Felder's hesitation. "What else did she say about me?"

"That your becoming her guardian was due to guilt."

There was a silence.

"Tell me, Dr. Felder," Pendergast asked at length. "Did Constance tell you of her existence between this earlier period and her very recent crossing on the ship?"

"No."

"No details at all?"

"None."

"Then I submit to you that, under a diagnosis of 295.30, schizotypal personality disorder cannot be assumed. At the very most, you should have specified a schizophreniform disorder for the Axis Two diagnosis. The fact is, Doctor, you have no prior history of her condition—for all you know, these delusions could have been of recent origin, perhaps as recent as her Atlantic crossing."

Felder sat forward. Pendergast had quoted the precise DSM-IV diagnostic code for paranoid schizophrenia. "Have you studied psychiatry, Special Agent Pendergast?"

Pendergast shrugged. "One has one's interests."

Despite everything, Felder found his irritation getting the better of himself. Why was Pendergast showing such interest now, when before he'd seemed almost indifferent? "I must tell you," he said, "I would categorize your conclusions as amateurish and superficial."

Pendergast's eyes glinted. "May I ask you, then, what possible reason you could have for vexing me with these questions about Constance, since you've *already* diagnosed—and committed—her?"

"Well, I—" He found those silvery eyes boring into him.

"Would it be out of idle curiosity? Or..." He smiled. "...in the hope of professional publication?"

Felder stiffened. "Naturally, if there is something novel in the case, I'd want to share my experiences with my colleagues via publication."

"And thus enhance your reputation...and perhaps"—Pendergast's eyes seemed to twinkle wickedly— "garner a plum appointment at a research institute. I note that you have been angling for an adjunct professorship at Rockefeller University for some time."

Felder was astounded. How could the man possibly have known about that?

As if answering the unvoiced question, Pendergast waved his hand casually and said, "I took the liberty of looking into *your* background."

Coloring at having his own phrase thrown back at him, Felder tried to collect himself. "My professional goals are irrelevant. The truth is, I've never seen a delusional presentation that has such authenticity. She *seems* nineteenth-century: in the way she talks, dresses, walks, holds herself, even thinks. That's why I've asked you to come here today. I want to know more about her. What trauma might have occurred to trigger this? What was she like before? What are her major life experiences? Who is she really?"

Pendergast continued gazing at him, saying nothing.

"And it's not only that: in the archives I found *this*." He opened a manila folder on his desk and removed a photocopy of *Guttersnipes at Play*, the engraving from the *New-York Daily Inquirer*, passing it to Pendergast.

The FBI agent studied it carefully, then returned it. "The resemblance is quite remarkable. The product of artistic imagination, perhaps?"

"Look at the faces," Felder said. "They're so real, they were certainly drawn from life."

Pendergast smiled enigmatically, but Felder fancied he could see a new respect in those pale eyes. "This is all very interesting, Doctor." He paused. "Perhaps I am in a position to help you—*if* you can help me."

Although he didn't know precisely why, Felder found himself gripping the arms of his chair. "How so?"

"Constance is a very fragile person, emotionally and psychically. Under the right conditions, she can flourish. Under the wrong ones…" Pendergast looked at him. "Where is she being held at present?"

"In a private room in the Bellevue psych ward. Papers are being processed for her transfer to the Mental Health Division of the Bedford Hills Correctional Facility."

Pendergast shook his head. "That's a maximum-security institution. Someone like Constance will wither away, grow increasingly worse, in a place like that."

"You needn't worry about her coming to harm at the hands of other inmates, because the staff—"

"It's not that. Constance has a propensity for sudden, occasionally violent, psychotic breaks. A place like Bedford Hills would only encourage this."

"Then what would you suggest?"

"She requires a place with an atmosphere similar to that she has grown used to—comfortable, old-fashioned, nonstressful. And yet secure. She needs to be surrounded with familiar things—within reason, of course. Books, in particular, are critical."

Felder shook his head. "There's only one place like that, Mount Mercy, and it's fully occupied. With a long waiting list."

Pendergast smiled. "I happen to know that a vacancy opened up not three weeks ago."

Felder looked at him. "It did?"

Pendergast nodded. "As the committing psychiatrist, you could jump the queue, so to speak, and get her in. *If* you insisted it was the only place for her."

"I'll . . . I'll look into it."

"You will do more than look into it. In return, I will share with you what I know about Constance—which is a great deal indeed, and which will exceed even your most fervent dreams in psychiatric interest. Whether the information is actually publishable or not will be up to you—and your capacity for discretion."

Felder found his heart accelerating. "Thank you."

"I thank *you*. And I bid you good morning, Dr.

Felder. We shall meet again—once Constance is safely ensconced in Mount Mercy."

Felder watched as the agent stepped out of the office and silently closed the door. Strange—he, too, seemed to have stepped out of the nineteenth century. And then Felder asked himself, for the first time, who exactly had orchestrated the meeting he'd so carefully arranged— and whose agenda had been satisfied.

EPILOGUE

Savannah, Georgia

Judson Esterhazy reclined in the library of his house on Whitfield Square. It was a surprisingly chilly May evening, and a small fire lay dying in the hearth, scenting the room with the aroma of burning birch.

Taking a sip of a fine Highland malt he had pulled out of his cellar, he rolled the peaty beverage around in his mouth before swallowing. But the drink was bitter, as bitter as his feelings at that moment.

Pendergast had killed Slade. They said it was suicide, but he knew that was a lie. Somehow, some way, Pendergast had managed it. Bad as the last ten years had been, the old man's final moments must have been awful, an unimaginable mental agony. He had seen Pendergast's manipulations of other people and he had no doubt the man had taken advantage of Slade in his dementia. It was murder—worse than murder.

The glass, trembling in his hand, shook out some

drops on the table, and he placed it down hard. At least he knew with complete confidence that Slade hadn't betrayed him. The old man loved him like a son and—even in his madness and pain—would have kept his secret to the last. Some things transcend even lunacy.

He had once loved Slade, too, but that feeling had died twelve years ago. He had seen a flash of another side of Slade that was just a little too close for comfort; a little too reminiscent of his own brutal father and the rather diabolical research of his that Judson was only too aware of. Maybe that was the fate of all fathers and father figures—to disappoint, to betray, to shrink in stature as one grew older and wiser.

He shook his head. What a mistake it had all been; what a terrible, tragic mistake. And how ironic, upon reflection: when Helen had originally brought the idea to him, an idea she had literally stumbled on through her interest in Audubon, it had seemed almost miraculous—to him as well as to her. *It could be a miracle drug,* she'd said. *You consult with a variety of pharmaceutical companies, Judson; surely you know the place to take it.* And he had known. He knew where to secure the financial backing. And he knew the perfect company to develop the drug: Longitude, run by his graduate-school dissertation adviser, Charles Slade, now working in the private sector. He'd fallen under his old professor's charismatic spell, and the two had stayed in contact. Slade was the ideal person to develop such a drug—he was a creative and independent thinker, unafraid of risk, consummately discreet...

And now he was gone, thanks to Pendergast. Pendergast, who had stirred up the past, reopened old wounds, and—directly or indirectly—caused several deaths.

He grasped the glass and drained it in one rough motion, swallowing the whiskey without even tasting it. The side table that held the bottle and small glass also sported a brochure. Esterhazy took it up and thumbed through it. A grim feeling of satisfaction displaced his anger. The tasteful brochure advertised the refined pleasures of an establishment known as the Kilchurn Shooting Lodge in the Highlands of Scotland. It was a great stone manor house on a windswept fell over-looking the Loch Duin and the Grampian Mountains. One of the most picturesque and isolated in Scotland, the lodge offered excellent grouse and partridge shoot-ing, salmon fishing, and stalking of red deer. They took only a select few guests, prided themselves on their pri-vacy and discretion; the shooting could be guided or not, depending on preference.

Naturally, he would prefer the self-guided shooting.

Ten years before, Esterhazy and Pendergast had spent a week at Kilchurn. The lodge sat in the middle of a vast and wild estate of forty thousand acres, once the private hunting preserve of the lairds of Atholl. Esterhazy had been deeply impressed by the empty, rugged landscape, the deep lochs hidden in the folds of the land, the swift streams bursting with trout and salmon, the windswept moorlands and the forbidding Foulmire, the heather braes and wooded glens. A man could disappear forever in a land like that, his bones left to molder, unseen, lashed by wind and rain until noth-ing was left.

Taking another lazy sip of the single-malt, which

had now warmed in his cradling palm, he felt calmer. All was not lost by any means. In fact, things had taken a turn for the better—for the first time in a long while. He laid the brochure aside and took up a short note, written in an old-fashioned copperplate hand on cream-colored, heavy laid paper.

The Dakota
New York City
24 April

My dear Judson,

I thank you most sincerely for your kind invitation. After some reflection I believe I will take you up on your offer, and gladly. Perhaps you are right that the recent events have taken a certain toll. It would be delightful to see Kilchurn Lodge again after so many years. A fortnight's holiday would be a welcome respite—and your company is always a pleasure.

In answer to your question, I plan to bring my Purdey 16-bore, an H&H Royal over-and-under in .410 caliber, and a .300 H&H bolt-action for stalking deer.

With affectionate regards,
A. Pendergast

Reading Group Guide

A Conversation with Douglas Preston and Lincoln Child

Why did you choose John James Audubon for this story? What attracted you to him?

Doug: He's a fascinating character, an American original (even though he was born to French parents in what is now Haiti). What gave us the idea was a trip I took to New Orleans, to Dauphine Street, to visit the site of the original Pendergast mansion, which is now a parking lot. As I was exploring the area at night, I came across an old, verdigrised plaque on a small cottage opposite the site, which announced it as the Creole cottage in which Audubon once lived with his wife, Lucy. I called up Linc on the spot and sent him a photograph of the plaque. Right there, standing there in the street, speaking like maniacs on the phone, we came up with the basic outline of the story.

Was there anything in your research about Audubon that you found interesting but weren't able to include in the story?

Doug: We always come up with ten times the material we can put in the story. What I found most interesting was that Audubon was furious at his printers and complained incessantly about the quality of the printing of *Birds of America*. If you go to the New York Historical Society and look at Audubon's original watercolors, you can see that Audubon had a lot to complain about, especially with the quality of the earliest prints.

How much of this story is true? Where does reality end and your fiction start; for example, is the Black Frame a real painting?

Doug: Almost all of it is true. The truth ends with Audubon's sickness and the Black Frame, both of which we made up. Even the part about Audubon's last days, his sinking into insanity and dementia, are true.

Helen Pendergast is a major part of this story. Why did you decide to focus on her and that side of Pendergast's life?

Doug: Many years ago, in our first book, we mentioned in an offhand way that Pendergast's wife had died under mysterious circumstances while hunting big game in Africa. For over a decade our readers have focused on that detail almost obsessively, wondering what happened and why. At one point a reader suggested her name was Helen and we said, "Of course." Linc and I mulled over the mystery of her death for years.

How do you structure the storyline to create a multibook arc? Do you prefer writing series to writing stand alone novels?

Doug: We like both. We generally write a broad narrative of the entire multibook arc, but save the details for the actual plotting, outlining, and writing. We don't like to over-outline a book because then it's no fun to write; it's like painting by the numbers. The multibook arc gives us the chance to develop a complex story, full of twists and turns and deep surprises, as well as a number of intertwined plot threads that enrich the story. Sometimes we like a self-contained story, something unique and different, such as in *Still Life with Crows*. But sometimes our minds expand an idea to the point where, unless we're going to write a 1,200-page book, we have to break it up.

Pendergast sometimes seems to cross the line morally in his search for the truth. What philosophical themes were you wrestling with in this book?

Linc: Pendergast does walk a very fine line at times in his pursuit of justice. Probably the biggest philosophical theme we deal with in *Fever Dream* is the nature of truth, which can be uncomfortably fluid at times. What Pendergast has believed to be true for many, many years turns out to be—as the book progresses—an ever more complex and mortifying tissue of lies, half-truths, and diversions. And yet, had he not—completely by accident—uncovered the first of these lies while cleaning Helen's hunting rifle—he would never have gone down the path of discovery chronicled in the book. He would have believed a very different truth and would probably have been a happier man for doing so.

You leave this book on a bit of a cliffhanger. Will we learn what really happened to Helen in the next book?
Linc: We would probably argue that it was more than "a bit" of a cliffhanger! *Fever Dream* is the first in the kind of multi-book series Doug discussed in an earlier question. The story of Helen Pendergast will be resolved in the next two books that follow: *Cold Vengeance*, which comes out in the summer of 2011, and the final book in the trilogy, which we are at work on now.

We know you are starting a new series introducing the character Gideon Crew. Is there anything you would like to tell us about him?
Linc: Gideon is in many ways the opposite of Pendergast. He is very clever, like Pendergast. He is a master of social engineering, which Pendergast can also be at times (although Gideon is usually more subtle about it than Pendergast, who favors intimidation). Unlike Pendergast, Gideon is musically inclined, an ex-art thief, and more than a bit of a rogue. He was great fun to put on the page! He makes his first appearance in the novel *Gideon's Sword*.

Dear Friend and Reader,

About a dozen times a year we send a short, entertaining note to a select group of our readers. It brings you information available nowhere else. We call it <u>The Pendergast File</u>. Each missive includes a surprise or shock: an outlandish bit of Pendergast history, a marvelous giveaway, a contest, hidden clues to buried treasure, upcoming book signings, snide and nasty comments about reviewers we dislike, and other amusing tidbits.

In short, <u>The Pendergast File</u> is not your ordinary "newsletter."

If you would like to sign up for <u>The Pendergast File</u>, please go to our website, www.prestonchild.com, and click on the sign-up button. You can opt out at any time.

With warm regards,
Doug & Linc

P.S. We will never, ever, under any circumstances, share your e-mail address or information.

When a murdered corpse appears
on his doorstep, Special Agent
Pendergast discovers an ancient
family secret—and a conspiracy that
can only end with his own death...

The following is
an excerpt from

Blue Labyrinth

1

The stately Beaux-Arts mansion on Riverside Drive between 137th and 138th Streets, while carefully tended and impeccably preserved, appeared to be untenanted. On this stormy June evening, no figures paced the widow's walk overlooking the Hudson River. No yellow glow from within flowed through the decorative oriel windows. The only visible light, in fact, came from the front entrance, illuminating the drive beneath the building's porte cochere.

Appearances can be deceiving, however—sometimes intentionally. Because 891 Riverside was the residence of FBI Special Agent Aloysius Pendergast—and Pendergast was a man who valued, above all, his privacy.

In the mansion's elegant library, Pendergast sat in a leather wing chair. Although it was nearly summer, the night was stormy and chill, and a low fire flickered on the grate. He was leafing through a copy of the *Manyōshū*, an old and celebrated anthology of Japanese poetry, dating to AD 750. A small *tetsubin*, or cast-iron teapot, sat on a table beside him, along with a china cup half-full of green tea. Nothing disturbed his concentration. The only sounds were the occasional crackle of settling embers and rumble of thunder from beyond the closed shutters.

Now there was a faint sound of footsteps from the reception hall beyond and Constance Greene appeared, framed in the library doorway. She was wearing a simple evening dress. Her violet eyes and dark hair, cut in an old-fashioned bob, offset the paleness of her skin. In one hand she held a bundle of letters.

"The mail," she said.

Pendergast inclined his head, set the book aside.

Constance took a seat beside Pendergast, noting that, since he had come back from what he called his "Colorado adventure," he was at last looking like his old self. His state of mind had been a cause of uneasiness in her since the dreadful events of the prior year.

She began sorting through the small stack of mail, putting aside the things that would not interest him. Pendergast did not like to concern himself with quotidian details. He had an old and discreet New Orleans law firm, long in the employ of the family, to pay bills and manage part of his unusually extensive income. He had an equally hoary New York banking firm to manage other investments, trusts, and real estate. And he had all mail delivered to a post office box, which Proctor, his chauffeur, bodyguard, and general factotum, collected on a regular basis. At present, Proctor was preparing to leave for a visit to relatives in Alsace, so Constance had agreed to take over the epistolary matters.

"Here's a note from Corrie Swanson."

"Open it, if you please."

"She's attached a photocopy of a letter from John Jay. Her thesis won the Rosewell Prize."

"Indeed. I attended the ceremony."

"I'm sure Corrie appreciated it."

"It is rare that a graduation ceremony offers more than an anesthetizing parade of platitudes and mendacity, set to the tiresome refrain of 'Pomp and Circumstance.'" Pendergast took a sip of tea at the recollection. "This one did."

Constance sorted through more mail. "And here's a letter from Vincent D'Agosta and Laura Hayward."

He nodded for her to scan it. "It's a thank-you note for the wedding gift and once again for the dinner party."

Pendergast inclined his head as she put the letter aside. The month before, on the eve of D'Agosta's wedding, Pendergast had hosted a private dinner for the couple, consisting of several courses he had prepared himself, paired with rare wines from his cellar. It was this gesture, more than anything, that had convinced Constance that Pendergast had recovered from his recent emotional trauma.

She read over a few other letters, then put aside those of interest and tossed the rest on the fire.

"How is the project coming, Constance?" Pendergast asked as he poured himself a fresh cup of tea.

"Very well. Just yesterday I received a packet from France, the Bureau Ancestre du Dijon, which I'm now trying to integrate with what I've already collected from Venice and Louisiana. When you have the time, I do have a couple of questions I'd like to ask about Augustus Robespierre St. Cyr Pendergast."

"Most of what I know consists of oral family history—tall tales, legends, and some whispered horror stories. I'd be glad to share most of them with you."

"Most? I was hoping you'd share them all."

"I fear there are skeletons in the Pendergast family closet, figurative and literal, that I must keep even from you."

Constance sighed and rose. As Pendergast returned to his book of poetry, she walked out of the library, across the reception hall lined with museum cabinets full of curious objects, and through a doorway into a long, dim space paneled in time-darkened oak. The main feature of the room was a wooden refectory table, almost as long as the room itself. The near end of the table was covered with journals, old letters, census pages, yellowed photographs and engravings, court transcripts, memoirs, reprints from newspaper microfiche, and other documents, all arranged in neat stacks. Beside them sat a laptop computer, its screen glowing incongruously in the dim room. Several months before, Constance had taken it upon herself to prepare a genealogy of the Pendergast family. She wanted both to satisfy her own curiosity and to help draw Pendergast out of himself. It was a fantastically complex, infuriating, and yet endlessly fascinating undertaking.

At the far end of the long room, beyond an arched door, was the foyer leading to the mansion's front door. Just as Constance was about to take a seat at the table, a loud knock sounded.

Constance paused, frowning. They rarely entertained visitors at 891 Riverside Drive—and never did one arrive unannounced.

Knock. Another rap resounded from the entryway, accompanied by a low grumble of thunder.

Smoothing down her dress, Constance walked down the length of the room, through the archway, and into the foyer. The heavy front door was solid, with no fisheye lens, and she hesitated a moment. When no third rap came, she undid the upper lock, then the lower, and slowly opened the door.

There, silhouetted in the light of the porte cochere, stood a young man. His blond hair was wet and plastered to his head. His rain-spattered features were fine and quintessentially Nordic, with a high-domed forehead and chiseled lips. He was dressed in a linen suit, sopping wet, which clung to his frame.

He was bound with heavy ropes.

Constance gasped, began to reach out to him. But the bulging eyes took no notice of the gesture. They stared straight ahead, unblinking.

For a moment, the figure remained standing, swaying ever so slightly, fitfully illuminated by flashes of lightning—and then it began to fall, like a tree toppling, slowly at first and then faster, before crashing facedown across the threshold.

Constance backed up with a cry. Pendergast arrived at a run, followed by Proctor. Pendergast grasped her, pulled her aside, and quickly knelt over the young man. He gripped the figure by the shoulder and turned him over, brushing the hair from his eyes, and feeling for the pulse that was so obviously absent beneath the cold flesh of the neck.

"Dead," he said, his voice low and unnaturally composed.

"My God," Constance said, her own voice breaking. "It's your son Tristram."

"No," Pendergast sad. "It's Alban. His twin."

For just a moment longer he knelt by the body. And then he leapt to his feet and, in a flash of feline motion, disappeared into the howling storm.

2

Pendergast sprinted to Riverside Drive and paused at the corner, scanning north and south along the broad avenue. The rain was now coming down in sheets, traffic was light, and there were no pedestrians. His eye lit upon the closest vehicle, about three blocks south: a late-model Lincoln Town Car, black, of the kind seen on the streets of Manhattan by the thousands. The license plate light was out, leaving the details of the New York plate unreadable.

Pendergast ran after it.

The vehicle did not speed up, but continued at a leisurely pace down the drive, at each cross street moving through one set of green lights after another, steadily gaining distance. The lights turned yellow, then red. But the vehicle continued on, running a yellow and a red, never accelerating, never slowing.

He pulled out his cell phone and punching in a number as he ran. "Proctor. Bring the car. I'm headed south on Riverside."

The Town Car had almost disappeared, save for a faint pair of taillights, wavering in the downpour, but as the drive made the slow curve at 126th Street even those disappeared.

Pendergast continued on, pursuing at a dead run, his black suit jacket whipping behind him, rain stinging his face. A few blocks ahead, he saw the Town Car again, stopped at another light behind two other vehicles. Once again, he pulled out his phone and dialed.

"Twenty-Sixth Precinct," came the response. "Officer Powell."

"This is SA Pendergast, FBI. In pursuit of a black Town Car, New York license plate unidentified, traveling southbound on Riverside at One Hundred Twenty-Fourth. Operator is suspect in a homicide. Need assistance in motor vehicle stop."

"Ten-four," came the dispatcher. And a moment later: "We have a marked unit in the area, two blocks over. Keep us posted on location."

"Air support as well," Pendergast said, still at a dead run.

"Sir, if the vehicle operator is only a suspect—"

"This is a priority target for the FBI," Pendergast said into the phone. "Repeat, a *priority target*."

A brief pause. "We're putting a bird in the air."

As he put the phone away, the Town Car suddenly veered around the cars idling at the red light, jumped the curb and crossed the sidewalk, tore through a set of flower beds in Riverside Park, churning up mud, then headed the wrong way down the exit ramp to the Henry Hudson Parkway.

Pendergast called dispatch again and updated them on

the vehicle's location, followed it up with another call to Proctor, then cut into the park, leapt over a low fence, and sprinted through some tulip beds, his eyes locked on the taillights of the car careening down the off-ramp onto the parkway, the screech of tires floating back to his ears.

He vaulted the low stone wall on the far side of the drive, then half ran, half slid down the embankment, scattering trash and broken glass in an attempt to cut the vehicle off. He fell, rolled, and scrambled to his feet, chest heaving, soaked with rain, white shirt plastered to his chest. He watched as the Town Car pulled a U-turn and came blasting down the exit helix toward him. He reached for his Les Baer, but his hand closed over an empty holster. He looked quickly around the dark embankment, then—as brilliant light slashed across him—was forced to roll away as the Town Car sheared toward him. Once the car had passed, he rose once again to his feet, following the Town Car with his eyes as it merged into the main stream of traffic.

A moment later a vintage Rolls-Royce approached and braked rapidly to the curb. Pendergast opened the rear door and jumped in.

"Follow the Town Car," he told Proctor as he strapped himself in.

The Rolls accelerated smoothly. Pendergast could hear faint sirens from behind, but the police were too far back and would no doubt get hung up in traffic. He plucked a police radio from a side compartment. The chase accelerated, the Town Car shifting lanes and dodging cars at speeds that approached a hundred miles an hour even as they entered a construction area, concrete pilings lining both shoulders of the highway.

There was a lot of chatter on the police radio, but they were first in pursuit. The choppers were nowhere to be seen.

Suddenly a series of bright flashes came from the traffic ahead, followed instantly by the report of gunshots.

"Shots fired!" Pendergast said into the open channel. He understood immediately what was happening. Ahead, cars veered wildly right and left, panicking, along with the flashes of additional shots. Then a *crump, crump, crump* sounded as multiple vehicles piled into each other at highway speed, causing a chain reaction that quickly filled the road with hissing, ruined metal. With great expertise, Proctor braked the Rolls and steered into a power slide, trying to maneuver it past the chain reaction of collisions. The Rolls hit a concrete barrier at an angle, was deflected back into the lane, and was hit from behind by a driver who rammed into the pileup with a deafening crash of metal. In the backseat, Pendergast was thrown forward, stopped hard by his seat belt, then slammed back. Partially stunned, he heard the sound of hissing steam, screams, shouts, and the screeching of brakes and additional crashes as cars continued to rear-end each other, mingling with a rising chorus of sirens and now, finally, the *thwap* of helicopter blades.

Shrugging off a coating of broken glass, Pendergast struggled to collect his wits and remove the seat belt. He leaned forward to examine Proctor.

The man was unconscious, his head bloody. Pendergast fumbled for the radio to call for help, but even as he did so the doors were pulled open and paramedics were pushing in, hands grasping at him to pull him out.

"Get your hands off me," Pendergast said. "Focus on him."

Pendergast shrugged free and exited into the sweeping rain, more glass falling away as he did so. He stared ahead at the impenetrable tangle of cars, the sea of flashing lights, listening to the shouts of paramedics and police and the thud of the useless, circling chopper.

The Town Car was long gone.

VISIT US ONLINE AT

WWW.HACHETTEBOOKGROUP.COM

FEATURES:

OPENBOOK BROWSE AND
SEARCH EXCERPTS
•
AUDIOBOOK EXCERPTS AND PODCASTS
•
AUTHOR ARTICLES AND INTERVIEWS
•
BESTSELLER AND PUBLISHING
GROUP NEWS
•
SIGN UP FOR E-NEWSLETTERS
•
AUTHOR APPEARANCES AND TOUR
INFORMATION
•
SOCIAL MEDIA FEEDS AND WIDGETS
•
DOWNLOAD FREE APPS

Bookmark Hachette Book Group
@ www.HachetteBookGroup.com